Liquid Kids

Scott G Buchan

F.M.F.T.M.C.

Published by Lulu.

ISBN 978-1-4092-2319-1

Chapter 1

"Amen."

Derek slumped back down onto the bench.

The minister began to tell the story of how the old man in the box survived a Gerry attack during the war. Derek had heard the story before, in a small yawl far out in the middle of the North Sea. He'd been around eleven years old at the time and had sat and listened with what possibly could have been genuine interest as his grandad, always the raconteur, took a break from pulling up creels and devouring cigarettes to tell his tale. Derek's dad had also been there, but that was about all the crew that that little boat could hold.

Fond memories of youthful summertime jaunts in The Searcher, however, were slapped about the face and molested by a hangover that he'd signed for the evening prior. The feeling of bliss usually summoned by recollections of three generations of Gibson men floating out on the big, blue pond was buried presently beyond his reach.

The minister's words bounced off Derek's eggshell forehead like apples. He felt like a tumbling knot of slugs. His attention zipped between the occupied box before him and the illness in his stomach. He avoided tilting his head back, as would've been required had he wished to watch the minister graft away at his pulpit like the best man at a dull and alcohol-free wedding. Prolonged bursts of concentration irritated the eye-wasps into perpetrating violence against him; but even so, Derek stared at the dark brown coffin.

Derek wondered why this occasion had taken so long to arrive. Big Stanley Gibson should've, by rights, popped his clogs years ago. It was testament to the man's strength that he had held on to at least shuffle his way through the past decade. The old man's brain surely ignored the complaints of his body, like a foot that walks off without the leg.

He recalled that The Searcher was sold to some biker when grandad's health deteriorated and his dad's time became greatly consumed with his proper boat, the trawler. And that was the end of it.

He had liked his grandad, and not just because he was genetically obligated to. Stanley was a good lad, by reputation and in person. Derek suspected that they would've been matey regardless of how they had encountered each other on this planet. He felt a mild pang of sadness, like a thud from under the floorboards of his sickness; his grief, though, probably didn't compare to the full-blown turmoil that his dad, sat to his left, would be enduring. Not that dad Gibson let any of that grass sprout to the surface.

Derek glanced around the hall. He had shirked from doing so until then for fear of forging pupilary chains with the army of the undead behind him. He didn't want to be exposed for being the hungover fool that he so blatantly was.

The church, a healthy-sized Protestant affair that Derek had been forced to visit each and every Sunday until he was ten, was about a third full, which he assumed was quite good considering his grandad's immemorial genesis. But then Stanley Gibson had always been thought well of by his contemporaries. Derek had gathered that much from chatting to elderly pissheads in his local.

The oldies could go on for hours once they started on about Big Stanley, fa lukt oot for aa bastard an' didnae take ony shite fae onybidy. They'd often get excited and fidget slowly on their stools like arthritic kids on cola as the nostalgic hue overcame them. Stanley was like their last link to a better time, when they were the protectors and not easy prey. And they would invariably add, oh, an' he liked a good dram, did oor Stan. This was perhaps the only characteristic that Derek could honestly say that he shared with his late grandfather.

The sea of wrinkly faces behind Derek acknowledged him dryly, as though some heavy canvass folding. There were only about a dozen or so non-OAPs sprinkled around the place, like grapes in amongst the raisins. He recognised a few of the oldies from The Tart. One man smiled as though they were at the bingo and he'd narrowly missed out on victory. The wrinklies were a dab hand at this sort of thing, he thought; as well they would be.

The month previously, Derek had been to a funeral for a young guy in this very same church. A junkie called Martin Aitkenhead, whom he'd went to school with, when he'd been of that age. Martin had been a popular, likeable sort – a solid and unshowy presence like your average defensive midfielder, and his overdose came as a melancholic, though hardly unexpected, blow for a fair portion of the under-thirty quotient of Fraserburgh town and the surrounding hick-nests. His planting had attracted a large crowd, with even the top tiers, unburdened this August afternoon, being filled to capacity.

The behaviour of Derek's peers had mostly been in stark contrast to the manner in which these wizened ladies and gents conducted themselves. The youthful crowd, mainly the girls, cried openly and, in some annoying cases, loudly. Ah care mair than you dee, professed each noisy sob, as the wails escalated in volume to the point that the mums in the Woolworths next door must've been startled into jabbing their scoops of pic'n'mix down the aisles, or so it had seemed to Derek. At best, it was merely off-putting; at worst, it reeked to the steeple of forced insincerity. Bunch o fuckin drama queens. Everything has to turn into a competition with these twats, except when it comes to singing the hymns, and then it all gets a bit quieter. The young folk won't sing sober, especially not about Christ and sheep and the like; unless they're fuckin mental and brainwashed, Derek thought. The hymns don't work at drug-death funerals; you just end up with three minutes of mumbling. The wrinklies were having none of that. They belt them out as though Simon Cowell's up there sitting on the coffin.

Derek noted that, unsurprisingly, his sister Tracy hadn't made an appearance. He was the youngest person in the entire church. And he wasn't that young. And he was really, badly, stinkingly hungover. And he'd never felt so much like a representative for his particular generation, surrounded by this vastness of senescence and potential wisdom. Here crumbles this naïve and disrespectful swine, who would think to show up for his grandfather's funeral – a man whom had been a war hero no less – mangled from a marathon boozefest the night before. Derek imagined the wrinklies climbing over the benches to get to him, howling and slobbering out of toothless mouths.

Derek considered that he was now flush out of grandparents. He sensed that something monumental had come to pass this day. Up until as recently as five years ago, he had had a full house. Now he didn't have any grannies or didies. The significance of this fact was something that his mindstuffs were, for the time being, unable to properly compute.

The hangover neared maximum strength. The thought occurred to him then that he was going to be sick, *definitely* going to be sick. Sunlight blasted through tall frescoes that crawled up the walls towards an ancient, pitched ceiling. Derek sweltered in his black suit. There was a mere inch of fabrics between him and his dad; tense and red-eyed, the man was compact and weighty like a cannonball. His dad must smell the alcohol that emitted from his pores as skunk cologne. If papa Gibson knew that Derek had been out on the ran dan the night preceding his grandad's funeral, then Derek would be up to his shaggy brown fringe in shite when later they got home, probably.

Nothing had been said thus far in regards to Derek's visibly weakened state. Neither parent had passed comment on the drive down to the church, not in relation to Derek or why he'd been struggling to stay vertical in the back seat of the smoothly driven vehicle. Maybe it wouldn't be an issue. Maybe this little thing could be forgiven. Maybe they'd let this one go and leave him be. It was just Derek being Derek. He means you no insult. Maybe. You never know. Just, at least, show mercy and leave the bollocking till tomorrow or some century after that. Derek, regroup. Don't be sick. Don't vomit in the church, Derek. Focus on achieving that meagre goal. You don't ever aim big. This is doable. Control your guts. That'll be enough. It should be enough.

Derek deliberated grimly over his having to carry the coffin out in the graveyard and then lower it into its hole, like construction work. Hard labour. He barely had the strength to raise his hands in an act of surrender.

"Scarred by the memories of that chaotic day so very long ago, Stanley would often turn to the Good Book for assurance and guidance from the Lord." The congregation listened courteously to the bespectacled minister, whose skin dictated that he'd be aged somewhere between Derek's dad and the latterly deceased and yet he had astonishingly black hair.

Although Derek wouldn't look again now for a closer inspection, he had noticed upon entering the church just how strained and puffy his dad's eyes were; like they'd been licked by cats, he'd thought. Derek had yet to see any actual tears from his father. Maybe he should conjure up some sorrow-saliva of his own and consequently elicit sympathy through his apparent profound mourning. But even crying would take more effort than he was willing to expend.

Derek's pinched, brunette mother sat on the other side of his dad and dabbed at steady droplets with the edge of a handkerchief.

His auburn aunt and her girlfriend packed out the remaining seats of this front bench. The two adamantly chic, though progressively thickening, madams were both historically adverse to Derek and had greeted his earlier arrival with the contemptible satisfaction of ones whom correctly predict bad news. It wasn't often that he had to withstand the company of Aunt Rosie, who was his dad's sister, and her special friend Sylvia, who had the fuller features and darker locks of the two, and all concerned were grateful for that. They mixed together about as well as ice cream and Bunsen burners, with the ladies masking their distaste of him only marginally better than Derek could his of them. In his defence, though, they had disliked him first.

The trousered pair had their own hairdressing business, which he'd never once frequented, and they'd heard all these stories from their clients; stories, which may or may not have actually transpired, that all failed to paint young knight Sir Derek in the greatest of lights. Obviously, there was all the stuff about his drinking. But then there was the morally questionable incidents involving married women and abortions and a girl who might have turned out, after the event, to be a smidgen underage. Things that they'd heard. Things that they believed to be true. And there were the things that the women *knew* to be true, such as his negative disposition towards motivation and ambition and his lifelong allergies to anything that resembled hard work. Bastard, drunken and lazy were words that his aunt and her lover had used in association with Derek on more than one previous occasion; although, rarely to his face. Tea and coffee would, apparently, be supplied at theirs after the graveyard. He loved the sound of that, as he did the idea of sucking the contents out of a pig's rectum through a straw moulded from foreskins.

Derek wanted to be invisible. However, he felt as though he must be glowing like the resurrection.

The hangover. The insidious little demon, ever ready to crush and humiliate its reckless host. The heat. The Broch gets one extraordinarily hot day a year. Today. Had to be. Sweat ran down the length of Derek's body. His ebony suit snatched every descending sunflake out of the atmosphere. Grease flowed through his hair; moisture gushed down his back. He sat in a shallow puddle, and Derek dearly hoped that it really was sweat as he'd presumed. He hadn't pissed himself this year. He couldn't smell urine, or maybe he could, but maybe that was just some of the old people. In any case, he felt like the warmth of the church was impacting upon him at variance to how it did all the other attendees, like they baked while he melted. Everyone else seemed crisp like pastry to Derek, and he envisioned that all their anuses were suction-cupped to the wooden benches and you could push them but they would just roll back towards you like one of those punching toys. The image did nothing to settle his rolling queasiness. Derek felt squelchy and ill and wrong and sorry.

Derek's insides scrambled about, in search of a way out; any exit would do for them. Derek sat upright. For the first time, his dad shuffled in his seat. The sudden motion compelled Derek to peep round. Anticipating a snarl of reproach in response, Derek was instead jolted by the uncharacteristically slack look that hung upon his father's lean face. The light gleaming through the man's short, fairish hair conspired to make him appear softer and more vulnerable than ever Derek was accustomed to.

"His son Adam told me how it was that he would often find his father immersed in the Book when he was feeling down. This became especially true after the loss of his beloved wife three years ago."

Derek could feel the sick rising. Time was milk in Derek's sieve. His body had turned against him, and his guts were on the march.

Derek studied the hymn sheet. They had already sung two of the hymns, listened to three prayers, one Bible passage and a couple of anecdotes. There was one more hymn to go, he reasoned. He would have to stand for that, if he could. He must've been swaying a bit through the last ode to God that they sang. People would have noticed. He was right there at the front. But he shouldn't be. He shouldn't be centre stage. He should be sprawled down a bench somewhere at the back. The heat and the hangover. He might faint there on his feet, collapsing and shattering like the 5'9" bottle of Buckfast that he basically was. He couldn't do that. He couldn't. Don't faint during the next hymn. Don't be sick. That would just completely fuck everything up. You can manage this. You could. You can.

He would, perhaps, manage to mumble his way through one final hymn.

*

And so he did. But after the box was wheeled from the premises and the organ stopped, signalling that the mourners were required to leave, his stomach barked him a warning that he'd be best to maybe think about making a dash for it. So Derek had lumbered up from the bench and past the oldies, out into the brightness. Thankfully, he hadn't knocked anyone down in the course of his escape. He wouldn't have been able to pause for apologies if he had. The town centre splashed at him from a bucket when he stepped forth onto the pavement but he could take nothing in for he was already sprinting around the corner into the side lane between the church and the Woolies and to where a man ate a sandwich in the cab of his parked lorry. Derek's legs locked when they realised that he was far enough down the hill so as to be out of sight of shoppers, while the lorry's trailer shielded him from any traffic on the left.

He could see some of the masts and sheds of the harbour from up on the brae, as well as fragments of piers and a sliver of the North Sea. The sky sat on the water like a feather on a pit bull's back; they were on the opposite ends of the blue spectrum. He fell towards a flat, grey wall. His right arm thought quickly to steady him against it. The vomit introduced itself like the police on a terrorist raid. Some of it, inevitably, rebounded onto his shoes. The bile streaked his tie. He loosened the garment, yanked it off over his face, almost breaking his nose in so doing, and crammed it into his coat pocket. He puked until he was empty. He scraped the dregs off his teeth with his tongue then spat, producing a yellow, frothy strand that dangled to the ground. He saw the hearse appear at the rear of the trailer then halt at the junction at the foot of the hill. The hearse moved off and to the right, where its progress was promptly concealed by a building that was as old as the harbour that spawned this town. The hearse was pursued by a silver Merc, which he, of course, recognised as belonging to his parents.

The lorry driver had shifted onto the passenger seat. The man's spherical, unpretty head emerged from the cab window. "Ye a'right 'ere, pal?"

Derek cut the spit rope with his fingers and wiped his hand on his trousers. "Aye, fine, ken? Funeral."

They'd left without him. The bus to escort the oldies out to the ceremony in the cemetery halted for some green sports car then vanished also southwards.

"Aye, chief, ye widnae happen tae be gaan oot tae the graveyard, wid ye?" Derek inquired of the lorry driver.

The man laughed. "Nah, sorry, pal. Ye stuck?"

Derek pushed out a smile. "It's lukin like it."

"Hard lines, eh?"

"Cheers onywye." Derek's hangover had more or less been vanquished, but he was far from feeling celebratory about the change in his predicament. He opened the top two buttons of his shirt and contemplated his options. He had to get to the graveyard; if he could just make it out there for the burial then maybe that would be enough to rectify things. But the graveyard was over a mile down the road. Derek certainly wasn't going to run there. He'd have to get a taxi, but he didn't have a phone with him. He'd chucked his last mobile into the harbour a couple of weeks ago, and he didn't have any change for the phone box. He'd have to go to the pub. The Tart was just down there, left where the cortege had gone right. Fat Ass Phil should be working; Derek would get him to book a taxi. But how long would that take? Plus, the fat swine would probably just encourage him to get pished again and forget about the remainder of the funeral, and that would be a really big mistake. Derek was on thin enough ice with his parents as it was. Cannae even get yersel intae reasonable shape tae ging tae yer grandad's funeral. Fit kina man are ye? He was nearly twenty-eight; he could do without any more of their tellings off.

This wasn't good, like insomnia in the build-up to some mentally taxing undertaking. This was Jimmy's fault; he was the arse who'd pestered Derek into drinking last night. Derek had had every intention of having a sober Sunday; but then Jimmy phones and drones on in his way, and now here Derek was. Was it too early for some Buckie? Was it fuck. Just the half, though. He needed to unkink his noggin, and he'd found that sometimes alcohol was the best tool for that specific task. Furthermore, there'd likely be some fucker who Derek knew milling about the Broadgate and whom could prove to be vehicularly useful to him.

Derek ascended the hill. The lorry driver expressed a good luck message with his eyebrows, which Derek countered with a 'shit happens' shrug. Having returned to the summit, Derek strode forth back onto the widened pavements of the town centre, feeling appreciably less inclined to hack up his intestines than when last he was caught by the full glare of the busy day. Retail outlets were wedged like plastic tubs between the spokes of parallel granite trains. Handbags swished between the few shops that the town had to offer, manoeuvring around the junkies who shuffled about on tiptoes seemingly at the ends of non-existent queues. Some teenagers loafed around a bench, scoffing the portions that they'd acquired from the nearby chip shop. A row of stars blinded Derek from the bonnets of parked cars. The seagulls screamed at each other from the tiled rooftops that had been soiled and washed many, many times. He was one of the few people not attired in a T-shirt and jeans. Some even wore shorts, though there was a nip in the air to suggest that naked calves weren't warranted.

Derek waited for a bus to advance before crossing the one-way street. Then he realised that that bus was headed south for the village of St Combs and would pass the graveyard on its way. He felt better than he had done, but still not well enough to be chasing after buses. Derek continued on and into the off-licence, passing a gaunt man asleep on his feet in a phone box as he did.

It took the coolness of the shop for Derek to remember how sticky with sweat he was under his suit. He retrieved a half-bottle from the fridge and proceeded to the counter, mindful not to graze and dismount the wine displays as he had certainly done at least twice before. He stood behind a red-headed man whom was vertically superior to him.

Derek remarked, "Ye sure ye're ginger enough 'ere, min?"

The man, who had been collecting his change from the petite female assistant for the packet of fags he'd just bought, spun around to confront his verbal assailant. The man's indignation broke instantly into good humour on identifying the culprit. "Aye aye, Derek, ye prick. Fit ye sayin tae it the day? You up in court or somethin?"

"Nope," he replied to the freckly chap. Derek was a year or two older than Dutty, and they'd become acquainted through random encounters in the arena of inebriation. Had Derek a mobile number to give, Dutty would have received it, though they wouldn't have exchanged texts. "Ah'm in the middle o a funeral. You drivin?"

Dutty stuffed the change into his jeans. "I certainly am. Nae fir lang, like. Meetin Ozzy in the pub in a wee while. You boozin later on, like? Or is 'at a stupid question?"

"Fuck knows. We'll see." Derek smiled at the girl behind the counter, then handed over the cash for his tonic wine. She was a new start. He didn't think that he'd seen her about the Broch. She was youthful, but she was legal; she must be, he thought, if she was allowed to sell drink.

"Ye needin a lift somewye, like?" Dutty asked.

Derek slipped the excess coins off the counter and pocketed the silvers. He slotted the browns into the charity box and winked at the girl, whose approval of said action was conveyed by a brief nibble of her lower lip, then a flustered toggle of her mouth-stud by finger. He committed her countenance to his masturbatory-depository for future reference.

"Aye, if it's nae hassle."

"Nah," said Dutty, "neen at aa. Faar ye gaan? The graveyard?"

"Yip."

The pair exited the shop. The scurries were gnawing each other's wings off to get at the teenagers' discarded chips. Dutty banged on the phone box door. "Waaken up, ye dozy cunt." The alternation between light sources clenched Derek's brain with a fizzy hand.

"Ye a'right 'ere?" Dutty asked, wafting his Celtic top out over his belly.

Derek followed Dutty to his car, a red one with angular contours. Although Derek's motor knowledge wasn't very extensive, he was aware that this model wouldn't have been their latest design. "Jist a bit fragile," he said.

They climbed into the vehicle and vocalised simultaneous complaints about the oven-like heat therein. Dutty sparked up a cigarette, bid one to Derek, whom declined as he did not smoke unless quite drunk, then started the engine, which chuggered with the declaration that it was born of the blood type diesel. The radio pounced. Dutty lowered the volume out of thoughtfulness for his guest. Derek cracked the seal of his Buckie.

"Bit early for 'at, is it nae?" remarked Dutty, getting them as far as the first set of traffic lights.

"Yip," Derek said, then downed the bottle in the time it took for the green light to appear.

"'At's fuck aal. Ah've seen you dee 'at wi a hale een afore."

"Probably."

Dutty took them down the town's main commercial street, the Broadgate. Derek settled into his seat. His town looked grand when it was lit like this. The place appeared mean in the rain, but the sun highlighted its handsome bone structure, lifting the tones of the rock. Too many of the shops, though, he noted, were boarded up. He couldn't always tell if that was because windows had been smashed or the business had gone bust. But that was part of the trouble with Fraserburgh. They razed things and didn't bother to conjure anything in their stead. Derek supposed that the people in charge of such things didn't value a place like this enough to invest in it with any kind of enthusiasm, and why the fuck should they? he thought. Fraserburgh, or the Broch as it was known locally for reasons unclear to even the majority of its residents, sat on the eastern tip of the bottom ledge of the great Z that was the upper half of Scotland. The Broch had a population of about sixteen thousand, if that, and was once bestowed with the esteemed title of being the heroin capital of Europe. Derek could forgive folk for not wanting to pish their pennies away on such a bulky nappy – he doubted that he would either. He himself didn't trust Brochers not to bugger things up for themselves. His view was that the airseholes didn't take pride enough in their town to justify a financial varnish. Anything new got broken and graffitied. The Broch was like that. Some fuckin nutcase even cut off a cocker spaniel's leg and left it to bleed to death the other week. What kind of a thing was that to do? he pondered. But when the sun was out and the Buckfast was in – and in the main, only in those circumstances – Fraserburgh didn't seem like quite the most wretched of pins under which to be stuck.

"Ye still at Toories, aye?" Dutty asked.

"Aye. Fuckin shite, like."

"Fuck aye, ah ken 'at." Dutty flicked his cigarette out the window. "Best thing ah iver did wis get oot o 'at fuckin place. At least ye got yersel a day aff work, though, eh? Ye iver think aboot gettin a job aff-shore?"

"Fuck knows. Dinnae really - "

Dutty stamped on the brake pedal to send the remainder of Derek's answer plummeting back down his throat. They'd turned off from the Broadgate and were travelling along the harbour road when Dutty dropped the anchor and swung their carriage to the right and to a stop, an act so sudden that it had traffic on both sides tooting their disgust.

"Fit the fuck are ye deein?"

Dutty did not respond to the question. Dutty jumped out of his car, leaving the key in the ignition and the engine still running, and bolted up to a small group of men whom had been puffing their fags by a pub doorway, jovial until they spotted the enraged newcomer. The four men were dressed as though their girlfriends had options and these guys knew that they had to present themselves to a standard. Dutty singled out one of the quartet, hailing the alarmed character with a punch that crumpled him to the ground. The three friends set upon

Dutty and were kicking him down the pavement when Derek unbuckled and removed himself from the vehicle.

"Hoi, 'at's enough o 'at," Derek shouted, leaning into the triangle formed by the car door and the roof.

The three men refrained from pummelling the now semi-concious Dutty to study their next opponent. Derek recognised the lads. He'd seen them about. They were younger than he was, younger even than Dutty. Derek could see their aggression constrict. These weren't normally the sort to engage in such scruffy behaviour. They appeared equally ashamed and confused.

"He started it," said one.

"Well, jist enough, a'right?" Derek replied. Some cars had slowed to witness the barbarity; their speeding away clarified that the matter had been resolved. The crew of one boat went back to their work. The trio returned from the bloodied spot on the kerb where Dutty had been disassembled to help their friend up. The pal needed no support in getting to his feet, however. The guy unfurled gradually; the gash above his right eye revealed itself on his ascent. He was slick with red from his eyebrow to his belt, like a hotdog with plenty of tomato sauce. His cream shirt would be for the bin. The blood leaped like newts through his fingers as he attempted to feel out the damage. He winced. A spasm of fury caused the man to pivot and aim a punt at Dutty, but one of the friends blocked him and he missed.

"Fuck sake, ye wanker," cried the bleeding man at the spud-sack. "Fit the fuck did ye dee 'at for? Ma face is cut wide fuckin open."

Dutty managed to drag himself up the pavement to slouch into the white wall of the pub. His eyes were on springs and his head lolled like a balloon with a pebble in it; Dutty, though, hadn't come off as harshly as he might have done. Had the three lads had any power about them, Dutty would have had more to worry about than a bruised cheek and a leaky scalp – the result of a cut sustained from his collision with the ground, rather than from any of the strikes allotted by the men.

"Hoi, min, ye a'right?" Derek asked of his chauffeur. Dutty looked over in the correct direction; he said something inaudible. Derek realised that Dutty, if not the man with the severed eyebrow, would need some assistance in getting up.

As Derek passed the four cautious gents whom his associate had launched himself at a minute earlier, the guy with his hand on the bleeding man's shoulder did a double take.

"You're Derek Gibson, aren't ye?" The guy had spiky hair and a pink shirt. "You used tae go oot wi ma sister."

"Ah might've deen. Fit's 'er name?" Derek bent down and took Dutty by the oxters.

"Lynne."

"Lynne? Nae sure. Oh, aye. Lynne. Aye, she wis a'right. 'At wis back in the academy, wisn't it?" Derek began to heave. "Aye, you cunts kin gie's a han', like. You fuckers did 'is; you eens kin lift 'im up. Ah'm nae fuckin my back o'er 'is nonsense."

Pink Shirt and his friend, the one with the streaks in his do, aided Derek in raising Dutty into a standing position. Dutty's pupils remained meshed in mist.

"Hoo is Lynne 'ese days?" Derek asked.

"Fine. Mairriet an' 'at. Twa bairns."

Derek held Dutty up by the chest. "'At's good."

"Mairriet tae an architect doon in Edinburgh."

Streaks also discovered that, on closer examination, he and Derek had some shared history. "Ah think you saved me fae gettin a hidin een night."

"Did ah?"

"Gazza Thomson wis gaan tae fuckin batter me 'cos ah happened tae luk at 'im in the bogs or somethin smaa like 'at," Streaks elaborated. "Like ah'd been lukin at his cock or 'at. Bit you were 'ere an' you calmed 'im doon."

Derek slapped Dutty lightly. "Good for me. Dutty, you 'ere, min?"

Dutty's faced tightened as though someone had grabbed a fistful of his ginger hair. "Ma cousin," he said. The morsels of his obliterated focus were once again starting to congeal. “Ye decked ma fuckin cousin.” Derek was no longer holding Dutty up, but holding him back.

“Yer cousin?” said the bloodied man; he, too, was being held back by his mates. “’At wee gobshite grabbed ma blon’s airse in The Peacock, so ah thumped ’im. The little fucker hid it comin. It wis the fuckin third time he did it.”

“Ye knocked oot his fuckin teeth,” Dutty exclaimed.

“An’ you split ma fuckin eyebroo. Ah’m gaan tae need stitches for ’is.”

Dutty relaxed back from Derek. “Ye think ’at’s us fuckin quits, like? No way, Jose. Ah’m awa up tae ma pal’s flat tae get a knife an’ ah’m comin back tae slit yer throats.” Dutty stormed off, disappearing around the corner. He did not return forthwith as they all thought that he might.

Derek turned to the group. “Ah widnae worry aboot it.”

“The boy’s a fuckin psycho,” said a man with golden shoes. “He’s left his fuckin car rinnin.”

“He’ll calm doon,” Derek said. “He’s jist hid three fuckers bootin intae ’im. He’ll be greetin doon a laney somewye. Onywye, enough wi these shenanigans; ah’m missin ma dide’s funeral ’cos o ’is caper.”

Streaks steered his aggravated friend round by the shoulders to investigate the wound. The bleeding man was less than amused by his physician’s summation, which was articulated as a pantomime grimace.

“We’re gaan tae hiv tae taak Steven-John tae the hospital,” Pink Shirt said.

“Aye, well, you cunts kin drap me aff on the wye.”

*

Derek stood by the cemetery gates. Streaks tore off in his Subaru to see if they couldn’t get their pal’s face sewn back together. Pink Shirt and Gold Shoes had come with them. Apparently, they were none too keen on testing Dutty's resolve by staying put. His Peugeot had been left to conk itself out in front of the pub.

To the right of the graveyard and past the mini-roundabout, there was a retail park with a Tescos and the like; and to the left, the road led out to the rival villages of Cairnbulg and St Combs. The golf course that began almost immediately after the graveyard followed the road part of the way. Beyond the golfers were the dunes and the beach and the sea. The bus that Derek hadn't thought to catch until it was too late completed its circuit, trundling behind him back into town. The other bus, the private hire one laid on for the mourners, was missing from the car park across the road, as was the silver Merc. Also absent were Aunt Rosie and Sylvia's car and any of the other vehicles that had stalked the hearse.

Derek fastened a shirt button. He gazed up the pathway between the green gums that shoot out glinting teeth to the far cement lip. The railings acted as a brace for this necropolis. He could see two men fill by shovel his grandad's grave; he knew that his grandad had reserved the plot next to his granny's. A third man hovered by the workmen, and though Derek could not hear what was being said from such a distance, he could tell that the two were humouring the third with polite disregard.

Derek watched as the man, satisfied at the conclusion of the one-sided chat, bid farewell to the pair whom did abstain from turning away from their job to trade in similar platitudes. The man sauntered down the path towards Derek. The man's smile of recognition opened rather than widened, owing to his age. Derek's Great Uncle Willie ambled up to him in a brown suit that appeared to have been borrowed from a taller friend and which had a chalky stain down one sleeve; he wore his tatty bonnet that Derek had always remembered Willie wearing. Willie was like a patchwork doll, consisting of the leftovers from when they'd manufactured his brother Stanley, and because of this Derek felt a fondness for his uncle that most of the rest of his family did not.

Willie congratulated Derek, in utterly unsarcastic fashion, on his exemplary execution of his graveside duties. Derek accepted the kind words without debate.

A bearded power-walker, rigged out in a tammy hat and tracksuit bottoms, which were both black, and a yellow waterproof coat, banged into the stationary Derek, nearly causing Derek to collide with his uncle. Derek hurled a grenade of vocal abuse at the man, whom did not retort or look back but marched on by the graveyard to the Cairnbulg road, chuntering away to himself something about control. The man did not even raise a mittened hand to apologise. His white trainers chugged off around the bend.

Unfazed by the incident, Willie suggested that they go now to Rosie and Sylvia's for a beverage and a biscuit. Derek saw no sense in standing about these gates all day and concurred. He had no desire to indulge further in the company of two women who hated him, but he would need to go there to see his parents and to converse before things got out of hand. Derek could even do with going back to his bed; this cloudless gleam was polishing away his flesh like a blowtorch on plastic.

Derek and his uncle journeyed to his Aunt Rosie's bungalow by foot. En route, they crossed between the metallic warehouses of the retail park, where they stopped so that Willie could talk to some bemused old lady whom didn't, Derek was quite certain, know the man. She was friendly about the encounter, though Derek was obliged to inch the pair away from her, assuaging the discomfort that he could sense but his uncle could not. His aunt's was only a couple of streets beyond that awkwardness.

On arriving at their destination, Derek saw that the silver Merc was not parked among the other familiar cars and decided against entering Rosie and Sylvia's house. There was much activity inside, with multiple bodies shifting around in the living room. Sylvia watched from the kitchen window as a stout man smoked in her garden, on the grass. Willie trudged through the flowerbed to shake the man's hand. The seldom seen Aberdeen cousin shook the offered appendage, though only after he'd taken another draw of his cigarette. Derek sneaked away as Rosie joined her lover at the window.

He strolled homewards, following a curving street that was lined with neatly spaced houses, much newer than the buildings of the Broadgate but somewhat older than the ones that had sprung up like acne across the by-pass. He cut through a lane to another street where the homes were of a greater height and width; expensive stables for oilmen and accountants, and fishermen like his dad.

He thought about what he might say or do so that his parents wouldn't go ballistic at him. He would just have to explain what had happened, and not linger. Get in, get washed, get changed, get out, and then go see Jimbo. But how could they be angry? They'd fucked off and left him. How was he supposed to get to the graveyard? Fuckin sulky pair o twats. It was always Derek's fault. He was fed up with their moaning.

Derek swapped pavements and scaled the drive of the street's largest abode. From his bedroom window, the whole of the Broch could be seen; it looked to Derek like a colony of seals, poking out through green clouds. He rounded the rear of a silver Merc. He halted when he was in view of the front door. He put his latchkey back in his pocket. He swore aloud to himself.

He collected the two hastily packed suitcases that awaited him beside the steps and departed.

Chapter 2

The bags were heavy. The handles prised at his grip like crowbars. The exertion required to carry both suitcases decimated his pace to an incremental waddle. He would spew again as he'd done outside the church, his innards assured him. It wasn't often that he felt ill through exercise, for none of his hobbies entailed much movement besides the hoisting of receptacles to a facial perforation and the slipping of bodily keys into female locks, and his being seemed to vibrate with this uncommon ache. He paused for breath halfway down a lengthy street of semi-detached houses and sat on some fellow's knee-high wall. He took his coat off and slung it over one of the suitcases.

His dad had taken little care in compressing everything Derek owned into those bags. His CD collection had jarred against him, hard edges stretching out from the tough black fabric. Tomorrow, light bruises would appear, crisscrossing the lower half of his legs like peach-coloured tartan socks. So at least he'd have that to look forward to.

He panted, then got back up to resume a scrap that he was losing. Derek leaned over and reacquainted his palms with the handles. He straightened himself out in a careless fashion that could've damaged his spine. A small twinge in his back alerted him to his disintegrating youth better than candles on cakes ever could. Derek hoped that he would remember to adopt a stricter hauling stance thereafter. He trudged on, trying to hide his exhaustion from anyone whom might be prying. An orange car sped up the street towards him. It flashed its lights in place of a wave; he nodded in reply and stumbled with the motion. The car halted and reversed. Derek let the handles go and wheezed.

Lee Johnstone grinned at him from the front passenger seat. Lee was slight of frame, though not in a sickly manner. Lee was groomed like a city person, as though his job demanded that his demeanour sparkled. Lee worked in a restaurant in Peterhead, had a potent phobia of moths and, as everybody but Lee himself would testify, was partial to anal insertions. The driver was female and raven-haired. Derek didn't know what, if anything, she did for a job, but she always seemed to be well stocked for petrol. Her name was

Catherine Somethingorother, and Derek had had some fun with her in nights of yore. She did not rotate her shades towards Derek. There was no one in the back seat. Lee proffered Derek a lift. Derek waited for Catherine to acquiesce with a smirk before bouncing aboard with his luggage.

Lee jokingly inquired if he was going to the airport. Derek asked them if they knew where Jimmy lived, and provided them with directions when it was announced that they did not. Lee spoke throughout the brief trip; Catherine said nothing more than to utter her disapproval at the protagonists' behaviour in the latest piece of gossip that Lee divulged, and to berate the skills of other road users.

Lee knew everything that happened in the town; he made a point of knowing. Derek descried the outwardly cheery and deceptively vicious chap to be entertaining company; but only in wee doses. It was from Lee that Derek had learned what had become of Jimmy's ex, Lori, and about her apparent new-found penchant for prostitution. Lee had told Derek that he'd spoken to a guy, some Nick character whom they both sort of knew through school, and this guy had, allegedly, bumped into Lori as she was punting it about in an alley in Dundee. Nick had been in the City of Discovery for a wedding, and he'd left the party for a drunken ramble when she'd propositioned him. According to Nick, he hadn't taken her up on the offer. Lori hadn't recognised him, despite her having been in his Modern Studies class. Lee had sworn blind to Derek that Nick had sworn blind to him that it had definitely been Lori. When next Derek and Nick had crossed paths, he told Nick to keep shtoom about the rendezvous, fearing how Jimbo might take the news that the love of his life was now a hoor, a professional one. Knowing what Derek knew about the girl, he was certain that it was all true; apart from maybe the bit about Nick keeping his wallet and his walloper to himself. Lori was a fair dame so she was, or she could be when she toned down the junkieness.

The orange vehicle turned into Jimmy's street. The co-pilot passed a derogatory comment, which caused the driver to snort. Derek had provoked her into vocalising a comparable sound when he'd spanked her with his belt. Jimmy lived on the ground floor of a block of flats; three homes stacked one on top of the other, with his pal holding the base card.

He had a front door, while the elevated tenants shared a stairwell on the side of the building. This meant that Jimmy was a prime target for thieves, or he would've been had he anything for the toerags to steal. The building was set like a dead tooth in a broken jaw. The dreary homes scrummaged around the car as though hobos encircling a corpse, each contemplating making their move for the unfortunate's clothes. A pair of teens stepped out in front of Catherine's bumper, causing her to almost stall the car. The shorter of the two had bleached hair, whereas his pal had a complexion like red paper ripped up and glued back down onto a larger white sheet. They glowered into the windscreen as they cut across the road, daring the occupants to remonstrate. If Derek had been driving, and had he a licence to do so, he thought that he probably would've ploughed straight into the pair. His hosts were not so inclined to court trouble. The car crawled to the kerb.

A dance song that Derek hated, but which was hugely popular, emanated from a mystery source. Lee took his mobile phone from his pocket and answered it.

*

Freddy greeted the caller with the enthusiasm that he would any interruption, regardless of the fact that his wife proved to be the most recent distraction that prevented him from getting these light brackets finally affixed to the hold of the bobbing ship. He had other jobs to finish around the harbour and it was already after four o'clock. He'd be working till midnight at this rate. He raised the hood of his visor firmly so that it stayed up this time and didn't swing back down from his ruffled blond hair onto his mobile-clutching hand. He held the welding rod away from him and put one boot against its portable generator. He stood beneath the opened hatch in the shower of light, still not quite far enough away from the ice-filled stanchion. Earlier, faces had appeared at the hatch to report of a fight that was happening over by Dunce's Bar, like he had the luxury of aeons to stand about watching idiots beating each other up. What was Kim needing with him now? It was the plumber, was it? Hadn't shown up to fix the bath as he was supposed to do, had he not? Well, Freddy would see to that. No, he didn't have enough on his plate, did he? He could see to this, couldn't he? His wife hung up, upset by his tone. Freddy stamped on the generator, checked that it was okay, then phoned the plumber.

*

Sylvia pointed at Rosie to mollify the hoover so that she could hear what was being said over the telephone line. Rosie shushed the contraption by stabbing a button as though she were opening an umbrella for the untimely rain. They had at last got the Aberdeen relative to vamoose. He'd lingered after the sandwiches had been eaten and the other guests had left; sipping his drink from the middle cushion of the sofa, the man had leered at the women like he was waiting for either of them to come to their senses and suggest a threesome. Rosie had lied about some function that they had to attend later; after a while, the man slipped away into his BMW with a look as though to mock their having missed out on something grand. Sylvia listened to the Asian man who told her that his name was Ethan and who pretended to be American and who began to list the benefits of his financial service provider. Sylvia expressed her disinterest by clicking the phone back into its handset. Rosie crossed the living room floor, crunching some crumbs into the carpet with her shoe. Sylvia rolled her eyes at the sound; Rosie slapped at her arm but did not connect. Rosie picked up the phone. Two children her brother had, and both were completely useless. Had she and Sylvia any kids, they wouldn't have let them become like the drunken imbecile and the drug-ravaged supposed-to-be mum that were her nephew and niece. She would have to, however, make this sympathetic call, stating her and her partner's solidarity with Adam and Suzanne, despite their misgivings over his and her parenting skills. Sylvia crouched to pick up the crumbs. Rosie dialled the number, and stretched out her foot to playfully tramp on Sylvia's hand. Sylvia smiled up at her as Rosie waited for someone to answer.

*

Mark instantaneously stiffened when he read the caller ID on the screen of his mobile: SexxyMilf. He knew by now that the thirty-six-year-old divorcee's real name was Chloe, but it was her Internet pseudonym that he stored in his phone. The words alone gave him a hard-on that could lift his desk and cause the mortgage forms to slide towards the empty guest chairs. He switched the mobile into his left hand and scooted further under the desk so that the camera in the top corner of his office would know nothing of the debauchery that he was apt to commit. Sometimes it was good not to have a view from one's workstation, he'd learned. Mark proceeded to read his monitor as though he were solving some customer's query. He untangled himself from his boxer shorts, trousers and tucked-in shirt; he grabbed hold. She told him in her Devon accent what she wanted him to do to her and for how long and how abundantly and with what specific implementations. He whispered his compliance. He gasped. He fired onto the underside of his desk. The other phone, his office phone, rang. He cancelled SexxyMilf's call, without a goodbye. She didn't expect one. He took a moment to let his voice tumble back down through the notes before reaching for the beeping handset. An underling knocked at his door.

*

His mother rapped upon the door. Derek pulled himself up into a sitting position on his bed. He checked under the duvet for visitors. He had, according to all signs, returned home alone. He waited to see if he was hungover or not. It appeared that he was not. He must've slept through the worst of it. The wilting light of late afternoon slithered in between the blinds. It was good to wake and for it to still be day. She knocked again and explained that it was the phone for him. It was Jimmy calling for Derek. She reminded Derek that it was his grandad's funeral tomorrow, as though he were the sort to forget such a thing, and left the cordless phone outside the door. He groaned at the thought that Jimmy would be phoning him, and it wasn't that he didn't like Jimmy. He liked Jimbo a lot, but he hadn't heard from him all weekend. Derek fancied that Jimmy would be going through one of his especially sinister phases. Calling Derek during such spells was equivalent to contacting the emergency services to free someone trapped down the sewers. But rather than bringing a fire engine and cutting tools and what have you, all that was required of Derek was his company and a few bottles of this, that and the other, and a willingness to be Jimmy's emotional dartboart for the evening.

For as long as Derek had known him, Jimmy had never been a particularly happy boy. Teen angst had hit Jimbo harder than most and by the age of seventeen his wrists had become bisected with macabre reminders of darker days. Hence why Jimmy never wore short-sleeved shirts on a night out. For a brief spell, though, Jimmy's condition improved. Emerging out from under a cloud of depression and low self-esteem, Jimmy approached his twenties with a newly unearthed confidence and belief in himself. Things were starting to look up. He was midway through his HND in Mechanical and Offshore Engineering and heading for university. In a few years, Jimmy would've been well on his way to making serious dosh. He would've done okay. Then, just a matter of days before his twenty-first birthday, Jimmy discovered that he had testicular cancer.

The poor boy lost a nut.

Feeling crushed and defeated once again, Jimmy forgot about completing his HND and got a job at CP's, handling putrefied fish guts for minimum wage. He never did go back to college. After that, things only got worse.

He met Lori. Fell in love with Lori. Then got totally fucked over by Lori.

Jimmy, along with Derek and the rest of the boys, was acquainted with Lori dating back to their time at Fraserburgh Academy. Indeed, Derek himself had had a short-lived romance with her all those years ago. Jimmy and Lori had spun in the same social circles for a long time without collision. It was on a Friday night in The Tart about three years ago when he and she really made first contact. For whatever reason, one took a shine to the other – a person couldn't be certain as to whom was the instigator, and they began to chat. Some doubted Jimmy's appeal, but Derek didn't think him a write-off. In Derek's opinion, Jimbo, although gangly and bearing a brownish mane that curled like smoke in the wind, wasn't quite the most godawful repugnant of people, and, when he wasn't too busy being steamrollered by the more sour attributes of human existence, he had a deadpan drollness that Derek found endearing. The forming couple's conversation would've started off breezily enough in their booth, taking in tales of school discos and mutual associates. Derek, who was mentioned in several of these stories, had watched from the bar with a scepticism that Lori didn't notice and Jimmy chose to ignore. The pair eliminated the barrier of the table, condensing the space between them like the blades of scissors closing through sticks. As the summer's flare had withered outside, so, too, had the tone of their discourse. His depressive nature and her accelerating narcotic habit were both touched upon. When The Tart closed for the evening and everyone else headed up to The Peacock, Jimmy and Lori slunk off to his parents' house. And thus it was that a grisly friendship, which somehow lasted for over two years, was born.

Whether or not she had ever at any point actually loved Jimmy was open to debate. His love for her, however, was beyond question.

Jimmy was infatuated with her.

He saw past Lori's minor imperfections – the spitefulness, the heartlessness, the heroin addiction – and saw something that was well and truly hidden from the rest of the world. So hidden, in fact, that nobody except Jimbo would ever know what that special quality was.

Derek suspected that it was maybe her willingness to receive.

Love. Money. Anything. Everything.

Jimmy was never meant to be alone. He needed to be in love, he needed to be needed. Lori came along and slipped into the role like a maggot into a gaping wound. She sucked his accounts dry, exchanging capital for blackened rolls of foil. A habit as ferocious as hers required more than what his pitiful salary could provide. She had tantrums. She punched him. She scratched him. She kicked him. She threatened to leave. He took out a loan. The money kept on vanishing like snow into fire.

His stereo disappeared.

She was happy.

No rent money.

She was happy.

Nothing to eat.

She was happy.

She was killing him. But she was there. Always there.

He was happy.

The bank wouldn't give him any more cash.

He turned to his folks; they turned their backs.

In the end, she left him. She took off without leaving so much as a text, with all the class and sentimentality of a parasite departing its dying host. Any kind of prior warning would've been too nice for her.

Lori's sudden disappearance aroused a wave of suspicious glances in Jimmy's direction. Rumours blossomed like tumours all over the Broch about violent arguments and shallow graves. The police questioned him. For a second, even Derek had got caught up in the swell of cynicism. Had Jimmy finally cracked and gone psycho in the tool shed? Derek wouldn't have blamed him if he had done.

A couple of days later, though, a late night call came through that completely exonerated Jimmy. From a phone box in fuck-knows-where, Lori called her mum to tell her that she was alright. That she just needed to get away. That she would never get any better being where she was and blah blah bollocks tit-wank.

According to the mother, Lori hadn't mentioned Jimmy once during the phone call.

Two years together and nothing.

Not a word.

Great stuff.

Needless to say, the ordeal had near finished Jimmy off.

Derek swung his feet off the bed and onto the floor. He still had his socks on from the Saturday night. His shirt draped the computer, which might've been switched on twice this year; maybe, if his parents had attempted to have a go at figuring it out. He'd given up on it. Derek didn't have an email address, and didn't have a clue what the girls were on about when they discussed their Bebo and MySpace thingamajigs. There were some music-themed posters on his walls, and stacks of CDs on the ledge by the twin windows. There was an expensive electric guitar on its stand that he couldn't play, and had never played, though he thought that he would like to be able to play it. He thought about Jimmy phoning him. He knew that poor Jimmy would be pining away in his flat on his lonesome, in need of a shoulder to cry on or an ear to sob into. But Derek didn't much want to be a shoulder or an ear. He was tired of acting as the sleeve upon which Jimmy wiped away his misery. Why the fuck was it always Derek whom Jimmy sought out for these monthly meetings? They'd get pished and Jimmy would rant about his ex, with Jimbo's opinion of whom veering wildly in relation to just how much of the booze had been guzzled. After a few beers, he'd be sobbing about how much he missed her and loved her and wanted to marry her. By the time that the last drop of alcohol had been consumed, Jimmy would be distressing the neighbours with screams of how much he fucking hated her to fuck and wanted her to die a painful fucking death the fucking cunt. A half-hour later and Jimbo would be asleep; tears and snot streaming down his face like frozen rivers. All the while, Derek would just listen. Derek was a sublime listener, or so the rep seemed to go. Basically, he knew how to sit quietly and not obstruct the flow of a person's oration with opinions of his own. He'd feign interest and nod when appropriate, and that would about do it. The indications were that this was sufficient for Jimmy. Derek would show up, drink, listen to his pal lose the plot for a few hours, wait for Jimmy to conk, then leave; possibly get a kebab on his way back to the castle. This procedure had occurred at a rate of roughly once per month since Lori had packed her bags forever ago.

Derek, like most chaps, felt a mite uncomfortable in the presence of any male nakedness, whether it be of the physical or psychological branch. This was not his forte. Derek was a knight, a slayer of dragons, a seducer of wenches. He was not a doctor.

The embarrassment that flowed between Derek and Jimmy the next time they met after a good crying session was always a treat. Christ, Derek reflected. Ye'd hiv thought they'd gotten blootered an' gunged each other's tonsils or somethin. But it seemed to put Jimmy back on an even keel again. After one of his venting sprees, Jimbo would be almost okay for a couple of weeks.

And Derek knew that his attendance at those seminars had far more importance than Jimmy would ever let on, drunk or nae. The Amazing Master Gibson was fully aware that his being there stopped Jimmy from wrenching open a vein or two.

But just why did it always have to be Derek? He didn't want to drink tonight. He honestly wasn't in the mood for it, and he had that whole funeral thing as well. And there was no way that Derek could deal with a distraught Jimmy in sober mode. The cordless phone awaited his response on the other side of the door. Derek didn't want to leave his room. Then again, he also didn't want to be the reason that Jimmy scurried off in search of the nearest packet of Bics.

Derek rubbed his thick mass of hair with one hand and clawed at his thigh with the other. He went to the door and opened it.

*

Jimmy answered the door in his dressing gown, which was purple and dirty. The flesh of his neighbourhood was scummy with a green sweat. He took a look down at Derek's suitcases then turned back up the corridor, turning right into the living room/kitchen. Derek noticed that his friend wore nothing on his feet. Jimmy was likely just out of bed, having been awoken by Derek's persistent knocking. Derek had thought to ask Jimmy why it was that he hadn't been to his work, then he remembered that Jimmy had told him last night that he'd been sacked from CP's. Jimmy had been made redundant as of last Friday. Derek had been quick to assure him on learning of this latest development that there were many more fishyards in the Broch; he'd even see about getting Jimbo a job with him at Toories, his uncle Tommy's yard.

Derek shuffled in sideways through the front door, holding his bags forward and behind as though he were a link in a ring of dancers. He closed the front door by thrusting the trailing suitcase back towards it. There were two doors on his left: the first led to the bathroom; the second, Jimmy's bedroom. Derek entered the door on the right-hand side, which was situated opposite the pair like a nose between eyes.

Derek plonked the bags in the centre of the room beside the furry settee. His coat flopped off a suitcase and onto the floor. He reacted speedily to remove the coat from the soiled carpet. He patted some filth off the garment then folded it over his arm. The curtains were united across the front window and a bulb had been tickled by switch into burning, and this was all in spite of the fact that the sun still skimmed in through the kitchen window. Jimmy stood by the sink, filling the kettle and looking out into the communal garden, at the end of which and before a high wall there was a wooden shed. Jimmy seemed to Derek to have been coloured in with Tipp-ex. In his robe, he looked like a blanket hung over a rocking chair: all edges and angles.

The enlarged and framed picture of Lori smiled at Derek with glazed green eyes, as though she were distracted by someone doing a wrist shake behind the photographer's back. The ex took pride of place on Jimmy's wall; the brunette received guests as a decapitated head floating against the wan background. She'd given Jimmy nothing but grief, stress, trouble and debt that he was still struggling to pay off, and yet he mourned her absence from his life as a remote control would a battery. Jimbo should've been doing cartwheels and banging on a tambourine now that he was shot of her. But no, no, no; that wasn't for Jimmy. That was too much like what a normal person might do. Derek hated the picture and thought less of Jimmy for having it mounted there like something that he needn't be ashamed of. He should be ashamed. Derek was ashamed of him, or sometimes he was. Presently, he was less concerned with silly pictures and more interested in securing shelter.

Jimmy didn't ask Derek anything. Why would he need to? Jimbo waited for the kettle to boil. Only after it did did Jimmy think to collect two mugs from the cupboard and spoon into them some coffee granules. The melody of suction and detraction was coherent as

Jimmy shifted his bare feet over the red linoleum, which only covered half of the room. It was grey carpet from the sofa to the TV. That TV had once belonged to Derek, and erstwhile it had resided in his bedroom. A kind, charitable act later and there it was, sat atop a straining cabinet, which itself was bestowed to Jimmy by a granny. Of course, it could be argued that Derek's donation had been motivated more by cold practicality than selfless generosity. Jimmy had been bereft of a television due to Lori having flogged his last one, and Derek wanted to be able to watch some of the European games here. The young knight had likely benefited from the gift just as much as anyone else had.

Jimmy offered Derek a beverage. Jimmy didn't tender him milk or sugar. He wouldn't have had any of either. Derek thanked him for the drink that he hadn't asked for and didn't particularly want. There would be no biscuits to go with this brew. It'd be futile rummaging through the flat in search of food. Jimmy bought just enough grub to stave off malnutrition for one more week and that was it. The guy's limited diet was imposed by a lack of financial resources. Anything edible would've been polished off by the pair the night before. Amongst the vacant bottles that littered the floor, traces of Sunday evening's banquet could be seen, none of which Derek could really remember feasting upon.

Jimmy looped the ear of his own mug with a stork-neck finger and gazed out the window. The sun leaked over the garden wall like some magnificent, disembowelled jellyfish. The mug loosened itself from Jimmy's hook and fell to the floor.

*

The ball rolled across the lino towards the toilets. Phil stopped it with his shoe and tossed it back onto the pool table where the two Latvian lads were playing. He made a comment to the duo about keeping their balls to themselves, in broad Doric, which they didn't fully grasp though understood the tone of well enough to respond with diplomatic laughter. Phil retrieved the latest copy of the Northern Echo from a table, along with some glasses, and went back behind the bar.

The Latvians completed their game and left with a wave as Phil read the newspaper to a finish. He'd been engrossed by a report in the midst of the local tabloid about a possible impending crystal meth epidemic in the Broch. The author of said piece also happened to have the same real name as a guy he used to be pals with; a guy they'd known as Pagan. Phil hadn't seen or heard from his old mucker since he'd moved down to England when they were but kids. He wondered whatever happened to Peggy. He'd be thriving at something or other, Phil speculated. Pagan had had that way about him. He'd had the brains and stuff; he was bound to be doing well for himself. Or he could just be dead. Phil sat back on his stool. He sipped his Guinness. He limited himself to just the two, at most three, pints through the day, so he savoured it. Phil knew that he could do without the excess calories.

He sat alone, in slack readiness for custom. The Tartan Rainbow was a small pub with only the two booths, one on either side of the entrance. The booths were coated with leather the shade of dampness. The proximity of the walls dictated to pool players which shots they could go for. The slats of the blinds peaked downwards as someone peering over a fence. Phil's face itched from having shaved that morning. The new girl had helped him to reach the decision that he needed to get rid of his beard. So now it was gone, and his face itched. He didn't think that the new girl was really right for this establishment. The Tart was a place of oak and whiskey rather than marble and cocktails. She looked like she'd be more suited to Dunce's Bar along the road there. But he was happy that she'd be working here, for however long her stay in Fraserburgh might be.

Crystal meth epidemic? That was just like the Broch; Brochers, fuckin numpties the lot o them. Phil was going to clear off from here this year. He'd spoken about it for long enough; this was the year to do it, before he was in his thirties and too old and fat to do anything. He sensed that he was becoming a bit of a joke with the regulars, having bored them all to tears for years now, *years*, about his plans to migrate to Australia or South Africa or Thailand or wherever, and then never doing anything about it. He felt as though he probably looked like something of a coward to them. He had to change that. He had to change this perception that people had of him as being a plump clown; an impression that was strengthened by his uncanny, and lamentable, resemblance to John Candy. Adrian Campbell was supposed to call the pub today. Adrian was originally from the Broch, and he was a proper globetrotter. Ades was currently in Canada; he was meant to phone and inform Phil as to what was happening over there in terms of digs and employment. Phil was just waiting to hear from the guy.

A patron entered the stuffy gloom of The Tart and swiped thoughts of overseas expeditions off the table. The man walked up to the bar. His every move implied the threat of violence: his slow, heavy walk; the manner in which his dense arms swayed as though in preparation for something. The stranger wore a T-shirt that accentuated his muscles. His legs were a couple of tree trunks wrapped in denim. The monolith's teak-whittled sneer complete with dark hair and week-old stubble brought forth to Phil the idea of an evil Superman. The guy looked the sort to have started a profusion of brawls, just to end them as savagely as he could. Having worked in the pub industry for the time that he had, Phil was accustomed to that mentality; but not previously had he encountered such menace encased so epicly. He stood a head taller than Phil, and Fat Ass was no midget. That would put the guy in the region of 6'5", maybe even taller. Phil had never seen this man in the Broch before. As the stranger cracked his mouth to speak, Phil did not know in which accent or language he might articulate himself.

The man addressed Phil in English, though with a gruff Scottish accent that wasn't quite of these parts. The man asked Phil his name and if he worked here. Phil answered, truthfully. The man then produced a photograph and inquired Phil as to whether or not he could identify the person in the picture. Phil stared at the photo and steadied himself for a lie. He adjusted his baseball cap over his black brillo-pad mop. He told the giant that he didn't know the person, and reiterated that assertion when he was asked if he was sure about that. The man slipped the picture back into his pocket and left the premises as if he were its new owner. Phil wasn't entirely certain that he'd convinced the man of his ignorance.

He sipped the Guinness to ease his tongue down from the roof of his mouth. The pub phone rang.

*

Derek put the phone back into its berth on the coffee table and disclosed to the sitting Jimmy that that was just Fat Ass calling. Jimmy could sense that he had more bad news coming his way. Derek stood over him, pausing to consider how best to relay the gist of Phil's story. There would be no alleviating technique. Derek told Jimmy about what had happened earlier in The Tart, and Jimmy didn't flinch at the revelation. There was some scary guy on the hunt for him. Jimmy scratched at a sticking thing on the cushion beside him and brushed it onto the carpet. So it goes.

Chapter 3

Heavy knuckles drummed against the door. The sound ricocheted through the flat.

Derek emerged from the bathroom, toothbrush in hand, with white foam lathered around his mouth like a rabid mutt. A dollop of froth dropped from his lips and onto his exposed belly.

Again, the fist fell upon the door.

Jimmy, who was now out of the dressing gown and into his uniform – a Dons top from some seasons ago and faded Levis, grabbed the last of the rubbish accumulated from Sunday's therapy session and tossed it into a rotund bin-liner beside the TV. He took the bat that he always kept handy under the sofa and entered the corridor.

Derek ducked back into the bathroom. He spat the remnants of the paste into the sink and wiped the thick splodge off his flesh. Derek noted the curvature of his belly. He looked like he'd just swallowed a bowling ball.

His eyes, boxed in a mirror above the sink, inspected his peculiar phizog. He was, as one girlie had put it, handsome in an ugly sort of way, which was quite the king of backhanded compliments. Aye, but that hadn't stopped him from nailing her until his final extrication made a noise like the removal of a foot from a wet boot. Derek surely wasn't a Bradley Pitt or a Thomas Cruise delicate beauty, but he knew that he had that something; the charisma and sex appeal possessed by the special few. Since the spots had slid off his face and he'd bid adieu to his stuttering teens, Derek had developed a gift for luring in the top chiquitas. In fact, Sir Derek was somewhat the Don Juan, as in the ladies Don Juan to marry him but they'd gladly engage with him in a bit of Saturday night slap and tickle. He couldn't really understand why he'd enjoyed such vast success in declothing the dames, and nor could any of his annoyed mates. He didn't have the best bait to begin with, though he always seemed to end up catching more than his quota's worth. Derek, however, was content to be grateful, rather than analytical.

The front door trembled.

Derek sorted his buckle, threw on an Iron Maiden T-shirt and met Jimmy out in the hallway.

Their eyes locked. The door shook. The cheap wood threatened to crumble like dry sand.

Jimmy's grip on the bat tightened.

Derek scrutinised the corridor for a makeshift weapon. There was nothing. The hall was bare. He turned to the bathroom. The closest thing to a blunt and dangerous instrument Derek could see was a jobby he'd left floating in the bowl. He flushed it.

Cheerio, sailor.

The door handle twisted. And twisted.

Ye're wastin yer time 'ere, pal. Derek had taken care to lock the front door posthaste upon receiving Phil's warning.

The door rumbled once more.

Phil.

Fat Ass.

Derek reached for the handle. He turned the key and pulled the door.

"Derek, fit the fuck are ye - " Jimmy's voice died in a flash.

There, bitter beneath a tarry sky, stood a large, familiar man.

"You cunts tuk yer fuckin time."

Derek could hear Jimmy mutter a mouthful of relieved curses behind him.

The tension dissipated, dissolving like aspirin in water.

Phil yanked off his hat and stormed into the living room. He settled down on the sofa; his considerable frame near folded the antique in half.

After a scan of the world outside – some paranoid children smoked under a streetlight, but no conspicuous hulk-types – Derek locked the door. He and Jimmy, ghostly and unamused, joined Fat Ass in the room that was now cleaner of carpet and fresher of smell.

"Did ye's nae hear me?"

"Aye," Derek replied, pushing his suitcases out of the way of Phil's giddy shoes. "Bit we wisnae expectin ye. We thought it wis 'at ither guy. Ye ken? The big cunt ye jist waarned us aboot?" Derek shook his head. "Ye fat pillock. Did ye hiv tae knock sae fuckin loud? Fuck sake. Ah near shat ma pants, ye gluttonous hoor."

The benign force of chub and jest writhed out of his grey fleece top, the flannel garment that he was fond of wearing and which made him appear even more mountainous than usual. Phil wore a T-shirt underneath that clung to his stomach like protesters to some condemned thing and highlighted his battle with the burger. Already, Derek could see petrolic semi-circles heading south from Phil's armpits. He was a fair size was Phil. But he was also a nice sort and reliable, in a way that Derek himself never professed to be. Considerate, useful, generous, kind: Derek regarded himself as being none of these things and less. The boy Derek was a knight, not a saint.

"An' fit's aa 'is aboot, like?" Phil spat a rag nail at the bags.

"Ah've bin kicked oot ma hoose."

Pause. Chuckle. "Seriously?"

"Aye, fuckin seriously, ye doup. Ah ken, ah thought it wis hilarious an' aa."

Phil's beardless face reddened. "Wis 'at onythin tae dee wi the funeral the day?"

"Hoo did you ken aboot 'at?"

"'Cos ye were gaan on aboot it aa last night. Ye nae mine 'at, ye drunken neap? Ye were girnin in the pub aboot hoo much ye used tae love gaan oot in a wee boaty wi yer dad an' yer granda. Ah thought ye wis awaa tae start greetin."

"Jimbo, kin you mine ony o 'at?"

Jimmy leaned the bat against the wall and crouched upon the sturdy coffee table. "Vaguely." He momentarily reminded Derek of an anthropomorphisised grasshopper in some cartoon.

Phil laughed. "What a bleezin feel ye are, Derek."

"Aye aye, Porky, an' faar's yer fuckin beard?"

"Jist fancied a change."

"'At's one wye tae slim doon, richt enough," Derek said. "Must've bin like shavin a sheep's airse." He scraped some toothpaste from his lip. "Ah thought ye wis supposed tae be workin the night."

"Sae did I." Phil picked up the bat and swished it about like a buccaneer. "Pretty cool. Faan did ye get 'is, Jimbo?"

"A while ago."

"The Internet?"

"Sports shop; Aiberdeen."

"So, why are ye nae?" Derek pressed.

"Nae fit?"

"Workin. Jesus. It's like pullin teeth wi you, ye sweetie-lovin tosser."

"Because," Phil put down the bat, "apparently ah dinnae work Monda nights onymair; okay, nosy bastard?"

"Fit? Dinnae tell me that you've bin sacked as weel."

"No. Ma oors hiv bin changed. They've got a new start."

"Fa?"

"Jist some quine," Phil replied, swiftly turning coy.

"A lady?" Derek assumed a hero pose, with his groin thrust out and his genitals visible through his jeans. Phil recoiled on the sofa, away from the sight. "Quit actin as though ye widnae want tae fin' oot fit 'is bad boy tastes like."

"Ah a'ready div," Phil said. "Lee Johnstone's shite, ye poofter."

"Get tae fuck. Hoo aal is she, 'en? Fit dis she luk like? Come on, Fat Ass, stop aitin the beans an' spill 'em."

"Ah dinnae ken fuck aal. God's honest."

"Ye must ken somethin, ye fat turd."

"Ah hivnae even seen 'er yet." Phil posted this mistruth as though guiding the blind with deodorant. "Ah jist ken that ah'm gettin Jessie's aal oors an' 'is new start's gettin mine. So ah winnae be workin Setterda nights onymair eether."

"Good," Jimmy remarked, though he was likely unaware as to what his chums were gabbing about.

Derek grinned. "Ah might hiv tae hae a wan'er doon tae The Tart sometime tae see 'is new barmaid, eh? She better nae be growlin. If she's you in a skirt, ye kin keep 'er."

"'At'll be right, ye fuckin drunk." Fat Ass sniggered. "Some o the beasts you've bin wi, ye probably wid ride me if ye wis drunk enough."

"Well, if ah wis drunk enough. Ye hiv got a wee bit o Josephine Brand aboot ye."

"Fuck you."

"Or a young, albino Oprah Winfrey."

Phil bellowed with mirth.

"With your succulent breasts and womanly hips," Derek continued, beaming at Phil's rapture. "Mind you, if ye squeezed your tits taegither, instead o milk squirtin oot, ye'd probably get choc-ices oozin fae the tips o those beauts. Or fuckin chip fat." Phil howled. Derek derived much entertainment from watching the man, engraved in the couch like a joyous planet, laugh so heartily; with his eyes bulging and his face beetroot, Phil began to choke for air as if he'd got a gerbil stuck in his gullet.

Although Jimmy was so near to the pair's merriment, he did not register the joke. Jimmy's mind was off on a tangent. His spindly body sunk into itself and his eyelids were padlocked to his cheekbones. His shoulders rose and fell with the rhythm of a tiger slinking through the bushes towards its prey.

The hilarity ebbed and a silence crept in. Derek and Phil glanced at one another. Derek shooed Phil along the settee and took his seat next to him. They sat opposite Jimmy.

Jimmy sensed their inquiring eyes on him. He raised his head.

"So, Jimmy," Phil ventured. "Fit exactly is gaan on?"

"Aye, Jimbo. Fit's the score, like?"

Jimmy gazed at the backs of his hands. "Ye've got tae keep 'is tae yersels." He levelled his eyes at the two stooges perched before him. "Ah'm serious."

They both nodded. The grins of anticipation on their faces were commonly worn by those whom were first in line for things.

"So fa's the big guy that's lukin fir ye, 'en?" Phil asked.

Jimmy rotated his jaw. "'At must've bin Lex."

"Lex?" Derek said. "Fit the fuck kina name's Lex? Is he a fuckin pornstar or a supervillain or somethin?"

Jimmy shrugged.

"Lex?" Derek repeated. "Lex fit?"

*

"Lex MacMurran," the man replied. The words came out soft and frail, befitting the man that birthed them. He hid behind Jimmy's pint, more wool than man. A scarf coiled around the man's neck while a bonnet drooped well over his brow, like a silver python had ensnared him and was in the process of devouring his skull. And though it was a warm evening and actually quite hot inside the pub, the man was fastened into what appeared to be the outer-body of a prime Alaskan bear. The man was ready for the next ice age.

"It's 'cos o his affliction," Lori had once told him. "It's like he's got a permanent layer o frost on his skin."

Jimmy could imagine her father's hardship. Cold wasn't pleasant; he could sympathise with that. Up until that very morning, Jimmy had worked in a fishyard. For eight-twelve hours a day, five-six days a week, he had had to endure real cold. Painful cold. Oceans of wood-like fish had passed through Jimmy's hands as he had slaved away in arctic conditions. The chill had gone through his being, fondling him with an agonising glee. Fingers. Feet. Face. They had withstood the worst of things.

The pain, however, had equalled money. Money he needed. Desperately so.

Jimmy had been contemplating his redundancy that same night when Lori's father had called. Recognising Charlie's voice after a beat, Jimmy had become instinctively cautious. The topic of conversation would most definitely be her. We hiv tae meet. The words were brittle over the line. Hoo aboot The Thistle at half seven? Jimmy had tried to turn off the tap that suddenly burst with pessimistic conjecture. He failed. Visions of Lori, pale and lifeless on a mortician's slab, had exploded from his subconscious. He could see Charlie sitting before him, welling up and telling Jimmy that she was gone. She's gone. Gone. Deid.

Jimmy had needed a whiskey before heading off to the pub, a pub that he rarely next-to-never went to. It was further up the town than the ones that he'd usually frequent, but at least this meant that he had less distance to walk. Jimmy couldn't afford to run a car and his bike had been stolen.

The news wasn't quite as bad as he'd been expecting. Nor was it anywhere near as good as he had secretly hoped for. There had been no tragic death. And there wasn't going to be any tear-jerking reunion. Instead, there were only surprises. Bleak ones.

"An' 'is MacMurran guy – he's aifter me?" Jimmy could feel the fight to hold on to his sanity wane. "Why?"

Charlie reached into his bear coat and pulled out a sheaf of paper.

This gentleman's bar, a saloon where he presumed that elderly freemasons would dwell peacefully like shells under feathers, struck Jimmy as being out-of-date and tedious and depressing; but then everything depressed him. Everything in this pub seemed to be of the gaudiest shades. He could envisage the fag reek that would have lingered like smog for decades, collecting as a liquid in each fibre of the curtains. Jimmy didn't go to The Thistle. It wasn't for him. Somehow the place reminded him of Bullseye and jokes about mothers-in-law and the use of the phrase nignog and football terraces being destroyed by men with perms and all manners of shitty things gone by. This place had been refurbished, but it felt to Jimmy like a failed exorcism. He half expected Bernard Manning to appear from the ether, microphone in hand, jowls loose, nose red, eyes adrift, slivering, drool dripping down to the tree-guts floor. Jimmy fuckin hated the place, but then he hated virtually everything. Apart from one thing.

Jimmy wanted to leave. Go home. Crawl into bed and sleep till Christmas. Fuck all this fuckin shit and fuckin crap and bollocks. Sleep, sleep; a coma *would* be nice. A cosy, wee pine mattress six feet under. Oh, fuckin fuck it. Fuck yer hole. Fuck it all. All you fuckin fucks and cuntish cunts. Cunts for everyone. Cunt to everyone. Everyone a cunt. Fuck ye's, the lot o ye. Fuck ye.

Behind him, Jimmy could hear a couple of fifty-year-olds arguing over a game of snooker. Four men, one of whom was a friend of Jimmy's dad, stood by the bar. He could hear fractions of their conversation. Something about fuckin fish quotas and useless bastardin governments. Everyone fuckin swearin. Fuckin nice. Three middle-aged couples sat to the back of the room. They were celebrating a birthday, Jimmy had gathered. They were happy and enjoying themselves. Jimmy had not received a single card on his last birthday.

"Read 'is. It came yisterda." Charlie offered the piece of paper to Jimmy. "It'll tell ye iverythin ye need tae ken." The man found something else to absorb his interest; anything rather than watch the lad read the sheet. It would only remind him of how his wife had reacted.

Jimmy took it. It was a letter. He examined the text. Some of the words were difficult to read. The letter had obviously been written in a state of frenzy. Yet he could still easily recognise the handwriting.

His heart crashed into the barrier of his sternum.

He gulped down the remains of his pint.

The snooker players settled their disagreement. "A'right, a'right" said one to the other, "ye're right. It wis a foul. You win."

Jimmy began to read.

Dear mum and dad,

I don't know what I'm going to say or how I'm going to say it. I just know that I have to tell you something. I've made a mess of everything. I'm sorry. I'm sorry. I'm sorry. Since I left things have just gotten worse. I can't really understand how I let my life fall apart this bad. I've ruined things forever. I can never go back. I can never go home and play nice.

I can never pretend to be good again. I can't tell you the horrible things I've done since I went away. I don't want you to feel embarrassed for me. Just know that I never enjoyed any of it. I did what I felt I had to do. I blame no one but myself. I'm stupid and I'm sorry. I got mixed up with the wrong people and I did filthy things. I feel vile and I don't know if the feeling will ever go away. The need is as strong as ever. I try but I always fail. I'm far too weak. I'm a born loser but I'm still trying. I did something really really stupid. I stole from bad people. I couldn't take it anymore. I couldn't do those things any longer. I had to go. I took a lot of money and ran off. I hope they never find me. I don't think they will. They would kill me. I think you could also be in danger. No one knows my real name. I told them my name was Joanne. They believed me. Then one time I told them that I was from Fraserburgh. I didn't mean to. I wasn't right at the time. I also told them about James. They took the photo I had of him. I'm sorry sorry sorry. They will send someone up to look for me. You should be okay. Please be careful. Watch out for a thug called Lex MacMurran. He's a nasty scumbag. You'll know him straight away. I'm sorry that I've caused more trouble for everyone. I'm a loser. I'm sorry that I was ever born. I can only try to be better. I have to improve myself. I'll keep trying. I have to forget about the Broch now. I can't ever go back. You have to forget about me. Don't forgive just forget. Imagine that I'm dead. That shouldn't be too hard. I was never really alive. I've told you everything that I feel you should know. I love you. I miss you. I'm sorry.

Goodbye forever,

Lori

The words enveloped Jimmy like a barbed wire suit.

He handed the letter back to Charlie and made his exit. He walked back to his flat. He opened the door. He entered. He sat on the sofa. He stared at the TV. He put his head in his hands.

He did not cry.

The weekend dragged itself along like a kneecap-deprived thing.

Jimmy left the sofa only sparingly. A half dozen times to go to the toilet and once to go out back to the dishevelled garden that he shared with the tenants above him, whoever they were. He returned from the shed with a sturdy length of rope. Saturday night through to Sunday afternoon, he sat, curtains drawn together, bathed in the dinginess; the rope in his hands.

Jimmy pondered his purpose.

Ultimately, he dropped the rope and picked up the phone. His finger jabbed at the numbers. He put the receiver to his ear. The dial tone echoed meaninglessly through his cube.

Jimmy's soul had been crushed by the weight of a solitary slice of page.

The telephone's chant was interrupted by a voice. It was the voice that Jimmy needed to hear.

The voice, inebriated and unhurried, yet always friendly and supportive, uttered, "Hello?"

*

"Fuckin hell, Jimmy, ye fuckin mug." Derek paced the room. "Faan the fuck are ye gaan tae realise that Lori's nithin bit a slag fa's made it 'er sole priority in life tae maak a right Mongolian-cluster-fuck oot o yours?"

Phil stifled a laugh. He kept his head down, careful not to make known his ever-stretching smile.

Jimmy also kept his head down, though it had nothing to do with concealment. He just lacked the energy. He had deflated internally as he had relived Friday night's discoveries. He felt like a used-up firework.

"Ah mean, ah've bit ma tongue a heap o times fin maybe a really shid've said somethin," Derek said. "Hiv ye ony idea o the amoont o shite she's put ye in? 'Ere's big guys caad Lex MacMurran, fir fuck sake, fa are comin up here lukin fir ye. He's probably roon the corner right noo. Ah mean, 'at's nae fuckin joke, Jimbo. 'Is is scary shit. 'Is is stupid shit, ridiculous, fucked up. Hoo else kin ah pit it?" He seethed. "An' it's aa because o 'er."

Derek fumed. He was pissed off, both for and at Jimmy. He was angry because of the never-ending merry-go-round of monkey nuts that was Jimmy's existence. But Derek was also enraged by the boy's reluctance to sever all emotional ties with the she-demon that was responsible for much of what was wrong in his life.

Derek approached the picture of Lori that had hung from the wall for near twelve forlorn months, a span of loneliness that chewed at Jimmy's nerves every day. The host mustered as much steel as he could and craned his neck. Derek stopped mere inches from the photograph.

Jimmy tensed.

Derek took down the picture with a care.

Phil's grin vanished.

There would be trouble.

Jimmy picked up the bat and got to his feet. His face twitched as though he'd munched into a pregnant spider.

Fear glimmered, briefly, in Derek's eyes.

"Pit the photo back faar ye got it," Jimmy said, with the indifference of an experienced hangman.

Derek stepped towards him, brandishing the framed picture almost like a shield. "'Is is the quine fa's ruined yer life, Jimbo. Luk at ye. She's still fuckin ruinin it."

Jimmy looked down at the photograph that he'd taken of her on the pier of a remote harbour. She smiled at him; her light brown locks curled down her fair cheek, and she smiled at him. She'd smiled at him. He said, "Pit it back faar ye got it."

"Jimmy, ye've got tae let 'er go," Derek said. "Ye've got tae throw 'is bloody thing oot. Move on, min."

Jimmy held the bat up at a forty-five degree angle. "Pit it back."

"Stop 'is fuckin craziness, wid ye?" Derek took another tentative step forward. "Ah've endured yer freakish obsession wi 'is slut fir lang enough an' ah'm tellin ye, it's time fir it tae fuckin end. Jist please stop fuckin killin yersel fir 'is quine an' jist move on. Dinnae be sae dim, Jimbo. Yer fuckin yersel up o'er the heids o 'er. It's nae right."

The bat was raised a further forty-five degrees so that it now pointed directly out at Derek. Jimmy recited his preceding order. "Pit it back." The gnarl in his voice was slight, but it was evident.

"Tell me, Jimmy, hoo mony times did Lori mention ye in 'er letter? Once? Fit dis 'at tell ye?" Derek saw something in Jimmy's face that frightened him. Intent. Jimbo planned to take a swing at his friend, if need be.

In a snap, Jimmy was wielding the bat high to the ceiling. He roared, "Pit it back on the fuckin waa NOW."

Derek balked and held the picture up ready to protect himself.

Phil dived off the sofa, sandwiching himself between his two pals. He wrested the bat from Jimmy and pleaded for calm.

Jimmy pushed Phil out of the way and snatched the picture from Derek's grasp.

The momentum of Jimmy's push had caused Fat Ass to fall back over the settee and land in a heap on the carpet. Pride hurting, Phil leaped to his feet and came within a second's loss of his senses from wrapping that bat around Jimmy's head. His composure returned just in time and Phil tossed the bat away, off into the far corner of the kitchen area, out of reach, out of temptation. Phil's hat had fallen off during his tumble. He retrieved it from the floor and stuck it back onto his curly crown.

Jimmy gave him an ill-fitting smile as though his face were distorted by staples.

Derek stood back, stunned by the abrupt escalation of Jimmy's temper.

Jimmy barged past Derek; he returned the picture to its nail. For a long time, he didn't turn around. He just stood there, looking at his photograph, pushing and prodding the frame until it was perfectly straight on the wall.

"She's gone," Jimmy said, after a while. "She's niver comin back." His voice was commensurate parts rage and sorrow. "Ah'd like ye's beth tae leave."

Phil and Derek divided a gauche hesitation.

"Jimmy, luk - " Derek was cut off by another scream.

"Get the fuck OOT."

Derek regarded Phil. The fat man was huffing and puffing, battling to get his engine to cool after all the commotion. His shirt was wound up and around him like a dishtowel, and, under dissimilar circumstances, he would've looked quite humorous.

Jimmy's appearance, however, was far from funny. His six foot-plus frame loomed by the picture. His mouth was twisted like the hinge of a rattly gate. Jimmy turned. He asked, most matter-of-factly, "You cunts still here?"

Derek could see that there was something absent about Jimmy, as if something had peeled away.

Lori wasn't the only one who was long gone.

Whatever Jimmy was missing, though, Derek knew that he wasn't going to get it back tonight. He took his suitcases and, with Fat Ass leading the way, left the flat.

When they were beyond Jimmy's path and onto the pavement, Phil confided in Derek, "Ah think Jimmy might be startin tae lose it a bit."

The door slammed shut with a bang that resounded through the street. Several navy squares turned yellow. A feline scampered down a lane.

Kicked oot twice in one day.

Great stuff.

Chapter 4

From this distance, the Broch looked like nothing more than a handful of tiny, slate blocks, with a couple of up-turned drawing pins for churches. Thin verdant strands flowed into the blocks from either side. To the left of his town, Mormon Hill was a knuckle; the scabs of its satellite dishes could not be discerned. Derek squinted his eyes. He could just make out the ginger of the beach. All else was blue.

The Searcher jostled along an amiable sea. The Earth's roof was an infinite azure, unbroken by the merest hint of cloud. Derek trailed his fingertips through the cold water. It glittered like a diamond caressed under the glow of a spotlight. It was a petite boat without a sail or a hut, and, being that there were only the three of them on board, Derek had room to stretch his legs and laze.

The sun glared at them; its rays were acute and concentrated like a torch beam blasted through a nail-hole on a sheet of card. All its power seemed to be focused on the Broch and a few acres of surrounding landscape.

Derek's grandad panted; he took a swig from his flask. The old man screwed its shiny cap back on and slipped it inside his coat. Stanley Gibson spoke, saying aloud to his fellow crewmen, "Fishing kills me exactly as it gives me life." It sounded to Derek like a quote, and probably a famous one, for all he knew.

The elderly gent gave the words the richness and depth of a Shakespearean actor in some black and white film. Derek embraced this idea of Stanley originating from an age before colour. The man seemed Biblical to his eleven-year-old grandson. He had a stature like Moses, or, at any rate, Moses as played by Charlton Heston. To Derek, Stanley Gibson looked as though he'd been fashioned from rock back when people were barely out of the caves. The man was old – Derek wasn't sure how old, but still few men would be dense enough to mess with this relic. And, for someone of his plentiful years, Stanley had an enviable head of thick grey-brown hair; although, admittedly, these days it was mostly ashen. The teenager at the front of the boat hoped to inherit his grandad's barnet, as opposed to his father's. The impressive pensioner also had a solid moustache that was near three times older than Derek was. Young Derek couldn't see himself ever suiting a 'tache. But this one hung proudly from Big Stanley's lip, a bristling raft on a sea of stone.

Derek's dad wiped his brow with his wrist and continued to row. Derek and his kin would've truly sweltered had it not been for the draught that whispered down from the North. The breeze gave the air some much needed bite.

It was still hot, though; hot as Derek could remember it being in this end of the world.

He felt like he was back in Florida.

Great two weeks that had been. Another fortnight with the giant, suit-wearing rat.

Derek's first foray to the magic kingdom was beyond the realms of his recollection. He'd been far too young at the time to form any lasting memories; random images here and there, that was about it. On that occasion, he and his parents had gone to America on a sort of double date with his Aunt Rosie and her then boyfriend Tim and a couple of his nieces. Apparently, when Goofy came over to say hello – and Rosie took tremendous relish in retelling this story at any and every family do – a four-year-old Derek Gibson soaked his shorties in fright.

Unsurprising, then, that Derek wasn't too keen on going back. But that was how he'd spent the initial fortnight of July. This time the trip was mainly for his wee sister Tracy, whom hadn't been born the last time that the Gibsons had crossed the Atlantic. And young Trace had sort of spoiled the whole thing by wandering off on her first day in the kingdom and getting herself lost. Then Derek's mum went over her ankle, and a pickpocket ripped off his dad. It wasn't all bad, however. He ogled some ravishing chicks, saw the new Arnie film and the rollercoasters were pretty amazing. He'd certainly enjoyed Orlando a lot more second time around. In saying that, though, Derek had given Goofy a bit of a wide berth. Something about that children's favourite made him uneasy.

The floppy-eared, buck-toothed bastard that he was.

"Oi, sleepy heid."

Derek broke from his daydream.

"Aye, you." There was no irritation in the old man's voice, only good humour. Big Stanley was propped up at the back of the boat like a grandfather clock in a trailer. "Throw in the anchor."

Derek's dad had stopped rowing, and the oars had been pulled aboard. Adam sat in the middle of the boat – the mean point of the Gibson trioca, and gave his son a wry look.

The green vessel revolved as though it were on display on a game show; small waves shooshed against its sides like an audience's applause. The boat was slipping away from its target: an orange globe the size of a football. Bizarrely, the fluctuating orb put Derek in mind of a marmalade-drenched duck. AG was penned on its bright skull; a rope looped through its centre descended into the murk.

Derek reached down to his feet and picked up the rusty weight. The chunky life jacket that he had to wear made this act more of a challenge than he would've preferred. He held the anchor. The elongated shape was heavy for his banjo-string arms. Mo said he'd seen a porno in which a darky had had a knob that looked exactly like it. Derek had dismissed the comparison until he'd seen the blue movie for himself.

The mass of the anchor strained on biceps yet to form. He plopped the weight into the sea; it vanished into the depths. The umbilical cord that linked the anchor to the bow, where Derek sat, slid downwards in hot pursuit.

The Searcher was manacled to the ocean bed. All it could do now was drift in Os.

Derek's dad reached for the buoy. The sleeves of his cardigan were rolled up to his elbows, exhibiting arms that were narrow but strong. A calloused hand gripped the buoy's neck and plucked it from the water.

Derek's visage glowed like the spherical eminence above. This was the moment that he looked forward to each year.

His dad stood up. He yanked the buoy into the boat; he pulled at the rope that cascaded down as a scratch on a record.

They had set the trap the night before, and now, the time it was, to collect their bounty.

The rope spaghettied onto The Searcher's floor. His dad's boots pushed against the boat as he struggled for leverage. The ship rocked and caused ripples that creased across the great face of the endless pond. Many times, Derek had seen his dad haul up the creels. Sometimes, Derek imagined him falling in and being gorged by some gargantuan sea monster. Christ knows what lives down there. His father, though, was as sure-footed as a leopard, and he would never lose his balance and go overboard. It would take quite the beast to topple Adam Gibson.

Adam didn't look too much like his own dad. He wasn't that tall and he didn't have a back that you could land a 747 on like Big Stan, but he had a grit and a toughness that couldn't be taught by a million Charles Norrises.

Derek could not yet see the living treasure chest emerging from the deep. He looked over to his grandad. The old man shared his excitement. His grandfather smiled and winked at him.

The taut line growled through his dad's hands. Bumps and ridges of muscle stood out on his forearms like the Himalayas as seen from the stratosphere. Thin lips were drawn back to reveal yellowing teeth. Brown eyes were no more than darkened slits. Sweat beads formed beneath a receding hairline that was becoming evermore like high tide on lonely sands.

Derek stared downwards. A pale stamp appeared, fluttering in the thalassic fog. The creel ascended. He couldn't tell what they'd caught; the prominence of his father's veins made it apparent that the creel wasn't empty.

Derek sat back.

The creel broke the surface. His dad leaned over the side and grabbed the front of the cage. He tugged it out from the marine soil and into the boat. Derek and his grandfather both shone with delight. The rectangular prison held a host of abnormalities. Lobsters, partans and other strange crabs fizzled and snapped with their michty claas.

His dad rested the creel on the centre bench and parted its side door. Fast but scrupulous, he yanked out the creatures. The pygmaean, inedible crabs were thrown back into the water. The lobsters and partans, however, were placed into separate boxes beside Stanley's feet for later consumption. Today's bounty had thus far amounted to three lobsters of fair size and two immense partans. That was good going for one creel, and they still had three more to pull up.

The grandad nodded his approval. His gold flask made another appearance, then dipped back into his coat pocket.

Nothing much remained of the bait. Parts of a jaw and plates of silver scale hung from a knot in the middle of the trap where a split fish had been lodged only last night. The crustaceans had had their fill.

The bait wouldn't be replaced today, though. Derek's dad was going away tomorrow, and so the creels would be returning to shore with them. Derek was disappointed by this. The last few days were the first of this year that he'd been out on The Searcher. Bugger knows when he'd be out on it again.

Enjoy it while you can, though, eh? That was his grandad's answer for everything. The old man was an optimist. "Live forever," he had once told his grandson, "or dee in the attempt."

Those words and their delivery had perked Derek up splendidly.

*

A quartet of wet, vacant creels hustled by Derek's rubber boots. Bemused crabs pruned cohabitants in the pitch black of their cells. Stanley rested his wellies upon the provisional abodes. Adam wound the boat around and aimed her for distant shore.

It had been a fine haul. The pot would be busy tonight; not that Derek was apt to eat the crabs anyway. His dad's mates and crewmen would be calling round later to see that their catch was scoffed. The day was still warm. It was a heat that would most likely carry on long into the evening. Dad and his cohorts would probably swill the maritime meat down with a few beers. Make a night of it. It was only a Wednesday, so surely the karaoke machine wouldn't be making an appearance; but you never did know. Derek had better scarper after supper, then. He didn't want to be marooned with a trawler's worth of drunken sailors.

He'd give Pagan and his muckers a phone when he got home. Organise a kick about or something. They hadn't had a proper game in almost a week.

Derek checked his watch. Garfield's upper limbs indicated that it was only a quarter to four. The somnolent sultriness made it seem later, as if their drifting had predated God.

He slouched over the bow. The torridity kneaded him into an ashtray. A dopey smile that he couldn't erase, however, clarified that he didn't mind. This is the only place I want to be, he thought. He believed it as well. Keep Florida. This is adequate. This is home.

The blueness fed his tranquil soul.

A cough crunched behind him. Over his dad's shoulder, Derek could see his grandad studying the handkerchief that he'd just wiped his mouth with. The old man's body shuddered with humour. "Oh me," Stanley said, as he showed the stained fabric to his son. Adam tilted both oars up in a V for vexation. Derek caught a glimpse of the hanky through a gap by the boatman's left side. Though his view wasn't fantastic, Derek could still perceive the red spot upon the silk square; it was a blotch the girth of a baby's toe.

Adam dragged the oars back through the water. A couple of seals popped their heads up a few feet away, and decided that there was nothing of interest here. The Gibson men continued homewards.

"Ah me," Stanley repeated, before tucking the handkerchief into his pouch. He noticed that his grandson's eyes were fixed on him. The boy's face now tallied with the pallor of the enfolding sea. "Fine catch, eh?" said the old man.

The frost over Derek's eyes fragmented. He awoke. "Eh?"

"Ah said 'fine catch'. Plinty labsters, eh?"

"Aye." Colour seeped back into Derek like trickling paint. "It wis a good day."

Stanley agreed. He sat up high at the stern, took a lengthy gander at the desolation around them, then produced a packet of fags from within his coat. He lit one with a match; he threw the burning splinter into the water. It died with a hiss. The old man drew on the cigarette; his lungs held the smoke hostage for such a time that his crewmates wondered if he would ever release it. The day had stolen Stanley away to raid the vault between his ears. Eventually, a tobacco cloud emerged from his lips and wafted off to the Broch, which was still nowt more than pebbles under siege by gangrenous warts. The grandfather took another suck of the paper straw; this time he blew out the reek far more sharpish.

"Ah thought ye tellt mam that ye'd stopped wi the fags," Adam said, not deviating from his steady rowing.

Stanley laughed out puffs of inky breath. "Adam, ye're an affa good boy," the old man replied.

The man in the middle responded as one whom concedes mutely to a superior opponent.

The grandad grinned over the rower's head at Derek. "Yer dad's an affa man, in't he?" Stanley smiled from the floorboards up. Derek also began to laugh; though he wasn't sure why it was that he did. The old man finished his fag.

The Searcher remained on its course.

A remote purser steamed back towards the Broch. It, too, was returning from the hunt with its spoils. The significantly more substantial boat may have been out as far as Norway or even Iceland, and had definitely been out for longer than the couple of hours that The Searcher had logged. Gulls like stringless kites chased and nipped at the ship. The scurries' skirls seared for miles, shaking the universe with their tumultuous squabblings. The sea sloshed. The crabs scuttled. A crewmate passed sporadic comment. The screeching of the birds dwindled into silence as the red purser reached the harbour, just out of earshot.

"Well, well, Derek. Well, well."

Derek had been watching the craft and its aerial entourage disappear behind the chalk border of the breakwater. He twisted around to acknowledge his grandfather.

Stanley sipped at his flask. He offered a tipple to his son. Adam rejected the proposal with a frown that Derek couldn't see. The old man then shook the flask at his grandson. Derek was about to decline in the animated mode of the startled when he realised that his grandad was just having some fun with him. That flask must nearly be parched by now anyway, Derek thought. His grandad's stomach was surely lined with gravel to be able to drink that stuff. Derek had tasted spirits once previously, at a New Year's party in his cousin's house, and he'd spewed immediately afterwards. The stuff had tasted like a mixture of paraffin and migraines. Derek couldn't fathom why anyone would want to drink that rubbish.

"It's a bonny day," Stanley said to his grandson.

"Aye."

"Kin ye imagine if it wis like 'is aa day lang ivery day o the wik, eh?"

The query stumped Derek. "Eh, nae really." Was this the whiskey kicking in?

Something of Stanley seemed to sail away from the yawl. His eyelids were roller shutters, hampered by fire extinguishers; he gazed northerly across the shimmering skin that led to the Pole. The twinkle had lessened from the old man's coins. Even his smile wavered.

And then he was back.

"Dee ye ken that o'er the neest few months, it's gaan tae be permanent daylight up 'ere?" Stanley gestured to his right. "The sun'll be oot twitty-four oors a day. Fit dee ye think o 'at, Derek? Strange business, eh?"

"Aye," Derek replied, intrigued. "So, hoo do they ken fit the time is?" The gap that followed his question alerted him to his having said something foolish.

Adam upped the oars and turned to his son. "They luk at their waatches." Derek couldn't defend himself from his faux pas and just had to wait for the laughter to subside. "Deary me, Derek," his father continued, "ah thought you wis supposed tae be the brains o the faimily."

"Ah me, Derek." His grandad let out a few more chuckles. "Aye. They luk at their waatches."

"Aye, okay, 'en," Derek said, running with his stumble in an effort to weaken his ignominy. "Bit dis it nae get a bitty confusin up 'ere, like? Ah mean, if it luks the same aa day roon, 'en surely it must be… confusin. Like. Ken?"

"Oh, aye, ma old cocksparrow." Stanley did transition effortlessly between voices, from jocular to authoritative. "Aye, it dis get confusin up 'ere. It could be twa in the aifterneen or twa in the mornin. Ye jist dinna ken. It aa luks the same."

Derek edged forward. "You've bin up 'ere, aye, granda?"

"Weel, fit dee ye think 'is aal-timer did durin the waar, eh? Guard bloomin lichthooses?"

There was a fact. Derek didn't have the slightest clue as to what his grandad got up to forty-odd years ago. It had never really entered his thinking before.

"So," the youngster broached the old man, "fit did ye dee durin the waar?"

Chapter 5

"Knocked the absolute livin fuck oot o some cunt," the one-eyed thug replied. "Ye ken fit like. Cunts get a bit moothy fin they're drunk, ken? Fit aboot you, eh? Fit the fuck did you get up tae at the wikend?"

Derek shrugged.

"Let me guess. Ye got fuckin pished, eh?"

Derek forced a smile. He refrained, however, from lifting his chin for his inquisitor, whom stood next to him on the steel platform; it was early, and Derek didn't want the sight of Gazza's puss riling his gut. The man's face, which Derek had had to endure most mornings for the last while, was bronzed with summer and broken with Saturdays. A black, leather pirate-patch covered the cave where his right eye once lived.

Want tae see ma hole? Ho ho ho.

Unknown was the account of how Gazza Thomson came to have that patch. He went on a stag-do to Newcastle a year ago and came back with it strapped across his skull. Sundry explanations abound, though none had so far been confirmed. Derek thought that Gazza revelled in every horror story that was concocted.

Derek could feel the swine's eye on him, like a thing on a web, waiting for a reaction. Gazza laughed; the mirth was of the kind that someone delivers to project their appreciation of a joke they didn't get. His laughter seemed more insincere than Derek's smile.

"Ah bet ye wis blootered," Gazza said with a baleful smirk. "Ye're aiwyes fuckin pissed, Gibbon."

Gibson. Gibbon. Every day was a comedy master class with good old Gary.

Derek continued to semi-ignore his workmate. He responded with the bare minimum enthusiasm to avoid slipping onto the stocky, stubbly macho-man's bad side.

Derek sank his mitts into the bucket of fish bits in front of him and got on with his job. The slimy, anonymous strips squished between his fingers. The cold chilled Derek's hands despite the gloves. He shunned the blossoming pain about as well as he could Gazza's teeth-grating attempts at humour and peeled the strips apart. Derek placed the strips down flat on the revolving belt before him and watched as they disappeared into the mouth of a massive refrigerator. Icy mist hovered above the belt and pinched at the workers' skin.

"Ye're probably drunk jist noo." Gazza looked around to see if his colleagues were getting a rise from his banter. They weren't. They hadn't listened to a word he'd said. They were working, tuned out to everything else, including the wide-boy ramblings of Mr Thomson. Gazza sank as when the owner hides a pet's toy behind his back. He gave Derek a lightish punch on the arm before turning his attention towards his own pail and the freezing belt that spun like a rusted bike chain, clanking along until Friday, when he'd be able to pan some new and equally deserving cunt in the dish.

Derek smiled, and without the need for any prior stretching this time. Gazza was as dumb as an elevator stuffed with bums, but he wasn't always wrong. As it happened, young knight Sir Derek actually was rather tipsy jist noo. He'd necked a half-bot on the way to Toories. Derek had slept in after an awful night's kip on the Fat One's sofa. Running late and with all the nonsense of the day before still swamping his head like a loose-fit u-bend, Derek had decided to pick himself up a little pick-me-up. And, Lordy Almighty, had it helped.

Derek lay another few slices of fish innards on the frosty belt as it inched past like chemotherapy. In less than an hour, those soppy strips would emerge as ivory at the other end, ready to package and sell off to some supermarkets or restaurants or whatever wherever. Not that Derek could give a salty sock where any of the fish wound up. He just got on with it till there were no more pails left to plunder.

Same as all the rest of these fuckers.

Derek watched the working world around him. Five others, Gazza included, fed the belt. Scores more carried out their tasks in the mammoth room where Derek stood. The room. One big, bloody shed with a roof as high as you like and where everything was white, silver or stone, except for the yellow of all those rubber boots. The granite carpet glistened like steak where the workers took root. They gutted the fish. They placed the fish on trays to be cooked in the kilns. They scraped the fish blood from the floor with squeegees. There were some locals and then there were, much to his cycloptic colleague's revulsion, some immigrants. For the most part, these migrant workers were from Eastern Europe, although some maltesers had found their way into this bowl of pandrops. No one enjoyed their jobs, apart from maybe the gaffers. Dialogue was sparse. The radio could not be heard. They all got on with their work. Their bodies were conditioned by mass hypnosis to disregard the cold, while their brains switched off to prevent insanity through monotony like a monitor that shuts down when not in use.

The indigenous women were all roughly the same shape. The years robbed them of their femininity; their shoulders broadened and their buttocks developed corners like microwaves. The short, squat ladies slaughtered each other in private and barked openly at the men-folk for being so slow and inefficient. The men pretend that the degradation of being harangued twenty-five hours a day eight days a week doesn't pare their pride as if with a blazing pickaxe. The dress code is adhered to by both sexes. Old jeans, pallid overalls, gory aprons and gloves, paper hats and those honeysuckle boots, which were either stuck on the same spot all day long like tent pegs or were scurrying about like chickens under constant stress from leaders who didn't know which way was forward.

Many of the unfortunates here in the yard have been so since they left school a spouse-and-bairns ago. The satisfaction of parenthood blunted the edge of work so grim, or so Derek hoped for the sake of this lot. Then they'd realise that wee Bowser's been tooting smack for the last two years and nicking the double-digit notes from their purse. The rosy-cheeked rogue that they raised from spunk has turned out to be as useless as they never could have dreamed that he would be. A lifetime of sacrifice and devotion has been rewarded with a blubbering junkie and no grandchildren.

Bollocks to that.

No ties was definitely the choice stratagem as far as Derek was concerned. No wife, no kids and no fuckin problems. He could be off to Morocco at the drop of a hat. If, indeed, he had a hat to drop and the money to do so. But that was why he was here, wasn't it? Save the baabbies and you're on your way. Fuck this responsibility fiasco. Derek was going to sacrifice nothing for nobody and devote his life to the modest pursuit of having something of a laugh.

The gaffer, a lady of fridge-like dimensions and whose paper hat was blue instead of white to signal her importance, was glowering up at Derek from beside one of the huge ovens. She gave him a look that demanded of him that he work harder.

It had occurred to Derek on occasion that perhaps he should have invested some effort in learning a trade. There was the Buchan Tech up the road where Jimmy did some of his HND, and then you had your pick of universities an hour south in Aberdeen. Derek knew that he wasn't that dim, and that, in his mid-to-late twenties, he wasn't yet past his prime. He could still be moulded to fit.

But what were Derek's special qualities, and how could they be most advantageously tailored for a career? Best list the cons, he thought. Derek was inept with his hands. This ruled him out of following in Freddy's footsteps as a welder. Plus, he was probably the least technically minded of all of his friends, even less so than Fat Ass, whom *did* have his own email address. And he wasn't much cop with numbers, and despised the idea of working in an office. Mo's bank job was safe, then.

So that left Derek with what options? Well, he was mostly good with people and was easy-going – up to a point. The majority of folks you ever did meet would like Derek. He first sensed this about himself when he began pubbing aged sixteen and noticed that everyone had a smile and a spare couple of minutes for the young knight. His main attribute was certainly his slick, slick charm. Slick as you like. Derek also had confidence. He was a confident sort, but, importantly, he lacked confidence's rich arsehole of a cousin. As a matter of no minor significance, Derek was devoid of the curse that plagued many ignorant and loathsome toss-bags. These twats whom, if they did possess this unpleasant characteristic, would likely never know it, or, if they suspected that they had it, and which was incalculably worse, they'd attempt to pass it off as some invaluable trait that was somehow synonymous with their imagined successes. Yes, indeed, Master Gibson had been born without that dreaded mark, more foul than three 6s on a child's scalp: the mark of arrogance. He would not exalt himself at another's expense. People regarded Derek as a total non-threat and opened up to him like hungry plants to a charitable star.

Perhaps, then, something in the field of public relations. Telemarketing? No. Door-to-door salesman? That wasn't any better. He would rather be a hitman. He thought that he would genuinely prefer to kill people than pester them.

There must be something else for a wondrous lad like Derek, though, surely?

Across the belt and through the mist, another fridge-creature gestured for Derek to get his head down and do some work. In complete seriousness, she – an Isabel Barclay, 46 – demonstrated to Derek in super slo-mo how to put the strips on the belt as though he hadn't been doing it every day for the last four months. She even unfastened her palms afterwards, in the style of a grand magician upon finishing a stunt.

Derek reached into his pail, made a show of searching through the fish guts, then brought out his middle digit.

Whaallaa.

Isabel was less than happy. She stared at Derek as if laser beams were about to launch from her goggles and Dr No him into cinders. Then she went back to minding her own business.

Aal Ritchie, jammy enough to be standing alongside Isabel for the day, gave Derek the thumbs up. Slyly, mind you, so that she didn't witness this insubordination. Derek winked back in appreciation of the older man's gesture. Ritchie was okay, as workmates went. Ritchie and young Chris Fraser – whom he had yet to see today, were about the only two people at Toories he didn't mind working with. The rest he could take or leave or tell to rin tae fuck.

The sadists likely had Chris out back again, tidying up the cold store. Poor mug. The gaffers gave up trying to persuade Derek to perform that chore after his first couple of days.

Eighteen-year-old Chris was as naïve as his numerics and school-gleaned sensibilities would suggest, and he had yet to develop the nerve to tell those clowns to rinse with Listerine and swallow his sac. However, the guy was obviously a clever chappy, and he purported to be quite the James Page on the guitar. Anyone who could play an instrument, Derek reasoned, couldn't be that worthless. That took a level of patience that Derek feared that he was born without. Chris also recently had had his hair styled into a blue mohican, which took some testes for this town and this factory, and Derek could admire that, sort of. The do obviously had to be bulldozed whilst he was at work, so that it would go under his hairnet, but it was a definitive statement that he aspired to be his own production. If, maybe, Chris could be somewhat lacking in the savvy department, he would learn. Despite the popular working-class sentiment to the contrary, Derek believed that common sense was a thing to be gained through graft, rather than inherited through lineage. In Derek's opinion, common sense was nothing more than tricks of the trade. It was simply a matter of adapting to your environment. Derek liked the boy and knew that Chris would do well at uni when his gap year was finally over and all his pretty pennies had been harvested.

Gazza was engrossed in his work now. That and some tune that he had clattering about in that melon of his, which Derek reckoned was like a cluster of elbows. The guy was bobbing about and humming in a none too shy manner, seemingly oblivious to the frigid milieu. The thrumming and burring of a multitude of machines and motors prevented Derek from identifying the song that Gazza muttered. Derek hoped that it would keep the chap occupied for a while.

Derek did not hate the guy. It was just that Gazza was an anus. Always had been, would be and is.

Derek had known Gazza since back when Derek was a virgin and Gary still had two eyeballs. Gary had always been a well-rounded thug, and on their initial encounter Derek ended up with a broken pinky.

Back then, Gary was entering his fourth and final year at Broch Academy, while Derek and his mates were just coming up from primary school. Never one to ostracise the puny or enfeebled, Gary made a point of welcoming Derek and his young friends on their maiden day. Namely, by pushing Derek down the spiral staircase that linked French to PE.

Shrieking and crying as he bounced down each and every step, Derek had done well not to piss himself. He eventually hit the floor, landing awkwardly on his left hand and causing the breakage to his little finger. Badly bruised and sobbing hysterically in front of a corridor full of laughing hockey players, Derek heard Gazza's evil grunt of a chortle for the first time. The bully's mirth boomed down from the top of the stairs; his pimpled face hung over the rails as though it were a ship's hull and Derek's foot were trapped by seaweed. Then it vanished when a teacher came over to scrutinise the weeping boy.

Derek, fearing reprisals, didn't tell his mum or dad about Gary; instead, he told them that he had tripped and fell by accident. The ensuing weeks were about the worst of young Derek's life, as he sneaked through this new church from sermon to sermon, compelled to conform through trepidation of the Devil. The thought of bumping into Gary Thomson again made him feel sick and terminal. Then, one afternoon, the oddness happened.

School was finished for the day, and Derek was making his way down the bustling English corridor when a digger-trough hand clamped down upon his shoulder. Derek thought that this time, undoubtedly, he would unleash urine. He turned, sheepishly, but still dry of pants. Gary Thomson recoiled his hand from Derek's coat. The look on his face emboldened Derek a tad. The six-feet of virulence, whom, as a teen, could already grow a sufficiently even beard, though opted not to, wore an expression that wasn't polar opposites from worried. Was Gary scared? Apparently so. Stranger yet, Gary held out his hand. Derek stepped back. Gary nodded, then reached the club out further. Derek barely noticed the crowds of cheery pupils whom flooded past. Derek looked at the out-stretched hand. That was a large paw, one likely to crush Derek's wee fist. Cautious as a man entering a smoky bath, Derek raised his hand to meet that of Gary's. Gary shook it, firmly yet sans malice. The bully's meaty fork fell to his side. He nodded once more. Then he joined the others on their way down the hall.

That night, Derek had entered the living room to find his dad watching some Western. Dad Gibson turned to see Derek, whose school bag pursued the boy like a diseased tail. "Hoo wis yer day?" Nae bad. His dad studied him. "'At'll be fine, 'en." He went back to his movie.

Somebody had, perhaps, been playing the amateur sleuth and, quite possibly, had had a word in some boy's ear. In any case, that was the end of Derek's two-month persecution at Fraserburgh Academy. Pretty much plain sailing after that. Apart from the schoolwork and such.

Although, for whatever reason, Gary Thomson's services as the school bully were no longer extended to Derek, they were still very much in effect. Jimbo had got the worst of it. Jimmy was tall for his age and softly spoken, and, for seven months, he got nonstop shit from Gary. Until, true to form, one day Jimmy just fuckin cracked and smashed a stool over Gary's head.

And that was the end of that.

There was a brief lull in the machinery orchestra when Derek could hear the tune that Gazza was humming. Definitely an Oasis song. Definitely one from Definitely Maybe. Fuck knows. They weren't so much his thing. The racket of the engines soon overwhelmed the room again.

A blast of cold water hit the back of his leg. Derek's jeans were soaked. He whirled around. As did Gazza. He, too, had been struck by the spray.

Dopey Robbie stood there, hose dripping in his hand, gormless look on his face, as though he'd shot his load in the waiting room. "Sorry, boys," he said, in his usual way. "Sorry, like. Nae hairm deen." Robbie sauntered off, slopping the stone floor. A Polish guy followed behind with half of a squeegee. The handle had been snapped by an enraged ex-co-worker.

Derek and Gazza turned back to the belt. Gazza shook his head. "'At guy's a right fuckin daft cunt." Derek hoisted his brow in agreement.

And fate did bring them together once more.

Derek had rarely conversed with his former oppressor since the big lump left school. Somewhere along the line, Gary transformed into Gazza, lost an eye and became more of an arse-divot than ever before. Derek had spoken to him maybe a dozen times outside of Toories, usually at the weekend. Pished, like. You'd have to be fairly numb to speak to Gazza for any length of time. His tough-guy posturing and self-aggrandising chafed within nanoseconds. And then, later on, after all the pubs were shut, you'd see Gazza and his hangers-on stalking the Broadgate for some unlucky bastard to pulverise. A winsome sort. Derek found it disquieting that such a character should ever command disciples. But Derek knew himself that it was wiser to be on friendly terms with Gazza than to get your cheekbones shattered by him. Manifold's the bleezinheid who's had to spend more than a couple of nights in the Aberdeen infirmary because of Gazza and his fan club.

To be perfectly honest, though, Gazza didn't scare Derek. Derek was certainly wary of the cyclops. You'd have to be stupid not to be. However, Derek had heard stuff about the so-called hard man that withered his stature considerably.

Lee Johnstone had told Derek the supposed *real* story about why Gazza had been kicked out of the army. The story Gazza let circulate was that he got the boot for fighting with two corporals or captains or some other high-ranking toodles. Lee had heard differently. Through a restaurant customer whom served in the forces, Lee discovered that Gazza had, essentially, left of his own accord. What made this whole story so especially funny was the reasoning behind Gazza's desertion. Apparently, the guys in Gazza's regiment begrudged his loudmouth ways and his swanning around the place and took a pick on him. Aye, the Fraserburgh hard man was getting beasted so bad that he had to phone up his mum and sob down the line that he'd had enough and that he was coming home. The homo.

So he took an E, fucked a drugs test and got himself turfed out. Gary Thomson came back to the Broch, never to leave again.

This tale had cheered Derek up enormously when he'd heard it. Oh, how he'd laughed. It didn't make the man any less dangerous. It just made him that bit more pathetic.

Okay, Gazza was bigger than Derek was. And you could tell that when Gazza stomped around in his basketball tops that he was ripped to shreds and that he had the pecs, and he was known to do the boxing thing. But that didn't phase Derek. He could take the witless jibes and the rare jab to the arm. Like it or lump it, that was Gazza, and Derek was never a one to go digging for oil without a bucket. He had the ability to let things go. In fairness, though, there wasn't really ever any venom in Gazza's taunts, and he suspected that the thug even had a certain fondness for Sir Derek. The pinky incident, which both surely remembered, was never mentioned, despite it being very much in Gazza's nature to gloat and antagonise. At the end of the day, however, friendship was a tower made of wax for Gazza; a moat of violence lay ready for absolutely anyone at anytime.

But Derek wasn't afraid. He wasn't eleven years old anymore and hiding on the stairwell between history and maths to dodge Gary Thomson. As far as Derek was concerned, the one-eyed twat, if he so wished, could bring it on down whenever he wanted to.

The gaffer pointed at Derek, then cooed him over with her finger.

An' you kin fuck off as weel.

*

Tommy's office was less like an office and more like a portaloo, where a body would be more inclined to deal in trade of the bowel variety than monetary. It was only marginally bigger than the sort of booth that a security guard might use. Situated somewhere between the car park and the loading bay, the office was a freestanding shed, separate from the factory itself. Weirdly, you got the rank smell of the fish worse out here than you did on the factory floor. Derek had noticed this anomaly before: that it wasn't until you were actually walking home at night that you realised how badly you stunk. In the factory, the smell was so overwhelming that, like gravity when you were on the ground, it could be ignored.

Derek sat, alone and waiting, in his uncle's office. He glanced around the place. The clutter constricted the room, like a spoiled girl's wardrobe. Shelves stuffed with files and folders bulged as varicose veins. Charts and graphs flaked like eczema. Behind Tommy's desk with the computer and bills and stationery junk and above the swivel chair, there perched a window. Derek's view out of the window was obscured from where he sat due to the blinds being half-closed, yet he could still just about make out the activity of the harbour. Men groomed the boats like fleas on horses. There had once been a whale in that harbour.

It was another bright day in the Broch, but it was nothing like as warm as it had been. This sun was a painted moon.

Derek pondered what Tommy might want with him. Probably something to do with accommodation, he supposed. Derek's mum would've been on the phone to her brother, enlightening him as to how she and Adam had decided to teach young Derek a lesson and had finally thrown him out. Scare tactics, indeed. They'd discussed it previously. His parents had already given Derek the sit-down talk at the kitchen table on the day after the night before. His mum would go on and on about how this was the final straw, Derek Gibson, and that if you continue to be such a drunken bounder, well, then, ye kin jist… fuck off. There, ah said it, Derek. It's the only language you un'erstan.

Aye. Derek had heard the speeches a few times, and now they'd finally followed through, as it were, with their threats. But Derek wasn't convinced that it would last. He'd likely be back in his old room by Friday. Maybe not Friday, though certainly within the fortnight. It'd be a travesty if things were to unfold divergently.

So Tommy would've heard all about the shenanigans in the Gibson household from his sister and, due to Tommy's generous soul, he would take pity on young knight Sir Derek by way of offering him sanctuary for the meanwhile in his country mansion. That sounds about right. That sounds like Tommy.

Tommy – and Derek didn't mean much disrespect by this – was a complete doormat when it came to family. Derek's uncle was a wee man; physically, he was as unimposing as bread. He was balding and podgy, and prone to avoid confrontation at all costs. Tommy liked harmony; he also liked his money. One could not mistake the intelligence and shrewdness that throbbed behind the horn-rimmed frames of his spectacles.

A habit of Tommy's was that he would often alternate between broad Scotch and queen's English during conversation. Derek knew that the proletarianism of the Doric tongue embarrassed many stratal Brochers. The language was designed to be spoken quickly and minus any substantial premeditated thought. Vowel chased vowel sought noise; punctuate this with a few swear words, concluding with an insult, and you had yourself a sentence. The Doric was not among the prettier forms of communication; Derek thought of it as being a kind of verbal graffiti. Any attempts Derek had made to *talk* in the past had resulted in failure. Like many men of the North, he became too self-conscious and frustrated by the gear-changes required to articulate himself into English. He felt imbecilic whenever he tried to slow down his speech and actually take the time to map out what it was that he was going to say.

Furthermore, his uncle looked older than he was. His appearance gave the impression that he was the father of three. The truth was, however, that Lisa had never borne Tommy any children. Derek thought that something of a pity. Whether it was a case of she would not or could not, Derek had never been divulged with that familial secret. She'd made Derek use a condom, he knew that much. Her fastidiousness, however, may have been actuated not by a reluctance to have babies but an anxiety over possible STDs.

Dear, dear Lisa. She flounces around the northeast doing fuck-knows-what with Christ-knows-whom and leaves sweet husband Tommy to run her parents' business. Her folks were too scrambled to be of any use to Toories anymore. Her dad was wrecked after a stroke left him with spazzy face, and the mother was just nutty, in that she was obsessed with collecting these petty things, like women's scarves from specific periods and unusual cat collars. Lisa had clearly inherited the bulk of her ingredients from Mrs Towers. Lisa was a handsome dame, but the screws had slackened as on a bridge over a quivering fault line. Thus, Tommy was the guy with all the responsibility; as far as Derek could tell, his uncle was fine with that arrangement. Tommy had married above his means, and why would he think to ruin his blessings by complaining?

Derek sort of regretted ever having gotten involved with Lisa. It would be a true shame if his uncle were to find out about that one.

Tommy was a goody, basically.

He could be a swine, though. Tommy was no fuckin sap, not when it came to his employees. And even then, Tommy wasn't a fraction of the prick that Derek had encountered in his years of coasting from yard to yard.

This was Derek's sixth yard in five years, and, although he'd only been at Toories for a few months, this was his favourite one so far. But that was much like saying which flavour of animal dung you preferred the taste of. You might be able to stomach it, though you wouldn't recommend it. It had helped that his uncle was the big boss man in these here parts. Initially, however, it was this family connection that had made Derek reluctant to go to Toories. What with the Evermore debacle still soiling his CV. After that incident, Derek had vowed never again to work for relatives.

Then he got the boot from Fishco half a year ago and had to do something. Unfortunately, there weren't many employers out there at the time who were looking for unreliable fuck-ups with no skills, training or discernible uses. Nepotism it would have to be, then. Some people got to be president; others had to settle for wading in amongst the minge-tang of aquatic vertebrates.

Derek got away with a lot more of his crap than erstwhile he might have done, and he wasn't treated like quite the reprobate that he'd grown accustomed to at the other yards. All the same, Derek still wasn't wholly in love with the place, but it was a wage, and they spared the castration if you dared to come in five minutes late. It would do for the meanwhile, he reasoned. Until he won the lottery, ken?

The door popped ajar. Derek flinched and sat up. He smiled a bit as his uncle took his throne behind the desk. Tommy ping-ponged the gesture back across the mess and nodded good morning. Derek's uncle wore a suit under his spotless overalls. The man also wore the standard white paper hat of the pleb. However, his hat was noticeably cleaner than anyone else's.

"Ah'm going tae maak this short," his uncle stated, locking his stubby fingers. "Derek, ye're sacked."

Derek pulled a blank. Inside, the sarky, dickhead voice of his subconscious croaked 'Surprise'. He drifted down the chair.

Tommy's expression didn't change. His smooth hands knotted together like some sausage decoration in a butcher shop. The paper hat hid his glossy dome.

The beep-beeping of a lorry in reverse chirped through the window.

"Eh, pardon?" Derek found his voice in the bin of mystification. "Fit the fuck dee ye mean 'ah'm sacked'? Is 'is a joke, like? 'Cos if it is, it's fuckin hilarious."

"This is no joke, Derek. Noo, jist calm doon. Ah've made up my mind. It wis a hard decision tae maak, bit I've made it. Towers Fish Processing is havin tae make cuts. Ye're nae the only een that we're goin tae have tae let go, Derek. There'll be other redundancies made through the week. Noo, ye can either finish aff yer day, or I've got a severance package put together for ye. It's nae brilliant, bit ah - "

"No, no, no. Jist wait a fuckin second here, Tom."

"Derek, the decision is final."

"Aye, ah fuckin hear ye, like. Bit wid ye fuckin listen, eh?" Derek was so far forward that he had his chair up on its front legs. "Did ye hear aboot yisterda? Did ma mam tell ye fit happened?"

"Yes. Suzanne tellt me exactly fit happened."

"So, ye un'erstan that ah'm noo homeless, aye? Eh?"

"Aye," Tommy replied. Derek could've grabbed his uncle's entwined fingers and splintered the lot of them. "Bit I'm sure ye've got plenty o mates that'll luk aifter ye."

Derek's hands clenched the desk as though he would bend the wood like plasticine. "No, listen, 'at's nae guaranteed. Ah wis sleepin on a pal's fuckin settee last night, bit ah dinnae ken if 'at welcome's extended tae the rest o ma fuckin life, like, ken?"

"Derek." Tommy leaned in to feel the heat of the lad's anger. "Naebidy owes you a livin. It's aboot time you realised that an' sorted yersel oot."

The nephew shook his head, thoroughly disgusted by this latest mishap to befall him. "So, fit the fuck's 'is aa aboot, eh? Why the fuck hiv ah bin sacked, like?"

"Would ye like a list?"

"Ah'd like a non-twattish reply fir a start." Derek leaped to his boots and snarled in his uncle's face. "'Is is nae fuckin funny, a'right? So fit's 'is, like? Get rid o us cunts an' taak in mair fuckin foreigners tae fill up yer fuckin flats wi? Ye fuckin chancer. Ah'm being serious here, Tommy. Ah'm nae jist gettin sacked fir nae fuckin reason."

Tommy remained seated. The disposable hat engulfed his bonce like fungus. "Well, let's try 'is fir size. Ye've bin aff five days in the last four wiks."

"Eh, ah wis at a fuckin funeral the ither day, in case ye for-fuckin-got, like."

"I wasn't includin yer grandad's funeral. Plus, Derek, ye're almost always late. Ye're supposed to start at eight, nae ten past eight, nae quarter past, nae half past, nae half way through the aifterneen. Eight. On the dot."

With the aspiration that a wee stroll might cool his jets, Derek paced behind his chair. "Is 'is aa ma mam's deein, aye? Did she pit ye up tae 'is? Ah bet she fuckin did. The tormentors."

"Derek, if it wasn't for ma sister, you would've bin gone lang before noo."

"Fuckin bullshit." Derek stormed to the door. He was about to burst from the office when the fury took hold and he twirled back; his finger was out like a bayonet. "'Is fuckin sucks."

"Derek, did ye even like the job?"

"Fit kina fuckin moron question's 'at, like? Of course ah didnae. It wis fuckin shit. Bit noo ah'm fuckin jobless and homeless. Ah cannae be fuckin beth."

"Maybe ye should try tae find somethin you're mair interested in." Tommy untied his digits and reclined. "Half the time ah saw ye in 'ere, you wis jist starin into space. Maybe somethin a bit more demandin wid help. Plan yer next step, Derek. You're twenty-eight years - "

"I am twenty-fuckin-seven."

"The point is: you're nae a bairn onymair, Derek. You have tae sort yourself oot sometime. This is as good a time as ony. If ye don't, ah shudder to think what'll become o ye."

Harmonious Tom was calm. He did have some concern for the wellbeing of his nephew. Derek sensed this. The rage and shock faded like steam on glass. Derek steadied himself against his chair.

"Work fuckin sucks," he grumbled.

Tommy quipped, "Well, just think, ye dinnae hiv tae dee it again for a while." The nephew didn't retort. Tommy reached into a drawer by his knee. He produced an envelope and tossed it up towards Derek, whose alertness deserted him and resulted in Derek having to collect the package from the floor. "There. An' 'at's nae fir drink."

Derek could feel that the brown envelope was thick with notes. The phone on his uncle's desk began to ring, as such devices had a tendency to do. Derek didn't have a phone. Tommy answered his.

Derek recalled the day that his dad had paid him off in a similar fashion. His dad had given him a cheque, a hefty cheque, which, owing to principles that Derek never knew that he had, remained unspent in a savings account. Unwasted on shirts and libations. The large sum given to Derek acted as his safety net through the past years' adventures of cocking about and tightroping with gaffers unimpressed. That pay-off was for a rainy day, his dad had said. Well, as surely as Derek knew clit from cloth, it was pouring now.

Derek's anger was gone. Most of it. A low washed over him, like when you arrive at a place after getting yourself lost, then remember that you don't want to be there. Derek shuffled towards the door. He inspected the envelope, though didn't open it. Behind him, he could hear that his uncle, phone call concluded, was now typing away on his computer. It was back to the gaiety of commerce for Uncle Tommy.

Derek turned. "Ah fucked yer wife by the way."

The typing stopped. Tommy's face rose above the computer. He laughed. "Really?" The typing resumed.

Derek left the office.

He stood outside in the simulated sun. Forklifts zipped about with box-mounted pallets. Workers tried to look busy. The loading bay door was up. Derek could see into the heart of the factory. The rolling belt. The gaffers. Gazza. Dopey Robbie. The fridges and the sullen.

Derek ripped off his paper hat and his filthy overalls and cast them onto the gravel. He strolled out the yard and through the gates.

Another time, fuckwits.

Chapter 6

Conversations with the Heavens

Raymond stared at the title. He poked his specs further up his nose. He itched under his chin and rubbed a grey-blue hand over his crumpled face.

Too pompous? he wondered. Too pretentious?

Of course it was, and all the better for it. It was the sort of title that lasted, and which enticed the plaudits. It puffed out its chest and demanded that you take it with a mighty grain of seriousness. Society's reverence will be stapled to its cravat for the centuries. Yes, it was pretentious. Incredibly so. But so, too, was the old man. He wanted to change the world. And, what was worse, he believed that he could. The title fit; it snapped into place with a satisfying click.

Beneath the title, he scribbled 'by Raymond John McLeish'. He turned the cover of the A4 jotter. Raymond switched the ballpoint to his right hand and stroked a '1' into the top left corner. He was always conscious of having to rotate between writing hands every so often. A seized-up claw was of no use to the Broch's would-be literary pride and joy. Chapter 1, he wrote, top and centre on the lined page.

Raymond shifted in his seat. His writing chair for the last couple of years was a lofty, lime, padded affair that was as hideous as it was snug. It didn't aggravate Raymond's back even after long periods of prose construction. The chair sat at an angle in his compact living room, directed towards both the television and the window. The window looked out onto the street: Sutherland Terrace, of all the places on all the planets that he could live. Raymond's was one of the few houses on the street that didn't have all of its front windows boarded up. A sheet of plywood, however, covered his upstairs toilet pane. A gang of bairns had caused that about a month ago: six or seven academy kids tearing down the street, whipping stones and shattering glass.

Raymond pushed himself up in the green monstrosity. The ugliness of that chair didn't contrast at all with the rest of the furniture. Every speck in the room had either come free or dirt-cheap, with most of the goods in the semi having been passed down from dead acquaintances. The TV's previous owner had been a poorly sighted friend, whom had stumbled drunkenly in front of a bus one Saturday afternoon; down in the Broadgate, so lots of people could see.

Raymond adjusted the pad on his lap. The afternoon glare pushed against his face like an oven glove. The pen tip palpitated above the page.

No framed photographs hung from these walls. No pictures of sons or daughters rested on the mantelpiece, and no portraits of grandkids either. These maroon walls stood bare. No loved ones anywhere.

Had there ever been any? There was a question. There was a book.

Raymond pressed the tip upon the page as if to write, then pulled it back when his mind flopped over onto dry terrain. He analysed the empty page. And the ninety-nine other sheets that hounded it. A grey-blue hand rubbed his crumpled face. He itched under his chin. The white expanse triggered that customary dread. It was not a fear that Raymond disliked. With that apprehension came simmering optimism.

And the pen will impregnate the paper with its black, black seed and give life to that which does not exist.

The void stared up at Raymond from the lap of his cream corduroys like the eye of a giant squid.

He could kiss the page, and with that kiss blow all the doors of the metagalaxy wide.

There was always the potential for brilliance. If he had it in him.

The pen tip dug into the page like a prospector's drill. He would not raise it again until he had the first sentence under his belt. For now, Raymond was done with the short stories and experiments that clogged up his cupboards and buckets. This was the novel that would amass his seventy-nine years on Earth; the sum total of over three-quarters of a century of thinking, drinking and sinning. The culmination of a life. The book, he thought, will be my tombstone.

Stipulations for the book: no swearing, of course. Debased and indecent language was for the illiterate and the inarticulate and not for these leaves of grandiosity. Every curse was a spark of frustration, spurting from the drainpipes of the ignoramuses. May the young writers swear till their tongues fall out.

The theme of Conversations? Existence in a nutshell. Let us waste no more time. This book will be *my* book, *the* book. They will talk of it. This novel should be a picnic in the haunted woods where pragmatism and idealism fornicate like bears with rabbits.

Raymond intended to pour tar into the sugary jar and watch the hordes choke on *his* reality. *Real* reality. The realness. What it really was to be. His would be the tome that the people reached for on the lousy mornings when the act of breathing was like a punishment levied by some unknowable entity for its amusement.

The clock above the gas fire caught Raymond like filaments snagging. Almost an hour had passed since he had written the title and still the page was devoid of word.

He made to write, when three light knocks splashed off his front door.

The idea vanished, crumbling away like soot into the night.

Anger rose and fell, sharply. Raymond closed the jotter and retracted the ballpoint with a click. He turned to his left and placed his tools on a lamp-sporting table, next to the dictionary, thesaurus and spare pens. The ballpoint rolled onto the pitchy ring where Raymond's coffee mug usually sat.

He peched as he pushed himself up onto his slippers. Raymond grabbed his cane from beside the chair. He didn't really need it for the short journey to the door, but it helped all the same. Raymond wasn't crippled. The stick just worked to take some of the pressure off of his lower back. Without his trusty cane, Raymond would be unable to go for one of his extensive walks. Thirty minutes sans stick and he'd be near paralysed.

The visitor knocked three more times.

Raymond had also discovered an alternative use for his cane as an anti-junkie device. A weasel-faced zombie-kind whom had tried to mug Raymond a while ago had ended up with a bloody mouth and a bust hooter thanks to the stick. Raymond now knew better than to answer the door without it.

He crossed the living room and down through the lobby, beyond his steep, and rather dangerous, staircase. Raymond's white, eight-year-old terrier took no notice of the old man. The swelling and thinning clod that was 'Gordon' napped in its basket. Raymond unsealed the front door, but, wary that Sutherland Terrace was on the other side of it, did not dismount the catch. The door parted just enough. He stared through the gap. No one. He looked down.

There she stood.

Raymond took off the catch and opened the door fully. The little girl in her school uniform stood on his doorstep and smiled up at him in the sunshine. In her arms, she held a clutch of paper, pages of hand-written meanderings. Raymond recognised the scribblings as being that of his own. She held the pages out to Raymond. He took them, graciously. Entirely, then, did his annoyance at being interrupted subside.

"Thank you, Rachel."

The girl stepped past the old man and entered the house. Raymond looked around his neighbourhood. 'Unwell' would be the best way to describe what it was that he saw from his doorstep. The sunlight hugged the land in an effort to aid its rejuvenation, though the embrace possessed scant warmth, like a consolatory gesture between recurrent enemies.

Gardens wallowed with football-concealing grasses and weeds that would never be displaced unless by the council's intervention. Homes appeared as hungover and strungout as their seldom viewed occupants. Raymond didn't know how many of these houses had residents. It was hard to tell with the windows blocked from sight as they were.

Nobody walked the street. No kids or parents loitered in their grounds and relished the weather, with chilled beverages accompanying barbecues, nor did any joyful sounds beautify the silence with their sonic cosmetics. No one eyed the old man with suspicion. No one scowled at the circumspect relationship that he had with the seven-year-old girl, whom was neither grandchild nor pupil. Nobody. Not a soul.

Unwell and close to death.

Raymond stepped back and shut the door. He slid the catch into place.

Rachel knelt over Gordon's basket, stroking the awakened mutt. It got up and licked her face. The small dog's tail flickered. It trotted after Rachel as she went into the living room. She sat in her favourite chair, which Raymond noted was the one with its back to the window. Gordon sat by her side, content to have its ear scratched by the young girl whom was both adoring and adorable.

Raymond entered and sat on his writing chair. He was acquainted with some of the sheets that the girl had handed him. They were his words and he knew them well.

It was one of his 'Tiggles McScone' shorts and was only a few hundred words in extent. In this episode, the heroic squirrel Tiggles is hypnotised by his dastardly nemesis Cpt Fantaztik. The bad guy convinces Tiggles McScone that he must drink every drop of water from every lake, river, stream and ocean in the world. Tiggles dives in and starts filling up like a balloon. Bloated, yet unable to stop drinking, our hero faces certain death. Halfway through guzzling Loch Ness, though, a butterfly lands on Tiggles's whiskers. This causes the squirrel to sneeze and shoot the water out of his mouth like a hose. The onlooking hypnotist is struck by the blast and whacked into the middle of the Atlantic, thus breaking the spell. Tiggles dries himself off and has a party with an assortment of his furry friends. The end.

Not the greatest of Raymond's 'Adventures of Tiggles McScone' stories, but not a bad one. It was certainly a lot better than 'McScone's Egypt Escapade', which he realised then that he hated.

Raymond lay the story on a coffee table, which was betwixt him and her. A bundle of pages remained in his hands. These were what Rachel had really wanted to show him. He looked at her. She was fixed on him; the drumming of her heels on the seat was the music of agitation. Even Gordon seemed to be watching Raymond with an anxious glint under its bushy eyebrows.

Raymond examined the pages. They contained drawings. Illustrations. They were pretty good as well. He guessed that they were exceptional considering the girl's age. The illustrations were nicely coloured. A mixture of crayons and felt-tip pens. The first illustration was of Tiggles: light brown fur, blue T-shirt and a grin like the spread wings of an albatross. Then Cpt Fantaztik: a nineteenth-century villainous type, kitted out with ominous moustache, top hat, black suit and cape. There followed seven A4-sized drawings that encapsulated a succession of plot points. Drinking water. Filling up. Sneezing. The best and most endearing of Rachel's pictures was the final sketch. It depicted Tiggles celebrating his victory over Cpt Fantaztik with the other woodland critters.

A gruff smile creaked upon Raymond's head.

"They're affa good," he said.

Rachel beamed as a thing that Raymond would expect to see escorted everywhere by a hovering halo. She refrained from drumming her heels. The girl was always nervous prior to Raymond passing judgement on her work. Once his appraisal came, however, she was back to being her chirpy self.

Raymond got up. He took the Tiggles story from off the table and, together with Rachel's pictures, put the sheets in a drawer by the doorway. The cabinet used to belong to his mother. It contained six other Tiggles tales complete with his neighbour's illustrations.

"Faan are ye gaan tae get 'em…" Rachel's cute face contorted comically as she strained to find the right word. Raymond didn't intrude in her learning process by interjecting. He knew that she would get there. And she did. "…published?"

Raymond was a hat stand by the door. His eyes strayed from her to the clock above the fireplace. "In time."

A smile encompassed her jaw like a bandito's neckerchief. It was the prettiest smile that Raymond could ever recall seeing in his life, so full of a hope and honesty that he'd known very little of.

"Hiv ye deen onymair Tiggles?" she asked.

He paused, in no particular rush to break the wee girl's heart. "No. There's nae mair."

The corners of her mouth slid downwards. "Why nae?"

"Ah'm writin somethin else jist noo. Somethin different. There winnae be onymair Tiggles stories fir a while."

"Fit aboot the book?" she said.

"It might jist hiv tae wait a wee filey langer."

Her bottom lip was pushed out as if to provide the birds with somewhere to rest. Ambivalence filled Raymond's thoughts. No one could look at that girl's face and not be troubled with stirrings of depression. But Raymond also felt twinges of delight around the edges of his disheartenment. Rachel was sad because he was killing off fictional characters that he'd created. He was having an influence over another human being for the first time in a long time. He and his actions were actually important to someone again. When was the last time that Raymond John McLeish had meant anything to anyone, especially to someone as special as that little girl undeniably was?

A while, at least.

"Rachel," he said, "hoo wis school the day?"

The sun encapsulated her in an angelic frame. The diminutive brunette had hair almost to her hips. Blue eyes pierced through a face that didn't look right being sulky. Rachel wasn't normally a one to grumph. She was a strong child. Her stoic nature was ground out from hardships in the home place. Seven years of neglect and mismanagement by the heroin addicts next door. The father was a drug dealer, no less.

The girl's sadness stabbed at Raymond just below the neck of his jumper. He tapped the drawer. The old man's supposed epitaph on the table beckoned him. Perhaps Conversations could wait. Or he could do both. How long did it take to write a Tiggles story anyway? A week? A fortnight? Five minutes, if he had talent. He could resurrect the squirrel at night. Carve his tombstone by day. Although, that was a lot of writing to do for an old man with old eyes and an old brain, and he didn't want to put off the writing of his One Great Novel any longer.

The blue eyes seeped.

Could he do both?

He could try.

Raymond cleared his throat. He murmured, "Well, there are a couple o Tiggles adventures ah've bin workin on. Ah could hae a luk at 'em. Sort 'em up a bit. Ah'll gie ye 'em later in the wik; if ye like?"

The churlish aspect that didn't suit Rachel very well was replaced with an elated one that very much did.

"Aye," she blurted out. "Ah mean, yes, please."

"Fine," Raymond said. "They'll be ready fir ye on Friday. So be sure tae hae yer crayons lukt oot."

Her ear to ear grin returned. A loving, genuine expression that made Raymond feel like he was almost worthwhile. For the recipient of such an exhibition of affection couldn't be that ineffectual of a creation. Could he?

Raymond sent the girl back a decidedly more dilapidated smile. She giggled.

"Hiv ye hid onythin tae ait the day?" he asked.

"Yes." She nodded. "Ah hid an apple at break, an' crisps an' a cheese sandwich at dinnertime. Ma mam packed ma dinner 'is mornin before ah went tae school."

Raymond thought it wonderful how she pronounced school as skoo-aal. He inquired, "Is yer mam an' dad in jist noo?"

"Aye. Ah mean, yes. Ma mam is. Dad's oot."

"His she made ye ony supper?"

"No," Rachel replied, fondling the appreciative dog's belly. "She's sleepin. Ah think she's bin nae weel again."

Raymond gulped his outrage for the child's benefit. "Well, ah wis jist gaan tae maak ma ain supper. Ah could maak you somethin as well, if ye'd like?"

"Yes, please."

"Fine. Hoo aboot yer favourite? Macaroni an' cheese?"

"Yes, please." She bit the inside of her cheek and resumed kicking her heels against the seat, spurned on by the pleasure of holding a rhythm as opposed to jerking through tension. "Thank you."

Twenty minutes later and Raymond reappeared from the kitchen with two portions of the savoury dish. "Waatch, it's kina hait." He gave one of the bowls to Rachel. She thanked him before quickly attacking the food with her spoon. Raymond sat across from her in his writing chair and picked at his meal. He noticed that his dictionary was on the cushion next to Rachel. She'd been reading it again. That was one of her things. Rachel would flick to a page then attempt to memorise each word with its meaning. One day, he thought, she will be an extremely intelligent and radiant young lady.

The dog raised its snout towards Rachel's bowl.

"Gordon, stop mooching," the old man barked. The dog groaned and lowered its beak. Rachel rocked with joviality.

After the food had been gobbled up, Rachel told Raymond about school. Ryan Simpson had snapped one of her pencils in half and blamed Peter McLean. But she'd seen Ryan do it and called him a liar. Ryan got told off by Mrs Docker and he started crying in front of the whole class. Although, Rachel also got told off for calling Ryan a liar, as it wasn't a nice name to be calling people, even when appropriate; however, *she* hadn't cried. Rachel told Raymond about sums and drawing. She thought adding was simple, though subtracting was less so. Painting was her favourite subject.

It had become boldly apparent to Raymond over the last while that the pick of his day was hearing about hers.

Rachel left Raymond's house smiling. She skipped over the miniature fence that separated hers from his and danced into her doorway.

The sun was still high in the sky when Raymond sat back in his chair and reopened his opus.

1. Chapter 1. Line. Line. Line. Line. All blank.

The ballpoint touched the page. Then started twitching. He wrote, The only thing that I know with any degree of certainty is that nothing ever works out the way that you expect it to.

Raymond closed the jotter and pressed the pen tip inwards. He placed them both on the table by the bequeathed lamp. He went to the cloakroom under the stairs. Space was limited; the room was populated with some coats and bonnets that he couldn't recall ever having worn. It was also littered with miscellaneous bits and bobs that must have found their own way into Raymond's closet. A spider's snare distended from the dangling bulb to the back wall. A grey jacket hung from a peg. Next to it, a brown suit that he'd had to wear the day before.

Goodbye, Stanley Gibson.

Raymond plied himself into the jacket. The cane stood by his writing chair. He took it. Gordon looked at him. Raymond whistled. The dog tore across the room; it jumped about and panted at its master's feet. Raymond bent over as far as was wise to do so and petted the terrier. "Ye fir a waak?" The dog ran to the door and sprung towards the handle. Raymond checked his appearance in an oval mirror in the lobby. He'd never been an attractive man. Passable, but far from dazzling. He scraped his silver hair with tarantula hands. He made his way out the door.

The light welcomed Raymond back into the fold.

*

But shouldn't it be A Conversation with the Heavens? Doesn't that sound better? It was a question that had crept into Raymond's mind every so often since he'd departed from the house. He was now past the Broch, about a mile-and-a-half deep into the countryside. His legs and his cane had followed the old railway line, while his brain had stayed at home with the book.

Fraserburgh itself was out of sight, hidden by the high grass verges that sheltered the path. No tracks remained. The horizontal ladder that had once unfurled all the way down to the city had either been wrenched up or was submerged under rocks and dust.

Gordon wandered off ahead. Sniffing at the air; scenting thorny bushes; bolting from side to side; halting suddenly; surveying the barbed wire that split the world into a Rubik's cube; chatting mainly through telepathy to the animals fenced within. Sheep, horses, cows and goats watched from their enclosures as their four-legged relation woofed its pleasantries.

The sun fired its rays from afar, ensuring that Raymond's patch of the quilt was bright and mildly toasty. The summer dwindled by the day, but there were still a couple of weeks left before the shadowy, early nights would really begin to tell.

The world was spectacular out here. The hills and the grass and the creatures and the sky. A blue tarpaulin protected Raymond's dimension from the blackness of the nothingness. The quiet. And the peace. Today, no grinding of tractor motors jarred at the serenity. Birdsong placated him like honey in his tea. There was no one out here to judge Raymond but himself. A couple of cyclists – a man and a woman – had whizzed past back when he was nearer to the clubhouse; otherwise, Raymond's world was merrily bereft of humans.

Rachel was fine, though. It'd be a glorious thing to partake in this world with her. But people would talk. And rightly so, he thought. An old man and a young girl whose linkage of one to the other did not extend beyond a shared partition had no business together.

Gordon touched snouts with a calf at the top of a verge. Their tails wagged. The lowest line of barbs hung mere centimetres from the animals' eyeballs.

A crow flapped its black-sock wings across Raymond's view.

A scream near burst his eardrums.

The calf ran off to rejoin its herd; all the creatures had been affrighted by the cry. Gordon stared down at its master; its ears were pricked up like felt triangles. The dog's gaze then followed that of the old man's, which was targeted on the path ahead. The decrepit track curved to the right less than a quarter of a mile down the line. A green wall stood at the end of Raymond's vision. Whatever had produced that shriek was around the corner.

Raymond pushed the cane into the ground and quickened his pace. The brave, wee terrier took off, galloping ahead with its stubby legs, like a pillow on lion's fangs. The old man wasn't quite so eager to discover the source of that unexpected din. It had been a male sound, that much he could tell. And it had been a squeal of immense pain. This worried Raymond. Possibly, a farmyard accident had transpired. Or the cyclist from before had tumbled from his bike and broken something or landed on something sharp. Maybe. And, perhaps, someone else had caused that scream. Had inflicted that scream upon the man.

Raymond's hand tightened around the head of his cane; he didn't allow his pace to let up. The aged tripod moved with as much speed and grace as he could; he jogged like a camera stand that had just been fished out of the harbour. The slopes of untended plant on either side seemed to converge on Raymond as he neared the bend. Gordon was already around the corner, yipping its confusion. The dog had traced the source. More screams were issued, though they lacked the excruciating urgency of that initial sound.

The old man followed the bend in the path. The curvature of the gravel road and the grassy dikes bent back into a straight that streaked across the land for as far as Raymond's ancient eyes could see. About a hundred metres down the track, there stood a bridge that Raymond had walked under countless times previously. The bridge tied together farms and fields, and was just wide enough to accommodate the trains that never ran under it anymore. It was a solid structure, like a troll playing leapfrog; the individual granite blocks could be distinguished in a style uncommon with the plurality of modern architecture. That bridge would've been erected earlier even than the date of the birth of the old man who hobbled on a cane. Underneath the bridge, Raymond's dog bounced around a dark lump in the dirt. The lump was larger than Gordon, and Raymond could see that the lump did move. This lump was the source.

Raymond couldn't see anyone else on the path or up on the verges or in the fields. The old man, the dog and the lump were alone. Unless, of course, there was someone hiding behind one of the pillars. He knew that there wasn't, though. This had been an accident, he thought. The lump had been on the bridge, admiring the view, and had fallen over, causing himself some agony.

Raymond was almost right.

He approached the lump. As he got closer, Raymond could hear the lump swearing to himself. Whoever had taken that tumble was in furious distress. Nearer still and Raymond saw that the lump was wearing faded jeans and what he was sure was an outdated Aberdeen shirt. The lump's eyes were pinned shut and his teeth were bared like a bamboo screen; the youth beat at the ground as if ants swarmed him. He sat on his rear; his long legs in front of him were at strange and unsettling angles, which put Raymond in mind of two telescopic rods he'd seen dumped in a skip. Raymond stood over the lump. He'd seen some nightmarish things in the duration of his life span, but still the old man winced.

The dog twinkled with energy. Gordon went to its master's side, momentarily, and then was off again, darting around the stricken lump as though it were a downed maypole. A cow the shade of Raymond's trousers moaned its monosyllabic catchphrase from behind a paling.

The lump's eyelids blew apart. He glared up at Raymond. He had the look of hell about him.

He was but a young lad. Under thirty, Raymond thought. The old man could see now that there had been no accident of the sort that he had first deduced. A length of rope slithered along the stones from the young man's neck to a pin that was flat at one end and jagged at the other. The noose wreathed his bloodied throat like Satan's grip.

Raymond looked up at the bridge, and then down at the boy's legs. It must have been a fair drop, right enough. Between ten and fifteen feet.

Snap: the support.

Whoosh: the rope.

Crack: the bones.

Oocha.

The young man growled. Foam bred around his lips. He lashed out at the dog that dashed around him. His fist struck Gordon's side with a thud. The dog yelped and scampered behind its owner.

"Hoi," Raymond protested. "There's nae need fir - "

The young man cut him off, roaring, "If 'at dog comes onywye near ma legs again, ah'll braak its fuckin spine." The youth continued to punch the terra firma as the pain fried his nerves. He shrieked and swore and cried for death. "Finish me aff, ye aal cunt," he screamed. "Get a fuckin big steen an' smash ma fuckin heid in. Go on. Fuckin dee it. Come on, ye aal fuckin bastard. Fuckin kill me."

Raymond stepped back onto his cane. Where was he? Had he taken a wrong turn somewhere? What had happened to the quiet? The peace? His brain frazzled with bewilderment. Raymond found words trickier to come by than when he was confronted with a blank page. He couldn't remember ever having been faced with such wild rantings, not since he'd become teetotal. What could he do? What could he say? How could he appease the suicidal without granting them that which they craved most?

"Fit's yer name?" Raymond said, interrupting the screams.

"Fit the fuck dis it maitter? Nithin maitters. Jist fuckin kill me. Fuck it. Jist fuckin dee it." Spit flew from the young man's mouth with every intonation.

"Luk, if ye tell me yer name, ah'll be able tae help ye."

"Jimmy. It's fuckin Jimmy, a'right? Noo, get a fuckin rock. Cave ma fuckin heid in. Finish fit 'at cunt up 'ere started."

Perplexed by the youth's delirium, Raymond turned once again to the bridge. There was nobody there.

"God, ye fuckin idiot." Jimmy got the old man's attention back pronto. "God's the cunt. He pushes ye an' he pushes ye an' he laughs fin ye fuckin drap. Ah niver used tae believe in the cunt. An atheist like aa ither bastard. Bit noo ah ken he's real. God exists, an' he's a fuckin cunt. He's a cunt, an' he fuckin hates me fir some fuckin reason. The fuckin…"

Raymond adopted the most serene voice that was presently available to him. "Luk, Jimmy, listen tae me. Listen. Jimmy, ye hiv tae calm yersel doon. Ye're in shock. Ah'll get ye help."

"Fuck you, ye aal cunt. Ye're gaan tae finish 'is noo. Ah'm deein the day an' 'at's fuckin it. Ah fuckin demand tae die."

The old man looked to the hills and the grass and the creatures and the sky. They were no longer of any use to him. He pushed his glasses into his eyebrows. Raymond sank into his mind, swimming through memories in search of support. But no experience had prepared him for this eventuality, and the memories were all muddled anyway.

The young man seethed beneath the bridge.

A flash, a memory, a recollection burst into the old man's head. There was a farm nearby. Aal George's farm was just over the field to his right. There would be people there. He could phone an ambulance. He would get assistance.

Raymond locked eyes with the tortured soul. "Fit's wrang wi ye, min?" the old man asked. "Why wid ye iver want tae kill yersel? Ye're only young, fir goodness sake. 'At's a good thing."

Jimmy cried his answer, stunning even the weather into stillness with his statements, "Life's shit. It's nae fuckin worth fuck aal. It's nae fair, an' it's shite. Noo, fuckin kill me."

Raymond could feel the man's despair clamp around him like a bedbug-riddled sheet. The young man had meant every word that he had said. "Ah'll get ye help," the old man muttered, backing away from the spitting youth.

Raymond clawed his way up to the top of the verge, muddying his knees in the process. The old man found a step along one of the railings and managed to climb over without catching his cords on a barb. The field he entered was full of mother cows and their offspring, and no bulls. Most of the animals munched downhill and paid little heed to the old man and his dog. The farm sat a short distance away in front of a small enclave of trees.

The old man journeyed onwards.

The sun blasted through the heavens.

The young man screamed about God.

Chapter 7

The golden poison wriggled in its crystal cage. The aroma burned at Raymond's senses when he rolled the glass in his hand. Memories floated back to him in the darkness. Raymond pondered in his lime, high-backed chair, as the streetlights gently illuminated the room. The whiskey and its smell sang to the old man, who was now a tired old man. His afternoon walk had maimed him. Clobbered him to this stop.

The bottle stood on the table beside Conversations with the Heavens or A Conversation with the Heavens or whatever shitty, pretentious title he had deemed to give it. It'd surely be crap, regardless of the name.

Raymond looked at the glass. The dog snored like a bus in the lobby. The street outside was grave like a forsaken hospital. No gangs of marauding teens tonight; no, not when he was ready for them.

The Broch was hiding at half past nine on a Tuesday evening.

Raymond raised the glass to his lips. He could taste the drink before a globule had touched his tongue.

How long has it been?

The whiskey washed his stomach.

Too long.

The old man poured himself another generous serving. Clang. Empty glass. Another, me thinks. Clang. Clang. Clang. Quarter past ten. Empty bottle.

This was an eventuality that Raymond *had* prepared for. After the ambulance had been summoned and the young man taken away, Raymond had dropped by the off-licence. A few of his pension-pounds had gyrated like crickets in his pocket. He'd felt the need for a shandy coming on. He'd been in no mood to fight it. He asked for a bottle. He remembered the old days.

Better maak 'at three, he'd said.

Raymond rocketed out of his chair and shuffled into the kitchen. Moonlight stained the white room blue. He left the light off, fearing that the trauma of electricity would burn out those discs of his that he needed for the intaking of data to be analysed by the mind mush. Everyone was a psychological hypochondriac. Raymond liked to make up words. He'd invented the word 'reflake': a noun that denoted the act of mistaking one's own reflection for another person. As in, the reflake caused him to wave at himself in the window. Although, Raymond did not do that. He did not wave at himself in the kitchen window. He knew that that worthless being was him, as in himself.

The spares were in the cabinet by the fridge. He took one. Then, to save himself a repeat journey later on, he grabbed the other. On his way out of the kitchen, Raymond bumped into the cooker. He apologised. He could feel the bruise grow. There was no pain.

The second bottle lasted a further hour. The third and final booze-capsule fell silent a little after two in the morning.

Aye. Naebidy fuckin drank like Raymond John McLeish, did they? Could they? No, they could not.

His slender, wrinkled frame was now melted into the seat. The brain rattled in its case like a maraca. The old man slivered. And smiled.

*

The drooling chimp awoke late on the Wednesday afternoon to discover that he had urinated in his sleep. From the soles of his feet to the hem of his plaid shirt, the irritation reeked and squelched. Raymond didn't bother to get up. He was in his chair. His writing chair. And though the piss had grown chilly over night, the old man couldn't complain. He was exactly where he felt that he should be. The faltering king upon his green throne. He grazed his facial clefts.

The maniacal buzz of the whiskey was as strong as it had been in the wee hours before he'd fallen into a transient death. He would be drunk for days now. But he should get more. Beers, maybe. Cheap lager, thirty pence a can, or less. And, perhaps, some vodka this time as well. Fill me to the gills with the Russian antiseptic.

Russia.

Bleak, cold, hungry Russia. The Communist bear with its Stalin and its poverty.

A memory tried to surface from the depths of Raymond's inebriation. The recollection fell away and drowned.

The sun tipped its hat through Raymond's window. Another fine mess of a pointless day.

Conversations sat on the table next to the old man. He tried his best to manoeuvre his left hand into picking it up. Twice, he was certain that he'd felt his skin pass through the book as though he were a spectre. Then his flesh solidified and he gripped the jotter. Raymond cracked it. He could not focus. In spite of the lenticular artefacts, his eyes drifted as separate geese flocks over the sentence he had written only the day before. The words were as jumbled and mangled as he was. His mind churned like a squall. The old, drunken man tossed the 'book' at the television. It fell short and landed as a smashed gull on the purple carpet.

Raymond snorted. A laugh.

Television. He exhaled, bitterly.

Trust a Scotsman to be the instigator of our demise, or at least a plagiariser of the instigator of our demise. Or was it the phone lad who was the thief?

TV was for people whom had already given up, he thought. Why live when you could watch some other bugger doing it? Living took effort. It was hard, hard work just to be alive. And that was the thing. That was the thing that none of these youth full bastards really understood or, as the old man mused, simply did not want to grasp.

Death is easy. It's as easy as pie; it's as easy as soiling yourself.

Puh.

Life. Hmmm. Why bother, eh?

The old man snorted.

A fifteen-year-old had a publishing deal with one of the majors. So he'd read in last week's paper. The boy – and, at fifteen, he was nothing more than – the boy's debut novel was to be released next February. White Man with Gun. A tale of highs and lows and sexuality and drugs and violence and war and love and death and madness and mayhem set in Manhattan. Fuckin New York stupid shits. Raymond had fought the urge at the time to tear the newspaper to shreds. He hadn't yet done that day's clueless crossword puzzle. Brando McGuigan was the name of this precocity. Brando. How could a person so young truly know something about anything? It defied belief. The journalist had signed off with the cliche 'Behold the birth of a brave new voice'. What utter faeces.

Fifteen.

Pah.

Fif-fuckin-teen.

Big things were, indeed, predicted for this bright child. Raymond felt like ploughing through the garbage to find that article just so that he could vomit and excrete on it. The old man was bitingly jealous, though he knew that he had no reason for feeling such ways inclined.

Raymond John McLeish was the one responsible for wasting his life. Nobody else could take the blame for that.

A starling swooped by the window. Either his drunken eyes were deceiving him or that bird did a loop-to-loop.

But how true was that?

Raymond was a writer nearing his eighties who had never had anything published, nor had he ever written an entire novel. He was a grey man with no roots. No family or friends, except for a series of drinking partners over the years. He'd been in love once, possibly twice, but he had never married. No kids. That he knew of. And no books. Raymond was a writer. He'd handed his life over to the craft, yet what had he produced?

A few fucking stories about a bloody squirrel. He essayed to granulate his false teeth.

But how true was that?

The old man had travelled. Had seen the world when it was still big. Continent to continent. Gathering and noticing and observing and interacting and trying to live. And drinking and fighting and losing and humiliating himself. And, somehow, winding up back in the Broch. A lifetime of odd jobs and low pay, and not a single novel under his belt.

He'd started a few, sure enough. Romance, crime, melodrama, fantasy, horror, sci-fi, semi-autobiography. But then the binges would kick in and the opportunities would shrink. The book would never seem as fresh as when he'd started it, and Raymond would soon lose interest. In time.

The old man was old, and he had yet to discover his voice. Raymond John McLeish didn't know who or what he was. This thought would've scared the old man to drink were he not already blitzed. He didn't know whether he was the cynical spokesperson or the impartial observer. What did he have to say? And how would he say it? He didn't know if he were a Hemingway, with his economy of words, or a Joseph Heller, whom mixed the dictionary with genius to produce seminal chunks of prose that burst with fantastically abstruse metaphors and similes. Two men whose work echoed between the ears of generations. I will be Ernest, he thought. Streamlined and vicious like a shark. That would do it. That'd work fine. That's who he'd be. Fine. Okay. I'll just be great, then, thought the old man. Simple as that.

The old man didn't know what he was thinking, or why. He couldn't desist. Enormous shards of glass crashed together in the neon of a charged nightscape and showered, endlessly, into the vast mire below.

The world had been a big place, massive even, and spacious like a newly built house.

He'd seen it. Opened it up and understood it. Raymond John McLeish had witnessed the world's transmogrification from a pumping, grinding whistle-bag of mechanical befuddlements to a lonely ball of cables and worry. He had seen it all, seen everything. He'd had and did done. Everything.

Raymond had actually met Hemingway, and had split a bottle of brandy with Papa himself at a port in South Florida. Raymond had owned, and been robbed of at gunpoint, a signed copy of Catcher in the Rye. He'd attended orgies organised by Dali. Had witnessed a bald man smother his head with Vaseline and disappear neck-deep into a model's vagina. He'd sailed through cyclones with men whom couldn't speak English, and swept by the shores of Antarctica. He'd seen men die, to the very death dead. Had almost died himself on at least three distinct occasions. He had watched a fat Elvis perform in Las Vegas. Had spilled a drink on Sinatra and called him an 'overrated, wop, mafioso faggot'. Spent a couple of night's in a Nevada hospital. Had watched as a man had ripped his own arm off in a vain effort to save his life. He'd seen things. He'd felt the ecstasy of existence in the morning and the misery of existentialism in the evening.

And yet, sincerely, he didn't know what the answers to anything were.

Nothing Raymond had ever done had been recorded, and, unless his index digit was retracted from his rectum posthaste, his stories would be melding with the oblivion that clouded his fate. He could feel incidents and events slipping under the blankets and falling into infinite rest.

And to all those wise and rebellious kids whom he'd seen wearing T-shirts with Che Guevara's face slapped on the chest, this old man had had a heated exchange with Ernesto in Mexico City, only just prior to the Cuba incident. After he and Fidel initiated their Latin-American revolution malarkey, Raymond saw a picture of the Argentine in a paper and identified him as being the aggrieved soul whom he had crossed ideological swords with. A single photograph framed Che forever as the freedom fighter for all times, but the old man hadn't cared for the youth very much at all. He had found him to be an idealistic rich kid whom thought that any idiot moronic enough to disagree with him deserved to die. Raymond could appreciate that this was a dangerous logic held by a great many other troublemakers whom had been coughed up into civilisation. Who knows? Maybe the doctor was right. We should all just kill our enemies; not that Raymond was significant enough a person to warrant having a nemesis.

The doltish youth, the one from under the bridge: his words shot back through the fog.

God is a cunt.

That sure would explain a thing or two about the ways of men, he thought. Us being in His image and all that.

Not that the old man believed in God. Perhaps he had done for a spell in his younger years; but religion was clothes that he'd outgrown. Raymond had learned to accept what may. Put your faith in each other and in doing right and let that be enough. Surely, you don't need folk from BTV telling you how to behave. There was something somehow entertaining to the old man, however, about the fact that two-thousand-year-old gobbledegook formulated by sand clans and the scientifically utterly ignorant was revered so mightily by a future people.

God, as Raymond had said on numerous occasions, mainly whilst drunk, was past its sell-by date.

But people, as the old man had known for centuries, were weak. They needed that bank where they could deposit their fears and desperation. Most people had several of these repositories. The two most common types could be found between the arms of a loving partner or in the hall of a church. Raymond functioned without access to either. Instead, the old man had his blank jotters and his lost words. And that had worked out beautifully, hadn't it?

He had dreamed of a life in which he was a Raymond Melville or a F. Scott McLeish, reaping wide acclaim a hundred years after his death. Shaping the world. His world. A world in which the old man had won prevalent approval and was beloved by all.

Those banks were never stable for long, though. Christ and the cunny were not always enough. Man has to be released into darkness to survive the light, as someone had said to him somewhere. A drink, maybe. A peculiar, sexual fetish. A random act of brutality against property or a person. Or a fire. Flames reminding us that we have mastered nothing. Drugs. Plenty of drugs. Your character, your strength of, your brilliance of being, is, ultimately, dictated to by your ability to survive this darkness. And how many of these weak-willed buggers whom scuttled around the Broch stealing and mugging could beat heroin?

But how true was that?

Raymond didn't support the argument that the Bible, with its stale pages and eager following, started fights, caused wars and drained the blood of many. He kind of liked the idea that you could put *any* two people in a room together and eventually they would get on each other's nerves. Some bestial people – and Raymond had met more than a few, just took things too far and always wanted to fight. Any excuse would do. Religion was as good as race was as good as geography was as good as tiddlywinks. There would always be the guy in the pub with a penchant for intentionally bumping into folk, then knocking them to the ground for spilling his pint. You couldn't point your finger at a book for that, he thought. That was no book's fault. That was purely human, and humans were irritable specks of volatile matter like everything else.

Free will, eh? And Raymond was positively convinced that the humans did, indeed, possess such a power. It wasn't always exercised, but they had it all the same. The free will, for example, not to pick up a rifle and not to shoot a stranger simply because someone tells you to. The free will to think and act as you yourself deem appropriate. The free will to spend your days on your arse in a pool of your own piss dreaming your life away, if you would so like.

But how true was that? Had the old man wasted his life?

That was a definite maybe.

And there's your book, eh, ye aal drunk? Raymond Pretentious rhapsodising about free will and atheism. Astonishing. Work this into your novel. Is it fiction? Is it anything? Already you can see the queues lining up like millipedes for the signings and the readings and the congratulating. The billions awed stiff by the originality of the old man's ruminations. Seeking out any glimpse that they can of the virtuosity that resides within this grey-blue, crumpled coffin.

Three light knocks splashed off his front door. Puh. Not now. Get up or don't get up. School must be finished. That'll be her. Tae fuck wi 'er. Little bitch. No. She's good. Answer it, 'en. No. Drunk. Sodden with urine. Can't see her now.

Three more knocks.

Ignore her. She'll go away. But she won't come back. She might do. She won't do. They never come back, Raymond. We'll see.

Knock knock knock.

Raymond wasn't sure how much thought went into his actions over the next few moments. The old man got up and stomped as though through a river towards the front door. He tried to rip it ajar; he'd forgotten about the catch. He could've broken the lock were he not so worthless and weedy these days. He took off the catch and prised the door properly. There she stood. There she was. Surprise surprise. Rachel smiling in the sunshine with a sheet of paper in her hand, her school uniform on and the ruins at her back. Her smile slipped for a second when she looked at the old man's trousers. She wouldn't have understood that a grown man could still pee himself and would have assumed that he'd fallen into the bath or something.

"Aye?" Raymond grumbled. "Fit dee ye want? Ah tellt ye Frida; 'is is only Winsda."

Though the girl's grin did not contract, it now seemed artificial, like one that had been carved into the side of a pumpkin. She offered the leaf of A4 to the old man.

He took it, snatched it, giving the girl a paper cut. She nibbled at the minute wound. Raymond glowered at the sheet. Another illustration. This time, Tiggles was, for some unknown reason, surfing. Oh, how she did like to draw the pictures with a beach setting.

Rachel anticipated a delivery of sunlight on his wintry puss, which would mean that she'd done well. It did not arrive.

The old man scrunched the drawing before her eyes and dropped it onto the concrete strip of path. "It's garbage," he said. "Noo, fuck off." He slammed the door in her face.

The old man staggered back to his chair; he almost trampled Gordon in its basket on his return. Raymond's shell opted for sloth while his internals sloshed, like magnets did bother a bottle of iron filings. He wept, now and then, but not much. It wasn't the first time that Raymond had thrust a door at a well-wisher; he knew, however, that it had been the last. Nobody would be rapping for this old man again.

And who could really give a shite? he thought. People equal hindrance.

'Unless a writer is capable of solitude he should leave books alone.' Steinbeck.

The whiskey pound was losing its sting. Pain would leak in if he didn't soon clog those holes with more bottles. To the off-licence. Steeped in piss? Get washed, then. Change your clothes.

The jewel of this solar system disintegrated over a thousand rooftops.

The old man groaned.

Go on, 'en, ye aal cunt. Get changed.

*

The sky was turning black in a slot of the interstellar toaster, at nine o'clock in the PM, when Raymond and cane trundled down a main road. Gordon sensed that something was off with the old man, and had abandoned its master soon after they'd exited via the garden gate. Raymond had not tried too hard to beckon the canine to bide by his heel. The scraggy mutt could fend for itself, then. And Raymond would be glad to be rid of it.

Although the whiskey was currently drying from his radiator brain, its smear was evident in the old man's walk: a loose, staccato stride that passed for sobriety about as well as shit did for chocolate. And thusly he made his way along the road that swung through the town and out again like a boomerang. Posts lined the street like a colossal insect in a state of rigor mortis; its lean legs stretched and curled, and bled yellow from their toes. The gulls fought over bedding rights as though they were at a hostel in December. He stumbled by buildings whose father was the harbour and whose mother was the sea. Some cars whizzed by. The youngsters raced about in their souped-up whatever they weres, producing a din as enticing to him as the burr of a lawnmower was to dandelions. Not many people walked their journeys tonight; not many solitary, English-speaking folk, he noted. The incomers did tend to bunch together like sparrows on telephone lines. Stories in the town paper had scared a lot of the public off the streets, possibly. Some people were too afraid to put a foot out the door in case it was lopped off. People afraid of people. Why should that ever be? That should never be.

Raymond John McLeish was many things, including a multitude of hyphenated adjectives beginning with self. A coward – he had managed to convince himself, however – he was not.

He deviated away from the main road and onto the Broadgate: Fraserburgh's commercial boulevard of charity shops and other such glamorous establishments that sat derelict with bandages over their eyes. He entered the off-licence. Inside the alcoholic-facilitators, stacks of the laxative whistled from the shelves at the emotionally constipated.

A young girl served a young man. She was maybe nineteen, Raymond thought. The man would've been in his mid-twenties. The twenty-something was flirting with the girl; he had a cheeky yet likeable air about him. He was probably the sort to never be fazed by being out and about in public, being watched by others. The guy got his change and his drink and left. The youth smiled and nodded at the old man on his way out. Raymond couldn't tell if the youngster had recognised him or was just being friendly.

Raymond had remembered the boy, though. From the funeral a couple of day's earlier. The youth had been up front at Big Stanley's wake. A grandson, presumably. The man lacked the size and presence of his grandfather, but he'd certainly inherited his confidence and charisma.

The old man ambled up to the till. The girl had an abhorrent piercing above her top lip; apart from that she was quite pretty. She was smiling as though it were her birthday, and she had more presents to come. Raymond got the leftover glow from the Young Turk's charm offensive. Her good cheer waned when the old man's fragrance jabbed her nostrils like rotten bananas.

Raymond took out his wallet. The leather pouch had not been in his defiled trousers at point of micturition; and yet, when he opened it, a sour stench was released that made the girl tremble as though he'd licked her hand. He had not bathed as he likely should've done.

There was ample cash at Raymond's disposal. He had no one to spend his pension on; he didn't eat much; he no longer smoked; and, until last night, Raymond had been on the wagon. The old man placed three sheets on the counter and pointed.

"'Ee o 'ose, please, ma quine."

The whiffy prescription was exchanged for his remedy. She looked repulsed as she picked up the notes and put them in the till, as if taking a squished thing to the bin.

Outside, the Broch was like a ruptured ink cartridge. Fraserburgh was a statue tonight, apart from those cars that paused at the traffic lights, as though halted by an invisible force-field, then zipped away when red birthed amber. Music like keyboards merged with dynamite blasted from the cars as if it were the battle cry of alien beetles. Raymond thought that even though he were a young man today, he wouldn't be able to listen to that nonsense.

And they zipped away. Up to the Leisure Centre car park at the far end of the Broadgate, or down along the harbour. Then up the by-pass. Around the Broch. Out to Peterhead, some sixteen miles south, if they felt adventurous. And then back. Part of a circuit. Like bubbles chasing the water as it swished down the plughole. A car could be a bank, like all things could be.

Raymond chose another route to head for home, opting for the back roads and inaudible streets away from the circuit. He carried both bags in his right hand. One bag held two bottles, and the other held one. The girl in the shop had double-bagged the one with two. The old man's left hand leaned on his cane.

Raymond passed the burned down Baptist church, which had been razed late on a Friday night in early June. Culprits had never been apprehended. Raymond thought that whomever the arsonists were, they should be praying that God doesn't exist.

The builders were in the process of rebuilding. They had been working fast, and their progress was manifest. The skeleton of the church reached from the grave. The back and side walls had been resurrected like a jaw in the gloom.

The workmen had gone home for the night to contend with their suppers and devour their wives, leaving a cement mixer and heavy equipment behind the portable fence that surrounded the site. Two sections of the steel fencing had been pulled apart at the front, just wide enough to allow access for curious fellows.

Raymond heard muttering and laughter exude from the mouth of the church. He stopped. The street was an otherwise noise-parched gully. If the circuit taken by the speedy drivers was a belt, then this street was a nugget of sweet corn inside the town's belly. The people in the flats above the contiguous butcher shop and newsagents would have their televisions down low so as not to give their neighbour's cause to complain, but loud enough so as to insulate themselves from the exterior environment. No cars went by. Nobody passed him or crossed the street to avoid him. It was just the old man, the insect legs and the mutterings from the church.

"Fit the fuck are you starin at?" A shrill voice cut through the evening like a dagger thrown from the work site.

The old drunk, though, wore his malt-fuelled invincibility cape. He stood his ground and stared into the bones of the House of God.

Some more mutterings. Laughter. Raymond recognised the sound as being that of mischievous teens, drinking on a school night.

The shrill voice returned, sharper as if by fracture. "Oi, ye aal bastard, ah said fit the fuck are ye starin at? Eh?"

Raymond swayed dumbly and didn't respond. He was away, surfing on that wave of youth. Rachel. Shadows filled the fissures of his old, old face like oil into an egg carton. This old man is proper old. Swaying dumbly. Gazing into that black hole. Surfing. Away. The little girl. Shadows. Old. Away.

"Oi. You."

The old man recoiled from his drift and looked back into the church. Four figures emerged. Boys. Teeth wobbling free from God's orifice. They were all grinning and chuckling and staring at the weak, old, worthless drunkard on the other side of the fence. They appeared younger than did the bestudded girl whom had served him at the off-licence. Each boy held a rhino's leg-sized bottle of cider.

They came out through the gap in the fence, one by one; they surrounded Raymond, as might chewing quadrupeds on the brink of a feeding frenzy. He still wasn't afraid. He was too drunk to be considerate of his health. These were events in a dream that had no lasting effect, like a henna tattoo, and where the bogeymen were just kids. Teens of varying ages. From fifteen to eighteen, maybe. They'd probably had pubes for less time than he'd managed to go without a drink, up until last night. Then he'd buckled like sliced tendons.

The four of them all looked the same to Raymond: skinny, acne-scorched youngsters whose pastiness was combated by the lemony tinge of the streetlights. They dressed, he assumed, as socio-economical factors inevitably coerced them into dressing. They wore the baggy sports clothes and flashy trainers that their even younger Asian counterparts would've killed themselves in a sweatshop to produce; a week's wage for Chong would enable him to purchase a sip of the sparkling bilge that these Broch lads utilised as transportation. Smirks were poised over their hairless chins like vultures on branches.

One boy wore that most common place of T-shirts: the top with Dr Guevara de la Serna's mug on the front. Raymond thought to treat the youths with an anecdote, when a lad attacked him with a question.

"Fit hiv ye got in the bags, aal man?" The boy in Raymond's face, the boy that spoke, was the one whom had addressed him from the church. This'll be the leader, then, he thought, absently.

"Aye, fit's in the bags?" Che piped in.

Three of the boys were of the same height, which was a couple of inches taller than Raymond was, whereas one was notably shorter and skinnier than the others. He was their chieftain.

The leader had a ratty visage, though it would be inexact to say that he was ugly. His features had an assured definition that some girls would be drawn to. His hair appeared to have been bleached, and he had a collar-up, chest-out manner that made him instantly unappealing.

Stanley Gibson, Raymond contemplated, would simply have picked this ruffian up by the eyelids and lashed him into a wall. The others would've taken this as their cue to scamper off.

A third boy, who had yet to speak and who was undoubtedly the spottiest of the quartet, said, "We asked ye a fuckin question. Fit's in the bags?"

Three of the boys revelled in their moment as generational warriors. The fourth, thin and with what Raymond's spectacles toiled to convince him was a neat, blue mohican hairstyle, stood at the back of the gang. He plainly wasn't deriving as much entertainment out of the harassment of this old man as were his pals.

The leader leaned in, with his forehead only a thumb's length away from Raymond's nose. "Are ye gaan tae tell us, or are we jist gaan tae hiv tae taak 'em aff ye?"

The three who baited the elderly drunk laughed like the hyenas of the dominant pride.

"Are ye a mute or somethin?" the spotty one inquired. "Can ye nae spick, like? Are ye feel?"

"Fuck sake." Che, who had the longest and swarthiest hair of the group, waved his arms about in exaggerated fashion. "'Is guy fuckin reeks o pish."

The hyenas made uproarious jest about how terribly the old man smelled, holding their snouts and wafting their paws as though trapped in a burning den.

"Ah ken," the spotty one said. "He fuckin smells like yer mam, Alex."

"Fuck you, Piggy, ye zitty cunt."

So Che was Alex and Spotty was Piggy – possibly due to his scarlet complexion, Raymond surmised. Piggy was like diced pepperoni.

The old man dreamed away and ignored the abuse being vomited at him by three youths. He thought about his book and about how he wanted it to end. It shall have a positive ending, he declared to himself. Conversations should leave the reader on a note of optimism. Society would be educated and redeemed by his final sentence. They would hunt him down and thank him for constructing such a marvel with his mind. Well done, Raymond. Well done, you spellbinding maestro.

A pink missile connected with the side of Raymond's face. His glasses were knocked for six and his cane popped out from under him. He collapsed in a heap on the pavement. The whiskey bottles smashed by his side. The old man's left cheek reddened, then swelled as though someone had blown into a valve in his ear.

The quiet chum protested. "Fir fuck sake, Scotty. 'Ere wis nae need fir 'at."

"Shut the fuck up, Chris, an' stop bein such a fuckin poof aa the time, wi yer gay fuckin hair." The leader cleaned his fist on his tracksuit bottoms. He had caught the old drunk well. However, Scotty now feared that he might've lost a knuckle. Bastard.

The other two rounded on their director.

"Scotty, ye daft cunt," Piggy said. The teenager was bulkier of frame than his cohorts were. "Could ye nae've tuk the drink aff 'im first, ye asshole? 'Ere's nithin left."

"Waatch yer fuckin tongue," Scotty snapped. "Ye cunt, ah'll wreck you fuckin neest."

The old man let out a protracted groan; he made no attempt to get back to his feet.

Alex expressed his disappointment with the outcome of this raid in a more settled tone than had his spotty accomplice. "What a fuckin waste, min. Piggy's right enough. Ye shid've got the bags first. Noo luk at the mess. Luk at aa 'at drink fuckin splooshed aawye. Could've fuckin sellt 'at, like."

"Luk, homos, if ye's dinnae stop fuckin girnin at me, ah'm gaan tae fuckin start slappin ye's aboot." The leader stated his case adroitly; the others sat on their words.

Blood percolated from the old man's mouth like dirt pushed through lattice.

The three for whom this was all fun shared nervous glances. A giddiness surged through them, like after the Twin Towers had fallen and people waited to see what would happen next. The fourth boy, Chris, stepped towards the unlit butcher's, beyond the steel fence that guarded the churchyard as the trellis on an American football player's helmet, to reassure himself that none of this had anything to do with him. He was about ready to sprint and leave these psychopaths and this situation for dust. He could not leave, though. He had to see how far things might escalate.

The tip of Scotty's trainer hovered above the old man's phizog, as though a winged pollen-seeker.

Raymond gurgled, and laughed out some fluids. "So, you wee boys are the impendence, eh? Scum like you rinnin the country?"

Scotty stamped on the old man. The bridge of Raymond's nose caved in. He gargled out yet more gruesome mirth.

"Scotty, come on, 'at's enough," Chris said, his plea not registering at all with his clansmen. "He's jist an aal manny."

"Gie me yer wallet, ye aal cunt, or ah'll gie ye anither hoof in the dish."

Raymond gazed up through runny lenses at his attacker: a midget transformed into a giant because of the unfortunate angle. He felt his petrol trickle from the corner of his lips and onto the road, as though he were some water feature in a garden. The old man hadn't bled like this in some time, not since he'd become teetotal. He considered how this incident could be adapted for his book. This certainly was as wearying a statement about where we were headed as anything that he'd ever need to make up. Did it require embellishment? Where we were, was, how, always had been, never till now, maybe. Something. Or the other.

The old man stared upwards. He mumbled, as though replete of mouth, "Stick yer heid in a blender, ye wee shite."

Piggy scowled. "Fit the fuck did he say?"

"He caad 'im a wee shite," Alex replied.

Scotty kicked out. Crack. Gurgle. Raymond's lips were obliterated. His gums had burst apart and his dentures were embedded in the back of his throat.

Chris could not watch. The others couldn't look away.

"Ye slag me, ye aal pishy cunt, eh?"

The old man held onto his consciousness long enough to spit onto the rat-faced youth's formerly white trainers, coating its logo with a syrupy wine.

"Fuckin kill 'im," Piggy screamed, as the adrenaline fizzed in his veins.

The leader disappeared from Raymond's sight.

With the guerrilla commander solemn on his chest, Alex shrieked, "Brick 'im."

Raymond looked up. The last thing in the world that the old man saw was a full moon breaking over a row of flats. He saw a chimney pot silhouette like a great door against the flat, pale surround.

Then nothing as a brick cracked open his skull.

Chapter 8

It was a national tragedy.

The incident occurred on the Wednesday night, and by Thursday morning it had infested the media like mould. Usual programming schedules were interrupted on all terrestrial channels as the story was told and retold throughout the day. The morning papers exploded with images and headlines that made the kingdom truly united in its puzzlement and grief. Men and women sobbed behind microphones. Randoms were stopped in city streets to gauge their reactions to this dire affair. Some radio networks were apologetic about playing any tune with a hint of cheer to it, being inappropriate as it was in this dark hour, whilst other stations had jettisoned portions of their playlist in favour of sombre reflection. Warblings of sorrow. Condolences came from the worldwide elite. Both the Prime Minister and the President had already extended their deepest sympathies at this loss. Today, the Earth cared. It bewailed this universal tragedy. For it affected us all. Every decent person under the Almighty's intangible shield couldn't help but be moved to tears by last night's events.

Derek yawned. He rolled onto his back and stretched like a dog. His Doors T-shirt spiralled scruffily about him; he pulled it over his head and tossed it to the floor, which was the blue-carpeted floor of Fat Ass Phil's spare room. Derek pushed the blankets to one side and sat up on the sofa bed, where he had slept for the past three evenings. He had fallen asleep with the TV on. He'd had a few beers. He could remember watching The Roy Complain Show.

That cunt was one funny fucker, he thought.

He'd slept straight through to the drowsy unpleasantness when his eyelids were winched apart at eleven. Since then, Derek had been watching the unravelling of the disaster that had stunned the nation.

The wide-screen television spewed out sadness from the wall like a chute of woe. This has really caught these chaps off guard, he noted. Derek was interested in the story – it was quite the tale; although, he did not share that sense of ultimate aggrievement, which the slide informed him that everyone else was currently sustaining.

The young drunk even found some amusement in the previous night's fatality, and he was certain that he wouldn't be the only person to have done so. Derek was not a particularly sick-minded individual, but the camera-phone footage that captured the happening, and which edited highlights thereof had been shown continuously on all the channels, was rather funny. Jesus alone knew how many jokes would already have been assembled on the topic, like fire engines to a blaze.

Derek's two suitcases were partially unpacked in this surplus room, which was more commodious and better furnished than Jimmy's living room-kitchen combination. There were no windows on the white walls but a skylight on the ceiling. The plot of bright blue had nudged Derek awake, like a cokehead trying to get by him for a cubicle. Another day of sun sunity sunshine.

Derek tapped upon his bare knees and smiled as the ceaseless mourning of the TV ran off him like drink off a drake. He stood up and scratched his testicles through the red cloth of his boxer shorts. He had a semi, which was not unusual given that he had yet to have his day's first urine expulsion. He went out to the bathroom in the lobby. This domicile was a capacious, lucre-wolfing abode, and as such was alike his parents' house; though the Gibson dwelling possessed a woman's flair for ornamentation and maintenance. The Ironside residence was unkempt, like hair that was habitually left to grow out for slightly too long between trims. Derek's parents' home was only about a street away.

He entered the bathroom and slipped off his pants. The vinyl was cold on his bare feet. He approached the bowl. He sat. Shat. Sprayed. Then had a wank. Derek fantasised about the girl with that piercing from the off-licence. It was all rim-jobbing and bum-shagging.

Derek spent a while in the shower, relaxing under its powerful blast. He sang everything from folk to funk. He sang both loudly and proudly. Derek, much like his deceased grandad, had a rather strong voice. Mother's Son reverberated down the corridors without a mumble of complaint.

It was an empty mansion. Empty on the account that Phil was off working in The Tart; the older sister, Claire, was married and lived in Strichen; the mother was a cancer victim; and the daddy, Grite Tam Ironside, was offshore, which suited Derek to a tee. The big man didn't much care for Derek. In fact, Grite Tam Ironside very much despised Derek; not only for being a perennial negative influence on his son's life, but also because of Derek's having inadvertently broken up Tam's wee quine's first marriage.

When Derek was only seventeen, he got a bit saucy with the just-married – and not at all fat of ass – Claire. It had been at her twentieth birthday party, in this same house. Lots of drinking. Lots of canoodling. A hearty laugh was to be had for the most part. Somehow, Derek and Claire ended up alone and naked and 69ing in brother Philip's room, when her then husband walked in. Derek spat out a hair and greeted the mortified man as though he were his best mate, and got a fair punch in the face. From Claire. The husband stormed off, and the marriage was annulled within the month.

From then onwards, young knight Sir Derek was canny to elude Grite Tam. Even after a decade later, with Claire contentedly remarried and a mother of four, Derek was still prudent about being in the house when Phil's dad was around. Thankfully, Grite Tam Ironside wasn't home that often and he wasn't expected to be back from his rig in Nigeria until next Tuesday. This gave Derek a few more days to sort himself out, get a new job and find alternative digs.

Fuck. Cunt. Bollocks.

To do. To do. To do.

Shite.

Much much much.

He turned off the shower and grabbed a towel from a rack. Derek patted himself dry and hung the damp sheet by the radiator. He then had the deplorable vision of Phil using that cloth to floss between his buttocks. He prayed that he had not rubbed any of his friend's skid marks into his resplendent flesh. He checked himself in the mirror. Nae too bad. A few days' worth of stubble prickled his intriguing physiognomy. He could shave. Or he could just leave it as is. The rugged manly look. And why not?

The full-length mirror arrested Derek's attention. A round one loomed above the sink, but that mirror was smaller, and didn't captivate Derek the way that this long one did. He could see the entire computer-tinted rectangleness of his body. Derek had a beer belly sure enough. He was lean and tight around the periphery, though. His working days had mostly consisted of heavy labouring work: pick up box and take it from A to B by way of Z. Derek had never done any weight training before, and he suspected that all body builders had a secret proclivity towards having their buns maleonnaised. The evidence would suggest, however, that he'd gotten a half-decent work out himself at his previous employers.

Pretty fit, ma manny.

Just like Bruce Lee. All muscle and no fat. Well, not much fat. Apart from the gut, which still didn't bear comparison to Phil's. Now Fat Ass Philip Davidson Ironside, he really was a fatty. A perfectly cordial gent. One of the absolute best. But a right proper lardy boy, like a Yank. And even the Fat Ass was dwarfed by his dad. Grite Tam Ironside was gigantic – a Phil and a half. Tam was like some mountain that had slipped off the range one day and developed limbs and a head and settled in Fraserburgh and started a family. Grite Tam was a biggun, and it wouldn't have been all just flab. He, like his son, was equipped with an unnatural natural strength. Grite Tam was a being to be wary of.

Naked, Derek waltzed from one end of the bathroom to the other. As he approached the door, Derek realised just how expansive this room was. The shower area itself was the size of Jimbo's bathroom, and this was only a spare. The main bathroom, with the jacuzzi, was upstairs.

Poor, poor Jimmy.

Thinking of whom, Derek hadn't heard from that lanky twat since the row on Monday night. He hoped that that clown hadn't done anything in character. Derek would have to beg pardon of Jimmy, despite him knowing that he'd been in the right. What Derek had said had been true enough, about Lori and the like. But he'd leave it a couple of days yet. Jimbo's life was on the fireman's pole straight into the shitter. There wasn't much that Derek could do or say that would perk Jimmy up at present.

And there had been no sign of that Lex MacMuppet fella either. Although, Derek feared that the Dundonian was still lurking about somewhere.

Derek, genitalia slapping about freely in the steam, grabbed for the door handle and opened her up.

Bolly olly ocks.

A huge man, shrink-wrapped in a black business suit, filled the lobby. The man stood before Derek like a vast tear in the very fabric of space. His mass clogged Derek's escape. Gravestones encrusted the behemoth's pothole mouth, which bent into something that was either a grin or a sneer.

Derek cupped his bits. He was too stunned to dart back into the bathroom and felt too ridiculous to stand scrot-naked in front of Phil's dad any longer.

Pool-ball eyes rolled in their sockets down to Derek's protective hands and then up again. The field immediately north of where Derek thought to cover himself was of similar design to the dark locks on Tam's head. Grite Tam Ironside's expression dangled between harmless incredulity and split-second eruption.

Derek quivered under the gaze and pondered how likely it was that he could just teleport from that spot. He analysed the situation. He postulated miserably. More than surprise could be derived from this latest calamity. It was confirmation that, whoever should be up there, He never missed an opportunity.

"Well," the fat man's voice boomed, "are ye gaan tae get a tool or fit?"

"Aye," Derek said, prising his soles from the wooden floor. He bolted back into the bathroom. He snatched the towel that he'd dried himself with, quickly vetting it for any discoloured streaks, and slung it around his waist. Derek emerged with the twitchy, boyish look that normally saw him pulled clear of difficulties.

The pool balls were targeted on the young lad. "Is 'ere ony reason why ye'd be waakin aboot nyaakit in ma hoose in the middle o the aifterneen, Derek?" The warmth and murder in the fat man's voice was carted out like melon served with shampoo.

Derek spluttered out his reply. "Ah wis jist haein a shooer, ken?"

"Oh?" Grite Tam said. "Is 'at it?"

"Aye."

"An' faar's 'at son o mine?"

"Workin. He's doon at The Tart."

"An' why are you nae workin jist noo?" Mr Thomas Ironside's ambiguous grin-sneer countenance didn't budge. "Get Thursda's aff, dee ye?"

Droplets that ran the length of Derek's body from his mop to his heels formed meek puddles on the floor. Both men acknowledged these pools. Derek shrugged. Grite Tam replied by narrowing his lids, like snakes swallowing eggs. Young knight Sir Derek lessened before this mountain.

"So, is 'ere ony reason fir ye tae be here ony langer than the time it taaks fir ye tae get dressed?" Tam asked the fidgety youth. "Eh?"

Derek's chalk squares flipped up to meet the pool balls. "No."

"Right ye are, 'en." The aloof enormity started down the corridor. With his back to Derek, he said, "Ah'll tell Philip fin he comes hame that ye've decided tae move on." Grite Tam Ironside disappeared up the stairs at the end of the hallway, taking with him a suitcase that had stood by the front door.

Derek bowed his head. A trail of saliva travelled down to accompany the puddles by his feet. His eyes followed the path that Grite Tam had trod.

You fat, fat, fat, fat

Arsehole.

The tragic events of last night played on upon the wide screen in the spare room as Derek jumped into his clothes. Some people cried, hysterically so, though never once for Derek. The cunts. Others vented their rage at this most galling, pointless of wastages. An elderly woman almost gave herself an aneurysm calculating the heartache of it all. School kids in classrooms blubbed. Broadcasters sucked back lumps and soldiered on. El Capitan addressed the nation from Downing Street. A luvvie recited a poem in a park and sniffled at its completion. The world shared the homosexual's tears.

It was a national, universal, trans-dimensional tragedy, which Derek really couldn't afford to give too much of a fuck about at the moment.

He did, however, have one last laugh when they showed that amateur clip for the millionth time. Derek laughed aloud with plenty of conviction as he watched the movie star dance like a lunatic upon the roof of the now world-famous London nightclub, screaming something about silver fishes and devine wishes again and again. The picture was hardly of the highest calibre, though you could just about make out the ultra discombobulated actor's ubiquitous face. Derek giggled and chuckled and roared with laughter as the super A-lister frolicked until, finally, he swan-dived off the top of that building. We do not get to see him hitting the pavement, nor the ensuing wreckage of the thespian's corpse. A significant leg has been cut from Hollywood's table. Many celebrities weep. With this and the economy and the terrorists, everything keeps getting worse and worse.

Derek grabbed the handles of his two bags, then did exeunt from Grite Tam Ironside's nearly empty mansion.

*

Derek sat on the bench along from the trees and the swings, and which overlooked the playing fields. The swings were lonesome this afternoon. The suitcases settled by his side. He half expected a crew-cutted retard to shuffle up alongside him and start casting his pearls of wisdom about like a kid in a leaf pile. That did not happen; though he did spot another simple squire whom was off on his own voyage. A bearded strange sort, whom he had recently encountered, bisected Derek's view, marching across the pitch at the foot of this park. There were no games being played, and, judging by the yellow-jacketed man's determined stride, the presence of footballers would not have caused him to divert from his chosen track.

Derek appreciated the brightness of the day, but, equally, he perceived that it was searingly cold. Autumn was making its presence felt like a bad smell leaking into a dining area. He wore his navy coat: the thick one with all the pockets. He could be thankful that his dad had taken the care to stuff it into his bag for him. If not for his navy coat, he'd be wearing his suit jacket, and that, in partnership with his jeans, would make it seem as though he were going for some fashion thing that he really wasn't. Like the rest of his clothes, his navy coat was decidedly rumpled from its journey in his case. He'd need access to an iron before long. He hadn't thought to do some ironing in Phil's. The weekend was only tomorrow away. It was Thursday already, fir fuckity sake. He'd also have to get to a washing machine. The plastic bag for his used pants and socks, which he wasn't overjoyed about having to carry around with him in a suitcase, was near full.

Derek would also have to get himself a bed. And a roof. And a job. And an actual reason for existing.

Derek's pocket bulged with the 'cheerio, waster' bundle that Uncle Tommy had given him. He'd already managed to spend about a third of it. The last two nights in The Tart had been humorous and fluffy; Derek was disappointed to have not yet met the new barmaid, whose hours, thus far, were noncompliant with that of his. It had just been him and Fat Ass who had guzzled the brews these past couple of uneventful evenings. There had been no cameo appearances made by the likes of Freddy or Mo or, indeed, even Jimmy to help bolster the cast of this young knight's saga.

The remaining wad in Derek's jeans would amount to maybe two hundred quid. After this weekend, he knew that there might not be a bump to inconvenience his denims.

Derek's head fell back. He exercised his facial muscles. Grey lined the clouds like the shadings of a ceiling rose. Derek's jaw lolled and froze agape. He roared a naughty word as mightily as he could, purely for the sake of it. His gob shut and his noggin slumped forward.

The concrete veneer of Fraserburgh loomed behind Derek. The woods that skirted the park like an acorn fence eclipsed the houses on either side of him. Ahead, the Earth was severed into multi-coloured bands of diminishing width. Park, road, park, road, beach, sea. The sky straightened out this rainbow with its coral-reef magnitude.

Derek stroked his nose.

Great Uncle Willie? Nah. Aunt Rosie? Nope. Mo? Maybe. But Derek doubted that his chum's parents would be happy to have another drunken pervert lodging with them. Freddy? No. That was a nonstarter. Frederick was sinking in the quick sand of family responsibility. Laura? The Laura who'd just found out that he'd snaked a couple of her pals when she was through at RGU? Tracy? That was a thought. Not a very good one, but an idea all the same.

Perhaps it wasn't that awful of a suggestion. It would give him a chance to reacquaint himself with his younger sister. Plus, as it was unlikely that Derek would ever, by any intentional means at least, have any children of his own, it was about time that he got to know the closest thing as: his niece. Aye, Rachel was supposed to be a clever wee tyke, and, providing that the reality of having two junkies for parents didn't destroy her irrevocably, it was forecast that she would go far. And the man of the house was a decent type as well. Considering.

Derek had always got on good guns with Donnie Wise. Most people, though they wouldn't think it, *could* grow to like Donnie; just as long as they ignored his dodgy dealings and made allowances for the dubious comments that he was liable to make in the course of a chat. One occasion sprung to mind where Derek had done especially well to bite his lip. Donnie had been defending his vocation and had gone on to slander 'the system' and remark how it was that he flatly 'refused to conform' and all that kind of stuff that Derek couldn't be done with hearing. A sober, on-the-ball Derek may have countered by asserting that, as Donnie was a heroin addict in a town reported to have more heroin addicts per head of population than anywhere else in the UK, then it was he, Mr Donald Wise, who was the conformist. As it was, Derek had been drunk and hadn't cared enough to contradict the man of the lengthy mane and the moustache.

Derek had once overheard Freddy compare him to his brother-in-law, saying that if Derek were a junkie, he would be Donnie Wise. Derek critiqued this equation and discovered how dispiritingly wrong Freddy was in his supposition. Donnie had a wife, a child, a house, a car and a steady job – sketchy as it was. Derek had none of these things. Where did that, then, leave Derek when he was lesser off than a skeg-fiend? If Donnie were comparable to anyone in the Gibson brood, then it would have to be to papa Adam.

Derek wheezed.

The gravity of his situation hit him with a greater force than when he'd arrived home to find his bags waiting for him. He'd played his final ace, the fat ace, and it hadn't quite come off for him. Derek was now truly buggered. His hands went to his knees. His head dropped between his legs. He stared at the floor beneath his brown trainers; the glass-infested granite anchored the bench to the park. Anywhere between five minutes and an hour elapsed before Derek decided that he wasn't really of the nature to cry or feel too sorry for himself.

Derek looked out across the green and the grey to the thin blue of the North Sea.

Live forever. Dee in the attempt.

"If life wis easy," his grandfather had also stated, "it widnae be worth doin."

Derek got up and took the handles.

And life was absolutely nothing at all like a box o fuckin chocolates, ye feel cunt.

*

The front door was wide to the wall so Derek walked in without invitation. He didn't like standing about on Sutherland Terrace with two heaving bags of precious things. Derek sensed that he was being cased from between the gaps of the boards that covered most of the windows on the street. He perhaps knew the majority of his potential assailants, but that knowledge assuaged his trepidation very little. Friendliness was no guarantee that they wouldn't sneak up on him with a balaclava and a knife and politely dispossess Derek of his luggage. Despite the outward peril, inserting himself into this home still felt as though he were putting his hand down a hole.

Derek closed the door behind him. Jackets on pegs halved the width of the corridor. A baseball cap hung from the cream bollard at the bottom of the staircase; a child's headband with glittery tentacles lay on the white carpet. The motif of this semi-detached house was light and fresh. An authentically homely place, and not grubby like you might expect. Balanced against Jimmy's flat, his sister's pad was about as ostentatious as the Playboy mansion.

To be mates with Heff. Aye, eh, ah'm kicked oot the hoose jist noo, like. Say no more, sport. Uncle Hugh'll take care of you. Pick a room. Go on in there; join the orgy. Derek would walk around wearing Miss October as a ski mask. June and July would make a dandy pair of gloves.

Ah, to see the world through the sheriff's Jap's eye.

The overtly polished beats of some new indie band bounced through the house from the direction of the living room, almost directly to his left. Derek couldn't hear any other voices or rumblings and so assumed, and hoped, that Tracy was alone. He wasn't in anything like the mood for the usual crust of fucked-up smackheids whom had a predilection for polluting her habitation and whose probable turnout restricted his visits to times such as these. Derek also wished for his little sister to be alive and coherent today.

It had been a while since Derek's last visit. The door to the living room was like ice cubes set in wood; it was ajar. He stood by the entrance. He let the suitcases rest on either side of him.

Some pirated Disney discs were spread out like lily pads in front of the television, which displayed not cartoons but a comedy film that couldn't be heard for the music, and which Derek knew was only just out in the cinema. A grand family picture above the mantelpiece presented three Wise kin to a room that was cosy and normal, bar its occupiers. His sister was home. She was not alone.

Several wan plates tilted up towards the intruder with gradual amazement. The candyfloss aroma of singed heroin laced the air. The junk was disseminated about the coffee table. The junkies encircled the room, welded into their chairs like soap. Derek watched as smiles undulated upon their faces as dislodged debris rising from the seabed. He sorta kina recognised all six of them, and they all knew of him.

Tracy Wise knew Derek best of all. She crawled up out of her seat and gave her big brother a big hug in front of her spasticated guests. The two skegged-out lads who'd book-ended her on the settee, and whom had been craftily gliding their mitts into ever more intimate corners of her person, were peeved. Tracy flopped over Derek and mumbled something about him being her favourite guy in the whole world. "Ah love ye, ah love ye." Her caramel hair went in his mouth. Derek was rigid to her cuddles, like paste on wallpaper, and endured her affections with actorly enthusiasm. He nodded and said his 'fit likes?' to the room as they muttered sincerely about hoo lang it's bin since we seen ye last, man. The gas fire was up full blast. Derek unzipped his coat to uncover a black triangle of T-shirt.

"Ye're a fuckin top guy, Dennis," croaked the boy with his back to the window. The lad wore a trilby and had one too many of his shirt buttons undone. Derek had seen the guy before, had seen him about town, with his hat. No idea what his name was, but Derek knew that the chap would be at least a good few years younger than himself. A beautiful girl of about fourteen sat, hazily, on the guy's lap. Derek wanted to slap the girl to the floor and punt that smug trilby-wearing shit through the window.

"Ah hivnae seen ye in ages," Tracy rasped; she clung to the collar of Derek's coat. Her brother suspected that she was entirely dependent on the strength of the stitching around his lapels to stop herself from sliding to the rug.

"Ma mate really fancies you," said a twenty-four-year-old mum of three, whom hadn't thought to take the joint from her lips before speaking. She sat off to Derek's right in a recliner, nearest to the fireplace. Her make-up sweat into face folds like a stack of bleeding pigs.

"Really?" Derek replied. "'At's great."

One of the molesters from the sofa was arguing with trilby kid. "His name's nae Dennis, man." He corrected his friend. "It's fuckin Derek. Sure it is?"

Derek looked at the youngster whom minutes earlier, and without substantial protest, had managed to slide a finger into the host's vagina. "Aye," said the proprietor's brother. "It's fuckin Derek."

The zoo quietened. The seated primates focused on the CD player, watching to see if the tunes would solidify into a matter that they could snatch.

"It's bin ages since ah seen ye last," Tracy said, whining into Derek's chest.

Right enough, if ye dinnae coont the twa times ah bumped intae ye 'is month a'ready. Derek noticed that neither his brother-in-law nor his niece were about.

"Faar's Donnie?" he asked, pushing his sister back so that he could see her face.

"Aiberdeen," Tracy replied; her mouth barely moved. "He's meetin some folk."

In the family portrait, the young girl was not despondent. Her father's locks were slicked back into a ponytail; his beard was trimmed. Her mother was in superior fettle to what she was outside of the frame. The little girl smiled as though she would not want to be taken away from them.

"An' Rachel?" Derek continued. The contempt ripped up his throat. The lighters and darkened foil in the middle of the room began to infuriate him, like vapour turning into bullets; the intensifying animosity resonated in his voice. The mammals didn't seem to detect this, or care if they had done. Derek wished that they did take umbrage. An excuse. A remark. Any comment from King Twat in the Hat and his ilk and Derek would fuckin demolish the lot of them.

Tracy responded, casually. "She's at school jist noo, Derek. Why? Is somethin wrang? Fit's happened?"

His sister felt like moist fruit in his clutches. Derek couldn't feel a beat in those bony shoulders, nor could he hear life in her creaky utterances. Tracy breathed her sentences out as chores, every word a needless pain. Derek stared through her; point a torch, you could see her organs. He wanted to spit in the face of this pitiful, withering clone, then throw her to the mercy of the apes.

"Fit's wrang?" Her eyes drifted like hollow weather. "Fit's happened?"

"Nithin," he replied. His grip tightened.

She whispered some agony. Derek wished to snap her into kindling. You got lost in Florida, he thought. But he was almost certain that they had found her again. They had, hadn't they?

"Why are ye here?" she moaned, softly. "Fit dee ye want?"

He saw the lounging dead, fading gloriously. His disdain was replaced, for a second at most, with an unbearable sadness. He could have choked.

"Nithin," Derek said. He let go of his sister. She stumbled back between the hungry youths.

Derek lifted his suitcases and turned. His leaving extracted no reaction. It had been a bad idea, and a vain one. He reached for the knob of the door that led to Sutherland Terrace. A knock emitted before him, as though the door had just suddenly sneezed at Derek. No sounds of distress or concern sparked up from the creatures in their pen.

Derek opened the door and nearly, very nearly, fainted.

Chapter 9

"Waaken up, ye dozy bastard."

"Come on, min; doon the wing."

"Cross it, ye dopey cunt."

"Waatch yer line, goalie."

"Shoot."

"Fuck sake, Fat Ass."

"Fuck you, ye wanker. Ah dinnae see you deein onythin."

"Fa's markin 'im?"

"Derek, finger oot."

"Hopeless cunt."

"Get tae fuck, lanky twat."

"Up the wing."

"Fit wis 'at supposed tae be, like?"

"Useless."

"Ye aimin fir the corner flag, ye ugly bastard?"

"Suck ma baas."

"Shoot."

"Beauty."

"Fuckin beezer o goal, Derek."

"Nae buther."

"Somebidy mark 'im."

"On yer own; 'at's the stuff."

"Shoot."

"'At's mair like it, boys."

"Piece o piss."

The gang sat on the pitch, lapping up the early evening sun in their mishmash of football kits, and toasted their victory. From their loose circle, they jeered their departing victims. Bottles crammed with the requisite H2O were passed around the strewn six. Derek poured the cool liquid over his head. A fine reward for a crucial brace. Phil, big Phil with the big ass, gargled and spat on the grass by Freddy's boots. "Aye, waatch it, fatty." Frederick Paul Taylor never required much provocation for a greet and a girn; his capacity to bleat was surpassed only by his willingness to insult whomsoever he should regard to be his pals. "Fat plonker."

Jimmy, bolstered by what he himself would describe as a devastating performance at the heart of the midfield, got up and strolled around the group with a playful menace. He crept up behind Mo and flicked the boy's arm out from under him. Mo reeled onto his back. "Fuck off, ye skinny bastard." Mark O'Connor took a swipe at Jimmy's exposed calf. James of the clan Stevenson bounded away from the slap and, as a result, danced upon Pagan's resting hand.

The blistering gold of the falling star revealed Pagan's horror. A grunt squeezed out of him as though a juicer had been twisted behind his eyes. Jimmy apologised through laughter and pranced away to the other end of the group. Pagan rolled forward on his rump, shaking his paw like a tambourine that's cymbals had been replaced with reddish budgies. "Aah, ye baass taarrd." He held the hand carefully in event that it should fall off, and glowered at his mirth-ridden mates. The glower melted into a pained smile when the agony of his enflamed claw dampened. It burned like an icy shower, then throbbed as if kissed perpetually by volcanoes. Miraculously, none of Jimmy's studs had broken the skin; Pagan did not think that any bones had been fractured, although they might have been.

"Ye a'right 'ere, Peggy?" Mo inquired, sincere despite his merriment.

"Aye." Pagan revolved his bad hand and upraised the longest of its digits at Jimmy. "Moron."

"Fit?" Jimmy objected, laughing and remonstrating in equal measure. "It wis an accident. If ye're gaan tae blame ony cunt, ye shid blame 'at cunt 'ere." James singled out Mark.

The blithe youth responded in kind. "Me? You kin rin tae fuck. Hoo wis 'at ma fault? 'At wis aa you, ye dick-splash." Mo was the smallest of the bunch; with his neatly kept black hair, some had often mistaken Mark for being the more unhesitatingly likeable younger brother that Pagan did not have. The two were not related, however; they, like the rest of the gang, were the same age.

Pagan dropped his paw as if to test the Earth's gravitational pull. The handsome boy smiled his forgiveness, as though a joke about his mother had landed *just* this side of acceptable.

Derek inspected a graze that he'd acquired during the match; his skin wept claret just above his shin guard. One of the opposing players – some lad who'd had an ear savaged by a dog when he was an infant – had caught Derek with a crunching tackle that had confiscated from him his ability to breathe for a few seconds.

"Ye shid jist be glaid," Freddy remarked, "that it wisnae Fat Ass that stood on yer han', itherwise the fucker'd be squaashed flat like a fuckin pancake."

Phil led the choir of appreciation for the quip, then chucked a daisy that clipped Freddy on the tip of his beak and sailed on towards Mo, striking him on the neck and falling down under his Man U top. "Fuck sake." Mo shook his collar so that the flower dribbled down his spine and back onto the grass.

"Ah tell ye, though; we need a new goalie." Jimmy changed the conversation as though switching between climates. "Nae affence, like, Fat Ass, bit ye're fuckin useless."

"Oh, neen taaken. Ye prick."

"Nah, he's right enough, Phil," Freddy concurred. "Ye are too fat, like. Yer airse wobbles an' slows ye doon. Ye think ye'd be perfect for it an' aa, wi yer bulk an' 'at fuckin blockin oot the net. Bit no; ye're jist shite, like. Sometimes ye luk like ye're rinnin wi bags o cement aroon yer legs. It's like waatchin a hippo tryin tae tie its shoelaces."

The boys erupted once more. Fat Ass, through much practice and experience, had learned, for the most part, to take their insults with good grace, and laughed along with veiled chagrin. Phil muttered obscenities, and whipped more daisies at the bobbing and weaving Freddy.

When the mirth dulled like passing traffic, Derek said, "We won, though, eh? 6-3, wis it?"

"Aye," Jimmy replied. "We humped those orra bastards."

Those orra bastards were a makeshift team from another of the town's primary schools. Freddy was first cousins with a member of the opposition; together, they had organised regular and, usually, fairly evenly matched games. The boys of the divergent schools got on well enough together. Derek's gang and their sporting rivals would meet up again soon at summer's end, when they'd all commence their academy days.

They'd become friends, fall out, fistfight, renew friendships, then part forever in the course of the next few years.

The last of the vanquished team disappeared from sight, through the woods at the top of the park. The roving greenery bustled near its zenith; the swings and the other assorted fun-apparatus were busy with parents and sprogs. Younger kids than Derek and his mob climbed on trees as though crabs on lurching kelp. A row of opulent domiciles stretched like a string of buoys, upstream of the infested trees and the cavorting families, and leered snobbishly down the hill. It was one of these mansions that Jimmy referred to as home. The pitch was like the settled pool at the foot of a waterfall. The six boys basked in the grandeur.

Jimmy blasted the ball, rattling the high chain-link fence that divided the grass and the tarmac and kept stray shots from popping under car tyres.

"It's jist twa wiks afore we start the academy, eh?" Freddy affirmed, brushing a daisy out of his blond hair.

"Twa an' a half," Phil corrected his chum.

Mo assented. "Aye, twa an' a half. Fuckin hell, eh?"

Pagan broke from his taciturn way: a manner that gave him an intelligent, respectable quality, which none of his pals would admit to for fear of it sounding too much like a compliment. He asked, "Hoo you boys feelin aboot 'at?"

Pagan's questions sometimes gave the impression that he was documenting his friends, rather than being one of them. Although they all liked having him around, they occasionally got the uncomfortable feeling of being examined. That they were in the company of a spy of some sort. A researcher even, from a separate species altogether.

Pagan was not nearly as lax of tongue as the others were. When Pagan did speak, it was often to spike meandering frivolity with a query that would then force their chat into more serious, and undesired, territory. It was also patent to them all that most folk's parents didn't warm to Peggy, though it was arduous for them to adequately explain why this was.

Pagan was never a body to instigate or apply pressure to peers, and, nine from ten, he kept out of, and away from, trouble. Mummies had no cause for gripe in that respect. He was never cheeky, nor did he ever misplace a please or a thank you, and he could always be relied upon to manufacture a smile for the sake of politeness. The list of Pagan's pro points was, indeed, rather extensive, like the packaging blurb for a calculator. And maybe that was part of the reason for the grown ups' subliminal disapproval of him.

There was just that something about Pagan. Something that niggled away at adults. Something maddening. The teenager annoyed his elders, and he sensed this in the disparate usages of language and timbre when the adults would talk to him and then to another of their children's acquaintances, as though moving from a work friend to a real world friend. He, too, was nonetheless baffled as to why this might be the case.

Later in life, in hindsight, the truth would emerge to him as crystal. A matured Pagan would articulate how it was that his younger self, subconsciously or otherwise, did condescend to and patronise not only his pals, but their mammies and daddies also. The elders, whom were somewhat overfamiliar with the tone explicit in their being humoured, could scent this condescension where their junior selves could not. He was not just a co-worker; he was after their jobs.

Jimmy gathered the ball and guided it back to his mates. He stood like a spare goal post while the others loitered like kicked-over buckets. All of them were still yet runtish in appearance, with the one obvious exception.

"Hoo dee ye's think it's gaan tae be?" Pagan asked of the group.

"It's supposed to be a'right," Phil said. "Ma neighbour says it's great, like. Much better than bein at primary."

"He's probably jist taakin the piss, Fat Ass." Jimmy flipped the ball up and gave it a thunderous volley against the fence.

"Nah," Derek said, picking at the dried blood from around his forming scab. "Ah'd say it's gaan tae be good, like. Jist think o aa that quines. Big tits an' hairy muffs."

"Aye." Jimmy pushed Derek over with his canoe-like boot. "Ye're some boy."

"They winnae want onythin tae dee wi you onywye, Derek, ye ugly toss-pot."

"Fuckin right they will," Derek replied, pitching himself up from the straggly mess of poles that Jimmy had reduced him to with a shove. "Bit ah cannae see them bein interested in a hackit-faced mongo like you, Freddy."

Insults were exchanged amongst the coterie with the best of intentions, like crackers being pulled across the dinner table. It was a fine night. The heat was concealed by a lid of clouds that resembled over-lapping crisps on a dish. The boys joked and swore in the park as the sun slid down the sky like a raindrop on a church window. It treacled and crept and was gone. For Derek and his mates, and owing to the age that they were, time had become an irrelevancy, almost. Their strict conversational diet of utter nonsense, computer games and quines they'd love tae ride had engrossed them to the point that they hadn't really heeded the supplantation of the sun with the moon until Mo opined that it wis gettin dark, like. The ignition of the streetlights had occurred like the invasion of germs.

The six youths mumbled their agreement that it was home time; grudgingly, the youngsters pushed themselves up off the ground. There didn't seem to be much left for them to talk about anyway. They'd exhausted the wheely bin of nascent teenage wisdom, and extolled the virtues of shagging one's pal's materfamilias till it all, nearly, seemed a bit chronic and jaded. The band splintered off into sub factions. Mo and Freddy said their 'see ye the morns' and headed towards the changing rooms and the general direction of the town centre. Jimmy collected his ball, waved to the remaining trio, then strode off alone up the middle of the park. The gangly boy vanished into the woods, apparently having been devoured by shadows. Derek, Fat Ass and Pagan lived in fair proximity of one another and wandered off south together.

It had been an enjoyable evening. Spirits were raised. Even the dark took on more of a benign appeal tonight, like an inmate moping behind prison bars. The world was a sweet and simple place this night and no sinister connotations could be derived from the black shawl that hid it now. It had been a day that they could feel merging with the scratchproof alloy of nostalgia even as they had lived it. Often times, in colder years to come, their minds would slither back to this evening with oppressive affection. Although nothing spectacular, or even particularly interesting, had happened on this day, the boys would long for it always.

The six of them had sat on that pitch and discussed neither their ambitions nor dreams but just stuff, with the inexorable optimism of young boys who knew that life was easy and things were fair and home was an actual thing.

Derek, Fat Ass and Pagan walked on, chatting and chuckling; it was the music that had played since the completion of their game, though performed acoustically and with fewer instruments. They left the park behind and entered the suburbs. Their neighbourhood was under investigation by short-sighted lampposts.

"Fit time is it?" Derek asked.

"The back o ten," Phil answered.

There was no alarm at the lateness of their venture home. Derek's dad had his crewmen round and would be drunk enough not to care that his boy had ambled in post-curfew. Both Pagan and Fat Ass wore their collars far looser than Derek did. Returning to their households in the low AMs was unacceptable; their reappearance at some time between ten and eleven, though, would not be met with major antipathy. Derek envied the slackness of their respective ruling regimes; he promised himself that, were he ever to become a dad, his kids would be liberated like scurries.

Phil bumbled along, whistling through the streets. Pagan strolled behind and contemplated. Derek noted how it was that that boy always seemed to be scrutinising something deeply.

Derek decided to speak. "Fin ah wis oot in the yaal the day, ma grandad started spickin aboot the waar."

"Oh, did he?" Phil replied, as if he were, without regret, forgoing an offer.

Pagan quickened his pace to match that of his friends. "Fit did he say?"

"He tellt me fit he did durin the waar, like." Derek stopped. His two companions followed suit. "Sit here. Ah'll tell ye's. It's pretty cool, like."

The boys sat on a harled dike in front of a napping bungalow. Derek decided that he and his story would enjoin more authority if, instead of sitting between the pair, he stood before them as their teacher. Phil gawked at him with a hint of impatience, as though he were hoping to carry through his toiletry duties before the adverts were done. To the fat lad's right, Pagan watched Derek with those studious peepers, bracing himself for an influx of new information to be digested.

Content with each person's positioning, Derek began. He told Fat Ass and Pagan what his grandfather had said out on The Searcher. Derek had the gist of the story; although, the more complicated, technical details veered towards the fuzzier side of things. Derek started, as his grandad had done, in Iceland in 1942. Waiting in sheds with Americans and Brits, for a call. The men drank and fought and were given short shrift by the hostile locals. The call came. Stanley, his ship and the various others whom were assembled as crew took off soon after with the food, oil and ammunition desperately needed by the Russians to stave off Hitler and his cronies.

"Eh?" Phil interrupted. "Ah thought the Russians were supposed tae be the baddies as weel. Why wis we helpin 'em cunts?"

"I dinnae ken," Derek replied, illustrating his ignorance by showing his palms. "They must nae've bin at the time. Okay?"

Fat Ass motioned as though the emperor telling the actors that they may proceed.

It was left for Pagan to heal the injury of his friends' unenlightenment. "Russia wis a communist state. Hitler wis against communism fir some reason. He invaded 'em. Fuck knows. 'At's aa ah ken."

Phil lifted his coils and swung them towards Pagan. "Hoo dee ye ken sae much aboot iverthin? Peggy, ye're a fuckin freak."

The boy laughed, though it was a proclamation of mirth as reticent as the street. "Ah dinnae ken iverythin. It's jist fae buks an' listenin tae ma dad an' ma brither. It's nae a bad thing, ye ken? It helps tae ken stuff."

"Onywye," Derek said, feigning irritation. "As ah wis sayin, ma grandad went o'er 'ere in his boat wi the supplies."

Stanley's boat had been one of many merchant navy ships employed for the convoy, which consisted of over thirty vessels, including trawlers and destroyers. Derek couldn't remember the name of his grandad's boat or the name of the convoy. Sixteen or seventeen, wasn't it? Anyhow, the ships and the supplies got about halfway to their docking bay at Archangel when another call came in. The convoy was ordered to scatter.

"Fit dee ye mean 'scatter'?"

"Fat Ass, wid ye shut the fuck up?"

Reports had leaked in at HQ that there were German warships on the move. The head honchos were worried that the Germans had planned to intercept this convoy and engage in an open sea battle. Not wanting to lose one of their destroyers at this pivotal stage of the war, HQ ordered the scatter, bringing their huge battle ships out of potential danger and leaving the wee supply boats to fend for themselves. The grand assault from the German ships did not materialise at that time. The Luftwaffe, however, did feel compelled to breeze in for a visit. They picked at the small, relatively defenceless ships like angry ravens. The bastards swooped by and sank Stanley's boat. People died. Much to Derek's surprise, his grandad couldn't swim. Stanley Gibson flailed and flapped in the freezing sea, and was near blinded by the glare from the sun's impact on the glaciers. The other boats had disbanded long ago, and Derek's grandad was alone. Then seconds, minutes or days later, Big Stanley was carved out of the water and hauled aboard a raft by his surviving crewmen. They sailed for an epoch in the interminable light. A U-boat appeared beside them. Its commander spoke perfect English and was, apparently, very civil and affable. He asked for their captain. He'd drowned, they replied. The German gave the survivors rum, cheese, loaf and directions to shore. The submarine sank and left them behind. With tremendous fortune, the raft sailed onto Russian shores. The men had another struggle in getting to Archangel, but they did, finally, manage to get there, and were later taken back home in an ensuing convoy.

Bits and pieces of Derek's tale must not have made much sense, for Fat Ass looked perplexed.

Derek sighed. "Fit's wrang, Phil?"

"Ah'm nae complainin or 'at, like, bit it disnae maak ony sinse. Ah mean, why wid the German boy nae jist shoot yer granda an' aa the rest o 'at folk?"

"Dee ah luk like a German submarine captain tae you, like? Hoo the fuck am ah supposed tae ken?" Derek bestowed Fat Ass with a frolicsome slap on the chops. "'At's jist hoo waar is. In't it? Ye dunger."

Phil lunged at Derek; the pair wrestled on the road. The husky lad, who possessed what his friends had termed 'fat power', hoisted his competitor, chest to chest, and crushed him midair. Derek spluttered as the bear hug crippled his ability to digest oxygen and discharge carbon dioxide. With his arms locked by his sides beneath Phil's mass, Derek could only wriggle in the state of a hooked annelid. He could always break his friend's hold by either kneeing him in the testicles or by aiming a well-placed headbutt to the face. But that wasn't par for the course. Derek endured the torture with choking glee, until, boomph, Phil let him go and he crashed onto the ground. Derek sprawled on the grit and sang out a low groan. He sat up. The grinning behemoth towered above him like a termite mound; he gave Derek a clout across the crown that was probably harder than Phil had intended.

Pagan leaned back, lost in the romance of the story recently told. Of the time, of the place, of the war itself.

"So, Pagan; fit are ye thinkin aboot noo?" Derek was bent over and picking the stones out of his kneecaps. The duo had finished with their tussle and were both puffing like fretting simians.

Pagan responded with a look of such intensity that it startled Derek, as when dogs spot each other. "Dee ye think we'll iver ging tae waar?"

"Ah dinnae ken," Derek said, gurning as though a child presented with a pictureless tome. "Ah doot it. Why? Dee you think we will?"

Pagan's retort did astonish his peers. "Ah hope so."

The three boys walked onwards a little further. The scuffling of their trainers up the pavements reminded Derek of a dentist's suction tool. Then, as they each lived on diverse streets, they split up. They scraped out one last insult and said goodbye.

Derek could hear the blare of the karaoke machine from the end of his driveway.

Chapter 10

Sutherland Terrace glowed piteously, like the cuddly tart who'd got herself pregnant – again. The car equivalent of a Romeo chav did crunch and grind and ping down the street, hardly braking to take the corner at the end. Some doof-deesh-doof type sounds punched through its shaded windows and competed with the rusty growl of the engine to torment the neighbourhood. This noisy bug could still be heard for a few seconds after the bazooka-sized exhaust had flashed from sight. A thin woman with brittle hair and tight clothing smoked a fag and pushed a pram. She was escorted by her posse of scowly Eastern European minders. An iffy bloke, whose hunched strut gave him the appearance of being much shorter and wider than he actually was, and who was definitely an original Brocher, jittered along the pavement: head down, hood up, hands in pockets, elbows out like a coat hanger. He glanced at Derek, then nodded. Without much thought, Derek replied in kind. A white terrier barked at nothing and squatted in the jungle of an adjacent garden. The high grass engulfed the dog like a Venus flytrap. Somebody wouldn't detect that mess until it was far, far too late.

And in front of this scene. A metre in front of Derek. Standing on the craggy path that led to Derek's sister's door. A person Derek hadn't seen in over ten years. A person who looked the same but different. No drastic changes in the decade that had elapsed. Hair perhaps darker. Hair just as impeccable, though; still combed to the one side. Face sharp and bright; blue where he was now required to shave. Taller than before. Just taller than Derek. Stockier than Derek remembered him being. Used to be quite slight. Now built to suggest that he could possibly argue with more than just the use of his dictionary. Dressed well. Derek couldn't recall having seen him in a shirt and tie before. No, he could do. At a funeral. Black shoes, grey trousers and a brown jacket, which all blended together like landscape. Dressed smartly, but not to flaunt; nor for a funeral. Professional. Business-like. Derek's old best friend was at work. His old best friend was smiling.

"Well, well, Derek; what are the odds?"

"Fuck knows, Pagan. Fuck knows. Astronomical."

Galaxies fell away and were reborn in the aeons it took for the swooshing daze to subside. Derek's brain warped like a room that's furniture kept on morphing into other things. Pagan seemed better equipped for this encounter. His handsome face was smudged with marvel. But he was not struck with the dumbness as was Derek.

The two men reacted to one another as castaways whom realised that, bless the heavens, they spoke of the same tongue.

"Fa is it?" It was Tracy. She was calling from the belly of the house.

Derek ignored his sister. Pagan peered over his shoulder. Derek answered his friend's silent query with a dour look.

Pagan began, "Is this your - "

"No." Derek hauled up the zip of his thick, navy coat. "Things are jist a bit fucked up at hame jist noo, like. 'Is is Tracy's hoose. Ye mine ma wee sister, eh?"

"Oh, yes. Tracy." Pagan glanced about him. "She lives here?"

"Aye. Bit o a shite-hole, richt enough."

Pagan laughed. A laugh that was ten years older than the one that Derek had heard last. The two old friends stood there. Ten years. Waves of memories hurtled between them, like tower blocks folding into each other. For Pagan, this chance reunion had come as a significant, though not wholly unanticipated, jolt. Derek, on the other hand, was trapped in a bubble of shock. As far as Derek was concerned, it was like bedding down in the Broch and waking up in the Bahamas. Absolutely and completely unprepared for. But nice all the same.

"Jay Soose Chreest," Derek muttered. "Ah cannae fuckin believe 'is."

"I know, Derek. It's been some time."

"Some time? Ten fuckin years, min. Then ye show up on ma sister's doorstep. In a suit an' tie, nae fuckin less. Ye're dressed like fuckin Wall Street or somethin." Paranoia crept into Derek's voice and wrinkled on his face like a gust through a wheat field. Derek briefly acquired that apex of eccentric thoughts that all people obtain at least once in their lives: that fleeting certainty that they are the only true thing in the universe and all else is fantasy, conjured by your inestimably huge mind. The thought retreated for now. "Nae affence, like, bit fit the fuck are ye deein here? Faar the fuck hiv ye bin? Ah mean, fit the fuck? Eh?"

Pagan tucked his hands into his trouser pockets, and replied, "I'm actually here chasing up a story. I'm a journalist. I started working for the Peterhead branch of the Northern Echo last Monday. I've been down South most of the time. Spent a few years in London: reporting, freelance work – whatever paid the bills. I moved back about a fortnight ago. Thought I'd maybe bump into you sooner or later. I'm staying at my grandma's house, while she's in hospital. You remember my granny, don't you?"

Derek surely did. She bore to Derek a keen resemblance to Roger Waters. He recalled how she would dispense her home-made toffee apples to their mob, with the stipulation that they firstly had to memorise and recite large chunks of the Bible back to her. When he was eleven years old, Phil could preach Leviticus verbatim. Derek did recollect his favoured biblical quote, procured from those far-flung days: 'I am the Lord thy God, which brought thee out of the land of Egypt: open thy mouth wide, and I will fill it.' Psalm 81: 10, King James edition.

Pagan took a hand from a pocket to run through his hair. "And that's about it. What about you, then? What's Derek Gibson been doing with himself these last few years?"

Derek laughed as he might do before surgery. "Eh, nithin much, like." He felt a murmur of shame at this admission, which was uncommon for Derek. "Weel, ah'll be fuckered. Pagan, eh? Dee folk still caa ye 'at?"

"No. Not at all, never. I haven't been called that since I left the Broch. Actually sort of missed the name. Always thought it sounded pretty cool. So you can call me Pagan if you want."

"It wisnae supposed tae soon cool." Derek resisted a yearning to prod the other man; to clarify that he was no hologram. He finished shaking his old pal's hand before realising that they were gripped. "A'right. Pagan it is, 'en. Fuckin jizz-cakes. The boys are nae gaan tae fuckin believe 'is, like."

"Oh, and how are the boys these days? How's Philip?"

"Well," said Derek, "he's still nae stranger tae a mince pie, if 'at's fit ye mean. We could ging an' see 'im jist noo; if ye like? He's workin at The Tart. The pub."

Evidently, the idea turned Pagan's mind into a grappling mat.

"Fit's 'is story ye're chasin up onywye, like? It's nae onythin tae dee wi 'at fuckin actor, is it? The cunt fa killt 'imsel. Opinions fae the gutter an' aa 'at kina pish?"

Pagan jousted with inimical thoughts. He responded to this latest query, "No, no. It's about the old man that was murdered last night. A one Raymond John McLeish."

Derek became a scrubbed slate. "Eh? Fit happened?"

"You haven't heard? Can't be too surprised, though. I suppose that movie-star story will be hogging the headlines today. But yes, an old man was found with his head staved in late on Wednesday night. Right in the middle of the street."

"'Is street?"

"No. Another street. This is where he lived. Just next door. I'm here to build up a profile of the man. Apparently, he's got no close relatives or acquaintances, so I'm just going to have to quiz some of his neighbours. Find out what kind of a man he was, and how people feel about his death. That sort of pish.'"

"Well, if ah wis you, ah widnae get ma opinions fae in 'ere." Derek joked, though the facetiousness was deficient in his eyes. "Ye'd get mair sinse oot o a packet o peanuts."

"What about your sister?"

"Junkie."

"Really? Wee Trace?"

"Yip."

"I'm sorry."

"Why? 'At's 'er fuckin problem." And things were not said that didn't have to be. "So, ye want tae ging an' see Fat Ass, 'en? Cannae say that ah ken 'is Raymond guy masel, like, bit ah'm sure 'ere'll be plinty o aal codgers in the pub fa might. Ah widnae mind gettin a baggy o chips on the wye doon eether, like. Fuckin starved, ken?"

Pagan's dilemma was over. "Yes, I haven't had my lunch yet either. Fine. Let's go."

Pagan turned down the path. He produced keys from his pocket. One click and a silver car lit up. In comparison to the other vehicles on the street, this motor was like a piece of cutlery in the toy drawer. Derek advanced towards the car with his suitcases. He left the door to his sister's house agape, like a frog waiting for flies. Let whatever scallywags and scoundrels enter as they please.

Pagan's machine shined as a ten pence coin in amongst a tray of ones and twos, yet there was nothing lingering or boastful about the reporter's manner around his car. He didn't pat the bonnet and look for praise, though he'd probably have got away with it. Derek didn't really know his cars. He complimented the vehicle anyway. Pagan replied with a bashful shrug.

Pagan opened the boot for Derek. "Going on holiday?" Pagan said, as Derek hurled in the bags. Someone previously had made jest to similar effect. Derek was gladdened by Pagan's jibe, however; as though it were confirmation that his pal's cleverness hadn't by now extinguished his inclination to crack wise.

"Nah, nah," Derek said. He closed the lid atop the suitcases. "Ah'm movin in wi yer mam. Did Bev nae tell ye?"

Pagan took the driver's door handle. He smirked at his own nebulous reflection in the window. "You're too ugly for my mum. I thought she'd told you that."

"Is 'at fit she said? Couldnae tell. 'Er moo wis full at the time, ken?" Derek rounded the car and slipped into the leather passenger seat.

Pagan laughed, and joined him inside.

*

The silver car slooshed through Fraserburgh like rainwater along drain pipes. Homes were increasingly up-market the further they travelled from Sutherland Terrace, and the more at ease you would feel about carrying your wallet in your back pocket. The car let out nary a phlegmy bark as it hissed by, only a fraction above the limit. The elderly, the middle and the truants sauntered about the Broadgate. Solar-powered pedestrians halted and speculated to one another whenever a cloud mugged the sun of its rays. They ranted, and stood back. The movie star. Dear God. Fit a waste. Sae muckle tae live for. The old man. Richard, wis it? Aye. Ah didnae ken 'im, like. Bit, oh, fit a shame. Fit a coorse thing tae happen tae a man. An aal manny an' aa. Fit's the world comin tae? Ah hope they string up faiver did it. They should bring back hangin fir stuff like 'is. Disgraceful. 'Ere's jist nae respect onymair.

By the time that they'd reached the chip shop, Derek had explained the events of the last few days to Pagan. His friend had essayed to keep a straight face throughout.

"It's nae funny, ye cunt. 'Is is ma life under review here, ye fucker."

They took their food parcels down to the beach esplanade. They parked a few empty spaces away from a white van containing a gaggle of paint-splattered men. They all waved. Derek nodded. He'd spent a few months, here and there, with the boat painters. Fine outdoorsy work, but the hours were too erratic, and it was, after all, only a seasonal vocation. Once the dark nights swept in, and those rascally air currents inseminated the sky, the brushes would be left in the sheds to harden into sundry-stranded knives. The van reversed, renouncing a pile of cola cans and chip papers: the outline of a terminally wounded elephant. It honked twice on its way. Derek launched into his dinner, scoffing his portion with his fingers.

They were parked before the railings, between fishyards and the café. A tuft of greenery hung over the water, next to the nearest yard. Caravans were situated upon it. Derek considered how the outlook from those portable dens would've been nice; the smell, less so.

Pagan gazed through the windshield. He took in a sight that he'd had to make do without for a canvass of time so great that it was difficult for him to hold up and study. His history was a map that he couldn't properly read, for his nose was still pressed against the paper. The view held him to his seat as though a pane of glass were tipped back against him.

The electric wool of the waves nagged at the curve of orange that slung three miles south to the tiny village of Cairnbulg. The sea had the complexion of a city as viewed from a plane. He had swum down there throughout his youth. He had picnicked on that fabulous beach with his mum and his dad and David, and would never do so again.

Pagan remembered Cairnbulg. That village had seemed so droll and exciting when he and Derek and the others were young. The bicycle expeditions of extinct summers had felt like journeys to a place of wizards and dragons and adventure. It was okay to be obtuse then, and have an imagination. Those were the days; that was the time. A time when life, frankly, had been less of a burden.

It's worth the hassle, though. It *is* worth the hassle. No. *No*, it's not. It has already been decided upon. Get the lighter and the petrol. Tonight. Tonight. No more hassle. No more delays.

"Ye gaan tae ait yer grub the day or fit?" Derek's question tugged his friend back from a daydream, pleasant and deranged. Terns spiked palings as tower guards. A yellow-eyed gull stood outside the car, like a diminutive border patrolman waiting to see some identification. A larger scurry relieved it of its post. Derek said to his pal, "Ait yer mait, ye peely-wally cretter 'at ye are."

Pagan regarded the package on his lap with distaste. His stomach must've stapled itself shut for he was no longer hungry. He watched Derek toss his container out of the window. The gull fled from the bomb's descent, then returned to drag the rubbish away with its beak, like a strong man meeting some orthodontic challenge. There were bins along the railings. "I'll save mine for later." Pagan placed his lunch on the back seat.

Derek wiped his digits on his jeans. "Quite a view; isn't it, Peggy, dear boy?" The remark lacked the standard sarcasm that was expected of any positive comment referring to the Broch. "Bonny beach, eh?"

"Sure is."

"Good tae be back?" The sarcasm had returned.

"It is," Pagan replied, honestly. "I haven't been home in too long. It's kind of crazy. Like, it feels like I'm really moving backwards. And rotating, like one of those tumbler attractions you sometimes get at fairgrounds."

"Ye haein flashbacks? Is it jist like Rocky IV, aifter Apollo Creed's bin killt an' Stallone starts drivin aboot wi 'at daft fuckin sang playin? An' he hid 'at fuckin robot as weel, mine?"

"Exactly." Pagan put his hands around the steering wheel, as though it were the face of some wilting belle. "You're not even sure if you're going to recognise anyone anymore, or if anyone's going to recognise you, or even want to recognise you."

"Fit? Ah could tell it wis you straight awaa, min. Ye're a bit uglier than ah remember ye bein, right enough, like. Apart fae 'at, though, ye're jist Peggy."

Pagan's pupils pursued the line of the promenade to his right, as freewheeling hubcaps after a crash. The café and shelters gave way to dunes that formed a high ridge the length of the beach, like an enormous green eyebrow over an equally immense sandy eyelid. The turf hitched up over Tiger Hill as though to express the land's suspicion of the gnawing tide.

"So it goes, Derek."

"Aye." Derek burped into his fist, then blew into Pagan's ear.

Pagan looked at his jaunty friend, the drunkard, with a sadness that proved for him to be tricky to bury. Derek evaded any possible out-pourings, a la Jimbo, by gently facing away from Pagan and his burgeoning sorrows. The reunited buddies watched the scene in silence. Business on the beach was slow. A half dozen dog-walkers traipsed around the curve. A couple of guys dozed upon their surfboards.

Derek thought about the golf course that sprawled behind Tiger Hill. Many of his muckers from the whiles gone by put forth the suggestion to Derek that he should take up the game. He didn't see much of those guys anymore. There were the incidental meetings, as brief as they were awkward. Hoo's the bairns, 'en, such-an'-such? *Nae bad. Fit you deein wi yersel the noo, like, Derek?* Nae much. Fuck aal, basically. *Oh, ye shid start playin golf,*

Derek. We'll get aa the boys taegither some time an' hae a gamey, eh? Aye. Right-o. 'At wid be a richt fuckin laugh. Cannae wait. To be fair, though, he reckoned that their invites would be genuine enough; but he could always sense that relief when, without fail, Derek would decline with a, well, it's nae really ma thing, ken? With a bit of luck, then, they'd manage to dodge each other for a few more months and spare themselves another one of these encounters. Old friends, he'd learned, could be like total strangers; ones whom just happened to have read your biography. Trying to reforge bonds with some people was as worthwhile an exercise as washing yourself with excrement; some other past acquaintances, meanwhile, submerged themselves back into the latter pages of your memoirs as effortlessly as a sharpened pencil into Playdo.

"So, you never got married, Derek?"

"Me? Ye fuckin jokin? No, no. Funnily enough, ah niver got lassoed, like. Ah mean, if ma dong's requestin fir a gusset tae plunge, 'ere's ai' doors ah kin knock on. Bit nithin too serious. Ye ken fit like. 'Ere's jist too mony quines. Mairrage is like pickin a finger an' cuttin the rest o the bastards aff."

Pagan laughed, eventually. "Quines. I haven't heard that one in some time. Sort of forgot how hard to follow the Doric was."

"Aye, fuck, sorry; hoo ye gettin on 'ere, like? Bit o a fucked-up language, in't it?"

"It's just a bit fast," Pagan replied. "It'll take some getting used to."

Derek grimaced. "Aye, ye're in the provinces noo, ma laddie. Better mine tae leave the Gs aff the end o yer words. They'll fry ye fir less than 'at."

"Probably. This is Wicker Man territory. It wouldn't surprise me in the least."

"Nah, that's the West Coast. Here, we dinnae need the appeasin o gods tae justify settin fire tae ye. We'll dee it 'cos we're cunters."

A Labrador dragged a studenty girl across the panorama. Derek assessed the lady's buttocks, quietly and to himself.

"An' you, Pagan: did you iver meet Mrs Right? Or is it Mr Right? Ah wis niver too sure aboot you, like. Thought ye might be a bit too wordy nae tae be a bum-inspector."

The passing girl slipped from Pagan's cogitations. "Yes. I met her."

"Ye're fuckin mairriet?"

"No. Came close, though."

"So, fit happened?"

"She was raped," Pagan said, "and thrown under a train. As is the way." He turned on the engine. "We going to see Fat Ass, then?"

*

The journey from the esplanade to The Tart was a short one. Pagan stopped the car just along from the smokers at the pub entrance, which was like the gap at the centre of a coiled armadillo. The pair got out and stretched upon the pavement. Then shivered. A cold snap barged off the North Sea and dug its knuckles into their sides. A red van beeped as it passed. Derek gave a compulsory wave, though he wasn't certain as to whom he had just saluted. The scurries, in their white coats with the grey arms, congregated in their ranks upon the roofs of the flats on this side of the road and upon the yards opposite them like a guard of honour. A man on a parked ship called for a younger lad on the pier tae get a move on. Derek led the pair inside, funning with the bedraggled smokers as he so did.

Derek thought The Tart unusually busy. The chill had pushed the people indoors, like a pizza slice stuffed into a tot's mouth. Giros were liquefied. A man and a woman argued by the fag machine, in a foreign dialect. An elderly gent sat alone at the end of the bar. A mullet and a skinhead hogged the pool table. An extended family, including two children, crowded around the booth nearest to the toilets. Their trainers fringed a sleeping dog like tattered petals. Three teenage guys stood by the fruit machine; one fed it coin after coin, whilst his mates observed this interaction as though their mothers were introducing them to a wall of shoes, all to be trialled. The gambler was the shortest of the trio, and had bleached hair. One of the pals had the pitted surface texture of an asteroid. Derek and Pagan sidled up to the bar.

Pagan viewed the room with ostensible discomfort. The place was too dim for the time that it was, he thought. The windows were stained with the trenches of blinds, which seemed to him as though a farmer had ploughed the day, enabling the crows to make off with its gleam. This left the task of brightening the room down to a few tiring bulbs. Those lights were too puny to support a world so heavy.

The twosome sat on wooden stools. Pagan tussled to unshackle his ocular orbs from this tank's inhabitants. Were these nocturnal creatures? Would the full blaze of the sun reduce these people to cinders? Pagan tried to look without staring, but a pointed glare from the man by the cigarette dispenser indicated that he wasn't succeeding. Pagan faced front, stung as though his dancing partner had flicked his erection and now gyrated just that smidgen further away from him.

Derek leaned over the bar, in search of staff. "Faar the fuck is Phil?" he asked. Pagan gesticulated as he would to an innocuous comment at the VD clinic. Derek noted how the establishment disagreed with his friend, like golden fields to a hay fever sufferer. "Oi, Pagan: 'is is The Tart. The best pub in the Broch. Sure it is?" Derek addressed the pensioner, whom raised a quivering glass in acquiescence. The loner sank his drink and pivoted his attention upwards, to the ample TV screen and the gorgeous, dead thesp whom adorned it. The jukebox, though, hijacked the airwaves. "See, Pagan? Best pub gaan aboot. Jist relax."

"This place is your local?" Pagan intoned, as if his order had been messed up for the umpteenth time but he still didn't wish to lodge a complaint. "A bit vintage. Isn't it?"

"Ah'm an old school kina chap; fit kin ah say? Once ye get past aa the stabbins an' the smell o pish an' bleid, it's nae too bad." Derek evaluated how steadily Pagan whitened, like he were the beneficiary in a toothpaste commercial. "Pagan, ah'm yankin yer baas. 'Is pub's a'richt. Simmer. Noo, fit ye drinkin?"

"There doesn't seem to be anyone to serve us."

Led Zep were interrupted by the clash of the flush of a toilet. The door to the gents opened and out waltzed Fat Ass.

"Ah might've guessed," Derek muttered.

The hefty man crossed a clingy floor. His puss transformed from indifference to mild contentment when he noticed Derek gesturing at him from the bar. Then his expression catapulted towards stupendous elation as the smiling face next to Derek's was refined into recognition, like the passing of an eclipse. Phil galloped over and planted a great hand upon Pagan's back.

"Holy shit," Fat Ass cried. Phil beamed like the porthole of a furnace. "Peggy. Pagan. Holy shit; ah hivnae seen ye in fuckin years, min. Fuckin hell, eh? 'Is is fuckin nuts." Phil appraised Derek; he, too, was ecstatic. Pagan, however, shrank, flustered by the scrutiny that their jubilation was eliciting. He could hear the hush generated by the contemplation of the various clientele, as though it were headphones rustling on his eardrums.

Phil's paw lifted from Pagan's spine, like a truck plucked by a crane. He clenched the besuited man's hand with his, cursorily, then paced back to his station behind the bar. Phil took off his cap to roughen up his curls, then screwed it back into place. The sleeves of his grey and crimson-checked flannel shirt were twisted upwards. Fat Ass was sweaty with excitement, or perhaps from his lavatorial toils. "Fit ye drinkin, Pagan? On me. Fit ye haein?"

"Ah'll hae some champers," Derek said.

"You kin get tae fuck. Ye a'ready owe 'is place enough, Derek. Ye cunt." Phil's composure loosened as though after a bend in the track. "Right, Pagan: fit dee ye want?"

Pagan hummed and hawed, hating having to rebuff his old chum's generosity. "Well, I'm actually supposed to be working just now. And I'm not really a drinker. And I've got the car."

"Ye're workin?" Phil said, heeling back in admiration. "Ah thought ye lukt a bit proper, like. Aa spivvied-up an' 'at. So fit is it ye dee? Insurance?"

"Nah. He's a journalist." Derek intercepted the query and ran with it. "He's jist started workin wi the Northern Echo – through in Peterheid, like. He's bin doon tae London an' iverythin. Oor Peggy's a real professional, ken? Like an adult."

Black eyebrows impinged upon Phil's forehead, like a draft propelling parachutes. "Aye? Good goin, eh?"

"Thanks," Pagan replied, playing with his nails.

"An' ye winnae taak a drink?" inquired the barman. "Why nae? Ye kin manage one, surely tae fuck?"

"No, really. I've got this story to do." Pagan rambled in his defence. "And, like I said, I'm not much use with alcohol."

"Nads tae that. Ye'll be drinkin wi us the morn's night," Derek said.

"Maybe."

"Maybe? Fit ye mean 'maybe'?" Fat Ass sloped over the bar, resting his piglet forearms in front of Pagan like safety barriers. Although to intimidate was not primary of Phil's intentions for adjusting his stance, Pagan was naturally inclined to be chary under the tint of such a voluminous canopy. "Come on. Ye've got tae ging oot on a Frida nicht, min. We'll hae tae catch up an' aa 'at."

"I'm not sure. Maybe. You see, I try to limit myself to one drinking spree every few months or so. Conserving the brain cells, you know?"

"Oh," Derek said. "An' faan wis the last time ye wis drunk, like?"

Pagan paused. "About a year ago."

"A year?" Phil asked.

"A hale fuckin year?"

"Yes. It's a long story, and I've got this job to do, so I'm afraid that I'm going to have to piss off now, for a while. Deadlines, you see?" Pagan rattled off his excuses as he stepped down from the stool.

"Wait, wait; faar ye gaan?" Derek swung round on his seat. "Ye've only bin here a minute. Come on, min. We've jist seen ye again aifter aa 'is time, an' noo here's you buggerin off aa o'er again. Fit's 'at aboot, like? Fuck me, ye dinnae hiv tae ging jist yet. 'Mon, Pagan. We hivnae seen ye in o'er ten fuckin years. Bide a filey. We'll hae a pint an' a yap. Catch up, like, ken? Ye dinnae even hae tae drink. We'll dee the drinkin; you kin dee the spickin."

"No, I appreciate it, but I've got to get this story finished and go through to Peterhead with it and get it typed up and ready for print. It's got to be done by three. I'm cutting it finely enough as it is. And it's only my second week at the job, you know? I can't really afford to fanny about too much with these people." Pagan appealed for empathy, as if he were fighting to inaugurate new rules to a common game. "I'll catch up with you guys later on, though; if that's okay?" The fatty and the lush concurred. "If you's would give me your mobile numbers…"

Derek shook his head. "Ma phone's fucked. Sorry."

"Ma een's gettin sorted," Phil said, with a tone that implied that they'd been fixing it for longer than had been avowed.

"Oh. Well. I could phone the pub," Pagan suggested. "Are you two likely to still be here tonight?"

Fat Ass and Derek unleashed some jolly abuse. If they'd had daisies to throw at him, they would have done.

"I'll take that as a yes, then, should I? Right, I'll see you guys later." Pagan made for the exit.

"Wait," Derek exclaimed, bounding off his chair. "Ye've got ma bags."

Pagan circled by the doorway. He was opaque in the middle, but the sunlight conspired to make his edges appear transparent. "That's okay. I'll drop them off at my house; if you'd like? I mean, it seems to be that you're in need of a place to sleep; so you can stay with me at my grandma's if you want?"

The proposal stimulated ardency. "Aye, fuckin right," Derek said. "'At'd be fuckin tops, like. Cheers. Are ye sure, though, Peggy? Ah dinnae want tae pit ye oot or 'at, ken?"

"My house it is, then," said Pagan. "Goodbye. I'll see you both later." His molecules dispersed in the radiance.

The cave dwellers shifted their concentration back to their own particular dealings. The barflies' squabblings whooshed up like the licking of the ocean's tongue on pebbles.

Derek sat upon his stool in cheerful fatuity. Phil was also rendered both doltish and giddy by the reunion. After more than ten years, and their having believed that they would see neither hide nor hair of him ever again, Pagan had regenerated. And then he'd swiftly hightailed it once more.

"'At wis kina brief, eh?"

"Aye," Derek replied. "He's comin back, though. He's jist got 'at thing tae dee."

"Ah noticed he *talks* these days as weel."

"Fit dee ye expect, Fat Ass? He's bin doon Sooth fir o'er a fuckin decade, ye feel. He's nae gaan tae come back spickin like Rab C fuckin Nesbitt, is he? Ye fat twat."

"Get fucked, ye gob-shite." Phil gazed at the door, as though at Santa's departure. "Pagan, eh? Wis 'at fucked up or fit?"

"Incredibly so."

"Faan wis the last time you thought aboot 'at cunt?"

"Ah cannae really mine. It's bin sae lang, ken?"

Phil wiggled his finger as though he'd cracked some case. "Ken 'is? Ah thought ah seen his fuckin name in the paper. Somethin aboot crystal meth. Bonny writer, like."

The tallest of the three by the fruit machine came over so that Phil could convert another note into shrapnel. The young lad's hair was of correspondent length to Derek's, though it was straighter and darker. He and his two pals dressed as Derek might have done at their age, just prior to his realisation that the ladies liked you to attire yourself in such a manner that it conveyed some level of sophistication, as though you could be trusted to spot a book in a library. The boy's blue shirt was acceptable enough, but his jeans were ridiculously baggy. The zitty youth who hung off the side of the bandit like a mug handle declared his stylistic illiteracy with his linking of gravy-shaded footwear and trousers with white socks. He was the only one of the three who'd thought to wear a jacket. The boy of the floppy hair and baggy jeans returned to his group and gave his pal the metal. The bleached-haired kid in the white T-shirt pulled at the unsteady waistband of his tracksuit bottoms, then slotted more coins into the machine. You could barely see the boy's pink trainers for the descending leggings.

Derek spun a beermat around on the adhesive oak of the bar. "Ah tell ye, Fat Ass: 'is really his bin a weird wee while. Ah'm jist won'erin fit the fuck's gaan tae happen neest, like. You're nae gaan tae turn oot tae be an android wi vag's for armpits; are ye, Philip?"

"Ah doubt it."

"Ah hope nae. Dinnae reckon ah could handle 'at."

Derek purchased a pint of lager; he bought the bartender a Guinness, for which Fat Ass was thankful. A delegate for the corner tribe propped himself up against the bar like a collection of knitting needles that had been unsheathed from a denim-scrap receptacle, and beckoned Phil for another round; a request that the barman did serve. This likely patriarch of the booth-based brood was a slovenly fifty-something with few teeth and fewer hairs on his bonce, like Derek himself might look after having been locked inside the washing machine for a week. Derek slanted his glass at the man, whom did respond with a nod that seemed rather fumbled to its recipient, as if the man's nerves had betrayed him in the presence of celebrity. The man took the tray of spilling libations back to his table. Pincers swooped in at the glasses like the spasmodic reaction of a poked sea anemone. The kids, wisely, kept to soft drinks. The mongrel slept on. The mind dust gathered in Phil's skull and formed concrete thoughts.

"Aye, Derek," Phil said, "why his Pagan got yer suitcases, like? Ah thought ye wis bidin wi me fir jist noo. Nae that ah'm buthered, like. Be fuckin glaid tae be rid o ye."

"Yer dad's hame, Gutzilla."

"Shite? Ye're jokin? Faan the fuck did he come hame, like, ye hideous hoor?"

"'Is mornin. Kin ye believe 'at? He came in faan ah wis jist comin oot o the shooer. Ma fuckin stroop wis oot an' aathin."

"Seriously?"

"Aye," Derek assured his friend. "Seriously."

"Fuck sake. Nightmare. He disnae normally come back early. They must be wantin 'im ontae anither job or somethin."

"Well, jist ma fuckin luck, he did 'is time, didn't he?" Derek gulped his pint. He dried his lips on his wrist bone.

"So fit did ma dad say tae ye? Did he kick ye oot, or fit?"

"No, nae precisely," Derek replied. "He jist made it clear that ah wis wanted aboot as much as a shite stain on the gweed curtains."

"An' fit did you dee?" Phil asked, with the black drink raised up to the lowest of his chins. "Ye didnae hud a cairry on, did ye?"

"No. Ah didnae. Ye vibrator." The two men sipped in tandem. Derek continued, "Ah got ma bags an' left, didn't ah? Christicles. Dee ye believe 'is? Hoo's 'is fir fuckin desperate? Ah actually went doon tae ma sister's hoose."

"Ye wis gaan tae bide 'ere?"

"Ah wis thinkin aboot it. Bit nah. Ah couldnae bide 'ere. Place wis fuckin mobbed wi junkies. Fuckin useless twats. Ah wid've ended up throttlin the bastards."

"Hoo wis yer sister, 'en? Wis Tracy a'right, or…?" Wis she fucked oot o 'er nut? Phil thought it better to leave the question unfinished.

Derek took another swig. He put his glass back upon its coaster. The old man asked for a refill; Phil dutifully complied. The mullet rejoiced over by the pool table. A thud. One of the youths had kicked the bandit. "Hoi, min." A shout from the barman was enough to quell any more disgruntled attacks.

"Philip," said Derek, "she's a fuckin mess."

Then Derek told the bartender how he'd met Pagan outside her house. Pagan had knocked at Tracy's door only for Derek to answer it. It was a fair coincidence, indeed; they'd both agreed about that. But that was life. And life was full of coincidences, ironies and chance happenings that were best not dithered upon for danger of making a man loopy. Neither of the pair believed in God or in Fate or in any kind of grand design; and this occurrence most queer was allowed to evaporate from their thoughts with a synchronised tipping of their brows.

The fat man and the drunkard took a taste of their drinks.

The foreigners ceased rowing so that the man could, in satisfactory English, bid for more beverages. Phil dealt with the man's order.

Derek's eyes swept upwards of the bottles and the mirror before him to the television. A Bad Company song, which Phil would certainly have selected, jumped from the speakers, trampling the voice of the sizeable screen. It was obvious, however, that the actor's death was still saturating the channels. Some Beverly Hills woman dabbed at her taut face with a hanky as if polishing a baking pan.

The till clinked and whirred as Fat Ass operated it. He handed the man his change. "Many thanks," said the male of unknown origin, taking the drinks over to an irate lady whom might've been stunning a few years earlier. The man offered his partner her drink; warily, in case she decided to slap the glass from his hand. He deflated with relief when she did not.

Phil saw where Derek's attention was grapple-hooked. "Crazy, eh?" the barman remarked. "Mintal wee bastard. Did ye see 'im jump aff the reef o 'at nightclub? Nuts as fuck."

Derek bowed, like an animal following a biscuit. He was facing up towards the TV, though he wasn't really watching it. "Aye, Fat Ass." His medals stayed, but his mind strayed. "Did ye hear onythin aboot 'is story that Pagan's writin aboot?" Derek looked across his pint at the barman, whose bulk threatened to buckle the till that he reclined against. "Aboot 'is aal guy that wis supposed tae hiv bin killt last night?"

Fat Ass Philip shot forward. "Did you hear aboot it as weel, aye?"

"Yip. Pagan tellt me. 'At's the story he's reportin."

"Aye," Phil said, gravely. "'Ere wis a couple o guys in earlier on spickin aboot it. Somebidy wis supposed tae hiv hit the aal manny o'er the heid wi a brick an' killt 'im or somethin. Och, aye. 'At's fit ah'm hearin, like. Ah wisnae sure if they were spickin shite or nae. Ye ken hoo the Broch is. Bit it's true, aye?"

"Must be."

"'At's nae real, 'at. 'Is fuckin toon's jist gettin worse. They'd better catch faiver did it, like. Or ah'll get the fucker masel. They shid guillotine the cunts." Phil thrashed the sprigs of his right mitt and chewed upon the nails of his left. The typically amiable barman was angered.

Derek tinkled his own digits around his glass, as though he were playing the piano at the base of a loch. Out of the corner of his eye, he noticed that the aged loner was perusing him. Derek shifted in his seat to greet the old man.

"Ye's jist dinnae care onymair," the pensioner crackled.

Phil spat out a nail, then replied, sensitively, "You said it, partner. Nae cunt's got ony respect 'ese days."

The old man pinched, as if the fluttering of bat wings had disturbed a web. He crept down from his stool and crawled out into the drained sunshine: sieved dry of its prerequisite heat. The pensioner hadn't even emptied his glass.

Fat Ass was bemused by the old man's indignation, when Derek called, "Oh, corpulent bar steward." He chinked his goblet upon the oak vivaciously. "Another, my obese compadre. I have become overwhelmed by this urge to get fantastically shitey-faced this eve'."

*

Rachel knocked on the door. He wouldn't still be in a bad mood, would he? Her parents also took to yelling and swearing at her on occasion, but their tantrums frequently concluded in hugs and ice cream.

She rapped once more. The rising wind nipped at her knees, which was the only strip of skin visible between the long socks and dark skirt that was part of the school uniform.

He had frightened her. She'd spent the remainder of yesterday afternoon sobbing under her bed. He wouldn't still be mad, though. Raymond had warned her that the hypnotic trance of Cpt Fantaztik was so astounding that it could even overpower the author himself. In this eventuality, he had told her, don't fret. For as long as Tiggles was on his side, he would emerge immaculate from any fray. He would be Raymond again by now, she thought.

She didn't want to go home yet. Those people were round. She was averse to them. They were scary and didn't seem to like her very much. They played that music too loud and they swore a lot. They were. They were in-tim-uh-date-ing.

Shade fell upon Sutherland Terrace.

Her fist struck at the door like the beater of a drum in a marching band. She unsealed the letterbox to discern if there was anything to be heard within. She peered through the crack, on her tiptoes. A bare corridor presented itself to her; it were as though the house had been lobotomised. She called his name. She received no reply. He couldn't still be ignoring her. She let the flap snap shut. She went flat on her feet. She pulled at her blouse to stop the warmth from escaping.

The white terrier sniffed at her shoes. Rachel knelt; she scratched the dog. Gordon gruffed its gratitude. "Walkies?" she asked. "Walkies?"

Chapter 11

There was nobody left to talk to, and thus he mulled things over. He thought about Thursday, last Thursday, and coming home from work enshrined with the uriney gale of fish. The subdued poise of his former house had accosted him. His mam sat in the kitchen. Her manner was akin to the taxi drive back from the airport at the closure of a holiday, and delivered the punch line before the comedian had set up the joke. "Derek," she'd said, "yer grandad's passed awaa. He deit in his sleep." He remembered not crying, or even feeling that sad. He'd thought, matter of factly, about how this meant for him a day off work. He showered, washing the stench of moderate graft from his person. Derek dried himself and got dressed. Ate his supper and got drunk. Went to sleep and woke up. Went to work and went home. Did this and did that. But did not really mourn.

He thought about the last time that he'd seen his grandad: a fortnight ago in the old folks' home. The old man had not been bedded, in his pyjamas, as Derek was forewarned that he might be, but was clothed, like a child's attempt at gift-wrapping; he was sitting there in front of his TV and nibbling at toast. This old man still bothered to get up and get dressed and eat. He recalled how his grandad had smelled. He'd smelled like the cold, as if he'd just come in from a winter's walk. Although, that could not have been so. Big Stanley hadn't said much, hadn't uttered anything compelling or worthy of recitation, nor been able to. His answers were short; his words battled free as buffalo straining from the river, away from the crocodiles. Derek made his small talk like a pop sensation visiting a fan in their ward. The old man's movements were that of an orangutan caught in a downpour. It had been as though his grandad was growing into his chair. Like two decomposing subjects forming some new compound. The old man tilted his head up to see his kin. White hair dangled down his brow like sheets over stored furniture. His moustache was like a twig on the ground of some deforested area. His blue eyes were as the headlights of a sinking car. Derek could see the old man's pain. He could tell that the bridge between mind and mouth had long since crumbled. Derek had smiled. Had said, "Cheerio". And had left.

Goodbye, Stanley Gibson.

He thought about the last time that he'd seen Pagan. Before today. So bloody many whiles ago. Could he remember? Was it too far back? Had the abundant picklings from then until now sullied the lens of Derek's telescope far too comprehensively? Academy. Nearing the end of. A divorce. Who was leaving whom? They both left. Dad went away. To Inverness, wasn't it? Mother moved to England. Back home. Reading, maybe? Took her boy with her. Waving goodbye. A Saturday afternoon? Shoddy weather. Bright but miserable, as though the sun were merely the adjustable roof at a match between wind and rain. None of the boys wept. Too self-conscious and insecure at that age. Sixteen, surely? There abouts. Didn't want to look pooftery. Pagan and his mum drove off. The car rounded a corner. And gone was.

After the divorce.

What divorce? Why divorce – what need?

Derek searched. He threw a couple of flares down the well. The flames splashed the walls and ate the blackness. Faces became illuminated. One face surged out beyond the others, like a fist pressed into latex.

David.

"Hoi, Phil. Div ye mine David? Dee ye mine fit happened tae David?"

No response.

"Oi. Fat Ass. Ah'm spickin tae ye."

Derek refrained from gazing, bewilderedly, at the bottles in front of him, and at his distorted reflection between them. He drilled his mind back to clarity. The nondescript drone of the jukebox jiggled back into melodic tunage. The generator hum behind Derek filtered into individual voices and conversations. The mirror swirled and then set, so that he could identify himself within its skin.

A pretty, young girl stared at Derek from behind the bar. She looked vexed, somewhat. Confused, Derek flipped the charm switch and smiled up at her. His sorcery bounced off like a bird into a window. Derek's grin died and was reincarnated as a shuffle, to formalise his carriage upon the stool.

"Excuse me?" she demanded. "Who are you calling a fat ass?" Her thin arms were crossed below a stout chest. Her pink top was revealing without being slutty. Her blonde-brown hair was tied back to unveil a lovely view, like the Alps as seen from a chalet in spring. Derek detected the lilt in her voice. A pretty, young Irish girl.

"Oops, sorry," Derek said. He chortled to consolidate his recognition of the error. "Ah thought ye wis somebidy else. Phil. The ither barmin. Bartender, fitiver."

"Did you now?"

"Aye. Ah did. Sorry again."

"So you think I look like this Phil fella, do you?"

"No, no," Derek replied. His hands were up to pacify her figurative kalashnikov. "Ah sweer. Ah jist niver lukt. Ah thought he'd still be here, like. Ye see, ah tend tae drift noo an' again."

The Irish dame defrosted. Her arms fell to her sides; her hurt faded into amused irritation. The irritation transfigured into a reluctant smirk as Derek grinned back at her.

The news was on the television. "Crazy 'at shit aboot the actor, eh?" Derek said.

She nodded.

"Some folk say ah luk a wee bit like him."

She said nothing.

"Probably even mair so noo." He watched her swallow the cud of her mirth. "Ye hivnae got the time, hiv ye?"

"It's just after seven," she said. "How long do you usually 'drift' for?"

Derek chuckled. A vacant pint mug and a dried-out nip glass stood on the bar like a couple of mismatched hombres in the desert. When had he moved on to spirits?

"Eh, ah dinnae ken," he said. "It depends. Wid ye be able tae fill 'is?" He handed her the pint glass. "Lager, please. Nae the black stuff."

She placed the tumbler under the tap and brought it to its head. Derek realised that he wasn't wearing his jacket anymore; his consternation was consoled when he conceived that he was sitting on it. Samantha looked at the pump and at the filling drink and at the other patrons, but never once did she glance back at the cheeky lad whom sat at the bar and smiled at her all the while. A redness bloomed about her like leaves, which her clippers fought exhaustively to contain.

She placed the rejuvenated beaker on his coaster.

Derek rooted in his pocket and excavated some coins. His fingernails tickled her palm when he placed the money into its cup. She swivelled away, as if at a police officer's torch. He thought that she giggled. Derek took a huge gulp of his drink. Refreshed, he was, like a reloaded web page.

"So," Derek inquired, in his finest Oirish, "where is it you're from, my wee Leprechaun?"

The girl hunched over the till and convulsed with a spatter of laugher like a troubled engine. She turned towards him, despising her disobedient lips.

"Let me guess: ye're fae Warsaw?" he said. "Plinty o them gaan aboot."

"Very funny," she replied.

"Ah'm jist jokin wi ye, ma dears." Up on the screen, a guy outside a nightclub laid a wreath beside many others. He may well have been Michael Caine. "So, you're the new bartender, eh?"

"That's right," she said. "I started on Monday night."

"But of course. Ye've got Fat Ass Phil's aal oors. Aye, 'is is the first time ah've seen ye."

"I've been working afternoons the last two days."

"Must've jist missed ye."

"Suppose so."

Derek raised his glass. "Aye. Ah supposey so." The chilled drink avalanched into his gut. "Ah'm Derek, by the way."

"Samantha."

"Samantha?" Derek pronounced. "Seriously? Samantha?"

"Yes," she replied.

"Ye're nae gaan tae believe 'is," he said, "bit ma mam aiwyes tellt me that ah shid mairry a bonny Irish quine caad Samantha."

"Oh, really?"

"Sweer on ma life."

Samantha wiped down the bar with a cloth. "Your friend warned me about you."

"Fa? Phil?"

"Yes."

"An' fit did Philip, Lard o the Pies, say tae ye?" Derek asked.

"He told me you were a bit fresh. Said you were a bit of a chancer. Good thing I listened to him."

"Och, dinnae listen tae Phil. He's got mair skeletons in his closet than a Jersey orphanage. He's a rare lad an' he means well an' 'at, bit the thing aboot 'im that ye hiv tae waatch oot for is his insatiable penchant for fraudulence. 'At an' his hygiene. Oor Fat Ass cannae button a shirt withoot startin tae smell like a packet o cheese an' onion crisps. An' he really is a compulsive liar. He's awaa geein oot the wrang directions tae strangers ony time he waaks doon the street. Cannae help 'imsel. It's genetic, like a St Combs' toe. He's a good singer, though."

"And you call him 'Fat Ass'?" she said.

"Aye. Term o affection. He's like the fat brither ah'm glaid ah niver hid."

"And you say he's your friend?" She appeared baffled, bordering on upset.

"Aye."

"So why would you call him something so cruel as 'Fat Ass', and speak so unkindly of him?"

"Because he's ma chum. An' he's fat."

Samantha didn't seem too impressed with this answer; nor did she find any comedic worth in the nickname that had served Philip Ironside so well since primary school. Fat Ass. Derek had not instigated the moniker, but he was a front bench member of its conservation committee.

He glanced over his shoulder. The drizzle of daylight had lessened substantially against the umbrella of the blinds. Some of the patrons from whence he'd been sober had been substituted. The mullet and the skinhead were gone, and in their stead a couple of flash guys contested their pool playing abilities. These two twenty-and-a-bit-year-olds were none too common to The Tart, and were likely here on this singular excursion to impress their girlfriends, whom giggled in the booth on the cigarette machine side of the entrance, with scant interest in the outcome of their men's game. The quartet wouldn't have looked amiss among the mannequins of the trendier High Street stores, thought Derek. Their overt self-awareness never dipped for chance that somebody somewhere might be taking a photograph of them. The resting pool player admitted Derek's fascination; an exchange of congenial head-pecks was transacted. The girls sipped their drinks through straws that Derek was oblivious that The Tart had, and then drew in towards each other like doubles tennis partners after the rescuing of a point. He knew that they'd be talking about him, and speculating.

In the other corner, in the booth that was right of the doorway, and where that brood innumerable had bantered like parrots in the afternoon, three recognisable oldies convened. They were: the guy with the small, shrivelled face who seemed to delight in the plight of civilisation; the man with the permanent frown and large, bumpy nose; and the jovial Englishman with yellowing hair whom had debuted in The Tart about a month ago and had made regular pit stops ever since. The reflection of bulbs on their lenses put Derek in mind of security monitors. The gents raised their drinks to Big Stanley's descendent. Derek lifted his pint like a trophy acquired from an amateur-ranked endeavour.

Two of the trio remained by the fruit machine. The ultra spotty youngster with the white socks and black shoes had departed. The bleached-haired boy continued to feed the bandit as though he were in a phone box, funding an international call. The kid with the floppy barnet did spectate as though on a school trip at the local water-treatment facility. They were both too peachy-faced and lean of years to be served any alcofuel, but the fruit machine was sufficient bait to keep them in this creel. Floppy sauntered off to the jukebox. Bleach Boy commanded him to put on two songs of his choosing – no, three songs. The duo seemed somehow familiar to Derek. Hadn't he encountered one of the pair at some stage on Monday? He wasn't for certain. Monday was a long time ago.

Derek decimated his pint with a swig. Samantha leaned against the till, admiring the door with glazed disinterest. She was roughly half the width of Philip. She could sense Derek beaming up at her, like a teddy on her pillow.

"Yes? What?"

"Eh? Fit ye spickin aboot?"

"What are you staring at me for?"

Derek slackened with surprise. "Why dee ye think ah'm starin at ye? Ye're a stunner. Wid a man be expected tae luk awaa fae a UFO?"

Samantha blinked as if she had utterly forgotten the name of a person whom she was set to introduce.

"So," Derek began, "fit are ye? Rangers or Celtic?"

She glared at him; her indignation, however, wasn't that convincing. "I don't watch football."

"'At's nae fit ah meant, sweetness."

"Originally, I'm from a village you've never heard of thirty miles south of Dublin."

"That would be Celtic, 'en," he said. "Hoo are those IRA rapscallions 'ese days? Ye dinnae hear so much aboot 'em noo. They even still on the go? Al-Qaeda kina showed up an' stole their thun'er, eh? Like a fuckin hot stepdaughter at 'er new mammy's weddin. Ken fit ah mean?"

Samantha recrossed her arms. "Whatever."

"An' fit brings ye here onywye?" Derek asked. "Tae the wondrous Broch. Why'd ye leave the Emerald Isle tae come tae Britain's smack capital? Ye go oot een night wi an orange han'bag an' a 'I heart Brian Laudrup' T-shirt, an' noo ye're in the witness protection programme or somethin?"

"I'm travelling," she replied. She intertwined her denimed pins so that her body became a wrung crucifix.

"Traivellin, eh?"

"Yes."

"With whom?"

"Alone," she said.

"'At's by yersel, in't it? An' nae some boif caad Alfred Ohn or onythin?"

A thud. The fruit machine had connived its way into receiving another boot.

"Hey." Samantha's protestations made little impact. "Excuse me?"

The reply seared back like a rock to a riot shield. "Fuck off."

Derek snapped, "Waatch yer fuckin tongue, ye soggy wee cunt."

Bleach Boy and Floppy both glowered at Derek. The room paused, as if a whisk had been taken from the bowl. The pool sharks halted play; their girlfriends ceased with their conjecture; and the oldies retracted their toes from the reminiscing pond. The Doberman growled on its stool until the puppies aimed their snouts back at their machines.

Derek reached for his drink. He finished it. What was it about these young pups, eh? They couldn't even swear properly. Whereas, for example, when either he or his pals swore, he thought, there was an inherent comical aspect and rhythm involved that helped cushion the blow, like a kiss on the anus before sodomy; but with these younger cuntos, the sound was purely antisocial and vile, as if to sign for a delivery using one's penis. Oh, how Derek did despair.

He could see that Samantha was further displeased with him. Great stuff.

"I don't need a guardian, thank you very much."

"Ah ken. Ah jist wanted tae shout at somebidy. Bin a rough few days." Derek shook his glass to indicate that a refill was required. "Choppity chop chop, then." She snatched it and shoved it under the tap. "So, faar aa hiv ye bin a-traivellin tae?"

"Pardon?"

"Where all hast thy been on thine gallivantings, my dear? It's 'is language o mine. It's like tryin tae spick through a snorkel filled wi chuckies. Gaan tae hiv tae get it fixed, like."

She returned his brimming tumbler to him. He gave her the money. "Around Europe: France; Germany; Austria. All over." She rebounded from the till like a dart hitting a divider. "I've taken a year off. Completed my degree in May, and been travelling ever since."

"With Alistair Owen?"

"By myself," she said. "I've met people on the way, though. In hostels and such. Travelled with groups here and there. But being on my own doesn't bother me."

"And why would it? Your delectable company is copious for anyone's enjoyment. Ah suppose it must be good fir buildin up self-reliance an' 'at, ken? Maak ye mair independently minded, like."

She laid her hands flat on the bar. "It has."

"An' fit's yer degree in?"

"Art."

Derek sipped. "Ah thought as much."

"What's that supposed to mean?"

"Nithin. Please. Less defensive, eh? An' so ye've bin tae Francois, Deutschland und fitiver them Austrians caa their country."

"Osterreich."

"Osterreich is right," he said. "An' fit brings ye tae the northeast o Scotland? A bit o an oddity for the itinerary, like, is it nae?"

Samantha put her elbows where her palms had been. "Not really. I'm making my way up to John o' Groats. I started off not quite at Land's End but in Dover and worked my way up the country, travelling by bus or train. But not by plane. That's my rule. No aeroplanes. I've been stopping here and there, and walked some parts of the journey: when it was safe to. Working in pubs and clubs whenever funds were low, which is always. Trust me, I've worked in rougher places than this."

"Brave lass. You're quite somethin, eh? So, faar ye bidin – where art thou staying?"

"I'm staying with a cousin," she said. "My dad's mother's sister's daughter married a man from here. I'd never met them. That was the incentive for me coming to Fraserburgh."

"An' fit dee ye maak o the Broch? Amazin, eh?"

"I like it." Her answer came swiftly; she knew that any hesitation would discredit her sincerity. "So far so good. It's a beautiful town."

"Aye, the Broch's nae too bad," Derek said. "It's jist a shame aboot the folk."

She smiled at the remark. "Why is it called the Broch?"

"Ah'm gaan tae be totally honest wi ye. Ah hiv nae idea. Could be some Gaelic pish."

Bleach Boy slapped a note onto the middle of the bar. "Change, eh?" Samantha took the cash and clawed the coins from the plastic trays of the till's stomach. The youth scowled at Derek incessantly.

Derek glared back. "If ye dinnae stop starin at me, ah'm gaan tae hiv tae punch ye in the face."

"Ah'm really scared," Bleach Boy sneered.

"Ah niver asked ye if ye wis scared, ye chocolate hat. Ah jist tellt ye fit ah'm gaan tae dee. Noo, stop fuckin starin. Tit."

Bleach Boy distended his spine so that his chest would protrude. "D'ye ken fa ah am?"

"Well, if it quacks like a cunt…" Derek sat up on his stool.

Samantha rushed in between them as though enmeshed in a pulley system. The boy snatched his coins from her and trudged back to the fruit machine. Floppy did not conjoin his line of sight with that of Derek's; he shrugged at his approaching pal. Bleach Boy shook his head and muttered some grumblings. They turned their aggression on the bandit; money was thrust down its gullet as though it were designed to tear up its intestines, and knobs were slammed as if they were temporary substitutes for something fleshier.

"Did Phil say onythin afore he left?" Derek asked. "Did he say if he wis comin back or nae? Ah cannae mine."

"I'm sure he said he'd be back around eight-ish," she replied.

Derek examined the clock behind her. According to that timepiece it was ten past eleven. The cheap swines couldn't even replace a battery. They liked you ignorant, they did, and leaving only when they themselves did dictate. Derek tapped his wrist. Samantha took a second to click.

She checked her watch. "It's about a quarter to."

"Goody goody gumdrops." Derek swigged. He contrived to spill onto his T-shirt. "So, then, hiv ye spoken tae Fat Ass much since ye started here?"

"A wee bit," she said. "I only see him when we're switching over. He seems like a nice guy, though. Shame for him to have such a name."

"He disnae mind."

"How do you know? Have you ever asked him?"

Derek tickled a lobe. "Nope. Bit he's the Fat Ass. 'At's jist fa he's aiwyes bin. He's used tae it. An' he's got tae lose weight onywye. The fatso cannae cairry on the size he is or he'll be deid by the time he's thirty. He's braakin twa o the deidly sins jist by stan'in 'ere: gluttony and sloth, and probably aa the rest o 'em an' aa. Once he loses some o his vastness, we'll stop caain 'im Fat Ass." He drank. "We'll caa 'im Tiny Cock Phil instead."

Samantha whipped him with a towel. "You're a nasty bugger, you."

"Aye," Derek said. "An' ah'm een o the better eens."

"A fella such as yourself be lucky to have friends."

"Pear haps, Miss Haps." He fidgeted on his seat. Cumbersome bloody stools. Almost as bad as those church benches. Samantha found some Scampi Fries that had gone spongy and binned them. Derek said to her, "Ah bet Phil fancies ye a'ready."

"What? He does not." She tried to rub the grease off her fingertips. "How would you know?"

Derek replied, "It's the wye he is. He's fat, an' he faas in love wi ony fine, bonny quine that'll gie 'im the time o day. You're jist his type. You're ivery man's type. A few lesbos' as weel, ah'd imagine."

A while elapsed before Samantha spoke again. She busied herself by tidying up around her workstation and rinsing out the used glasses. Derek watched her trying not to watch him. His accumulator was flung around its container like a reverse bungee jump. He could already feel himself falling for this Irish lassie.

Derek's best buddies beside the fruit machine slipped their last coin into the robotic thief. Still smarting from their earlier affront, the pair marched out the pub, with their heads down as though to elude the paparazzo by the courthouse steps. The pool players downed their sticks onto the table and sat next to their lady friends in the booth. The guys then bought more drinks: pints for themselves; fruity bottled campness for the chicks. Chunks and lines of chatter cascaded through the beat of the jukebox like javelins through a blizzard. AC/DC, it was. The bell-ends had good taste, he considered. So to speak. The young couples spoke about cars and tyre treads and about going down to Edinburgh at the weekend. *Ah cannae believe Frida's the morn.* The oldies, meanwhile, prophesied glumly. "They're gaan tae close the North Sea," said one. "'Ere'll be nithin fir naebidy." Dire warnings of worsening spells ahead reverberated from the aged corner of The Tart like the clatter of a stairwell tumble. Derek preferred the song of the heavy-metal expats, and did what he could to attune himself principally to their frequency.

Derek nursed his drink, killing her softly a sip at a time. Feeding his buzz with teaspoon portions. Waiting for the Fat Ass whom had, incredibly, managed to maintain his lifelong streak of being late for everything. Thinking of Pagan. Wondering. Nursing and sipping, and waiting for Samantha to speak to him again.

"So, what is it you do?"

Derek's thoughts were severed, as when a passing aviator momentarily blocks the sun's route into a room. He looked up at the Irish girl, whom had floated into his life at some point that day to bolster his dam. It was still Thursday, wasn't it? "Eh?" he said.

Samantha repeated her inquiry. "What do you do?"

Derek smiled. "Ah get drunk an' maak a dick o masel. Ye nae noticed?"

"Apart from the obvious," she said. Her interest in this youthful man was growing, despite his boozy manner and near impenetrable jargon. He was even rather attractive, in the way that dolphins were smart. "Where do you work?"

"Ah dinnae."

"You're unemployed?"

"Aye," Derek replied. "'At's usually fit they caa somebidy fa disnae work, aye. Ah did hae a job, like. Ah'm nae a complete simpleton. Ah worked in a yard along the road 'ere. Until Tuesda, ken? Toories, they caa it. Ah worked 'ere, an' then ah comes in een mornin 'is wik an' ma uncle gies ma the old heave-ho, like."

"Your uncle fired you?"

"Yip." Derek witnessed a singer from a group he did not cherish cry live on TV. "Ma uncle sacked me. Which is nae fuckin great, like."

"That's awful," Samantha said. "Why did he do that?"

"Because, tae be perfectly honest wi ye, ma darlin, ah'm a bit o a useless cunt." An ill humour flourished briefly on Derek's face, as if the dye in his veins had changed tincture.

"That's a bit harsh, isn't it?"

"Nah," he said. "Ah'm sure if ye got tae ken me ye'd un'erstan."

Samantha cut away from Derek to serve an oldie. The elderly sort, whom Derek had seen in The Tart many times before, spoke to the lad as he waited for his order to be processed. "The Broch's on its last leggies, eh?" enthused the gent with the small, shrivelled phizog, and whose name was Patrick Hendry. Derek acceded unreservedly, which pleased Pat like a flood after he'd had the foresight to bring his wellies. The old man transported his cargo back to his wrinkled gathering in the corner.

"What are you going to do with yourself now, Derek?" Samantha was satisfied with her having remembered his name.

"Fuck knows," he said. "Somethin ai' comes up. Ach, it's nae like me tae worry o'er muckle."

The door creaked. Then shut. The conversations did moulder as if the movie had commenced. The concern that glimmered in Samantha's eyes triggered a mild panic within Derek, like the appearance of a bee inside a car. He wanted to zip round in his chair and see what had just entered The Tart. His good sense, however, did overrule any impulsive desires. The alcohol-suit peeled away from him, uncovering a Derek that was better prepared for whatever trouble had tracked him down.

Heavy steps pulsed leisurely across the floor like approaching thunder. He saw Samantha take a tiny step backwards. She glanced at Derek. Her fear became his. A figure halted at the bar, suppressing Derek's view of the television, as a telephone pole could conceal a satellite. One side of the pub vanished behind the newcomer. Derek turned a cautious ninety degrees to his left. There stood a dark giant. A brick-shaped man with a face like a tombstone. And he was bearing down on Derek.

The hum of chitchat found its level, and was quieter than previously. No one wanted to be loud and aggravate this terrifying stranger. And nobody wished to arouse paranoia by whispering.

The giant pulled a stool up beside Derek. He sat, seemingly, a foot taller than the drunk, whom was relatively minuscule.

The fashionable foursome collected their coats and slunk off into the night. The boyfriends had proved their mettle quite sufficiently. The oldies viewed the ongoings at the bar from their table, as though at a tide that had to be minded.

Derek doubted not that the man next to him, peering over him like a cliff, was the Lex MacMurran that Jimbo had been warned about. Fat Ass had been right. The man did look like an evil Superman.

"Hoo ye deein 'ere, pal?" The man intonated as though his throat were barricaded with sandpaper.

Derek sipped from his libation. "Nae bad," he said. Samantha had retreated to the till. Derek attempted to conduct a front of calm and bravery. He did not prosper.

Lex reached one spade into his black leather jacket and produced a photo. He showed it to Derek.

"Ken 'is guy?" the giant said. Derek wasn't sure if the utterance had been truly meant as a query.

Derek pushed the boat of his bottom lip down the slip. "Nope, cannae say that ah ken the guy, no. Fa is he, like? Ah taak it he's nae yer beau: the airse crack fa got awaa?"

The stranger's face didn't disclose any shift in emotion. The giant continued to stare straight through the weedy youngster, like he were land to be remodelled into roads. "Ye sure ye dinnae ken 'im?"

"Aye," Derek replied. Lies usually came to him so much easier than this. "Ah've nae idea fa he is, like. Fit, is he a chum or somethin? Did he dee ye wrang?"

"So, ye definitely dinnae ken 'im, no?" The voice quaked as though cuffs were excised upon the train tracks. "It's funny, like. He's fae the Broch, ye see? An' it's a newish photo, an' he luks tae be aboot the same age as ye. Funny that ye widnae ken 'im; especially considerin that 'ere's only one secondary school here, an' that ye must've went tae school wi 'im. 'At's funny, eh?"

"Nae affa funny, no." Derek thought that he might pass out and hover with the intangibles. Thankfully, inquisitive coppers and attentive dads had prepared Derek for such a fraught interrogation. He did not panic, and he did not faint. He just had to hold his nerve and rely that the mounting mistruths didn't catch his feet. "He must jist hiv went tae anither academy, like," Derek said, judicious not to spit out his refutation. "A lot o Brochers ging tae Mintlaa Academy, ten miles oot the road 'ere – the wye o Aiberdeen. Mair standard grades available or some shite like 'at. Fuck knows. Bit ah kin assure ye that ah've niver seen 'at skinny cunt afore in ma life."

A twitch. That was it. The first physical clue that the giant was losing his patience. Lex had already arrived at some conclusion and was simply waiting for Derek to meet him at the intersection.

Samantha could feel the spaces between herself and everything else thicken, like she could take a bite out of and be nourished by the air; though the taste would've made her sickly. The oldies were now focused solely on pisshead and Goliath, abandoning any pretence of discourse.

Lex clamped the photograph between the broad cables of two fingers. He moved the picture a couple of inches closer to Derek. It was very nearly touching the tip of his nose. The giant asked once again, "Ye sure ye dinnae ken 'is guy?"

Beneath a layer of dread, Derek felt the initial pangs of resentment. "Aye, ah'm sure. Ah tellt ye that ah've niver seen 'at fucker afore."

"Ye sure, now?"

"Fir fuck sake, aye; ah'm sure." He hadn't intended to swear then. It was a blatant sign of stress, and Derek had regretted signalling his tense state as soon as the grubby rebel had absailed from his gob. "Luk, ah dinnae ken the guy. Ah dinnae ken fa he is, fa you are, or fuckin onythin, a'right? Ah'm jist sittin here, haein a pint an' tryin tae get bleezin in peace. Ah've tellt ye fit ah ken, which happens tae be a fair amoont o fuck aal. 'At's it. Unless ye want tae rin up tae the Chinker's an' get's some chow, 'en 'at's the end o oor affairs."

The giant's gaze held firm like steel sheets over potholes. The photo disappeared back into his coat. "It's funny," he said, after a lengthy silence, "ah heard 'is wis his local."

"How's 'at funny? An' fit mug tellt ye 'at?"

"Some fella ah asked," Lex answered. The hound was gaining on the fox. "Apparently, the guy ah'm aifter hings oot here a lot. Disnae seem tae be here the night, though. Unless ye's hae got 'im stashed in the bogs." Lex's stare broke from Derek like a stalactite to appreciate the rest of the pub. The oldies dropped their sight to consume drinks. This pub was, indeed, the exact same sort of shit-hole that Lex had graduated from since becoming a teetotaller. He said, "Come here aften yersel, like?"

"No. Ah'm jist back fae helpin the peer bairns in Africa."

"'At right?"

"Aye," Derek said, sensing that his teeth were on the cusp of gritting. "'At's right."

Lex frowned as if to a refractory student. "The boy ah wis spickin tae: he mentioned the guy's chums. Said they hung oot here as well. Described a couple o 'em. Beth in their mid-twenties. One really fat; the ither, a Jim Morrison wannabe, wi an average build an' scruffy broon hair. A dafty wi a quick moo. Soon like ony bastard you might ken?" The giant gripped the bar, as though it were a ledge that he could thrust himself from. "Funny, eh?"

"If ye're lukin fir funny, awaa an' fuck off an' Google Joe Pasquale: he'll be right up your fuckin street." Derek reclined on his stool. "'Is is nae funny. 'Is is jist a coincidence. Normal build? Broon hair? Fuck me, fa wis ye spickin tae? Lucian fuckin Freudy? He fairly fuckin narraed it doon, eh?" His mouth was in the form that would result in his prompt dismissal from a position. "Aye, ah mean, fir fuck sake, 'at must be me, 'en, eh? An' nae the ither three billion punters fa's fuckin profile 'at fits."

"Said the guy's chum wis caad Derek," Lex continued. "Fit's your name?"

Derek measured his response. "Gertrude." He leaped off his seat and went straight to the pool table. Derek grabbed one of the cues and held it baseball style. "Come on, 'en, ye fuckin twat," he roared. Even as he stood there, with the stick in his hands ready to swing, Derek knew that this was not an act motivated by courage. This was adrenaline, unconfined, and perceptible in his propulsory brain and the acid that gelled into a paste around his gums. "Airsehole, ye want some?" The taunts flew one-way across the room. Lex sat still. The giant's leering amusement, however, was gone. Samantha was distressed. The wrinklies winced and braced themselves for a massacre. Poor, poor Derek. But his grandad would be proud.

Lex reared up; his massiveness shrank the pub. He kept his distance from this idiotic youth, whom was only probably trying to influence the barmaid's affections with such foolish gallantry. She was, Lex did concede, very pretty. "Listen tae me, dough ball," said the giant.

"Ah couldnae gie a fleein fuck aboot you or yer fuckin pal James. Ah want tae ken faar his aal girlfriend is. An associate o mine. She said 'er name wis Joanne, bit ah've got a feelin that she wis tellin me porkies, like. Ah'm sure you ken fa ah'm spickin aboot, an' ye'd better fuckin tell me fit ye ken aboot 'er – fuckin sharpish." The giant was unguarded about the details of his mission, spinning his yarn regardless of the three wrinklies and the barmaid. All potential witnesses for the prosecution. If they'd be so dumb. "Ah need tae fin' 'er. Ah'm gaan tae fin' 'er. She tuk a lot o money fae me, Derek, an' ah'm gaan tae get it back. So, ye're gaan tae hae tae help me oot here by tellin me somethin fuckin useful."

"Aye, a'right. Ah'll tell ye somethin," Derek replied. "Yer breath smells like semen. Suck less dick an' brush mair aften. 'At ony eese tae ye?" He held the cue tighter than ever. "Ah dinnae ken fuckin onythin. Jist leave ma mate alone, ye big prick. Jimmy's hid enough shite in his life withoot cunts like you comin up an' geein 'im mair grief. Noo jist fuck off."

"Tough guy, ah dinnae think ye ken fa ye're speakin tae here."

"We'll pit money on 'at, will we? Ye're some monkey sphincter fae Dundee caad Lex MacMongofuck or some shit. Ah couldnae gie a bag o wanks fa ye are, or hoo fuckin hard ye're supposed tae be. Ye got me on the wrang fuckin wik, chummy, ah'm tellin ye. An', ah fuckin sweer it, ah will wrap 'is fuckin stick aroon yer gigantic fuckin heid. Cunt, ye'd best jist scamper while ye kin still fuckin waak."

The lad's jibes were pushing it, to say the very least. Lex didn't know whether to laugh or hobble the guy. Probably the latter then the former. He said, "So, ye ken ma name, eh, Derek? She must've bin in touch."

"She wrote a fuckin letter – 'at wis it. She could be in Aca-fuckin-pulco fir aa ah ken, or care fir 'at maitter."

"Funny, ah dinnae believe ye." The giant took an area-gobbling step forward. They were a mere whisker from striking range of one another. "Faar is she? Faar's yer fuckin pal? Faar's ma money, ye wee fuckin jobby?"

The barmaid, the oldies and the pool cue-wielding drunkard did concentrate squarely on the giant whose voice alone would often times be weapon enough to secure the fulfilment of his aims. They could plainly see that Lex's forbearance was worn to the nub, and that Derek was either going to have to drop the stick or use it.

The door burst open. Merriment bulged inwards from the darkness. The eye of the pub shifted to the entrance and to the three figures that came vaulting in like the circus.

Derek's hands loosened around the pole. The sight of his friends had precipitated his resoluteness into tottering. This blip enabled Lex to make his move. The giant pounced at Derek, ripping the pool cue from his grasp. He clutched the chest of the lad's T-shirt. Requiring only his right hand to do so, Lex hurtled the young man at the entering trio. The power of the throw, augmented by the weight of Derek, was enough to floor Freddy and Mo. Phil stood, knotted of tongue, over his fallen comrades; mirth had turned to alarm in an instant. He looked at the bartender; she shared his horror. The snarling giant, whom had paid Phil a visit a few days earlier, snapped the stick over his knee and thumped the shattered pieces off the linoleum.

"You, ye fat fuck," the giant yelled, and brought out a gun that had been hidden beneath his shirt and the waistband of his jeans, "lock the fuckin door."

Chapter 12

The society of men fractures, and two significant fragments are left awaiting judgement in the dust. Each man cowers upon his designated half. On one side, those who have killed; on the other, those who have not. Simplicity. Fifteen-year-old Scotty Thomson now shared the ground with the murderous minority. He had actually killed somebody – how nuts was that? Whatever else he got up to in his life, they could never dispossess him of that fact. Wee Scotty was a killer. It elevated and swelled the 5'3" boy to know that he had snubbed out the internal spark of some piss-scented, probable paedo. Even big brother, for all his notoriety, couldn't claim to have killed anyone. But Scotty could. He was now a murderer. He certainly was. Say it.

"Ah'm a fuckin murderer."

"Whoa." Alex fired an arm across Scotty, as though to save the poorly sighted at the pavement's edge. "Dinnae be crazy. Ye cannae ging aroon sayin 'at, Scotty. Some cunt'll fuckin hear ye."

Scotty swatted away his tall friend's slender bough. There's yer waarnin, pal.

Alex began, "Ah wis jist sayin - "

"Well, dinnae," Scotty concluded. "Ah dinnae fuckin need you tae tell me aff, beanpole. So fuckin shut it."

Alex unleashed his exasperation at the chastisement with an array of facial contortions towards the boats; his bitter scorn blended with the gloom like exhaust fumes in a tunnel. Scotty was far too riveted with last night's adventure to reprimand his sulking chum. Greet if ye like, faggot. The pair proceeded down the harbour road with nary a cloudy comment to be said. They shivered in their garments. Although Alex had the more padding, wearing a vest under his blue shirt, it was Scotty, with only a white T-shirt to soothe his torso, who appeared to be the better insulated.

The duo's contrast in height was punctuated by sunless lustre. Alex may only have been a year older than Scotty was, but the sporadic passer-by in the night would mistake the shadowy pair for being father and son, until immediate proximity revealed otherwise.

The brick.

In Scotty's claw; he had brought that brick downwards. He'd smashed the pishy cunt three times on the napper. Mushy yoke had seeped through cracked slivers of skull, like a gas main had ruptured through a city street, directly below a fruit and veg stall. He'd never seen a brain before. The others – the bunch o gays that they were – had scampered. When the lights had popped awake in surrounding windows, Scotty, equipped with the perfect presence of mind, had picked up the sodden rock and bolted. He had known then that the old man was either dead or dying: too messy to be anything other than. Euphoria had surged through Scotty, better than any E. Friskier than any Buckfast. Scotty remembered well how he had dashed for it. The road had pushed his soles along, faster and faster; flight. He'd felt both streamlined and enormous; unburdened and emboldened. He finally caught up with Alex and Piggy behind Central Primary School. Chris hadn't stopped. The coward had run all the way back to his doorstep. Scotty wasn't fond of Chris: the swotty knob-end. But Chris could play guitar, and Scotty couldn't. If Scotty was going to be the frontman in a band, he'd need to keep the mohicaned prick on side. Alex and Piggy had been panting in the moon-soaked courtyard, buoyed by the utter extremity of Scotty's actions. They had always treated their pint-sized chief with the fear and respect that he'd asked for, and their deference had been justified. Scotty's rule was now reinforced, like a potted plant had become a forest.

Afterwards, the three academy kids had went down to the harbour, prowling out of sight of the ambulance and police cars that would have scalped the roads in response to this unnerving turn of events. Scotty felt brilliantly gratified when he thought of the emergency services crawling at his feet. He'd chucked the brick as far out as he could into the rippling black. Then they had gone for a bag of chips and strolled home; the murder gleamed ever more explicitly subsequent to the initial sibilant haze. They each knew that they had passed under an archway that evening that most would never even approach. They were hardcore. A plain above.

The pair continued onwards, minus the need to communicate aloud. But where was Chris tonight? Scotty pondered. Piggy had work. He'd gone off to stack shelves for peanuts until midnight in the supermarket. Shite job. And Alex was always free. Rich wanker had never worked a day in his life. But Chris? Hiv tae get up early, ken? he'd told Alex. Toories, ye see? Too tired tae muck aboot the night, ken? Excuses, excuses. Scotty didn't want to have to start worrying about that cunt.

Christopher's disfavour of their treatment of the old man had been conspicuous at the time; but would the sissy flounder and go sobbing to the coppers? Hopefully, Mr Fraser would think better than to implicate himself like that. Chris was, however, something of a paradoxical commodity. He was shy and extroverted, awkward and outgoing. The twat was three years Scotty's senior, and was, as Scotty enjoyed telling him, aa brains an' neen common sinse. Chris wasn't like Scotty. Much to Scotty's chagrin, Chris had the ability to appeal to Alex and Piggy's kinder and soppier dimensions. He was a bad influence.

Too tired? Scotty had a milk round that he had to get up at the crack of dawn for, and then he was supposed to go to school. Scotty's brother told him that they more or less all just slept on their feet at Toories, so undemanding was the job. And this was going to be the year that Scotty sat his standard grades, and they were projected to be tough. Not that he cared about the outcome of those exams, but if anyone had cause to complain about fatigue, it was Scotty. He likely wouldn't even sit his exams; if he could get away with it. Then he'd be straight up to the college to do his fishing course. He'd get a birth aboard a trawler or, if he was lucky, a purser and make some money. Then he'd be able to bankroll his band when he was onshore. He'd even put some of his raps down on paper. His friends agreed with his assessment that they were quite great.

The one negative aspect of last night's enterprise was that the old troll had spoiled Scotty's good trainers with his blood. He'd tried washing them in the sink. Unfortunately, Scotty had triumphed only in modifying the tint of his footwear to a hue that would absolutely not be of his own choosing. He wasn't going to throw them out, though. They'd cost him a fortune, and they were still new. The old bastard had paid him back, however, with the contents of his wallet, which The Tart's bandit was now in custody of. Collections were tomorrow night; the customers' tips would assuage his grief.

Luk at 'em boats. Big fuckers. Smaa fuckers. Masts. Caibins. Wheelhooses. Their hulls sexy-danced with the tyres that rimmed the piers like liquorice on novelty cakes. Scotty could handle that. Alex necked a couple of pills. Scotty couldn't handle those; they gave him too much of a sore head for his rounds. They were okay, though, if you didn't have to get up at half past four in the morning. Alex didn't have to worry about anything. He'd get on a rig with his dad and rake in hundreds of grands a year for sitting on his arse and checking the occasional dial. The affluent dick.

Vicious cunt as well, though, to be fair. Credit where credit's due. Like that Setterda nicht faan they were aa millin aboot up on the Broadgate an' 'is junkie came up to 'em an' started lippin aff. Alex wis the first een tae smack the cunt. They kicked the livin fuck oot o 'im, like. Alex, Piggy, Chris – aye, Chris an' aa – they aa threw in a few punches, like. It wis a fuckin right beatin. The skeggy bastard. Aifter knockin the fuck oot o 'im fir aboot quarter an oor, the junkie gets up an' rins awaa. Fair enough. So, fit happens? The gleckit cunt braaks a shop windae an' comes back doon wi a golf shoe. A fuckin golf shoe. The boys jist fuckin laughed at 'im an' gave 'im anither beatin. Fucked his jaa up pretty bad, ken? Clicks fin he spicks, or so folk were sayin. Serves the cunt richt, though. If ye're gaan tae fuckin mess, like, ye taak fit ye get. Fuck me, ye even learn 'at shite at skweel. 'At wis the physics.

And, sure enough, Scotty had gone to school today, even if it was just for the opening act of it. He'd been eager to get a feel for the hate and anger and confusion propagated by the murder that he himself had perpetrated. Scotty had been punctual this morning. Aye, his fellow pupils and the teachers and the rest of the Broch and Britain and everywhere else would be disconsolate and enraged due to the old man having been annihilated in the street like that. Such inhumanity. Scotty couldn't wait to hear their bleatings. But then, of course, the movie star had burst his balloon by doing the hari-kari on the same night. Moneyed fuckin asshole. What a cunt. The girls were all weeping and bubbling because of that fuckin cock, and not because of what Scotty had done. Only a handful of his peers had discussed the old man and had argued that his demise was an even bigger tragedy than that of a selfish thespian whom had dived into his grave. Scotty had assented, aggressively. The day had riled him up. The majority hadn't heard, or had the capacity to care, about Scotty's work of violence, such was the response to the dead celebrity. Bastards. Bunch o bastards. Scotty had killed a man and he could hardly gloat. It wasn't right.

Although, Piggy had phoned to inform him that there was a sublime write-up in the evening's Northern Echo. Piggy could tell that it was well written because he'd needed to consult with the dictionary for, seemingly, every other word. Scotty had found this most heartening, and ordered his mate to keep a hold of the newspaper. In fact, keep a hud o a few o 'em fae yer work. He'd sign them for his disciples after he'd broken through. The piece was, as he'd been notified, joint front-page material. There were also, apparently, pride-filling snippets on the Scottish news. Scotty's handiwork was wedged between a Perth fire that had killed a family of four and Billy, a seal that thinks it's a dog, which had been adopted by a Stornoway community. There were bits about a blossoming crisis in the North Sea. Shrinking quotas threatened the existence of fishing as an industry, allegedly. Then it was back to the late prince of Hollywood.

A bobby on the TV had insisted that he would apprehend 'Raymond's' killer or killers. "We are currently following up several leads into our inquiry. We urge the public to come forward with any information that could lead to possible arrests." Fat chance, ye fucker. Nae witnesses. Nae weapon. Neen fuckin arrests. Only he, Alex, Piggy and Chris knew the truth. All could be trusted, Scotty thought. Surely, surely.

And even if they couldn't be, and he was caught, what did that matter? He'd get a couple of years in Polmont – wherever the bollocks that was? Scotty would just have to slash a weegie or two on his first day; he'd be the daddy before supper time. And having that kind of a back story wisnae really gaan tae dee his rap-star credibility ony damage, wis it? In saying that, however, Scotty thought that he would, perhaps, rather not go to prison; given the choice. Scotty, then, would prefer that his accomplices kept their traps shut. They'd better do.

Alex had stopped to urinate in the doorway of what transpired to be a solicitor's office. "Got a light?" Scotty asked him. Alex rummaged about in a bottomless pocket of his baggy jeans with his free hand. He then delivered the plastic lighter to his pal. "Got a fag tae ging wi it?" Alex passed him his cigarette packet. Scotty took two fags: one for his lips; the other for behind his ear. Alex zipped himself up. Scotty handed back the woodbines. He lit his cigarette. The wavering flame decked Scotty's features as a moving spotlight, searching for escapees. In the background, crow's-nests and antennas scratched at the tarry heavens like quills loafing in ink bottles. Alex didn't bother asking for his lighter back.

Scotty had finished his cigarette and had cast it at a careering motorcyclist when they'd arrived at the entrance of their destination: Dunce's Bar. The exterior of this building was more welcoming than that of The Tart's. If The Tart was a pillbox, Dunce's Bar was the medical tent. Alex never wanted to be the first to enter grown-up establishments. He hung back against a white wall, allowing Scotty to swan in before him. Alex shuffled in closely behind his friend, like a ladder hiding behind a step. The hardened paint that was the frost upon their skin disintegrated at the door. Alex considered with relief that the pub was a lot less busy than normal. He'd a tendency to feel nervous and out of sorts when adults were about. Young adults. Especially ones like that wanker from The Tart. Alex and Scotty had been reduced to looking like a right pair of twats. The cunt would've been trying to make himself look big in front of the barmaid. She was a babe.

The Tart incident would be rectified shortly, however. This was the bonus of socialising with Gazza Thomson's wee brother: access to a free and effective bodyguard. Plus, as the happy sack of weekend jollies halfway down Alex's leg would attest to, Gazza was a handy middleman.

Like the outside, the interior of Dunce's Bar was far more hospitable than the edifice from whence they'd come. This pub was larger and was endowed with novel suggestions in regards to its decor. The place was fresh like a nunnery; everything was unspoiled and sanitary. Fluorescent blue bulbs slid down the walls and hung over the twin pool tables, which were not in use. The Dunce's approximation of beatnik chic was complemented by framed effigies of deceased jazz musicians that were dotted around the room like the studs on a hip girlie's belt. The pool tables got moved off to the side at the weekends to forge a makeshift dancefloor. Alex knew this from experience. He made fists inside his pockets. He need not worry. He had his fake ID with him.

Encephalon. Demolished brains. The colour of the old man's devastated thought-palace sprang back before his eyes like windshield wipers. As it had done during Alex's morning maths class. His teacher's bald, moustached head had started to leak before him, as though something were being hatched prematurely. Mr Jappy had witnessed the boy's sudden tremor of revulsion and had sent him off for some cold water. The episode had inspired Alex to skip the afternoon with Scotty and Piggy. This wasn't some kind of guilt-manifestation either, because, genuinely, Alex didn't care that the old man was dead. He didn't. He really couldn't give a thimble full of rat jism for the old, dead cunt. Scotty had bricked the guy. And Alex had egged him on. So fuck. But the image of spilled brains was driving him to distraction.

The pills did not aid him as they might have done. Alex's mind seemed to be stuck on a loop.

It was sort of like that night about six months ago when they'd all been sitting about in Alex's house watching films and that documentary had come on about those kids who had Progeria or whatever it was called and everyone had started laughing and taking the piss because the children looked like aliens on account of their shrivelled skin and bulging eyes that was as a result of their disease that he was sure was called Progeria and that made them age ten times faster than normal and they'd all laughed and joked and everyone went home and that night he couldn't sleep because those kids' faces kept appearing like bumper stickers on the inside of his skull and he'd begun to snivel and cry and he'd had nightmares for the rest of the week.

He'd felt guilty then: he could admit to that. That must've been guilt. But not now, not in this instance. They'd been disabled bairns, those Progerians. That had been different. This was different. Last night, it was just some old drunk. He couldn't care. Care couldn't care care couldn't less.

Alex blinked hard several times, as though attempting to get the lock of a sliding door to catch. He opened them again. The lumpy red gore was replaced with the indigo and purple of Dunce's Bar.

A projection screen absorbed the far wall beyond the pool tables. It exhibited a panel of D-listers in an UK studio offering their cogitations about the dearly departed. In front of the screen, there was a head: a block over which you could bend the wing of a jet. Scotty and Alex approached the head and sat around its circular table.

Alex sat with his back to the screen, facing both Thomson brothers. He did knead the denim around his knees. Big Gazza was about twice the age of Wee Scotty. They were, indeed, closer in appearance to parent and child than actual brothers, and even then they didn't resemble each other that much. Same mother; diverse fathers. They'd shared a mixer, but it was disparate builders whom had shovelled in the cement.

Gazza wrapped his fingers around his half-empty pint and chugged it down. His brown leather coat grabbed Gazza like caramel laced over video tapes. He'd confiscated the jacket a while ago from a fool who'd issued a drunken challenge to him; he'd confronted the apologetic man when both were sober, and had received the garment in lieu of dispensing any permanent disfigurement. His good eye rolled from Alex to Scotty. The pirate-patch still gave Alex the creeps.

The barman was engrossed in a book at his post. Alex, principally, had to be alert when the bouncers were on, which was, in the main, on a Friday and a Saturday night, and sometimes a Sunday if there was a holiday. Some other guys capered at a table, though their behaviour was stilted, as if they were seated by the grannies at a function. One of them had a bandage across his eyebrow.

Gazza was unreadable. Was this subdued anger? Wordless rage? Inward reflection? Equanimity? Was he amused by something? Or disappointed? Or was the hard man simply tired? In Alex's observations of the subject, Gazza's moods were so erratic that it was impossible to predict his state of mind during the periods when the lunatic was just sitting still. The instances whereupon he was jumping around and attacking people made for facile prognosis.

Scotty's disposition was easier to deconstruct. Alex's short-ass chum was glowing with the immortal confidence that sprouted out from his nasty soul like a nicked artery whenever Scotty was near the myth, the legend, that was his older brother.

"Fit you boys up tae the night?" Gazza asked. He lifted his frightening gaze above Alex to the animated sheet.

"Nae much," Alex replied, wishing that he hadn't sounded so soft. Alex did a second take. "Fit are you up tae, like?"

Gazza spoke at Alex, as though he were really addressing some imaginary figure behind the floppy-haired youngster. "Waatchin TV." Alex noticed – although, he could've been wrong – a lull in the wrecking machine's voice that was, in part, sorrowful. But Alex refused to believe that Gazza could be depressed over one dead ponce.

Scotty, blind to his brother's anguish, leered in like vermin at the boundary of the dump. "We wis jist o'er at The Tart the noo, ken?" The teen lingered upon the story, anticipating his sibling's wild reaction. "We wis playin the bandit, like. Fuckin thing's rigged – ah'm fuckin sure o it. Lost fuckin heaps. Onywye, we wis playin the bandit, right? Jist playin awaa. Then 'is cunt starts in wi his shoutin an' sweerin. We're jist standin 'ere like 'fit the fuck?', ken? Bit the guy keeps on geein us shit, like. He threatens tae punch us an' iverythin."

"He threatened ye's?" The panellists grieved above Gazza. The feedback that Scotty had educed was similar to when someone strives to talk with another at a deafening gig. The eruption of fury that Scotty had expected had materialised as more of an apathetic dribble. This didn't pass Scotty by undetected.

"Aye, he wis richt fierce, like." Scotty leaned towards propaganda to whip up some hysteria. "Really startin trouble an' 'at. He wis a proper dick. Ah tellt 'im fa ma brither wis, bit he said he couldnae gie a fuck. Says he'd knock the fuck oot o us an' you, nae buther."

Curiously, it was to his brother's friend rather than to Scotty himself that Gazza looked for confirmation of this account. Alex shrugged, then nodded, humbled that Gazza should seek his opinion.

"'At's pretty much fit he said, aye," Alex concurred.

"Is he still at The Tart?"

"Should be," Scotty answered; his fervour grew once more. "Think he wis tryin tae get awaa wi the quine ahin' the bar."

"Fit dis he luk like?" Gazza inquired. His passion for strife was sluggish today. "Wid ah ken 'im tae see 'im?"

"Ah think ah've seen 'im afore, like," Alex replied. "His name's Derek, ah think."

"Derek?"

"Aye. Ah think so."

"Broon, scruffy kina hair?"

"Aye," Scotty said, as if having glimpsed movement from a hibernating pet. "'At's 'im. Said he'd kick yer ass aa o'er the place. A richt big moo on the cunt."

Gazza watched the people on the screen. They moved about and said some stuff, none of which Gazza found to be very interesting. He barely registered the existence of Scotty and his pal. Some of their dispatch had stuck, however. Most of the time, though, Gazza had been thinking about his ex, the army and the fact that this time tomorrow he'd have been made redundant.

"Derek, eh?"

"Aye."

Fuck it. A fecht's a fecht. "Let's go."

Chapter 13

"Ah said, 'Let's fuckin go'," the giant bellowed at Derek and his mates. "In 'at fuckin booth wi ye's." As none of the three oldies were adjudged by the Dundonian to be anything of a threat, they were allowed to remain settled in the far corner; not that there was a 'far', specifically, in the cramped lung of The Tart. Samantha from Ireland, France, Germany, Austria and Dover froze behind the bar; the outburst of menace had impaired her hinges and melted her stomach into a lava lamp. She saw Derek, Phil and the other two, whom she had yet to make the acquaintance of, slip around the booth at the left side of the doorway. Only the slighter friend whose black hair was whipped into a side-parting bared his palms in obedience to the pistol, which the massive stranger extended towards their faces. Its sight followed their stuttering progress. The young men trundled around the horseshoe bench as though they were being ushered home by the police. The black-haired man's eyes did not avert from the mechanical cyclops. He caught his navy cords on the table. His blond pal prodded him to keep moving. Phil, in his enormous coat, was the first to sit; he scooted round, anti-clockwise, so that Derek, Mo and Freddy may do the same.

"Fit's aa 'is aboot, like?" Mo asked; his hands were still raised while the others' were down by their sides or resting on the square table in front of them. Freddy scorned him with a look. Mo let his mitts fall. They pointed downwards like the collar that emerged from the neck of his green jumper. He asked again, "Fit's gaan on here?" Mo was like a granny, badgering the postie about a hike in the price of stamps.

Lex's frothing temper simmered as a pot placed on another hob. "You," he gestured at Mo with the gun, "shut the fuck up. An' you," the gun addressed Derek, "faar's ma fuckin money?"

The blond man reclined as though someone under the table had yanked at his jeans. "Oh, is 'at fit aa 'is cairry on's aboot, eh?" Freddy exclaimed. His jigsaw was complete. "So you're the guy fa's lukin fir 'at bitch Lori: Jimmy's aal quine?"

"Lori?" The sight shifted. "Fit aa dee ye's ken aboot 'er? Faar is she?"

"Fuck knows, pal," Freddy said, able to relax more now that he had some sort of a handle on things. It was as though it had just dawned on him that he did, actually, have an alibi for the authorities. His grey T-shirt eased away from him like a vehicle in reverse. "No, no, like," he continued, "naebidy kens faar she's at. Aa fucker's better aff withoot 'er, like, if ye ask me."

Mo was wholly unenlightened about Jimmy's present tumult, having missed out on the update that Fat Ass had entertained Freddy with in the welder's car only ten minutes prior. Phil and Fred had arrived at The Tart at the same time as Mark, but they had travelled down separately from the banker. They'd phoned Mo's house when they'd been out on his street, set to give him a lift to the pub, as had been the plan. Mo had had to decline as he had SexxyMilf on his mobile; though he did not bid them that as his excuse for finding an alternative means of getting to The Tart. They knew nothing of her. He had to speak to his dad about something, he'd said. He'd walk; he'd meet them down there, and he had done. Before their convergence, however, Freddy had parked himself and Phil somewhere secluded so that Freddy could bind and smoke a joint. That was when Frederick had been made privy to these latest developments. Mo had sacrificed knowledge for phone sex, and he was baffled and clueless and scared. "Wid somebidy please fill me in here? Fa is 'is guy, an' how dis he ken Lori? Aa ither bastard seems tae ken fit's gaan on."

"We'll explain aifter." Phil's eyes drooped like pears under the visor of his hat.

"Anither time, Mo," Derek said. He was hunched behind the pint glasses and fruity bottles that the booth's previous occupants had excavated and denounced. His temper was still there; though humbled like an animal flogged. He noted Lex and the gun that could purge his loft in a second. "Ye dinnae need tae ken aathin jist noo."

"Mo," Freddy began, irrespective of Derek's proposal, "ye mine hoo Lori fucked off an' became a hoor?"

Mark nodded.

"Well, she's up tae 'er aal tricks. She ripped aff 'er pimp or dealer or…" Freddy pleaded to the giant for substantiation. "Fa did she rip aff?"

“Me. Faar is she?”

“Ye’ve bin tellt,” Derek replied. “Naebidy kens.”

Mo’s top lip squirmed like a crested wave. “Fit? His Lori ran aff again, like? Wi ’is guy’s money?”

“Aye,” Freddy said. “She tuk ’is lad’s pennies an’ ran tae buggery.”

“’At soons jist like ’er. Ken ’is, ah niver liked ’at quine. Thievin slut.” Mo, as Freddy had done, spread loose now that candles guided their shady path. “Is she in the Broch the noo?”

“No,” Derek snapped. “We dinnae ken faar she is. Naebidy dis.”

Mo scratched his vertex as though her location could be found within the neat folds of its turf. “Well, hiv ye tried ’er mam an’ dad’s hoose?”

“Mo, ye dildo, wid ye fuckin zip it. We’re nae on this bastard’s side, ye ken?” Derek roared this last statement into his friend’s ear.

Lex tipped forth with the gun. “Dinnae be aggravatin me, Derek.”

“Jeepers.” Mo twiddled a digit in a head-hole to squelch the reverberating words. “A’right, Derek; ’ere wis nae need fir ’at, min. Ah’m sittin right next tae ye, ken? Ah wis jist sayin that Lori could be wi ’er mam an’ dad. Okay? She could even be at Jimmy’s. Hiv ye tried ’ere?”

Derek looked to the ceiling for guidance. Then he glanced beyond Lex to Samantha. He wanted to smile at her. He exhaled.

Fat Ass made an effort to allay his chum into taciturnity. “Mo, please jist hud yer weesht, wid ye? Jist for the noo, eh?”

“An’ fit hiv ah deen, like?” Mo protested. “Ah’m jist tryin tae help us oot here. Ah mean, ah’m on the side o faiver’s pointin a gun at me at the time. Ah’d raither ’is guy fin’s Lori an’ gets his money back than us gettin shot wi bullets. Dee you eens want tae sit here wi a gun in yer face aa night?” Mo picked at a label of one of the bottles on the table. “’Is is jist shite, like. Ah dinnae like ’is at aa.”

"Hoo much did Lori steal fae ye, like?" Freddy asked the pillar of denim, leather and stubble.

"Too much." The gun hung in Derek's direction. "Faar dis Jimmy stay? Fit aboot the mam an' dad: faar dis Lori's folk bide?" He said her name distrustfully. "Listen tae yer pal, 'ere, Derek. The sooner ah get ma money, the sooner ye's kin get back tae waatchin yer cartoons an' playin aboot in the dubs. 'At'll maak aa cunt happy, eh?"

Derek laboured to keep his voice reasonable. "Bit ah a'ready tellt ye, she's nae here. The only correspondence ony cunt's hid wi 'er his bin through one letter, an' 'at wis jist tae waarn 'er parents that some twat might be lukin for 'er. She niver said onythin aboot hoo much she tuk fae ye, or faar she's gaan tae next. She jist said that she's stolen some cash an' that she's leavin fir good. Aye, niver comin back. 'At's the absolute truth. Fit mair kin ah say tae prove that ah'm nae fuckin leein tae ye?"

The jukebox whistled away on a full stomach. On the TV, one could only guess at the reverence with which the dead movie star was being lavished.

"Gie me the addresses," Lex said.

"Get tae fuck," was the response. "No."

"Derek," said Freddy, "stop mouthin aff tae the boy. Ah'm nae losin ma life for Lori or Jimmy or ony ither fucker. Ah've a faimily, ye cunt."

"Freddy, suck ma nuts."

"Dinnae spick tae me like 'at, ye feel hoor."

"Ah'm nae fuckin jokin wi ye, sunshine," the gun proclaimed. "Ye'd better start coughin up streets an' numbers. Ah'm losin patience here, an' ma finger's gettin a bit nervy roon the trigger." To illustrate this assertion, Lex tapped his index finger against the side of the black pistol. "Ah'm tired o 'is bloody cairry on, a'right? Ah want tae fin' 'er an' get the fuck oot o 'is fuckin mess o a toon."

"Says the cunt fae Dundee."

"Twice 'is wik ah've driven up here tae to luk fir 'er," Lex said. "'At's a total o eight oors in four days; right up tae the bastardin back o beyond. Ah'm nae exactly delighted aboot 'at, even though ah dee like taakin the motor for a spin." The giant rubbed his chin. "Noo, ah'm fairly sure that ye's hiv seen 'is scenario in some gash film or ither: ah'll gie ye three seconds tae tell me fit ah need tae ken. If ye's dinnae, ah'll shoot the four o ye's between the legs. Straightforward, eh? An' 'at is the fuckin truth."

The black hole attached to the giant's hand stared at Derek. It instilled within him the image of a U-boat periscope. Derek could feel the room drawing delicately away from him, as though he'd inquired of its inhabitants if anyone had seen the pin for his grenade. The seriousness hit; the instinct for self-preservation took over. Both Mo and Freddy's buttocks elbow-shuffled gradually along the cushion. Fat Ass moved a touch to his right. No one, for all their compassion and affection for the young drunkard, wanted to be showered in a geyser of his exploding fluids.

"One."

"Tell 'im, Derek," said Mo. "He disnae luk like he's prickin aboot."

Derek was still.

"Ah'll fuckin tell the guy if you winnae," Freddy declared. "Lori's nae oor problem."

Derek pressed his fingertips into the table as if about to perform a song.

"Two."

Phil recalled how Jimmy had been a few nights ago in his flat. He enlisted the enthusiasm that a person invents when being interviewed for a job that they really don't want, but need. "Derek, we'll hiv tae say somethin. Jist gie 'im the addresses. Fir fuck sake, it's oot o oor hands noo."

Derek winked at the lovely Irish lass: rendered inert.

"Two-an'-three-fuckin-quaarters, you stupid arsehole."

A voice blurted out, "55 Kennedy Crescent." It was Mo who had bent under the pistol's arrogant gaze. "'At's 'er mam an' dad's hoose."

Derek yelled at him. "Mo, you fuckin halfwit. Why'd ye tell 'im 'at?"

"He wis gaan tae shoot ye, ye dog's egg."

"Wis he fuck," Derek insisted. "Wi aabidy here? He wis testin ma mettle."

Fat Ass agreed with the neat fellow. "Ah dinnae ken, like, Derek. Ah think he wis gaan tae ging fir the trigger."

The giant's gun was lowered, as though one of the ropes holding it to its port had been released. The weapon remained aimed, vaguely, at Derek, however. The tension did not flutter. The oldies and the barmaid watched the activity around the far table with something of a fixed wince.

"Wis ye really gaan tae shoot 'im?" Freddy was disgusted, like his father had just come out to him.

"Ah still might." Lex's bubble-free sink barely hinted at a torrent of ardour, and, likewise, his reply gave little indication of any hidden depths of sentiment. "A'right; 55 Kennedy Crescent means precisely fuck aal tae me, so een o you buffoons kin taak us 'ere."

"Hear 'at, Derek?" Mo felt thoroughly vindicated. "See? He wis gaan tae shoot ye."

"No," Derek said, disregarding Mo's comment. "Lori's parents are decent enough folk, despite fit they spawned. Ye're gaan tae leave 'em alone."

The gun rose, like a grandad's cane to reprimand his progeny. "Dee ye want tae die, son? Is 'at fit it is? Did somebidy pinch yer pencil case wi the Transformers mannies on it? Ye really depressed aboot it an' noo ye want tae end it aa? Is 'at it? 'Cos ye're in luck, pal. Ah kin help ye oot 'ere."

"No." Derek smirked at the giant, as when he'd discovered that the blood on his sheets was not from a scrap but a screw. "'At's nae it at aa, ye giraffe testicle."

"Derek," Lex said, "they've got a sayin up in Orkney: dinnae wave yer fud in yer brither's face faan he's got a drink in 'im. Comprende? Quit wi the lip. Ye're nae a fuckin hero."

"Ah'm nae tryin tae be a hero," Derek replied. "Ah'm aboot the least heroic cunt ye're iver likely tae meet. It's nae in ma nature. Bit 'ere's nae need fir ye tae be butherin 'er mam an' 'er dad. 'Em folk hiv suffered plinty o'er the heids o 'at quine. An' 'ere's nae need tae be geein Jimbo a hard time eether. He's anither cunt fa could dee wi a break, like. Lori's nae here." Derek scraped his tines back across the table towards his wrists. "Face it, ye grite fuckin lummox: she's got yer money an' she's gone. Ah'm sorry, bit, by ma reckonin, 'at's jist your tough titty."

Mo employed a calculated spot of grovelling to facilitate the termination of this situation and to encourage the peevish character to head south once more. "Luk, we'll help ye oot, mister. Derek, wid ye jist stop bein troublesome? We jist want rid o 'is guy. Nae affence, like. Dinnae provoke 'im."

"Troublesome? Mo, ah'm nae a fuckin mortgage. 'Is tosser's nae a client. Ye're nae brokerin ony deals here. 'Ere's nae commission. 'Is guy kin get fucked."

The gun descended: a danger only to the floor. "Ye're in a brave mood the day, ah'll gie ye 'at, Del Boy. A bad wik, did ye say?"

"Fairly awful, aye."

One of the oldies spoke up. "He buried his granda on Monda." It was the gent with the small, shrivelled puss. Patrick Hendry, an ex-fisherman who craved nothing more than a good, solid moan about anything and everything. The room looked at Pat, like he'd come crashing in on a bike. The old man's glory wilted. The attention returned to Derek and his immense interrogator.

"Yer grandad died, eh?"

"Aye."

"Hard luck."

"Ah'm touched."

"Right," Lex said. "'At's ma sympathies oot the wye. Ye're comin wi me tae meet Lori's folks. See if they're ony mair use than you four fuckin bam-pots. If no, like ah said, ah'll shoot ye."

"Aye? Wi seven witnesses?" Derek replied. "Ah'm sure ye will."

Something of a laugh had thought to flee from Lex then didn't, like a horse that had halted just before the jump. "Derek, ye wee twat, dinnae suffer under the misconception that ah'm nae well versed in 'is sort o thing. Ah kin assure ye, ah am. 'Ere's nae empty-gesturin wi me, cunt; ah'll hollow oot yer heid wi a blunt knife an' dee the same tae ivery ither fucker in 'is room, if need be. An' ah'll get awaa wi it. Experience, ken? Ah'm cliver enough tae be sly, an' dumb enough nae tae be hassled by a conscience. An' dee ah honestly luk like the kina cunt that's feert o jail? Ah'm the reason prisons are scary. So aa 'is pissin aboot'll come back tae haunt ye, gobby. Ah will, hooiver, feel slightly less inclined tae dee awaa wi ye if, by the end o the night, ah've got ma money back. Noo, ye gaan tae steady yer gums an' be o some assistance, or fit?"

The audience willed Derek to choose the box that they all knew to be the correct one. But Derek was on the alcohol and roused by his slide down the vertical groove, and he was ready for mischief. Young knight Sir Derek was in a less than co-operative mood. He replied, with crevices between each syllable, "Fuck you, cock-slit."

The audience cringed, as if the failure buzzer had rung. The giant's arm swung up as though his fist had been fired from a clay pigeon sling. In a flash, the pistol went from pointing at the floor to being pushed into Derek's forehead. Fat Ass, Freddy and Mo recoiled further from their friend. It was as if the datum relating to a cohort's soiling of themselves had only now coagulated into a smell. Puny squeals crawled out from their shrinking chests like fox cubs too meagre to leave their lairs. Derek stiffened against the cyclops. Its tough rim bit into his brow like an eagle's beak.

A scream. "Don't."

Lex scythed the gun towards the wellspring of that feminine cry. He pulled the trigger. A vodka bottle blew up less than a foot from Samantha's head. The whine and crash of the bullet mingled seamlessly with the jukebox. A shriek lodged in her throat like a pen lid; a tsunami of spirits and glass splashed behind her. Small red trails appeared across her neck and the left side of her face. She stroked her flesh; she felt the damp. Samantha whimpered.

Lex turned back just in time to catch Derek in the middle of a noble lunge. The giant brought the heavy gun down upon the youth's skull. The dry thud was chased by a wet smash as Derek's body collapsed onto the table and thwacked the tumblers asunder.

His pals didn't move. The oldies didn't stir. The girl sobbed.

"You," Lex shouted at the barmaid, his gun in the air, "turn aff 'at fuckin machine. Cannae hear masel fuckin think." Samantha reached out; she flicked a switch as though she expected it to grab her when she touched it. The music was superseded by the quiet, incessant chatter of the television, like avian flirting across a digital field. A celebrity chef warbled on about her admiration for expired what's-his-face. "You his fuckin woman or somethin, eh?" Samantha thawed and responded; she shook as though from hypothermia. Phil melded his hands together. "Next time," the giant jerked the pistol like a can of spray paint at an underpass, "ah winnae fuckin miss."

Fat Ass, Freddy and Mo watched the limp body of their friend. They waited for any sign that he was still alive and that the giant hadn't belted his cognitive faculties clean out of his coconut. Mo placed a wee hand on Derek's back, and impelled a long, sleepy lament from Derek's lips, like a bovine's gaseous rectal expulsion. Derek didn't move. He sprawled across the table in a pistol-whip doze.

The gun sliced the air as if to parry a sabre. Mo put up his forearms as though to block a jab. His porcelain features were like a gathering tempest.

"Ah taak it you boys hiv niver seen a gun afore, far less hid one pinted at ye's?" There was a touch of the cybernetic-organism to the giant's delivery; he didn't appear to enjoy or abhor his role. "It's nae fine, is it?" Lex said. "Nae cunt likes haein tae talk intae a shooter. It's embarrassin mair than onythin else, isn't it? Aye, ah ken it is. Fuck aa ye kin dee aboot it, though, is 'ere? Jist hiv tae sit 'ere an' dee fitiver the guy wi the gun says. Mair tae the pint, ye hiv tae aiwyes assume that the boy is willin tae use it. Well, get 'at intae yer heids right noo. Ah'm nae a nice guy, an' blastin you bastards disnae really pit me up or doon. Ah hope 'at's clear tae ye's." The boys conceded this declaration without pause. "Right, you – fit the fuck's yer name? Is it 'Mo' they've been caain ye?"

"Aye: Mo. Or Mark."

"Mark?"

"Aye. 'At's mair like ma business name, though."

"Right, Mo, ye're comin wi me. We'll go past yer mate Jimmy's hoose, 'en we'll see fit like 'at fuckin hoor's mam an' dad are. Get the fuck up."

Mo complied. He stood up, feebly, like when he'd removed himself from that hospital chair after learning of the tragic outcome of his cousin's Aviemore skiing accident. His knees clattered between the table and his friend's legs. The gun followed him to the door as though the weapon and the banker had related aerials.

"You two," Fat Ass and Freddy scrutinised Mo as he trudged towards the door ahead of the giant, "stay here, 'cos ah'll be comin back. Nae fuckin aboot. An' ah dinnae think that ah hiv tae tell ony o ye's nae tae phone the pigs. If ah come back here an' smell bacon, ye's must ken fit'll happen. Right? Right. Move it, asshole."

Mo went to turn the latch.

"Wait," Phil called. Unbelievably, Lex mused, the fat beaker of excreta got to his feet. Lex dropped the pistol to his side. None of these stooges were worthy of a slap, much less a pellet.

"Fit dee ye want?" Lex said, seeing all sides of the room without having to shift. He could see the old men to his right, braced as though at the induction of a fifth ace in a high stakes game. Lex saw the pretty barmaid, somewhere behind him, crying softly into a rag that she had used to wipe her cuts with. He could see the weakling clutching at the lock in front of him; everyone was aware, Mo especially, that he wouldn't try anything intrepid or sneaky. And he studied the barman on his left; he whom had lied to him earlier in the week.

"Fit are ye gaan tae dee fin ye fin' oot that Lori's nae in the Broch?" asked Pavarotti in the baseball cap. "That naebidy really dis ken faar she's at?" Lex was glad to hear that this fatso, big as he was, lacked the insubordinate vim of the concussed mop-top. "Are ye jist gaan tae caa it quits an' leave?"

"Ah kin assure ye o one thing," Lex replied. "Whether ah fin' Lori or nae, somebidy's gaan tae pay me. Ye got 'at, fat fuck?"

"Ma name's nae Fat Fuck." Phil unfastened his coat to display his favourite flannel shirt. "It's Fat Ass."

Lex thought that the pub might subside into neurotic hysteria, which he also would quite possibly lose his spine to. But the room stayed silent and fearful. The lardy boy's quip wasn't enough to undo the canny ambience of terror that Lex had hewed into their souls.

"Right, Mo," Lex said, stuffing the pistol back down the waistband of his jeans. "Get it deen."

Four rhythmic slaps fell upon the entrance. Mo let go of the latch and looked to the giant for further instructions. Lex clasped a thumb to his belt. The Tart concentrated on the door and puzzled over who this latest visitor could be. Was that Alfie, or perhaps another of their contemporaries? the oldies wondered. More drunks? More trouble? Samantha thought. Pagan? pondered a depleted Phil. Lex knew, at least, that it wasn't the police. It sounded like a sloth was rapping at the door; the weight of its arm and its customary idleness hindering the speed at which it knocked. Thirty seconds passed. The lingering, open-handed strikes returned. The visitor was persistent in his lazy way.

Lex nodded to Mo. The young man reached for the lock and twisted it. Lex's thumb didn't leave his belt. The door crept inwards. Freddy craned his neck round the booth to get a first peek at this evening's newest gift. It might, he thought, be a person to bring some jocularity and logic to proceedings.

The door yawned. The visitor appeared like a lump of coal in a pocket. The harbour lights and the blue wash of the moon made him glint in places. The man was no bigger than Mo was, but appeared to be of a sicklier condition than the banker. His pale features emerged from a tangle of dark facial hair like dollops of cream cheese dripped onto a litter of pumas. The vines that began at his peak cascaded down as far as did those that started around his muzzle. His fashion style was as indeterminate as his purpose for arrival. A knee-length, black, leather coat overhung a vest and polyester bottoms. He also wore brown sandals with white socks. Just the way that he stood there, as though bereft of vital bones, spoke of ravaged health. He was like a papier-mâché doll that was sinking into itself. The man stared at the pavement; sporadically, his body quavered. Was the man crying? Lex queried. The Tart gazed out at the man as if they all shared a lens of pay-to-use binoculars upon the ridge of a tower. In time, the man's legs warmed into slush and he broke into a nimble stride. The Tart's most recent customer went straight to the bar, giving the Dundee behemoth not a glance.

Lex inspected this newcomer as though he'd just been slighted. The man held onto the bar like it was the handrail of a ship. Under his scraggy hair, the man was plainly older than 'Fat Ass' and his cronies, though was, possibly, younger than the giant himself. Lex could tell by the looks that ricocheted between the trio of young men that they knew this pathetic stranger.

Sensing that this likely heroin-fancying butt-perforation had nothing to do with his adventure, Lex gestured for Mo to leave. Mo skulked out of the pub as if he were stepping into the headmaster's office with bruised knuckles. Derek was still out cold. Lex departed with a warning for Fat Ass and Freddy: "Nae fuckin aboot an' 'ere'll be nae mair trouble." The door pursued him with a bang.

To the relief of the oldies and Samantha, the giant was gone. But to the despair of Philip and Freddy, their mate was gone with him.

"Fit the fuck we gaan tae dee?" said Phil; his pitch wobbled throughout the sentence, like the line on an adulterer's polygraph test.

Freddy got up and pulled Derek into a sitting position. "Fuck knows, Fats. Ah jist went oot fir a pint, min. Ah ken it's the Broch, bit ah niver thought ah'd be riskin ma fuckin life." Derek's head slumped back; he drooled some strawberry juice onto his black T-shirt.

"You boys okay?" The oldie with yellowing hair approached their table.

Fat Ass knew the globular man rather well. He was English Bob Schell. The man and his wife, whom had yet to set foot in The Tart, were caravaners. Dangling midway into his sixties, Bob was a youthful oldie. He was a pensioner, but he breathed an optimism that glowed in his red cheeks and inflated his smile. He had a shine to him that either endeared him to people instantly or never at all. Although Robert Schell was, indeed, English – Lancashire somewhere? Phil thought – there weren't many of the pub regulars whom didn't appreciate the man's company.

"Oh, dear," Bob said when he saw Derek. "The poor fellow must've took some wallop. You'd best lie him down; make sure he's breathing properly."

Phil hauled Derek by his armpits while Frederick Paul Taylor grabbed hold of legs that flopped like eels. Carefully, Fat Ass backed out and away from the pool table as though a bus retreating around a corner. "Watch out for - " But Bob's notification came too late, and Phil tripped backwards over a shard of the broken pool cue. He stumbled and lost his grip. In turn, the dead-weight casket of their friend was yanked free from Freddy. Derek whacked down onto the floor like a lead chandelier. All of the men involved in shifting the body, from the delegate to the grunts, flinched. Samantha gasped and rushed over from behind the bar.

"Phil," Freddy barked. He always reverted to the Fat One's Christian name when they were in the presence of more senior grown-ups. Truth be told, Freddy thought the nickname a bit childish.

Derek gurgled to life, like an unblocked lawnmower. He groaned as he moved onto his side. His eyelids flickered as rotors and sucked at the miserable light. "Fit the – Hoo the – Why am ah – "

Eager to atone for his blunder, Phil collected the Guy Fawkes doll of his pal. Adopting the movement and speech of a man who has been awoken from his nap in the sunshine by having his hammock overturned, Derek swayed and mumbled. The strange room and strangely familiar faces twirled like hurled soup. Phil guarded the rear like a forklift truck; his prongs were out ready to catch Derek should he fall again.

"Relax, my boy," the jolly old man with the custardy quiff said to Derek. "You took quite a knock from that big fella. Best get you cleaned up." Derek put a digit to his brow, tentatively, as though a chimpanzee's initial encounter with a keyboard. He felt the scarlet ooze slalom down from a gash on his scalp. A horn rose in the midst of his hair. Everywhere did hurt. Samantha's cuts also seeped, like a raspberry brushed over a grater. "You'd better get cleansed as well, my lovely."

"Aye," Freddy said. "You twa shid scrub up in the lavvies. Ye's are beth bleedin, like."

Samantha regarded the men. Her face was like the first day back at work after the reporting of some scandal, in which she was incriminated. The bullet. The glass. She did well not to cry, and she wouldn't for as long as she was part of this aggregation.

"It's a'right," Phil told her, taking off his coat. "Ah'll get the bar. Ah'll maak sure the glaiss an' aa the rest o 'is mess is tidied up. Get yer cuts seen tae. They dinnae luk too bad."

Samantha took Derek's wrist and guided him to the toilets, past the two seated oldies. They greeted the young pair as if they were beaten hometown boxers. Derek shuffled by as the old-timers would transport themselves.

All this tomfoolery, meanwhile, was taking place on another planet to the one in which Donnie Wise inhabited. He held onto the bar as though he were windsurfing. Donnie wailed like the reservoir beneath the bonnet was parched, and ignored the furore beside the pool table. Obscurities slogged behind him and disappeared into the gents.

"So, Freddy, fit are we gaan tae dee noo?" Phil asked. His chum replied with an expression like a snow-covered roof. "Quick, use yer mobile. Phone Jimmy's. We'll need tae gie 'im some waarnin."

Freddy ripped the phone out of his pocket and pecked at the buttons. He put the tiny device to his ear. He grazed a nostril.

"And who was that that was threatening everyone?" Bob inquired. "He was a rough one, eh? Not a friend of yours, then?"

"No," Fat Ass said. "An aal mucker owes 'im money. He's pesterin us tae fin' 'er."

"Oh, dear."

"Aye."

English Bob Schell tugged the creases out of his patterned cardigan. "And what about your pal that went with him: do you think that he'll be alright?"

"Dunno," Phil said. "Jist dinnae ken."

Freddy wheezed brusquely. "Come on, Jimmy. Pick up, ye lanky twat." After countless uninterrupted rings, Freddy pushed a button. "Ah'll try his mobile." He did, but it went straight to voicemail. “Fuck.” He slipped the phone back into his jeans. The old man was looking at him. “Sorry.”

“Sorry?” Bob almost chuckled. “Friend, I’ve heard a lot worse than that in my time, believe you me.”

“Is he nae pickin up?” Phil asked. The question was redundant. “Ye’ve got yer car ootside. Fit if we bomb up ’ere aheid o ’em an’ maybe ambush the guy? Get ’im wi a stick or somethin?”

“An’ kill ’im, aye?” Freddy spoke as though he’d been tendered some magic beans. “Ah’ve a wife an’ kids. Ah’m nae gettin involved in ’is cairry on mair than a hiv tae. ’Is is mintal. Hoo did aa ’is shite happen?”

“Blame Lori.”

“’At silly cow.” Freddy clenched his jaw. “We dinnae ken, though; maybe ’is guy will jist skedaddle once he fin’s oot that she’s nae here. He probably jist wants tae maak sure that we’re nae fibbin, like.”

“He said it ’imsel, Freddy. He’s gaan tae get the money one wye or the ither. ’At bastard’s here tae caas trouble.”

“Fa the fuck are we tae solve aathin?” Freddy said.

Phil tossed his coat over the bar. “He’s got Mo an’ he’s got a gun an’ Christ kens fit he’ll dee, like. Ah’m startin tae worry a bit here.”

English Bob observed the two panicky youngsters. “Well, what about the police? For my money, that’s looking to be your best option; if not your only option. They’ll know what to do better than any of us. And this doesn’t appear to be the kind of situation that you can just pretend’s not happening and hope will sort itself out. The coppers’ll have to be told, you know?”

Fat Ass suspected that the old man was right.

Freddy was less certain. “We cannae dee ’at. The bastard’ll start shootin iverybidy if the rozzers show up.”

"Do you really think that he would?" Bob asked. "I might be wrong, but that sounded like a lot of macho talk to me. Maybe your friend was correct to doubt him."

"Derek? Aye, then the guy caved his heid in," Fred said.

"Yes, but he never shot him, did he?"

"No," Freddy replied. "Bit he shot at the barmaid, did he nae?"

"He shot at her; he did not shoot her. There's a difference." Bob pocketed a hand. "It's conceivable that he's been bullying you guys with hollow threats."

Freddy looked away as though from a picture that he did not like.

"Well, at any rate," Bob remarked, "the guy said he'd be back, so you've got time to plan. Do you think that you could, perchance, outmanoeuvre him?" The old man could tell that the youths felt as though they were sandwiched between a lorry and a wall. "Bugger me, does this type of thing occur regularly around here? Might have to tell the missus we'll be moving on."

"Niver seen a gun afore in ma life," Fat Ass said.

"Me neether." Freddy was solemn with anger, like a power cut had struck minutes before kick-off.

"No, not in a pub, I certainly haven't." Bob had a gander at the sniffling wretch whom was propping up the bar. "And who's that fellow? He doesn't look like he's had the best of nights either."

"'At's Donnie," said Fat Ass. "Derek's brither-in-laa."

"Ah won'er fit's the maitter." Freddy moved away from his fat friend and the concerned oldie. "Better see fit's wrang wi the cuh – guy."

"An' ah'll hiv tae get the glaiss picked up afore the boss comes in aboot an' starts in wi 'er questions an' stuff."

Bob did as his name prescribed. "Right you are, lads." The old man moseyed back to his booth to apprise his peers.

Freddy drew up to Donnie; Fat Ass heaped the debris from Derek's collision with the table. Then Phil got the wee brush and shovel from behind the bar and began to sweep.

Donnie didn't acknowledge Freddy straight away. There was nothing hostile or rude about the snub: Donnie was cocooned within his problems. He was like an oil-slicked shore. The good junkie was transfixed by his own fiddling fingers, fiddling as if through boiling water. Freddy watched the man for a while, trying to solve the bearded bewilderment's quandary for himself. Then Donnie turned to him; he pitched the tent of a smile with butter for posts.

"Fred, man, hoo's it gaan? Ah niver saw ye 'ere. Fit like?" Donnie's drawl couldn't hide the desolation that was plastered from 'burn to 'burn like a billboard on a forgotten street.

"Eh, nae bad," Freddy replied. "Fit like yersel?"

Donnie took a beat to consider this query. "Nae good, Fred. Fuckin nightmare, man."

Crouched behind the bar, soaking up vodka and gathering glass, Fat Ass heard Donnie and stood up. "Fit's wrang, like?"

"Boys, ye's cannae tell ony cunt 'is." The dealer's words rolled out like turtles after the hare. "Serious, boys, ye cannae tell onybidy fit ah'm awaa tae tell ye's or ah'm fucked, like, ken?" The guys bobbed their foreheads, as if to a doctor. What else could be going wrong tonight? "It's Rachel." Clothes pegs clamped upon the tips of their ears. Derek's niece. "She's disappeared."

"Eh?" Freddy said, nearly shouting. "Fit happened?"

"Aye, boys, ye's hiv tae keep 'is doon, like." Donnie was suddenly mindful of the old-timers behind them. "Pigs hear aboot 'is an' ah'm fucked, ken? They'll taak 'er awaa fae us fir good, man." He drifted then returned, like a raft swinging back into the pier. "Tracy says Rachel came hame fae school a'right. Ah wis through in Aiberdeen at the time, ken? Aye, weel, Rachel drapped aff 'er bag an' then went oot again. She usually dis 'at, ken? Fuck knows faar she gings, like. Usually safe enough, though. Then ah comes hame the back o seven an' Rachel's still nae hame, like. Tracy's gaan schizoid. Ah started baalin at 'er, man. She's jist like 'fuck you fuck you', ken? Ah fuckin went nuts, like. She's sayin 'phone the pigs phone the pigs'. Ah'm like 'fuckin no way'. Fuck 'at, like. You boys ken fit like.

'Em cunts: they couldnae fin' a bulldog's airse in a saasage roll factory. An' the fuckin social workers are a'ready waatchin us like fuckin haaks, ken? We phone up an' say 'aye, eh, ken somethin? We've lost the bairn'. Then fit the fuck happens? We lose Rachel, man. Ah cannae fuckin hae 'at. Couldnae fuckin live withoot ma wee quiney. Love 'er tae death, ken?"

Freddy peeped at his watch. It was after nine. "Hoo lang's she bin missin for, Donnie? Since the end o school, aye? 'At's o'er five oors she's bin oot 'ere."

"Fuck sake, Donnie," Phil said. "We really are gaan tae hiv tae phone the coppers."

"No, no. They'll taak 'er awaa fae us, Fat Ass, man."

Freddy seized Donnie's jacket, not in an overly vehement manner, but harshly enough to convey some of Freddy's anxieties. "Luk, she could've bin fuckin abducted. Onythin could've happened tae 'er."

"Oh, dinnae say 'at, Fred. Ye're freakin me oot noo."

"Ye're gaan tae hiv tae luk fir 'er," said Fat Ass. "She could be in a bad wye."

"Ah've bin lukin for 'er, man."

"Hiv ye got yer car wi ye, Donnie?" Freddy asked.

"Nah." Donnie clawed at his greasy locks. "Fuckin battery's flat. Left the stereo playin fir too lang withoot the engine on full tilt. Stupid bastard ah am. Is Derek aboot? He'll be able tae help."

"Derek's a bit o a meese," Phil replied.

"Fuck sake."

"Aye," Freddy said. "Luk, Donnie, ma car's ootside. Ah'll taak ye roon aboot the Broch tae luk fir 'er. Bit if we dinnae fin' 'er aifter sae lang, we're gaan tae hiv tae ging tae the fuckin cop shop – a'right? Rachel could be fuckin deein oot 'ere."

Donnie's silence broadcast his acquiescence.

Freddy spotted Derek's navy coat draped over a stool. He pilfered it. "You'd better stay here, Fats." He slipped his pal's jacket on. "Ah'm taakin 'is. Come on, Donnie. It's nippy ootside. It'll be gettin caaler."

Donnie muttered his sort of compliance. Freddy led them both like a kid harrying an elderly guardian into the fairground, before the queues got out of control. The pair exited The Tart.

"More ado?" Bob said aloud, swivelling his chair a touch so that he could see the default bartender. "Is that more mayhem transpired upon your lives, friend?"

Fat Ass looked at the door as if it spun to beguile him. "Aye."

The Englishman sighed. "It's turned out to be a night fraught with obstacles, hasn't it?"

"Aye." Phil ambled over to the section of the wall that used to be masked by a large translucent bottle. The wood was splintered and damp where the bullet had made its stunning entrance. The bullet couldn't be seen, so far had it burrowed itself into the beam. Fat Ass touched the ragged hole. They'd been fortunate that Lex had not aimed to hit the mirror, or the girl. The bottle's neck remained in its handstand position like a masochist's wine glass. He grabbed its smooth underside. He ejected the remnants from its plastic holster. He fed the bucket.

Chapter 14

And this was it; this was where 'Lori' had lived for a time. Lit up like the seedier section of the shop and mute like rot, the street recalled some extravagant, on-the-nose, postmodern monument to baseline affront. Lex knew plenty of neighbourhoods like this round his way. In his business, sojourns in such shit-holes were unavoidable. Concrete cells held back the indolent and the incompetent and the downright bloody useless; scum of only one walk of life: the poor. He got out of his two-seater, pea-green sports car, and scoffed at the surrounding feculence.

"Is 'is fuckin it?" he asked the puny man-boy whom was emerging on the road side of the motor.

Mo answered in the affirmative. His fretting had passed on into grim acceptance, as if after being told that there was no known cure for what he'd contracted. "'At's the een 'ere." He nodded towards the three-storey block of flats behind Lex. "The een wi nae lights on." The curtains were drawn together.

The giant turned. "Disnae luk like he's in, eh? 'Is is the right place, in't it?"

"'At's definitely Jimmy's flat." Mo was at least chuffed that he'd brought a jumper out with him tonight. "Cannae guarantee that he's in, though."

"He fuckin better be." Lex shut the door of his prized vehicle as though wary that he might catch a toddler's fingers with it. "Right, let's see if yer pal is faar he shid be." He walked up the grey aisle to the flats, never once leaving the path for the unpredictability of the grass. Mammals were about tonight. Despite the bottom bunk being ostensibly sans people, Lex let his fist fall upon the ply, like golf balls driven into a van. Lex contemplated that the door might last a quarter of a second in a raid.

Mo stopped on the path, halfway between Lex and the pavement. "He might be oot, ye ken?" he remarked, after the fifth unrequited thud. "Jimmy's nae bin seen aa wik. He's probably buggered aff tae the Cairngorms or somethin. Jimbo aiwyes spoke aboot hoo much he'd like tae ging campin an' 'at, ken? Niver did onythin aboot it, though. 'At's 'im maybe gone jist noo."

"Yer pal: he a heavy sleeper?"

"Jimmy? Nah. The boy's an insomniac. Hisnae bin able tae sleep proper fir years, like. His heid's a bit fucked up, ken? Bit o a shame fir the guy; bit 'ere ye go."

Lex wouldn't stress much over the plight of that duplicitous slag's boyfriend. He stooped to peer through the letterbox. No irradiations emitted from the hushed abode. Lex confronted Mo. "So, ye reckon yer chum's awaa, dee ye? Oot an' aboot, is he?"

"Must be. Ah mean, if he's nae answerin his door, ken?"

"Aye? An' fa dis he hing aboot wi fin he's nae wi you an' the rest o 'at muppets fae the pub?"

Mo shrugged. "Naebidy."

"Ah see." Lex glanced at the mouldy mat on the step, and at the dusty plant pots and ornaments along from it. A cat mewed for a mate. "You bein a good pal o his an' iverythin, ye widnae ken if he hid a spare key hidden awaa somewye, wid ye?"

"A spare key?"

"Aye. A spare fuckin key."

Mo found that he was unable to do anything other than conform. His hand raised as if lifted by flies. "He usually keeps a kye under 'ere," Mo said of a ceramic hedgehog. "In case me or the boys want some place tae crash on a Setterda night, ken?"

"Good." There was no enthusiasm in the reply. Lex awarded Mo's service with the aloofness its predictability deserved. The giant kicked over the garden decoration. A key embedded in the muck shone like a worm. He reached for it and slipped it into its place. He turned the key. The click was succeeded by a push. The door was spread into the ebony lobby as though it were the lid of a peat bunker.

Mo watched the giant enter Jimmy's flat and reflected upon how much more he'd prefer to be sat in front of his computer with a clump of loo roll in the one hand and his tackle in the other. Worriment had desiccated his mouth like a coalman's glove since he'd entered

The Tart that evening with Fat Ass and Freddy. His back was moist, however, as if he'd had to leave the shower in a hurry. Mark O'Connor had brought an unknown danger right into his friend's flat, like a scorpion that he knew to be poisonous, just not how so. He could merely pray that Jimmy wasn't home. But then, maybe he was out. It was, after all, peculiar for Jimmy not to answer his door. The gangly scoundrel was not apt to discourage assembly, so lonely was he. Perhaps he'd gone to see his parents. Unlikely. They never really got on these days. Although, it was possible that Jimbo, without telling a soul, had gathered some equipment and made for the hills. It was, Mo reasoned, exactly the kind of thing that Jimmy would do. As much as Mo could tolerate and was almost quite fond of his dour chum, he thought Jimbo rather an odd cucumber.

Yellow burst forth from the tunnel of dark like a bag of seeds. Lex had found the light switch.

The giant paused to study the corridor and decipher the layout of the flat. There appeared to be no sign of this 'James' character, but Lex still had to be cautious of any stealth attack that could be lurking with bat or knife – a gun would be most unexpected. Those pansies could have rung the guy up to forewarn him of Lex's imminent arrival. Lori, silly girl that she was: she had alerted her beloved.

Oh, how she did love her James. In her weakest hour, the girl had confessed to Lex about her romances and regrets. Lori – he found it difficult not to think of her as Joanne – had produced the picture of her beau that he kept with him now. In it, the guy, this Jimmy nitwit, looked gaunt yet content: a happy corpse. She tended to have that effect on a man. Her sting produced an endorphin that convinced men to be satisfied with their slow deaths. Lori, Lori, Lori. Dropped her panties and fell to her knees for the hypodermic needle and its quick release. Where the fuck will you go, you disloyal twat? Far away so the bad types can never find you, or home for help: hugs and kisses and all? She could be here now. Behind one of these few doors, any one; lurching and lingering, with a nice long blade at the ready, desperate to slash big Lexy boy's throat to ribbons.

Lex beckoned Mo soundlessly to join him in the hallway. Mo complied, as there was no qualms that he would do. He advanced hesitantly into the building, as if to exchange the packet of condoms that he'd purchased earlier for a smaller size. If Jimmy were home and naïve to the hazard that he faced, Mo might be able to intervene with his skills of diplomacy to prevent carnage. Heinous tragedy. Michty me. Mo's mind purred with ideas as how best to resolve this situation without call for any more brutality. He hated violence, truly abominated it. It made him queasy, like drinking a cocktail of milk and snot. In spite of this, however, his thoughts invariably pulled towards finding a jagged object and burying it in the giant's spine. Not that he actually would do that. That wouldn't do. Won't do. For a start, Mo would wind up imprisoned, and, more importantly, killing people, weel, 'at's jist nae richt, is it? Back to blackboard time, then. There didn't seem to be any way of ridding the town of this guy other than by paying him what he was owed, and Mo had yet to establish precisely how much that was. Oh, Christ, and all Mo had really wanted from this night was some Ovaltine and a bath. And maybe another chat with SexxyMilf. He'd have to organise a meet with her one of these days.

"You," the giant said, as prudent as he'd been in all the hour that Mo had known him. "Is 'at his bedroom at the end 'ere?"

Mo closed the entrance to the narrow corridor. It dawned on him then just how long it had been since he'd last paid Jimbo a sober visit. He dimly recalled this lobby from a Friday night about three weeks ago, but he couldn't remember a time before that when he'd popped in simply for a chat or to watch the football. European fitbaa an' a couple o cans: 'at sort o thing, ken? And this trend didn't swing towards Jimmy exclusively. Mo – an assistant manager: hoo the fuck did 'at happen? – was gradually seeing much less of Derek, Fat Ass and Freddy, and, regrettably, he couldn't blame that on his having a girlfriend, because he didn't really have one. He rarely saw his mates at weekends and seldom-to-never during the week. It wasn't that he was too busy doing other things with other folk; he just wasn't out that often anymore. The only reason that he was out tonight was because Fat Ass had promised him a huge surprise. Some surprise, like. Over the phone, his buxom chum had alluded to a mystery reunion of sorts. Mo didn't know about that, but what he did, undoubtedly, know was that he and the boys were growing apart, like the ice shelves. He occasionally felt like a goose whose heavy wings were causing it to slip irrevocably behind its flock. The realisations saddened him, or might have done if weren't shitting himself with fear.

"Aye," Mo said. "Second left." He, too, was whispering: a fellow plotter.

Lex snuck down the hall as best he could. He rapped upon the bedroom door. No reply came his way. Not a whiff of bodies readjusting themselves could Lex detect from behind that door. He did not remove the gun from his waistband. He rotated the door handle and gave it a thrust. He braced himself for a surreptitious offensive. Lex discovered that he was disappointed when none came. He hadn't experienced some proper bedlam for a while.

Little and Large stared into the bedroom from the lobby. The excitable light whipped past them as if at the return of its owner; it betrayed that the room, which featured neither a resting Jimmy nor a prepared Jimmy, had been destroyed. Holes had been smashed into the walls; cupboards and closets slept on their sides; a leg of the upright bed poked through into the bathroom.

"Fit happened here, ah won'er?" said Lex, an inverted capital L in the lower-case o of the doorframe. "Yer mate got 'imsel some mair enemies than jist me, then?"

Mo didn't wait for the giant's cue to explore the communal area. He crossed the corridor. He barged into the living room/kitchen and punched on the light. Mo felt like he'd stumbled into an electric fence. There was more devastation, and still no Jimmy. Mo could feel Lex's footsteps enter the room beside him. The giant surveyed the damage also. The broken walls; slaughtered furniture; the wrecked creature that used to be a television set. The sofa had been hacked up; its entrails were strewn across the floor like a detonated cloud. Everything was demolished. Mo knew, as he knew anything, that it had been his friend himself whom had turned upon this house. He'd even had a go at wrenching out the kitchen sink.

A sole artefact had survived the reckoning unscathed. Gazing at the door as it had always done, the decapitated head of the framed photograph continued to hang. And slashed into the wall beside it, like a telegram from Beelzebub, letters the height of wee Mark screamed bloody fury. The two words were carved deep into the plasterboard. The steak knife that had been used to inscribe these words was stabbed into the wall after the final letter of Jimmy's statement. Those two words, from the pith of the tormented, announced to the world, 'Fuck God'.

*

"Goddammit, Donnie, faar the fuck is she? Think." Freddy's stuttering, spluttering co-pilot was proving to be not much of a use. They'd already knitted and weaved through the bulk of the Broch twice, and as yet no silhouette of the missing Rachel had been sighted. Aside from the obvious schools and parks that Donnie had suggested that they should cruise past, the distraught father was ignorant of any distinctly Rachel places where the young girl might be. The limited gap between smack and sense had closed fast, and Donnie was bankrupt of further proposals. Freddy was driving around the same residential area that they'd inspected ten minutes prior. "Come on, Donnie," he pleaded, when they passed the piled-up fortress of the academy again, "is 'ere ony place ye kin think o faar she could be? 'Ere must be some special somewye she likes tae ging tae, Donnie? Ah cannae bide oot aa oors o the night. Ye've got tae think." Freddy had to convince himself that the girl was either lost or hiding; anything beyond that was too repulsive to ruminate upon.

The alternatives, though, were already rattling about in Donnie's thoughts. His brain revolved as if on a kebab spike. "Ah dinnae ken, Fred," he whimpered. "Ma quine could be onywye. Ah mean, man, ye ken? Ah'm nae sure. Maybe. Ah'm tryin tae… Some pervert could be - "

"No," Freddy blasted. He steered his blue car around the streets off Sutherland Terrace. Dogs cursed the metal beast and chased it from their territory. Kids on a corner emanated smoke and jostled with each other. A hump-backed lady doused the egg remnants from her splattered porch. "She'll be lost an' confused. Ye ken fit like bairns are: they ging aff fir a wan'er an' forget 'emsels." Freddy couldn't tell whether Donnie was nodding in agreement or being bullied by the road.

Donnie phoned home. Rachel still wasn't there, his wife had informed him with piercing sombreness. He hung up. He put his head on the dashboard. A conception evolved in his frazzled mind, like someone surfacing from a landslide a couple of days after the event. "The beach," he muttered. He sat back. "She likes the beach, Fred."

"The beach, aye?"

"Aye."

"Right, 'en, Donnie. We'll try the beach."

Freddy headed south, away from the habitational terrain to the promenade at the town's edge. He slid into the car park and killed the engine's buzz. Freddy's was the only car at rest; other vehicles zipped behind them at growing intervals, along the road that took you either left and out of the Broch or right to the pubs and yards by the harbour. Those cars would be heading home on this late night. Freddy heaved with envy for every light that flashed across his rear-view mirror. Home to wives and to cuddles and to sleep, whilst Freddy would have to endure whatever mishap the cosmic prankster had in store for him next.

It seems she was right. For a change. Really, if a quiet pint could result in this level of nonsense, he would have to discontinue these drinking bouts with Derek et al. A long time coming. Tomorrow, Freddy would be steaming through the waves from the start, which would have to be an early start. It was important that he had that pipe job done by the weekend. Big weekend. He'd need sleep. Bed before late. Before twelve? Tonight? Here's hoping. He couldn't spare this Saturday morning to finish the task. Husband, we *are* going to get the drapes *this* weekend, nae excuses. Big, big weekend. Aye. Ginormous. Kim wanted her new fuckin drapes – for the spare living room that his grotty self circumvented if he craved not another row. The shopping and searching and sizing and spending would take up the best part of his Saturday. Sunday as well, probably.

Since we're here, fit aboot new paper fir the bairns' room? A computer fir the hoose? We've a'ready got a Playstation. *A proper computer, wi the Internet an' 'at.* Fit for? *Aabidy else's got een. An' the boys, they'll be needin it shortly. Simon's at the school noo, ye ken? Or hiv ye nae noticed? Too busy oot gallivantin wi yer muckers. Bit ah suppose oor Simon'll manage withoot it. Ah'm sure he'll dee a'right sittin in the corner o the class wi his slate an' his bitty o chaak. It'll suit 'im fine, bein ahin' the times, jist like his dad.*

There is an Almighty, and his job it is to tie all the reigns to Freddy. He's yer mug, 'at's right. Dinnae worry aboot it. Work? Mair work? Guns in ma face? Missin bairns? Nae buther. Bag 'em up. Ah'll dee 'at, ah'll dee yon, ah'll dee the neest thing. Fa am ah tae complain?

Derek: he's the cunt. He's got it sussed. Nae commitments. Nae cares. Lucky twat.

"Fuck sake," Donnie groaned. The beach and the dunes rolled on like fused tubes. Thankfully, though, the moon was full; the scene before them was coated with its bleary affections.

"Shid wi get oot an' luk, 'en?" Freddy said. He fastened the navy coat up to his chin. "Hoo wi gaan tae dee 'is? Ony ideas?"

"Ah dinnae ken, Fred." There was, in fact, a vast amount of ground to cover: three miles of sand and grass to Cairnbulg anyway. "Fit if we split up, like? Wid 'at help, ye reckon? Ah kin taak the beach an' shit, if you hae a luk o'er the dunes an' 'at, ken, up in the san'y braes an' stuff? Aye?"

"'At soons a'right tae me, Don. We'll hiv tae be quick, though. We cannae prick aboot deein 'is, like. She's gettin fair caal oot 'ere. Ye ready, 'en?"

"Aye, bit first..." Donnie brought out a fold of glinty paper from inside his leathers. Freddy thought to protest but didn't. Carefully, carefully, Donnie unwrapped the tinfoil. A sable maze graced the silver. Freddy found himself pursuing the murky snail trails as though trying to decode a conundrum. Donnie placed upon his bottom lip the tooter: a straw, which was also fashioned out of tinfoil. He held the shiny field in one hand; he flicked his lighter underneath it with the other. Donnie burned the pathway. He followed the line of the bubbling crust with his straw, sucking up the fumes like a brain surgeon doting over a patient. Slaked, stable and confident once more, Donnie crashed meekly backwards. That cosy, cosy seat seemed to clasp him as if he were its child. Every particle of Donnie recoiled, as though a blissful missile had been dropped within him. Vapour from the discharge wafted from his upper orifices. His eyes closed. With those eyes closed, he pushed his hand up through the air. His hand wavered as though pawing at a ball of string, then parted the straw from two numbing lips. Lips numb. Lips. Libs. Libs? Libbies. Lips. Lips opened. He blew out. The frost succumbed. Sweat bailed from his skin like a burst dam.

Donnie turned to the driver. He smiled as though hovering cherubs held the ends of his mouth. He offered his friend Freddy (a sort of friend, an old friend, associate, an old associate – that was it) the hallowed quilt.

Freddy cracked the jacket to his chest. "Ah hivnae deen 'at fir a while," he said.

"'At's a'right, Fred. Fred, man. 'At's nae problem," Donnie said. "Nae problem wi 'at, Fred. Fit's the problem, like? Nithin wrang wi 'at. Fit dee ye mean, Fred. Fred, eh?"

Freddy made an attempt at a refusal of some kind, but found that his fingers were already curling around the brim of the foil.

*

"Need a light?"

"Aye, cheers."

Derek accepted the girl's lighter and sparked up his fag, despite it being against the law to smoke in such premises and him being a non-smoker. Although, a cigarette, he would often attest, went frightfully well with the alcohol; if not a little too well. He was certain that there must be some complicit jiggery-pokery involved between the barons of the dissimilar legal drugs, which made them interlock like turds and arseholes. Derek didn't have any alcohol with him now in the white-tiled hub of the Tart gents; the bleach smell of which nipped at both his and Samantha's eyes. Derek had somehow sustained the will never to take up the old fagaroos professionally. However, he did seek out its pacifying reek when the wear and tear of conventionality took its toll, or he was, for example, clonked on the pate with 10 lbs of metal.

"Thanks." He passed the lighter back to Samantha. A tile behind her was split like the inside of a tree. She did osculate upon her own cancer-magnet. Derek had never thought the spectacle of a chick choking on a fag to be especially fetching. He was, though, amenable to change.

"Are you feeling any better now?"

"No, nae really." He felt groggy like a thousand Sunday mornings. His bleeding had ceased, though; as, too, had hers. She had been charmed. The nicks had vanished after a wee ablution and a buffering with toilet paper. She wouldn't spoil. She'd be okay. He, on the other hand, perhaps would not be. "Feels like ah've went twelve roons wi Michael Tyson. Ah hid ma airms strapped tae ma sides; he hid spanners in his gloves."

"Do you think maybe you've got concussion?" When she was down almost to the filter, Samantha tossed her cigarette into the bowl of the doorless cubicle, which was the only cubicle that there was.

"Ah suppose it's possible, like. Fuckin feel sick an' ma heid's still spinnin a bit, ken?" He was about to pitch his fag into the middle urinal, then realised that she would likely have to fish it out again to veil their criminal activities from her employer. His tabby splashed beside hers in the bowl. He flushed away the evidence. "Ah better get back oot 'ere an' see fit's happenin. Fuck. 'Is wik, ah tell ye. 'Is flippin wik."

"Relax, Derek. There's no hurry."

His tail began to wag. "Ah think maybe ye're right 'ere, Samantha. Ah shid taak a meenty here jist tae sort masel oot." It was true that his nerves and mental strength were as the spheres in a bingo machine. He reclined against the sink. The soap dispenser had yet to be reattached beside the scored mirror. "Cannae see 'em killin each ither in the next twa-three minutes. Ah div need a break, like." He grinned. "Since we're here, 'en, ma dears, fit aboot ye tell me aboot yersel?"

Samantha reacted as if she'd sat down to the wrong exam. The anguish caused by the bullet and the flying glass still skipped in her bones. "What do you want to know?"

"Well, tae start wi, ah dinnae even ken yer last name."

"It's Kemmet."

"Like the frog?"

She made no pretence of hiding her amusement on this occasion. "No." Samantha was uncertain whether it was the boy's joke, which she had certainly heard variations of in the past, that was the real reason for her laughter, or if it was purely the aftershock manifesting itself as mirth.

The roar of the evening's proceedings was suppressed. There floated upon her beauty a sunrise of an expression. "Kemmet, eh? Fit aboot yer hame toon? Fit's 'at like?"

"It's alright. Quite pretty; a bit bland. Boring, really. I had to leave. It just wasn't me."

"Ye reckon ye'd be mair o a city person, 'en?"

She reset the band around her blondish hair. "Maybe." She evinced her pearly whites. "Just somewhere different to where I was."

"Ah see."

"And what about the Brock?"

"It's the Bro*ch.* Ye hiv tae maak it soon like ye're bringin somethin up fae the back o yer throat." Derek demonstrated the *ch* sound on its own.

"The Broch," she corrected herself, for which Derek awarded her an appreciative wink. "Is the Broch always this obstreperous?"

"Ah'll pretend ah ken fit that word means an' say 'yes'. Bit forget aboot the nicht. Ah want tae ken aboot you. Hiv ye ony brithers or sisters, Samminton?"

"Two sisters. One older; one younger."

"Sammy in the middle?"

"Yes."

"How cute." He could see the light hairs on her forearms. The blood hardened on his scalp. His thoughts glided towards his pals and the giant. He may presently be needed. But then what could Derek do? Derek couldn't do anything. Couldn't he? Could he not? Time tells. Would there still be discord when he decamped from the toilets? Derek was in no great rush to find out. He had already accumulated his fair share of war wounds, and was aware that pain could be quite sore. Derek was not of the mood for another dose. A current of desirability exuded from the girl, drawing Derek's sails back to her. "Two sisters? Lovely. Hoo aal are ye, if ye dinnae mind me askin, like?"

"I'm twenty-four. It was my birthday last week."

"Last wik, eh? Well, a belated happy birthday to you, my darling. Ah'm twitty-seven masel, like. Twitty-eight neest month." Ordinarily, he'd be more averse to divulging such discouraging information. "Fit aboot loves? His there iver bin a monsieur Kemmet on the cards?"

"There was one who had the potential."

"A ceilidh-boogying Mick, was he?"

"No, Canadian actually."

"Canadian, eh? They nae jist like a Matalan American?" Derek moved away from the sink to be nearer to Samantha. The two were parallel to each other in the porcelain box. "He wis yer 'one', aye? Yip, 'ere's aiwyes one."

"Oh," she said, "and who was yours?"

"Naebidy worth mentionin noo, sweet maiden." Memories of Laura couldn't defeat the spell of such an enchantress. Let's push the boaty oot, he thought. "An' fit aboot yer fantasies? Iver drunk a bitty too much reid wine an' woken up the next mornin wi a mooful o yer best friend's muff hairs?"

Her eyes looked as though they'd been poured into a frying pan.

"It's a legitimate question."

"No." She spoke as though to downplay the scale of her astonishment.

"The cruncher: hiv ye iver thought aboot it? Nae lees."

"Possibly." Samantha would test this force of heterosexuality. "And maybe you've had fantasies of that nature yourself, Derek?"

"Ladies lovin ladies?" He brushed an eyebrow with his thumb. "Eh, once or twice, aye."

"I meant with other men."

"Cock up ma arse? Ah dinnae think so."

Her glow was overcast. "How manly," she replied.

"Fit?" Her tone had struck him like nettles. "Ye think jist because ah dinnae want tae be buggered that ah'm some oot-o-date yokel? Ah'm nae, ye ken? Ah'm no philistine. An' ah div ken fit 'at word means. Ah'm wise tae the world, like. Wise enough, ah think. Dinnae tell me fit's gaan on, 'cos the Derek kens. Believe it. Folk kin be buffties if they want. 'At's nae ma problem."

"I'm sure gay people everywhere will be glad to hear that."

"No, bit ye believe me, though, eh? Ah'm nae jist some gleck fae the back o beyond. Ma aunty's a clam merchant. 'Ere's gayness in ma faimily; jist nae in me. Ah'm sure ye probably think, like, ah'm the worst kina dottled Jock stereotype, bit ah'm nae. Weel, nae entirely. Ah might nae've traivelled 'at much – ah dinnae globetrot – an' ah'm sure that ah hivnae seen as much o Europe as yersel, like, bit ah'm fully conscious o the fact that the universe disnae stop an' start wi the Borough. Ah think. Ah read. Ah hivnae read onythin recently, like, bit ah kin assure ye that ah've read a fair few buks in the past. Mestly horror stuff, like Richard Laymon an' 'em kina cunts, bit it's still readin. Ah used tae ging through a buk a month. Seriously. Brain food, ken? Bit nae fucker's likely tae say onythin that's nae bin said afore by some ither twat by noo, or that ah hivnae thought o masel, like, so ah jist dinnae read sae much as ah used tae. Serious as fuck. Ah'm intae culture, nae cunture. Ah'm nae feert o the arty stuff an' change an' free will an' aa the rest o 'at pish. Ah'm tellin ye, Derek Gibson's nae like aa 'ese ither cavemen. Ah've niver kicked onybidy's heid in. An' 'ere's aa 'is cocaine whippin aboot like Pamela Anderson's pube lice; I niver touch the stuff. I give two fucks aboot fit happens tae Columbia, even if nae ither cunt dis. Ah taak a drink, 'at's it. Ah dinnae even hardly smoke hash onymair. Derek Gibson's a'right. Ah mean, is that hoo ye see me: jist a moron? Ye've met me fir, like, a couple o oors an' ye're judgin me a'ready. 'Ere's somethin wrang 'ere, like. 'At's nuts. Crazy. Ye need tae open up a bit – an' 'at's nae me bein smutty fir once. Ye cannae jist judge folk like 'at; ken fit ah mean, like? Mintal."

Samantha regarded Derek with an amusement that lacked any derision. "You finished? Is there any more, or shall we leave it there?" She chuckled, as though confounded by persistent flukiness. "What on Earth was that about?"

Derek's self-belief climbed back up the charts. "Ah dinnae ken. Northern stigma or somethin. Happens noo an' again. Usually aroon smarty foreign sorts, jist like yersel. Ah'm nae sure."

"Oh," Samantha said. "Well, if it helps, I don't think you're a moron."

"No? Cheers. 'At's probably the best thing onybidy's said tae me in a while. So ah'm homeless, jobless an' concussed, bit at least ah'm nae a moron. Ah'll hae to update the CV."

"Don't hold me to that. I'm normally a good judge of character. Please don't prove me wrong." They gazed at one another. They touched fingertips. "I don't want to sound rude, but *how* do you know who Lucian Freud is?"

"Am ah nae allowed tae, like?" Derek grabbed her hands. "Ah'm an enigma, playin on the fiddle, eatin a beefsteak pie. Noo come here so ah kin kiss yer face aff, ye saucy bint."

Derek enveloped her with his arms and latched his mouth onto hers. Her eyelids fell like shoddy masonry; her heart jolted as though beating at too high a speed for the gear. "Derek," she murmured, unsure whether or not she said it to protest. His hands massaged her shoulders. She didn't push him away, nor did she say to refrain. He kissed her cuts.

"Ye tried tae save me earlier."

Samantha cupped his elbows. She kissed him back and blocked his words. He gripped her behind; his tongue thrashed against hers. The slimy swords duelled on the castle ramparts. Derek drove her back into the cold, hard wall; his hands were now welded between the tiles and her perfect curves. They kissed like two snakes trying to consume each other. His left hand moved upwards from her bum. He yanked off her pink top and flipped down her cups. Splendiferous breasts jiggled forth. He met her nipples with his teeth.

"Ah want tae fuck ye," he gasped. "Ah want tae fuck ye right here. Right here against 'is fuckin waa." He groped her buttocks and delved beyond; she ground herself tightly against his crotch. The cement had set fast across his groin. He could bore a hole into the future with this erection. Derek feared that he would explode before he even got to the main course. He tore at the buttons of her jeans; a pale triangle of panties was revealed. His left mitt searched through the wiry hairs and found the wet ravine. With her back against the wall, balancing on her tiptoes, Samantha rode his digits and groaned. This was too much, too sexy too soon for her, but she'd be fucked if she'd stop now.

Two expert fingers did thrust instinctively. The boy and the girl rocked and lunged and became greasy with various bodily effluents. She moaned and pulled his head back to her breasts. He felt his rocket ready itself to wipe out half the town. Oh, you dirty, filthy turn for the better.

A phantom cry: "DEREK."

Eh?

The toes of her trainers skid forward. Her back misses the wall. She falls to her rump. As she descends, Derek realises that his left hand remains sealed between her crotch and her jeans. His and her eyes are like plates serving solitary peas; their jaws hang like the entries to mine shafts. She's slumped on the floor with her legs adrift. He arcs above her; his wrist peers out from her panties. Two of his fingers are perpendicular to the rest of the bunch. Derek barely has the space left in his head to deliberate over whom it was that might have shouted his name from the bar. Samantha wriggles her denims down so that he may free his paw.

The whole disaster slips out into full view. He unsheathes the first two fingers of his left hand. She winces and turns away in revulsion. Derek can't think to scream. He stares at his damp, crooked digits with ashen-faced repugnance. Samantha rises to her feet. She fixes her clothes behind him.

"DEREK."

His head tilts wearily in the direction of the door. Samantha looks at him for answers, though she can't yet bring herself to speak. The voice, Derek thinks, is not friendly, and nor does it belong to the giant. He recognises the voice as being that of an acquaintance, an associate, an ex-work colleague of the brand Gary Thomson.

Chapter 15

It was only ten o'clock, and here was more bloody trouble. Phil had just binned the broken pool cue when the pub door was flung open. In the trio marched, surging up and into the barman's face. Gazza at the front; the two kiddies stood behind him as though they were in any way intimidating. They examined the room, like velocoraptors out for a meal. It was evident to Phil from the outset that Gazza was on the warpath with someone, but that individual didn't appear to be either himself or the three old men.

"Faar is he?" Gazza slammed the bar, as if expecting it to shatter at his touch alone. He snarled again, "Faar's yer fuckin chum, eh?"

Despite the one-eyed troglodyte's reputation and foul temper, Phil couldn't muster the same fear for him as he had done for the giant. This guy, scary nonetheless, never, for as much as Phil knew, carried a gun. He could afford to relax, especially seeing as the shillelagh was at easy reach under the bar.

Phil scrutinised the two teens at the back. The taller of the pair knuckled his temples. "Fit's the problem, like, Gazza?" the barman asked.

The oldies' glass tumblers were as fence posts over which children watched a cowboys' dispute.

"Luk, Fat Ass," Gazza pointed a stocky finger, "ah ken yer pal's here. Noo, faar is he? Faar's 'at cunt hidin?"

"Eh? Fa ye gaan on aboot?" Phil had an idea as to whom it was that the thug might be looking for, though he'd yet to ascertain why it was that he would be. "Luk, ah dinnae ken fit's gaan on, bit, Gazza, wid ye please jist calm yersel doon?"

This proposition was, to Gazza, very much a scarlet scarf for a bull. He took hold of the oak and pushed himself forward, supporting his weight like a growly gymnast. "Tell me tae calm doon again an' ah'll smash yer fuckin face in, ye fat cunt. Got 'at? Eh?" Gazza showed off his set of cornflake gnashers, so impressed was he by this demonstration of his own strength.

Phil didn't give the guy the satisfaction of blinking. Gazza was built like a cube, being about as wide as he was tall. Fat Ass, too, was a big lad, however, and not accustomed to threats. Lex had put him in his place earlier – he could just about handle that, but now this hard-on was aiming to do the same thing. Actin the boy in front o the bairns – the prick that he wis. Phil could feel the red mist begin to rise. Rising. Blinding. Derek and the rest of the Broch may be able to stomach this twat; Phil no longer had the tolerance for such kowtowing. The red rose further when he contemplated the length of time that Derek had been in the toilets with Samantha.

Samantha: she seemed okay. She wasn't just okay. She was stunning. And she wasn't only that. She was a sensible lass as well. Nae a hoor like mest o the rest o Derek's quines. And she was a brave one. Been all over the continent, she'd said. Here, there. Where have you been, Philip? Eh, jist aboot, like, ken? Where to next? Eh, nae sure, eh. Eh. You should just go, Philip? What's stopping you? Pack your bags and leave. That's what I did. That's what you should do. Do it. Kin ah ging wi you? he'd like to ask her. But he wouldn't. He was still waiting for Adrian Campbell to phone. Girls loved Phil as a friend; they didn't like the thought of him as a lover. He hated that. He sometimes cried when driving by himself.

So the fat bastard fancied himself as a bit of a hardnut tonight, did he? Fuckin toughy, like? Eyeballin's his game, is it? A threat from Gazza should be sufficient to cow a donkey. Such insolence demanded action. Gazza felt greatly compelled towards laying the barman out with his brow. Right fuckin now. Would have to. The fat cunt's recalcitrant stance was made the more aggravating due to wee Scotty and the skinny pill-head being there to witness this insurrection. Studying it all. Oh, dear, dear, deary me. Here we go, here we go. Gazza was definitely – definitely – going to end up slapping this obese bastard. This fat fucker, this fat cunt – but hold on a second, boys: fit wis 'at? Fat fuckin Phil's pupils had rolled like dice to Gazza's left and to the door of the gents. Ah. Ha.

Gazza let himself fall back onto his feet like a mallet onto a nail head. "Bogs, eh? He in 'ere, aye? Fat loser. So 'at's faar yer fuckin pal is, eh?" He laughed like ferrets gorging on kittens. Gazza hollered at the door, roaring out the name of the guy whom he would be pasting in ein momentum.

Plan of attack, plan of attack. Gazza would come in close, that was a given because of the patch – fucked-up sense of depth perception, did he have? He'd give the guy a few solid uppercuts. Get the brain spinning in its pocket. Then the boy's head goes down; Gazza's straight in with knees to the dish. Improvise. Use the wall; shun the sharp corners. Don't wish to murder the poor guy. Some mess, though not dead. It's nae the winnin that coonts, it's the taakin ye apart.

That would be adequate. Leave it be after that.

Derek was, after all, in Gazza's good books. But wait – history. Hadn't there been previous grudgings? There certainly had been. A warning of some venom had been imparted, had it not? 'At's fuckin right, the bastard. Years ago. School days. The bastard's dad had threatened to pulverise Gazza if he gave Derek any more shit. So why the leniency? Fuck it, enjoy 'is; hae some fun, pal. Ye owe it tae yersel. And if Fat Ass wanted to join in, aa the better.

"DEREK," he shouted. His sidekicks looked to be having fun also. "Derek, get the fuck oot o 'ere. Stop bein a fuckin pussy. We've got some settlins tae deal wi, eh?"

Phil made his final plea. "Oi, Gazza, 'at's enough."

Enough?

Gazza swiped a half-pint from the old men's table and belted it across the room at the barman. Phil just managed to get an arm up in front of his face. Alcohol and glass burst over his elbow. Déjà vu clicked in his noggin.

There ensued a reflective second of post-shitstorm shock. The moist spread over Phil's flannel shirt; the agony reached into his fingertips. The shortest of the boys spurt out a giddy chuckle. The taller teen ruffled up his floppy hair as if digging through a hedge. Gazza smirked: a joyful challenge. Fat Ass accepted.

Phil grabbed the misshapen clump of wood from the shelf beneath the bar and swung it heavily at Gazza. The knobbly stump missed the thug's mouth by a maggot's breadth. By the time that Gazza had realised what had happened, Fat Ass was charging around the bar with the club raised in preparation for another strike. Scotty got wise to the barman's onslaught and pulled a blade out from his tracky bottoms. Phil raced towards Gazza, but, having noticed the knife, he instead aimed his assault at Scotty's hand. The knife shot out of his palm; the youth collapsed holding his wrist. The bleached-haired boy gulped back his tears. Phil was left exposed after the swing; Gazza used this opportunity to mount his own attack. The cyclops deployed a series of vicious smacks to Phil's side; his face endured a brief, though furious, pummelling. Blood rained down from his lips. Fat Ass slouched away from the blows. Dazed yet clutching the weapon firmly, Phil unleashed a backhand skelp that docked flush on Gazza's beak. The room resounded with the crunch, like vertical and horizontal doors colliding.

Bone glistened from the tear, formed afresh beside the thug's eye-patch. The muddy pulp made Phil want to wretch. Gazza staggered as though filleted. Fat Ass was reeled back into the veritable world; he was apprised that there would be repercussions for such a sacrilegious act. Gazza never endured any defeats lightly. The letting of his blood signalled the inevitable spillage of much more from the responsible parties. Tomorrow and the days after would be worrisome tests for Fat Ass. But tomorrow would just have to wait. Tonight's dissensions had not nearly reached their resolve.

Smash.

All that Phil had seen of the blow was an indistinct flicker, and then he was on the floor, with the skinny teen looming above him. The youngster looked confused, as though he himself didn't know how the stool had wound up in his hands. Despite the frizzy sensation that spread throughout his head like the chain reaction of spontaneous combustion in an anthill, lulling him into unwanted rest, Phil remained conscious. His baseball cap had been no substitute for a helmet. He could feel Gazza yank the club from his grasp. He saw that gruesome square of reformed rage wield the weapon high. That decisive thump never came, though. With immense relief, Phil watched as Gazza backed away and lowered the shillelagh.

The tip of Scotty's penknife pressed against the side of Gazza's neck, threatening to penetrate skin. He felt himself being steered in reverse, towards the pub entrance. Gazza couldn't believe it. Who had him? Who had him? It couldn't be, could it? Nah. Yes. It was. One of those old cunts, the sneaky cunt, had nabbed his brother's blade and used it to shackle him.

"Come on, you two, over there," ordered a voice an inch or two behind Gazza. An English voice, matured. He'd been neutered by some fuckin guffy pensioner. What a joke. Some bastard wis definitely gaan tae get their puss rearranged fir 'is fuckin malarkey.

Having neutralised the risk of either teen flanking him, Bob halted. "Right, you pair, stand over there. Come on, you. Get up." He gave the kneeling Scotty a wee prompt: a kick up the arse to get him shifted. "Go on, now. Over there." The sneering kid clambered onto his pink trainers. Alex planted the barstool back where he thought that he might've found it. The pair plopped themselves down around the same booth that Phil and his mates had sat in earlier. The barman pulled himself up onto his rear. "How about you, big man? How you doing?" Phil nodded as if he were wearing a neck-brace. "Now, you, fella, drop the stick." The cyclops complied only after the blade had withdrawn a minor ball of blood from his throat. The shillelagh fell. Its bump on the lino demolished Phil's slumberous passivity. He reached for the club and leaped to his feet. Phil met the bleeding instigator with a look of pure bile. Bob drew Gazza further backwards. "Come now, friend, there's been enough trouble. Put that thing back where you found it, and we'll have dialogue, yes?"

Fat Ass comprehended then that tomorrow could go fuck itself. Consequence was void at this juncture, for Phil, with his aching cranium and seeping elbow, wanted nothing more in the world, in the world or in the gents, than to embed this club into the thug's spouting hooter. Phil was startled to see that his train of thought had been recorded by Gazza's eye, decimating the hard man's ferocity to a snivel. The cyclops grovelled away from the poised stump and into the chest of English Bob Schell.

"Fit ye's deein? Dinnae fuckin hit the cunt, Fat Ass. Ye aff yer heid?"

The old men, the young men and the teens turned to the voice. By the toilet door, there stood Derek and Samantha: pretty youths serving their apprenticeships in adulthood. He and she were doleful and mystified and tired, and, inexplicably, the boy's left hand was kinked as if it held aloft an invisible goblet.

The addition of Derek and Samantha to the mix was exactly the shift of focus that the scene required to enervate a portion of its ugliness. Phil's madness subsided, lost was his lust to inflict death, while Gazza did then cease with his struggle to emancipate himself from the elderly guff. Bob, who disliked his positioning almost as much as Gazza did, put a slight distance between the knife and the man's neck. Scotty scowled from his seat. The expression, Derek noticed, after identifying him and his spaced-out mate as being those same kids from before, was identical to the one that he'd worn after Derek had had to yell at him. The two old men in their booth, Patrick Hendry and Albert Thatcher, with their grey domes and prune faces, sipped and observed and remained silent.

Derek stared at Freddy, Mo and the giant who weren't there, then at his bloodied-up ex-work colleague who, for some reason, was. "Wid it be okay if ah asked ye's fit the mucky fuck's gaan on, like? Ah'm kina baffled here."

Bob shooed Fat Ass away to the bar with his free hand. The old Englishman whispered to his captive, "I'll put this knife in my pouch if you go and sit with your friends and behave. Does that sound alright to you?" Gazza agreed. "Good." The blade dropped to Bob's side. A shove sent Gazza bumbling towards his brother's table.

Gazza felt the sticky droplet on his neck. He rubbed the goo between finger and thumb. He seethed at the aal guffy an' the fatty an' Derek, the howlin cunts. "So fit noo, eh?" Gazza spoke as though both nostrils were pinched. "Ye think 'at's it, dee ye's? Fuckin shaak han's an' 'at's it, like, eh? Aathin's cricket? Eh? 'At yer fuckin game, eh?"

"Again," Derek interjected, "fit's aa the trouble aboot noo? Faar the fuck is aabidy else 'at? The Dundee dick-vein? Ma pals? Faar are they? Fuck me, hoo lang hiv ah bin in 'ere for? Are the humans still in charge? Fit's gaan on?"

Gazza gestured towards the Munro in Derek's jeans. "Fit the fuck's 'at aboot, like?"

"'At's nithin." Derek couldn't look at Phil, whom appeared to have been sucking on a ketchup bottle. "Ah got images in ma heid o Lindsay Lohan in amongst the minge. It sometimes taaks a few meenties fir the bad boy tae de-Hulk. So, fit's the crack?"

"Ah dinnae ken, like, Derek," Phil addressed his answer to Samantha. He turned his attention away from the Irish minx, as though she were a cousin that imbued libidinous thoughts, and on to Gazza. "Fit are you sayin, like? Dee ye want some mair, eh?" He brandished the club. "Is 'is the end o it or fit? Come on, Gazza, fuckin say it. Say it's feenished wi, or ah'll lay ye the fuck oot?"

"Feenished wi?" Gazza's laughter was truncated by the pain in his nose. "Ye must be fuckin jokin, fuckin daft bastard. Pit doon 'at stick an' 'en we'll fuckin spick, eh? See hoo 'at goes, eh? Fat fuckin clown. Rin tae fuck. Ye're fuckin deid, Fat Ass. Aa you bastards are fucked. You, ye aal cunt, ah'll pit your dentures up yer hoop fir cuttin me. Think ye'll pit a fuckin knife tae ma throat an' get awaa wi it, eh? Nae chance. An' you, ye cunt, you're deid as weel."

"Me?" Derek was bamboozled. The residual wetness on his fingers made it toilsome for Derek Jr to deflate, regardless of the misery of the fractures. "Wait a fuckin second here. Fit the fuck hiv ah deen, like?"

The short, bleached teen in the booth was as smarmy as one released on a technicality. Gazza singled out the loathsome midget. "'At's ma wee brither, Derek. Did you gie 'im shit earlier on, eh? Ye threaten tae batter 'im, eh? Fuckin come the hard man wi ma wee bro, eh? Eh?"

"Wait, wait, wait. Jist shut the fuck up." Brither? Nae fuckin doot. This was proving to be a tricksy night. Derek continued, "'At little dip-shit wis bein a knob. He wis moothin aff tae the quine. Ah wis mair than entitled tae admonish the fiend."

Gazza took a bold couple of steps forward. Bob raised the penknife with a limpness bred from his reluctance to use the thing. Phil shook the club: a promise.

The optically singular mess gave his pointing digit another workout. "He's ma fuckin brither. Naebidy fucks wi ma mates or ma fuckin faimily, eh? Ye shid ken a lot fuckin better than ’at, Derek, ye daft cunt. Ah cannae fuckin believe the fuckin hidin ah’m gaan tae gie ye fir fuckin wi ma wee brither. An’ you’ll fuckin deserve it.”

“Gazza.” Derek stretched out his back. “Lick ma fuckin chod, wid ye? Gie it a rest, eh? Firstly, you hivnae got ony fuckin mates. An’ second o aa, dinnae be o’er proud tae announce that ’at rectal-blemish is yer faimily. If onythin, ye shid ging hame an’ slap yer mam fir nae abortin the cunt. Failin ’at, taak ’im roon tae the charity shops an’ see fit they’ll gie ye for a second-hand prick. Noo, sort up yer fuckin face an’ jist get tae fuck, eh? ’Is is the wrang night fir you tae be in here shite-steerin, ye bum muffin.”

“Bum muffin? You fuckin cunt.”

“Luk, Gazza, you ken me: ah’m nae the kina cunt fa gings aboot startin trouble, right? ’At’s your domain. ’At’s fit you dee. You’re a cunt; ah’m nae. If ah threatened ’at wee fart-goblin ’ere, ye ken it wid’ve bin his ain fault. He’s an airsehole; ah’m one o the goodies. An’ thus it’s always been. ’At’s ma bit. Ah’ve said ma thing. Cheerio. ’Ere’s bigger poops sweellin aboot the boul the nicht than you an’ ’at pair o twats. Noo, please, jist fuckin fuck off.”

Gazza went for Derek. The barman stepped in, slamming the club against the pirate’s chest and buffeting him back. Gazza staggered, almost tumbled, but did not. He dug his soles into the floor like a horseman into stirrups. Gazza held himself as if ready for the starter pistol to go off. Derek didn’t move; weary, much much too too weary-like.

“Listen tae me, pal,” Derek said, as though talking to a virus that he alone was immune to. “Kin ye nae taak the night aff, Gazza? Maybe hing up the angry hat fir the noo, ken? Ah mean, is ’ere ony reason why ye hiv tae be such a root-polisher? Dinnae tell me that ye’re here defendin the honour o ’at wee cunt. ’Ere’s got to be mair on yer mind, surely tae fuck. Unfortunately, dear Gazza, ah hivnae got the time tae hear it. Ah’m sure it’s fuckin fascinatin, like. Ah’m sure ye’ve got a good excuse fir ivery twattish thing ye’ve iver deen. Ma chums seem tae be in a bit o a pickle, though. Shit’s faain apart, like. Faain tae bits, like icin on aal cake. Bad wik. Or bad wiks. Feels like ma mind’s haein its period or somethin.

"If yer wee brither disnae like bein tellt tae 'fuck off', 'en 'at's his fuckin problem. Ah'm really fuckin sorry, like, bit ah'm sure 'at blond fuckin feltchin-straa'll be tellt 'at plinty mair times afore he's deid. Cunt'll jist hiv tae grou up, eh? Get used tae it. Ah, personally, couldnae gie a fuck. Dinnae gie a fuck. Seriously, ah couldnae gie a fuck. Ah mean, seriously, dis ony cunt gie a fuck? No, ah didnae think it, like. Ah seriously hivnae got the time tae gie twa shites aboot 'at cunt's hurt feelins.

"Ma name's Derek Gibson; ah'm fae the Broch; ah'm nearin thirty; ah'm nae mairriet; ah've got nae ambition; nae real potential; an' guess fuckin fit – ah couldnae gie a fuck. Fuck it, ken? Ye see, 'is pub an' 'is fuckin toon an' your fuckin faimily disnae maitter tae me. Ah've snapped ma fingers, like. Snapped, ken? Snapped."

Derek's drone became narcotic; the utterances that fell from his regurgitator soothed and bemused the patrons with utmost equality. The sounds did trickle long after Derek had conceived that he didn't actually know what he was babbling on about, and that none of it was relevant in the least. Plainly, he could've been gibbering in tongues. The steady roll of the words, however, dried the well of indignation. His words were of a soft and pleasing drum. Pleasing to the ears of men after such commotion; they broke their fall from the heights of aggression. "Ye ken? Dee ye's ken? Aye. Eh. Like. Fishin, eh? Fuck me. Crazy shit. Fa gies a fuck? Fa fuckin gies a fuckin fuck? The Broch's nae got a future. Orlando. Ah think 'is might be the meltdoon spickin."

But only fleetingly could that well stay barren. The tracks of his speech met a verge that flipped the cart. Derek listened as his voice shimmered then disappeared. A cupboard of recognisable dishes cartwheeled onto the road. Where had he gone? Was he home? Where was was? Where were all the aliens? A thought occurred to him then; a thought that might not ever have betided him previously. Had he just 'cracked'? Derek mouthed the word as if to entrap some tangible credence.

A stillness endured like the pyramids.

"Drunk. Ye're a fuckin drunk, Derek." Gazza's embarrassment at the oddness of Derek's lullaby rant obligated him to say something. "Fit the fuck wis 'at aboot? Fuckin pissheid, eh? Ye dinnae maak sinse onymair. Ye're a richt neep. Daft cunt. Ah'm fuckin sick o ye, Derek. Ah'll kill ye, eh? 'At's fit ah'll fuckin dee tae ye, Gibbon. Fuckin kill ye deid. You as weel, fatty. An' you, guffy. Fat prick. Aal English cunt. Fuck off back tae Stratford-on-Avon. Ye's dinnae deserve tae live. Neen o ye's. The sye's oot 'ere. Ah'll droon ye's. Ah'll knock ye's oot then droon ye's. Wid ye gie a fuck 'en, ye wanker? Ah'm fuckin sure ye'd gie a fuck 'en, eh? Widn't ye? Eh?"

"I widnae gie a fuck," Fat Ass replied. He'd wreathed his right sleeve to check his elbow. It was bruised like a November afternoon. "Ah widnae gie a fuck 'cos you widnae be able tae knock us oot, or droon us. Nae even wi the help o 'at twa spunk-buckets sittin 'ere. Ah dinnae gie a fuck 'cos ah'm nae feert o a man like you. Ye dinnae scare me, ye one-eyed numpty. You're nae the toughest in the Broch."

"Fit?" Gazza said, as if the airport staff had declined his passport. "An' you fuckin are, are ye?"

"Did ah say 'at, like?" Phil shouldered the shillelagh like an axe. "If you think ah worry a fuck aboot the likes o you, then ye'd be nithin bit a fuckin idiot."

Gazza enlarged his chest as though to stop a bus with it. "Fuckin idiot, eh?"

"Aye," Phil said, "ye'd be a fuckin idiot."

Scotty was up like a meerkat. "Dinnae caa him a fuckin idiot, ye fat bastard. Ah'll kill ye an' aa."

Alex fondled his earlobes beneath his oily mane. He looked at his table.

The carousel of threats and insults made English Bob feel spinny. The penknife, aimed at nobody, targeted the bleached youth. "Sit," he commanded: an authoritative belch. Phil motioned to Gazza with the club; he, in turn, gestured to his wee brother. Scotty stood down, with the optimism that he'd be picked for the next game. "Please, for the love of God," said Bob, "we all need to sit and air out the room with some pleasantries. Let's see if it's not possible that we can't open our mouths and let some good spring forth for once. Please, now, everyone sit. I'm sure we can obtain some perspective on all this."

Sit. Sat. Sitting. One by one. Fat Ass set his pillows down on the nearest stool. He put the shillelagh on the bar, and tapped it: an indication to all whom it may concern that it was still well within his reach. Samantha, who'd yet to speak since leaving the toilets and the setting of her lowest instant, went up to the bar, not to sit, but to hide, to blend with and recede into the oak. Derek didn't move. With his transparent cup, Derek beheld Gazza in a manner as to illustrate the sincerest nonchalance. Gazza glowered in return, then, pondering why it was that he didn't either fight or fuck off, plonked himself down like he'd stepped off a gangplank. He took his place on the padded booth beside Scotty and his fidgeting mate. Bob Schell's relief left the nest and soared for the brightest circle. He was tempted to smile given the insanity that had served to prelude this climb-down. The old man looked at Derek. Derek wasn't sitting, and nor was he likely to sit. But the woebegone, young man didn't seem inclined to throw any tantrums either, so Bob let the fellow be. The Englishman folded the knife and put it in his trouser pocket for safekeeping. He sat on his stool, which was diminutive in comparison to the lofty ones by the bar. Across the table from him were his two contemplative drinking companions, both of whom were senior to Bob by a decade apiece. The backrests of the booths were not so high as to screen the oldies from the delinquents.

Bob dragged his seat away from the island of his table. Bob could confer with everyone proficiently from his new moorings; although, he had to pivot round to see Derek or Samantha.

"Can we talk civil now?" he asked the room. "Phil – it is Phil, isn't it? yes – Phil, if you would, get the man a cloth for his nose, please. That looks to be a sore one. Probably need stitches later."

Phil responded as though he'd just been enjoined to run a marathon. The barman snatched a rag from where the nip glasses were kept. He threw it at Gazza as though to take out a wicket. Gazza caught the towel and held it to his damage. Astute reflexes had been all that had prevented further distress to the thug's weeping schnauze. Gazza's eye slanted above the darkening cloth in gratitude to Phil's bittersweet act.

"To start with," Bob commenced mollification, "might I suggest that there not be any more hassle from anyone. I know you Scots are known for being a tough folk and fond of a ruck – any view to the contrary could've been dismissed tonight, but let's get a grip on things. Can we go five minutes without a gun or a knife making an appearance or a fist being thrown? Please, if you's can, no more agitations. Let's just calm things down a tad."

"Fine by me." Phil settled upon his high chair. "Ye winnae get ony hassle fae me as lang as aa ither cunt behaves."

Gazza considered the gore on the towel. He said not a word and revisited his wound with the sodden textile.

Pale and placid, Derek gazed ahead. At no one and nothing, and said, "An' fit exactly's gaan on? Sorry, ah must've drifted or somethin. Ah forget."

"Your hand, son? Goodness me, what did you do to your hand?"

The Tart door opened then closed. The huddled masses had only a second to mull over the noise of the influx. A bare-chested man of mid-to-late twenties strode fast into the pub. He carried a sloshing orange container with one sinewy arm. The smartly coiffured chap passed Fat Ass and the taxing trio. He took the fire extinguisher down from the wall. The man landed on the pool table; his grey trousers dangled off its ledge. His youngish face was handsome, though scattered with some mute disturbance. The fire extinguisher, he placed on the ground behind his black shoes; the container, he uncapped and poured over his head till he was soaking. At first, the liquid appeared to be water, but the substance gave the man's defined torso a heaviness and gloss that dispelled this notion.

Derek emerged from under his own near mental downfall.

The man discarded the container. The last of the petrol splashed from the tub, leaving a wall sprinkled with chip-paper stains. The dripping chap produced a yellow lighter. He held it to the ceiling: a torch for the attic.

"To life," Pagan exclaimed. "To the grand existence."

Chapter 16

"Luk at 'is; it's wee Derek." Wee Derek shrugged, blushing like he'd won an award, and waded through the tangerine living room. The crewmen laughed and beer bottles were jostled. Burly men on sofas and stools roared, affably, at each other. His dad yelled over them, into a microphone: singing, supposedly. The men gave cheer as the scrawny youngster in the football strip passed through. He countered their boisterous inquisition with a timorous smile, tapering like dank masking tape.

"Aye, fine. Playin fitbaa. Eh, neest month. Shid be a'right. Aye, see fit the quines are like. Aye. Eh? Aye, caught some labsters, like. Aye. Ah maybe wid ging fir a job at the sye. It's a'right, like. Ah'm nae sure. Nae bad. Were they? 'At's good. Might be. Ah dinnae ken. Nae sure. Aye. No, ah widnae fancy gaan tae waar, like. Nah. Aye. Maybe. We'll see fit like. Right, cheers."

"Derek," his dad had finished his tune, "is it nae aboot time ye went tae yer bed?"

Derek exited via the far door. The house was smaller than their prospective abode, but this room comfortably seated the eleven men of the Odyssey. This house was no bigger than Pagan's or Phil's, and was even bested in size by Jimbo's parents' domicile. The Gibson residence did not impose itself upon the surroundings as their subsequent castle would, from its mount atop a street that didn't yet exist. Derek's friends weren't poor. Their households tended to attract coin from either oil or fish, one way or the other. Mo's father was an accountant, and mainly drew his pay from skippers; amongst his client roster, incidentally, was a prosperous Adam Gibson. In ten years, Adam would sell the Odyssey, own the Evermore and become one of the wealthier men in the northeast.

Derek bumped into his mum in the corridor: clementine. An orange mansion, her suggestion. She shuffled in her lavender robe. Her slippers were trimmed with white fluff as though she'd stepped into a sheep. She said to her Derek, "Ah hope ye left yer boots at the front door, an' nae on the kitchen fleer like the last time."

"Aye."

"Good, Derek. Ye awaa tae brush yer teeth?"

"Aye."

"Ye hae a good night?"

"It wis a'right."

"Did ye win?"

"Aye, mam. Ah aiwyes win."

She crossed her arms, and yawned. "Ye sure are cocky enough."

He looked at the staircase beyond her.

"Ye aa set fir the academy, 'en? Is 'ere onythin mair that ye need? Buks? Pens? Dinnae be leavin iverythin tae the last minute tae tell me."

"No, mam. Ah think ah've got aathin."

His mum was dressed for bed, but she wouldn't have been sleeping. She would've been reading, if she could concentrate for the din of his father's guests. "Noo, you mine, if 'ere's onythin ye're concerned aboot at aa, ye come see me or yer dad."

"Aye, mam."

"Listen tae me, Derek. Dinnae be smairt. We're nae jist cash machines an' chefs, ye ken? It's a serious thing ye're awaa tae start. If ye've ony problems, ony at aa, we're here fir ye."

"Mam - "

"Dinnae 'mam' me, Derek. Ah ken fit ye're like. Ye jist want tae bottle iverythin up an' get on wi it. Jist like yer dad. Niver complain or say a thing, 'en it aa comes oot at once. Bloody men. Aa as daft as een anither."

Derek eyed those steps behind his mother. To escape from this awkward exchange.

"Derek, you listenin tae me? Why dee ah even buther? Tell me 'at?"

"Mam, ah'm fine."

"Oh, an' hoo wid ah ken 'at? Ye niver spick tae me. Jist 'cos ye're grouin up, disnae mean ye hiv tae ignore us."

The fishermen bellowed and sang and drank in the room to his rear, oblivious to this moment between mother and son.

"So, Derek, are ye lukin forward tae 'is new school? Wid ye tell me 'at much?"

"Ah dinnae ken, mam. Suppose it'll be a'right."

"Better you remember that 'is is nae Sooth Park onymair. Wi a bit o luck, ye'll be split up fae Freddy an' Mark an' Philip an' aa them lot. 'Is is a new page fir you, ma lad, an' ye're nae gaan tae muck 'is up. Ye'll meet in wi aa kines o folk; folk 'at dinnae think it's funny tae cairry on and act the goat wi teachers. Folk that are gaan places. Cliver folk. Folk 'at want tae achieve things wi their lives. Derek, dee ye hear me? It's a grite muckle world oot 'ere; 'ere's heaps o opportunities fir a boy like you. An' ah dinnae want tae be bad-moothin yer chums; ah ken ye've bin pals wi 'em fir a filey noo, an' ah'm sure they're a fine bunch fir the mest pairt, except fir 'at droll cretter, the quaet een – ah dinnae care much fir 'im. The thing aboot yer chums, though, Derek, is that they're nae gaan onywye. Broch's jist a tiny wee pairt o the world an' 'at's fir they'll bide tae the day they dee. You ken 'at. They aa ken 'at. Bit ye've got the brains, Derek. You could be different. Aa yer teachers say the same thing. They say hoo cliver ye are an' hoo far ye kin ging if ye stop the play-actin an' muckin aboot. Aye, ye're affa smart lippin-aff tae the teacher, gettin a rise fae the classie. You're better than 'at, Derek. You could dee somethin wi yer life, or dee ye nae want tae? Dee ye jist want tae be like yer faither – oot in 'at bloody boat fir the rest o yer days? Well, go on, Derek, show some sign that ye've actually listened tae a word ah've said tae ye. Dee ye want tae dee somethin wi yer life or nae?"

Derek tuned back in when he sensed that she was winding down to her question. He thought it rather hasty to be hounding him with such a query. These things were bound to resolve themselves in timely fashion. "Mam, ah dinnae ken." To bed. Sleep. Dreams of space and space girls. "Fit dee ye mean? Ah mean, ah dinnae ken."

"So, it's the sye wi yer dad, 'en?"

"Maybe. Ah dinnae ken. He maaks money, dis he nae?"

His mother fought hard the impulse to slap him on the head. “It’s nae aa aboot money, Derek. Money’s got nithin tae dee wi it. Money disnae maak ye happy, Derek.”

“Ah dinnae ken, like. Probably wid. It sure as fuck widnae maak me unhappy.”

“*Fit*?”

“Eh?”

The spare woman seemed to tower above him like the inside of a tyre. “Derek, fit did you jist say tae me?”

Derek was genuinely perplexed by his mother’s rapid vexation. He’d simply stated the obvious: money = good. Punctuated the remark with a curse. The ‘f’ word. Oops.

“Sorry,” he mumbled.

“Dinnae you iver sweer in front o me again, Derek.” Her eyes were crystallised lakes. “Ah’m nae yer dad, or yer granda.” She finally blinked. “You’d better ging tae yer bed, ma lad, afore ah tell yer faither fit ye jist said tae me. My, my lad. An’ waash yer bloomin knees.”

He looked down. There were patches of green and brown on both legs. He picked a blade of grass from the side of his calf. The door to the master bedroom slammed shut. The jollification of his dad’s party broke apart, then repaired itself. Derek trudged upstairs. By the final step, his mother’s oration had all but crumbled and blown away into the cogwheels of his mind. He stared out the skylight. Pondering exotic suns and their infinite escapades. There’s the life. A traveller, a lone gun in his interstellar ship, sailing through the cosmos, stopping over at planets to foil the deeds of galactic dictators. Rewards of gold and women, or their equivalents. The thoughts fomented and swirled like Van Gogh’s starry, starry night.

He entered the bathroom and peeled off his socks. The upstairs lavvy was not so grand as the one downstairs; it was used, primarily, by him and wee Trace. Tracy, a young seven, had the room across from his. He stood in the tub; he cleansed the worst of it from his knees. The boy whose ear had been mutilated by a dog had made a mess of his shin. That gash would take long enough to heal. It didn’t help that Derek liked to pick at his scabs. He dried his legs, then went to his room. Arnie posters adorned the walls, which were, thankfully, not a shade of orange but blue. A little girl in pink pyjamas sat on his bed, on his Superman duvet cover.

"Fit dee you want, Tracy? Ye're nae supposed to be in ma room; ye've bin tellt 'at a hunner times. Get oot or ah'll saafen ye."

The streetlights shirked the bouncers of the curtains and threw her outline to the floor. The girl's bare, tickly toes prickled above the grey carpet. She hugged her bear: a brown bear with one eye missing. He'd cut it off after she'd thought it funny to pee herself while sitting on his cabinet. The eye was in a sack with his marbles. "Ah cannae slee-eep," she said.

"So? Ah'm nae readin ye a story, Tracy. Get tae yer bed. Ah'm nae jokin. Ah'll get mam." He flicked on the light, and moved aside to unveil the doorway. "Oot."

"Why wis ye arguin?"

"Fit? Fit ye on aboot, ye freak?"

"Mam said ye hiv tae stop caain me 'at."

"Fit?" Derek feigned profoundest confusion. "A freak? Bit ye are a freak, ye little freak."

"Maa-AAMM. "

Derek dove towards the bed and clamped Tracy's gob in a game-saving catch. Her shriek could have brought more havoc upon his crown. "Shhhush."

His palm became sticky and damp with his sister's spittle. She giggled into his hand. He recoiled, disgusted, and dichted his mitt on the carpet. Derek regarded the young scamp. She smiled an adorably horrid wee smile. He sat back on the bed next to her.

"Fit the fuck dee ye want?"

"Mam says ye're nae supposed tae sweer."

"Okay," Derek reiterated, "fit dee ye want, ye monkey?"

She rested her chin on teddy's bonce, and said, mischievous-like, "Why wis you an' mam fightin?"

"We wisnae fightin. Fit ye gaan on aboot?"

"She banged the door."

Derek did sigh. The Terminator watched over them. “Tracy, ye winnae un’erstan. Groun up stuff. Come on; aff tae bed. Get.”

“Fit dee ye want tae be fin you grou up, Derek?”

“Eh? Shut up.” Derek rocked forth back onto his soles. “Stop listenin in tae folk’s conversations. Ye kin get intae trouble fir ’at, wee Trace.”

She swallowed her bottom lip then spat it out. “Derek disnae ken fit he wants tae bee-ee.”

“Shut it.” He paused. He looked at his posters. “Ah want tae be a time-traveller. ’At’s why we wis arguin. She thinks it’s too dangerous.”

Tracy appeared to have chewed on a lemon slice. “A time-traveller? ’At’s stew pit.”

“Ye’re right,” Derek replied. “Noo, awaa tae yer bed.”

“Ah want tae be an actress in films.”

“Best o luck. Get oot.”

“Ah want tae be rich an’ famous an’ bide in America.”

“Why?”

She was stumped. There was no ‘why’.

“Ah’ll be tap-dancin on the moon afore you’re in films.”

Her eyes mushroomed. “Ah want tae ging tae the moon an’ aa.”

He lifted her by the oxters and carried her out of his room.

“We kin maak a film on the moon taegither,” she said, as she was hoisted across the landing. “Kin we dee ’at, Derek? We’ll maak a film aboot a princess? You kin be the hero?”

“Aye, a’right.” Derek chucked his sister onto her bed. She let out a yelp of delight. “Sleep.” He closed the door.

“Nighty night, Derek.”

He cleaned the spit from his palm, as well as all the unwelcome hair and dirt from his rug that had bonded with it. He had a couple of pubes now, he’d been thrilled to inform his friends. He looked in the mirror. On his chin, a red dot. His first spot. T’would be the first of many, he feared. Derek prayed that he wouldn’t end up ravaged by acne like that guy down the road, whom he'd heard the older kids refer to as Plook. He went to his room, switched off the bulb and lay on his bed.

When had been his last attempt? About a week and a half ago? Indeed. The light of the night was reassuring. A diffident hand slid under the band of his shorts, as if there might be something with fangs down there. Wakey, wakey. He flapped it between two digits. The dopey soldier got to its feet. He rod his fist up and down the stalk, like he was taking the Brasso to a clarinet. Upwards and downwards, but without much sensation. He pushed and pulled: pushing the skin over the bell, and pulling it back to base. That familiar dullness. Derek decided to change tact. He clenched the anaesthetised carrot. He upped the pace, devoting more to the pull than to the push.

There you go.

After numerous failed experiments, this trial run did make known its fruitful nature. Derek was definitely feeling something this time. His claw fired away faster, as if these creels *had* to be taken up swiftly. Visions appeared. He summoned to his mind those two lesbians from Interracial Honeys – a vid, a true gem from Mo's dad's collection, which all the boys had watched last week in conspiratorial glee. The blonde had actually tongued the ebony babe's anus. Whoa, boys. They'd cracked up. Tongue. You're so good, babe. Baby, lick me. There. Woosh, woosh. I want to lick you there. There, there. Woosh, woosh. My turn. Oh, baby, you're making me cum. Cum. Come, comes the cum. Woosh, woosh. His right arm, tight and loose, tight and loose, became one with his prick: a bond that would serve him now forever well.

Honeys. Slurping. Munching. Thrusting, thrusting, hammering.

Stop.

Freeze.

Spasms.

His body jerked, jolted; he'd have sworn then that he could feel the rapture even in his toenails. The semen flowed, massacring his hand and his shorts and his pubes. A noise like a draft in a cave issued from his throat.

We have lift off.

*

Two hundred, about two hundred, young heads face front. The rector in the black cape at his podium welcomes them en masse.

“I know that you will all use your time here at Fraserburgh Academy wisely.” A new chapter. New leaf. So begins a new beginning. I see all this potential. Humming with positive energy. My pleasure to see how you all progress. Bright smiling faces. Good luck.

Derek watches the other pupils. Unknown faces; kids, even, from outside of the Broch. Potential friends, enemies or, not quite yet, shags. Faces not bright, but mostly dimmed with foreboding; some, though, did glare with roguery. Columns of heads and backs, like broom handles jabbed into turkeys, cooked or otherwise, were heedful of the strange adults perched by each line, sniffing out the bad uns: the chucklers and the chatters. All kids face forward. Parents’ words resound. You behave. Maak a gweed impression, you.

Derek spots Jimmy near the front of the hall, the tallest in his row. The nerd stands out like a bratwurst among chipolatas. Mo, he can’t see, nor Pagan. Freddy kicks at the legs of his metal chair. Derek won’t turn around. Phil fills the seat next to him; his pal will be in most of his classes from now until they leave in four years’ time. Folds of ass fat spread to the side of Derek’s chair. He scoots over to avoid the slow-moving avalanche of lard. The plastic-encased hooves squeal across the floor.

The rector’s flow is disrupted. Faces turn. Faces face Derek; he deflects their looks onto Phil with his thumb. Their accusing peepers shift, tunnelling into the bulky one instead. Fat Ass clouts the back of his neighbour’s melon. Derek rolls with the blow; it was the best way to keep his own visual-receptors in their sockets. The wallop echoes to the ceiling. Faces enliven. Murmurs ascend.

The rector calls for a silence that is delivered forthwith. Faces face forward once more.

Their adult points at them. Children quail from that red nail's path as if to evade a laceration. Mrs Pedersen will allocate the pair their first detention on their first day at Fraserburgh Academy. The boys mutter their grievances to their trousers.

A wary laugh behind Derek. "Neeps."

*

"Yes?"

"Ah dinnae un'erstan 'is."

"Pardon?"

"Ah mean, I don't understand this."

"What don't you understand now, Derek?"

"I'm just nae sure why X equals 6."

"Well, if you'd been paying attention like the rest of the class, as opposed to gawking out the window for the last half an hour, maybe you would."

"Aye."

"Pardon?"

"Yes."

*

"Come on, Derek. Dinnae be a poof."

"Fuck 'at shit, like."

"Ye might as weel, ye cunt. The teacher's nae here yet. It's noo or niver."

"Nah, fuck it, Freddy; you go if ye want. Ah'm nae. Ah'll be fucked if ah get caught."

"Ye winnae get caught. Come on."

"Ah jist ken that ah'll be the een that gets fuckin busted. Ma mam an' shit'll go crazy an' 'at, ken? It's nae worth it."

"Fuck sake, Derek. Hoo'll they fin' oot? Ah tellt ye, Colin's a master at forgin notes. Come on, Derek. We'll hiv tae ging noo. Cunt's waitin on me. Come on. Ye a homo or somethin?"

"Fuck you, ye cunt. Ah jist dinnae want tae get grounded again. It's a'right fir you. Your folks let ye aff wi murder."

"Yer mam an' dad winnae gie a shit eether. It's only RE, fir fuck sake."

"Aye, they will. They'll ging nuts."

"Well, ah'm gaan. Last chance, ye comin?"

"Ah said 'no'."

Quietly. "Oh, shite. Too late. 'At's your fault, ye dick."

"Now, I gather you all did your exercises from last time. Let's have a look." Rustles paper. "Yes, Philip?"

"Eh, please, Mrs Lawrence, kin I be excused tae go tae the toilet, please?"

"Which number?"

"Eh, fit number's poopin?"

*

"Ma face is sair wi laughin."

"Ah kin hardly breathe."

"Holy shit."

"Derek, 'is stuff's fuckin lethal. Good, like."

"Strong as fuck."

"Ah tellt ye's."

"Ah cannae stop thinkin aboot He-Man."

"Eh? Is 'ere somethin ye're tryin tae tell us, Fat Ass."

"No. Nae like 'at. Dee ye's remember Skeletor an' shit? Nuts, like."

"Fuck, aye. Mine She-Ra?"

"Oh, aye. Ah wid've well fucked 'er, like. Fuckin right."

"Mo, you're a creepy bastard. She wis a fuckin cartoon, fir fuck sake."

"Fuck off, Freddy; you wid an' aa."

"Ride a cartoon? You're aff yer heid, min. Hoo much o 'at shit hiv you smoked, Mo? You're fuckin wasted, ye little cunt."

"Am ah fuck. You fuckin are. Check yer een, Freddy."

"Holy shit. They're pinned tae fuck, like."

"Dinnae you start, ye fat cunt. You're fucked as weel. 'Is fat bastard wid probably taak Bugs Bunny up the flume if he hid the chunce."

"Aye, right; luk at you, ye cunt. Ah'm fuckin decked at ye, like, ye spotty twat."

"Ah bet ye wid, though."

"Wid ah fuck, Freddy. Ah ken you wid. You'd wrap his lugs aroon yer waist an' ging like fuck."

"Pair o fuckin imbeciles."

"Oh, checks cool guy Derek 'imsel."

"Hoi, ah'll admit it. Ah wid gie She-Ra a good shaftin."

"See? Derek's wi me."

"'At's 'cos ye's are beth fucked up. Pervy bastards."

"Spotty twat."

"Aye, boys, cool it wi the zit remarks, aye?"

"A'right, Freddy… ye poke-marked spasmo."

"'At's it, ye fat cunt - "

"Shit."

"Fit?"

"The manny Slessor's comin."

"Quick, fuckin chuck it. Flush the bastard."

Silence.

"What you boys up to in here? Did you's not hear the bell? Eh? Off to your classes. And you, Master Gibson, get that smirk off your face."

*

"Ye sure 'at's right?"

"Aye. Ah think so. Fit's wrang, like?"

"It disnae feel right."

"Well, it wis you 'at guided the thing in."

"Ah ken, bit it disnae feel like it's in the right hole."

"*Eh*?"

"Oh, Derek, jist get on wi it. Ma chums are waitin on me."

"Sae are mine."

"It's Baltic oot here. Could we nae've went back tae your hoose?"

"Ma folks are in."

"So? Ah could've sneaked in."

"No. 'Is is a'right."

"Says you."

"Fit? Ah'm deein ma best. Ah hivnae deen 'is afore eether, ye ken?"

"You said ye hid."

"Well, ah dinnae ken; ye must've heard me wrang or somethin. 'Is is aa new tae me."

"Jist shut up an' dee fit ye're gaan tae dee."

"Okay, okay. Woo-oo, eh eh eh eh eh. 'At's better. Here we go. 'At's the wye. 'At's the stuff, eh?"

Groaning. "Derek, it's sair."

"Aye, it's, eh, supposed tae be, like."

"'Is sair?"

"Ah dinnae ken. Ah hivnae got a fud, hiv ah?"

"Right." Wrestling. "'At's enough."

"Wait. Fuck sake. Lori, come back."

*

"Yes, Derek?"

"Can I come in now?"

"Derek, you may come in once you've learned how to behave in a manner befitting my classroom, and not a second earlier. Is that understood? Bearing this in mind, do you think that you're now ready to come in and join these other respectful pupils?"

"Yes."

"Well, I'm terribly sorry, Mr Gibson, but I'm afraid that I don't agree with you."

"Suit yersel."

"Derek, just you sit there and think about how you should grow up. And don't dare interrupt my class again for whatever reason. Unlike you, your classmates might want to learn something which they may be able to implement towards the betterance of themselves at a later date."

"On ye go, then. Teach awaa."

*

"Teacher here yet?"

"No. Why? Fit's the plan, fat man?"

"Ma dad's awaa. You got ony o 'at stuff left, Derek?"

"Indeed I do."

"Ye groovin?"

"But of course."

"Let's shoot, 'en."

At the door. Class watching. Along corridor. Mr Strachan approaches.

"Where, may I ask, are you two going? Another appointment? One to hold the other's hand? I've got your test scores here to give you back."

"Did we pass?"

"Somewhat extraordinarily, no."

"Then fa gies a fuck?"

Through the swing doors. Past the canteen. Into the Broch.

*

Night. A soggy bus shelter. A hobo's shack of raggedy brick, close to the Leisure Centre end of the Broadgate. The cider bottles pass from palm to shivering palm. The boys, eight strong, will be the worst of pals until their early twenties when most will fall by the wayside, either escaping the group for marriage or heroin.

Toot toot. A car halts. The passenger window unwinds. Derek smiles at the beaming pan revealed. He advances from the shelter.

"Aye, aye, Derek."

"Fit like, 'en, Davey?"

David: handsome, wholesome and thoughtful – a funkier version of his more recent imitation. "Nae bad."

Derek bends, careful not to kneel in a puddle. He nods at the driver: a callous platter havering by the wheel. The driver responds as though to a fellow train passenger whose eyes he happened to meet. The guy has no time for those younger than himself. The back seats are empty.

"Fit you boys up tae the night, 'en? Ma brither in 'ere?"

"Nah. Pagan's swottin up, like. Exams the morn. Ye ken fit like he is. We're jist prickin aboot, ken?"

"Oh, aye. 'At's right. Exam time. Cunt, eh?" Laughter. "Pagan. Why the fuck dee ye's caa 'im 'at onywye?"

Derek strove for the answer. "Ah cannae mine."

"Ah, me. Shid you cunts nae be revisin as weel, 'en?"

"Fuck it. It's only French. 'Em fuckin frogs want tae spick tae me, they kin learn tae spick English. Bunch o faggots, though, in't they?"

"Ah suppose 'at's one wye tae luk at it, eh, Derek? Fuck the French, eh?" More mirth. "So, fit's 'at you boys are drinkin?"

Derek raises his cider. "'Is shite."

"Fuck 'at, like. 'At pish gies me fearsome hairtburn. Ye's shid try 'is stuff. Fuckin good, like."

David brings a dark bottle into the reach of the streetlight.

"Buckfast? Fit dis 'at shit taste like?"

"Hae a sip."

Derek takes a swig. He winces. "Fuck me. 'At's fuckin orra."

"Ye get used tae it. The taste grous on ye."

"Ah doot it. Fuckin horrible."

"Trust me, Derek. You'll hae a thirst fir it een day."

"So, why you hame the noo? Ah thought you wis at uni?"

"Aye. Day aff, like. Thought ah'd come hame fir a lang wikend. Cannae get enough o 'is toon; ye ken fit like, eh, Derek? It's jist too great a place."

"Aye. Amazin."

"Nah. It's a bit o a shite-hole, right enough."

"Too fuckin right. Ah'm leavin 'is place as seen as ah can."

"See, Derek? Ah kent you wis een o the cliver eens."

"Ah dinnae ken aboot 'at, like. Nae proper school material. Aye, so hoo ye gettin on through in Aiberdeen, 'en? It's, eh, architecture ye're deein, is it nae?"

"Aye, 'at's right, Derek. Interior architecture. It's gaan pretty weel. Cheers fir askin."

"Nae buther. Yer brither wis sayin, like."

"Oh, aye?"

"Aye. Says ye wis deein really weel, like. Winnin competitions an' shit."

"Aye, Derek, ah'm deein a'right. Nae too bad. An' hoo's ma brither gettin on?"

"Ye ken 'at cunt. He's like a fuckin super brain or somethin. Ah hardly see Pagan at school onymair. The cunt's in aa the tap sets fir iverythin. Ah'm stuck wi 'ese mongos in the dumb-fuck classes." Derek gestures behind at the squabbling, fag-illuminated characters in the shelter. "He's a cliver cunt, like."

"Aye. He's a bright kina guy, like, is oor Pagan, eh? He shid dee a'right wi 'imsel. An' fit aboot you; fit dis young knight Sir Derek want tae dee wi 'imsel?"

"Fuck knows."

"Ach, weel, nae rush, eh? Plinty o time tae worry aboot 'at shit aifter."

"Aye."

"Right, well, Derek, ah'd better let ye awaa. We'll probably see ye aboot."

"Aye, right-o, David. Cheerio."

"Cheers, Derek. Taak care o yersel."

*

Same night. An hour forward. Tearing through the rural, the remote. Raining like a gutted whale. The car skids off the road, trapping an elderly woman between the bumper and a telephone pole. A Buckfast bottle goes through the driver's neck; he dies within seconds. David flees the scene; panicky legs stride through swamps; barbed-wire fences hunt him. Mud hides the cuts. The old dear gurgles her last cry a further hour forward.

*

Lies. Lies. The who, the what, why, where, the whens. No, no, no. David had been dropped off long before then. Crushed you say? Split in half? My, my, how frightfully ghastly. How awful. Awful. Ye kin tell me, Davey: fit happened? Wis ye 'ere? Seriously. Really. Come on, ah winnae say onythin tae ony cunt. Did ye leave 'er tae dee? Wis she a hoorin meese, aye? Ah mean, ah could un'erstan, like. Ye freaked oot. It happens. Ah might've deen the same.

Fuck off, fuck off, fuck off.

David immerses himself in his modules. Blocks, buildings, models. He can't concentrate for extended periods, however. Nothing sticks. People and ideas slip off the side of his brain and into the pools of his stomach. He whimpers at night, leaking from his handsome, wholesome phizog until three-four in the morning. This is guilt, no? His flatmates give up on him; he gives up on his course. David finds his blanket.

*

Sucking up the sugary smog. One of Fraserburgh's earliest heroin addicts, David spends his days wrapped in wool. He no longer walks; he hovers to where he wants to go – which happens to be nowhere. David disintegrates for the world to see, and he is euphorically unaware that he should be ashamed or pained by his reluctance to live. David pre-empts the cliché, setting the blueprint for all junkies to come. He doesn't work, wash or worry. Moans when he's down; babbles when he's up. Steals from his relatives and associates. Lies, lies. Lies when confronted. A deceitful, crusting cask smothers a hurting soul.

Ah wis 'ere, he confides to his brother and Derek one evening, gate-crashing their horror matinee in Pagan's bedroom. Ah seen 'er screamin. Bleedin. Guts an' stuff. We'd been drinkin, like; dinnae tell ony cunt, like, man. Boys, ah ken you's widnae; ye's are beth cool, eh? Aye, man, Derek, hoo's it gaan, mate? We'd bin boozin aa night, ken? Ah left 'er. Dinnae tell ony cunt, please. Ah left 'er. Deid.

The old lady had died.

Neither his brother nor Derek told anyone.

Parents ran the gamut. Concern. Alarm. Annoyance. Anger. Disappointment. David, both me and your father think it's time for us to cut our loses and tell you to leave.

*

"Oh, aye, Derek, fit like?"

"Nae bad."

"Ye finished school or somethin, man?"

"Nah. It's ma denner oor. Jist awaa tae the chippies."

"Oh?"

"Aye."

"Crazy."

"Aye, David, so ah heard ye've moved oot."

"'At's right. Kin ye believe 'at? Fuckin nuts, like. They think ah'm on drugs, man. They're fucked up, like. Skeg? Fuckin idiots. You fuckin ken me, right? You ken ah'm nae like 'at? Dee ah luk like a druggie tink tae you?"

"Nah. Stopped yer course an' aa, aye?"

"Aye, aye. It wisnae fir me, though, ken, Derek? Ach, it wis a bit shite, like. Piss-borin. Ah'd hid enough o it."

"Right-o."

"Aye, so, Derek, ye dinnae mind if ah ask a smaa wee favour o ye, eh? Hiv ye got a couple o quid ye could maybe gie me a len o, aye? Ye'll get it right back, ah sweer."

*

Broch's first smackheid supreme was found on a dry afternoon in the family shed. He had excrement in his pants and a needle in his arm. David the junkie had lasted barely two seasons.

*

"It is with great hope and bitter reflection that we must turn to the heavens at this time and pray that this terrible reminder of the destructive nature of drugs which has befallen us will serve to dissuade youngsters from pursuing the same unfortunate path as David."

Derek sits in the last row at his first funeral. Philip, James, Frederick and Mark hog the bench along with other acquaintances, most of whom are here purely for the day off school.

Derek doesn't enjoy this funeral. He watches Pagan at the front, hunched and speechless. Derek can't emulate the sadness felt by the first two rows. Death doesn't work for him at this stage. It doesn't really mean anything. The coffin could be vacant. He'll surely bump into David again sometime in the street. He'll be there to bum another few quid off of him.

David's death could not hit Derek as the permanent absence of a fixture in his weekly timetable would. He'd likely miss his bedside lamp more. A parent dead – there was a loss. You couldn't not notice one of your folks never being around for ever more. If it were a Fat Ass or a Jimbo whom were to be buried, that, too, might make Derek teary. Maybe even make him cry a bit. He supposed that it would do. Might. Possibly.

Pagan shudders, in a low-key style.

The greying district supervisor of Team God floats above the box. "We must stand mightily forth and accept this challenge from the Serpent. With the Lord's love and divine strength we will smite this terror, and thus ensure that Fraserburgh's fate is one that is heroin free."

The parents are stiff with dejection and the crushing knowledge that here lies a waste. A waste to be dumped in the soil, to be reduced to worm shit. Derek feels their grief as though it were a creeping presence, like a window, somewhere in the house, did splinter. A cushion pushes hard against his chest until a liquid secretes by the corners of his eyes.

Someone sniggers.

The eggy stench of a ripe fart enfolds the rims of his nose.

*

"Well, boys, ah guess 'is is it, 'en."

"Aye."

"Probably be back sometime."

"Yip."

"Good luck an' stuff."

"Aye."

"Ah'll miss ye's."

"Eh, aye."

"Well, ma mam's waitin."

"Right-o."

"See ye's."

"Okay."

*

"So, 'at's yer chum awaa?"

"Aye."

*

"So, 'at's yer academy days feenished?"

"Aye."

*

"Gaan tae college, 'en? University?"

"Ah dinnae ken."

*

"Work wi yer dad?"

"Suppose so."

*

"Hoo wis yer first trip?"

"A'right."

*

"Hoo did he get on?"

"Hopeless."

*

"Derek, the boat leaves in an oor's time. Ye gettin up or fit?"

"Cannae. Sair heid."

"Aye?"

"Aye."

"Well, please yerfuckinsel."

*

"Derek, yer dad thinks that maybe ye'd be better aff workin somewye else. Dee ye want me tae spick tae 'im once mair or fit?"

"Ah'm nae buthered."

*

"'At's a cheque."

"Aye? Fit for?"

"'Cos ye're nae eese fir fishin, an' ye're nae eese fir ma boat."

"Aye?"

"Aye. Ye kin spend 'at hoo ye want tae, ah couldnae care, bit ah recommend ye try tae save it. 'At's the last money ye'll iver see fae me. Dinnae buther askin me fir onythin again. 'At's yer last, Derek. So dinnae be greetin tae me or yer mam fin ye're skint jist 'cos you cannae stick a job. 'At's your fuckin problem. An' ye kin thank yer mam that ye still bide under ma reef. If it wis up tae me, ye'd be oot 'at door quick as ye like. Right?"

"Aye."

"Right?"

"Fair enough."

*

At fifteen years of age, Tracy Gibson embarks on a controversial affair with the rather much older Donald Wise, to the significant consternation of her parents. A renowned stoner and widely perceived ne'er-do-well of the North, Donnie's beardy features, in conjunction with unruly sideboards and lengthy black locks, prove irresistible to young Tracy. Miss Gibson is smitten with the hirsute lothario. They fornicate. They fall in love. She allows herself to be led astray. Together, they flirt with danger, romancing the edgier opiates. Who cares what the others think? they thought. Life's for livin, man. Try, don't deny. Es. Coke. Skeg. Higher, higher. Harder, harder. Much much more more more. When

Mr fills Ms.

Impregnated by Donnie, Tracy finds herself ostracised by her family, except for Derek. It would appear that Derek isn't really fussed one way or the other. She moves in with the father of her unborn child. He sells the stuff to get the stuff required to run the house. Rachel is born. Her grandparents on the Gibson stem never once do visit.

*

Yard to yard. Works to drink. Drinks to party. Parties to fuck. Works whenever he feels the need. Never dips into the account where the cheque, the pay-off, lies. It sleeps undisturbed to prove a point. Some point. Unclear.

Derek checks his watch. Years spill away like kids down chutes, water from boots, timber waistcoats, racing speedboats. Working. Sacked. Working. Sacked. Drinking. Drunk. Drinking. Destroyed. Smooching the girls. Twirling their curls. It's all a waste of time.

Probably.

*

Standing by the bar. Some fun in a glass. Steeper in nightclubs. Sombre thoughts take him. He exists now only in that fist-sized box between his ears. The dancefloor is some futuristic war zone. Drunken and drugged-up mugs are shot and molested by wicked lights, all strobes and probes in the gloom. Aye, aye, Derek. Fit like, 'en? Fit like, 'en? Battling the urge to attack every fifty-quid-shirt-and-sharpened-trousers-wearing bloke that comes grinning up to him. With their heads covered in styling wax. And their pupils like tadpoles gnawing at their larvae sacks. Nae bad. Nae bad. Fit like yersel? Oh, cannae complain. Cannae complain at aa. We'll see ye aboot. Enjoy yer nicht. Same tae you. Right-o.

Girls: open blouses, short skirts, looking for affection, a kiss, a cuddle, a husband; and boys: just after something more than a wank for a change. The men whoop and sing like they'd redirected a comet, pulsating with a rented happiness that'll dissipate once they're out in the cold, scrambling for a taxi. Guys dance to music that they shouldn't touch five out of seven nights of the week. Derek would be joining them soon. Once this negativity erodes, he'd be out on that floor, like a boar after truffles. Hopefully, he'd have had his snout in the bush by the time that the downer resurfaced in the morning.

Which morning? Sunday. Sunday? This was Saturday, wasn't it? Eh? No, no. This was only Friday. Friday, so it was. Pace yourself, Sir Derek. The young knight has another eve' in which to drink the finest wines and engorge the fairest maidens before he must return to his dire quest to procure the riches to once more enjoy another eve' in which he gets to drink the finest

Derek feels the dread. Oh, no. He observes those possessed beans leap and ping, knowing that any misdirected elbow or flailing paw could cause an argument could cause a shove could cause a fight. Bouncers would wade in, smart-like with their bowties, and throw the scrappers out to settle their strife in the car park.

Friday – Saturday? – night in The Rocking Peacock. Rocking, though there weren't any guitars here; it was all this Euro gubbins, which was to Derek the noise of music passing a bowel movement, and it splashing back up.

Godfuckindammit. Godfuckindammit.

I hate this fuckin place. This time. This bland chink of the universe. Drinking up these fond memories. These were the best of times. We earned this night. The right to impersonate retards till Monday morning. Appreciate it more when older. That seems to be the way. We hid some fuckin good laughs, eh? Ivery wikend, eh? Mine fan you spewed? Mine fan yer tits fell oot? Mine hospitalisin yon boy? What a time. What fun. And now I am old, and the girls I would've been nailing are wiping my arse.

Hope less.

Inconsequential. Insubstantial. Goldfish. Here's your reward for half a century of nine-to-five. Sprinkle me now with your sex and sound. Fuckin, fuckin, fuck it.

And tomorrow he'd forget it all.

*

"Fit's wrang? Ah tellt ye, ye kin bide wi me until ma dad comes back fae the rigs. Dinnae worry aboot 'at."

"Ah'm nae, Fat Ass."

"Fit is it, 'en? Ye've hardly touched yer pint."

"Slow starter the night."

"Come on, ye twat. Jist get it doon ye. Ye'll feel a lot better."

"Maybe."

"Oh, no, Derek. Dinnae tell me that ye're depressed. 'At widnae soon right comin fae you."

"Why nae?"

"'Cos 'at's jist nae fa you are, is it? Dee ye think ye're depressed, like?"

"Ah'm nae depressed, ye fat turd. 'Ere's jist a lot gaan on the noo."

"Nae awaa tae burst intae tears, are ye?"

"No, Philip, you portly butt-blurt, ah'm nae. Bit thanks fir yer concern. It waarms me right in the middle o ma chest."

"Nah, seriously, though. Ye a'right?"

"It jist kina feels sometimes like ah'm tryin tae get through ma life wi ma cock tied tae ma ankle. Ye ken?"

"Things'll pick up."

"Ah dinnae ken. Ah mean, Fat Ass, did ye iver think that maybe yer life wis leadin up tae somethin? Ah think ah aiwyes jist assumed that somethin good wis gaan tae happen tae me, ken, sooner or later? That if ah jist kept ma een peeled, like, things wid start tae – fit's the word ah'm lukin for? – converge. Nod if ye ken fit ah'm spickin aboot."

"Aye, Derek. Ah think ah div ken fit ye're gaan on aboot. An' no, Derek, ah dinnae think that ye're the chosen one."

"'At's nae fit ah meant, ye prat. Ah dinnae think that ah'm special."

"Then fit the fuck are ye gaan on aboot?"

"Ah'm nae sure. It's jist that it's startin tae sink in that maybe ah'm really nae gaan onywye, ken? That maybe ma life is leadin up tae nithin."

"Fuck me, Derek, ye're a slow learner. Noo, hurry up an' finish yer pint. Ye're fuckin bringin me doon, ye ugly cunt."

Chapter 17

Think about. Would you? This. Sort. Out. Your.

"Mark"

Had: been surprised.

"He's one o James's friends, ah think."

He did: meet up with both Fat Ass and Freddy. To get drunk, moderately so. Four or five jars. But didn't get drunk. Why?

"Ah ken 'at, Charlie."

Because he was: held at gunpoint; embroiled in some fatuous farce involving whores and giants. Pros and cons. Missing money. Stolen.

"He's Sandra's boy."

Prompting him to: lead the giant to Jimmy's (engravings in the walls: fornication with the deity?), then to Lori's. Kennedy Crescent: restful; mansions overlook mansions.

"He works in the bank."

Watched the giant: exit the green car; walk up to a doorway; enter the dark house. Followed him.

"Mark, Mark, come back tae us. Listen tae me."

Heard: creeks; groaning stairs ahead; Lex stop, go pensive, inquire the black. 'Fa goes 'ere? Switch on the light. Nae need fir trouble. Dee ye hear me? Answer me.' A click.

"Mark."

Witnessed: a flash; a burst of Zeus's palm; a house of money blast into sight. Then all fades. Back to black.

"Hear me, Mark. Ye're okay."

He'd felt: the warm spray; a falling trunk; the beanstalk crash upon him.

"'At's the car ready. Ye'll need Mark tae gie ye a lift."

"Noo drink," the man in the bear coat said, handing Mo a hot mug.

"'At'll bring ye roon."

Mo took a taste of the extra strong coffee contained within the walls of a 'World's Greatest Dad' cup. The man, barely a pair of eyebrows under his assortment of woollen garments, sat across from Mo at the kitchen table and waited for the caffeine to pummel the lad from his daze. The man swept the tail of his scarf away from his own mug. The woman couldn't keep still, pinballing about the laminate floor in her floral dressing gown. She went out into the lobby; up the stairs; down the stairs; into the garage; back; she bleeped out her requests and orders like a malfunctioning boiler. Mark sipped his drink. He looked at the rifle, pungent with use, as it leaned against the thingamajig-dotted fridge. The weapon was like a security guard that lingers in the crowd as its client greets the cameras. A chunky gold picture frame was poised on a unit, between the microwave and a knife rack. The daughter was captured behind its shield. She was pleased in the photo, but it seemed to Mark like her upbeat aspect was derived from relief rather than a general gladness about her state of affairs, as if she were finally going to her bed after being up for days.

Charlie ignored his wife; Lesley didn't mind that he disregarded her. This was a unique scenario. She continued to splash through the house; Charlie was much too far up the beach to care about her waves. He stared over the table. Mo felt obliged to chug the remainder of his beverage and speak.

"Is he deid?" Mo asked. It was as though he'd surfaced into a net. "Did ye kill 'im, mister?" He referred to those denimed legs, stretched out along the corridor. "Ye niver killt 'im, did ye?"

"Ah think maybe so."

"Shid we nae check? Shid we phone an ambulance?"

"Ah think maybe no."

Mo didn't know how to proceed. He knew, however, that he no longer wanted to meet the gaze of the man opposite him. The man who had been prepared for a visit since he'd received a letter of warning the week before, and had decided to launch his own offensive with immediate effect upon first sight of the thug whom had been involved in the soliciting of his daughter, his missing girl. This man who neither slouched nor rigidly sat in his chair. The man who contemplated and comprehended, and had allowed for majestic melancholy to suffocate him. That man. This ghosting man.

"Fit noo?" Mo inspected the silt at the bottom of his mug.

"Ah dinnae blame ye, Mark."

Mrs Mackintosh was busy finding things to keep her busy. She was currently in the shed digging around for the heavy-duty stain-remover. Blood in abundance had congealed in the hallway. Soap wouldn't take care of that. They might have to bung out the carpet.

Mo turned back to Charlie, whose expression reminded him of a frozen pint glass. "Fit? Fit dee ye - "

"Mark, Mark, it's fine. Relax. Ah'm sure ye hid nae choice bit tae taak 'im here. He disnae luk the type ye argue wi, eh?"

"No. Sorry aboot 'at, like. Ah really am."

"It's fine."

Mo utilised the comb of his nails. His hair was matted in parts with the giant's vital fluids. "He hid a gun."

"Ah believe ye."

"He keeps it in his belt."

The pint glass fractured into a smile. "We'd better get it, 'en."

Mo needed to unfurl himself. "Right." He stood up. "Then fit?"

"Ah think then maybe we'll hiv tae get rid o the body."

The body wasn't dead. Crimson syrup slurped from a hole on its torso, like an overflowing petrol tank. Lex couldn't speak; he could only move vaguely. His eyes twitched as if their lids couldn't quite close but wished to. Mo had missed his supper, as he was prone to do; otherwise, he would've vomited.

He and Mr Mackintosh said little to one another as they heaved the giant up onto his rump. Lex did not resist their efforts. Other than suggestions as how best to manoeuvre the giant out of the lobby and onto the drive, talk seemed wholly inappropriate. Mo, at any rate, didn't feel capable of chitchat. At the back of his throat, a road sign, a red one, had been erected. Mrs Mackintosh bustled over and behind and all around them. She had a thin, worn face that was given to angry contortions, and her hairdo was marginally shorter than what she'd asked for. Lesley had a wet cloth; she attempted to salvage the carpet as the two men dragged the other man. That man looked a cert to be dying. She rinsed the rag in a bucket, squeezing free the gore. She dabbed at Mo's face with the same cloth; he withheld his ingratitude.

The giant was hauled over a step; he thumped against the peat path, which poured up to a double garage and down onto the street, itself neatly submerged with the greenery of controlled wilderness. Every garden had high, suspicious walls.

Lex's sports vehicle was at the foot of the Mackintosh drive. It watched on helplessly at the disaster that had struck its master.

The Mackintosh car had been reversed up to the front door. A back passenger door hung ajar. The wife had also thought to leave the engine running and ready.

Mark and the Mackintoshes admired the haggard giant, as though their rocket hadn't quite made it to beyond the pylons. The lobby light presented this image for anyone to see, but everyone was asleep, or unfazed by the squib-bang of the earlier gunshot. The ears of the neighbourhood had chosen to discount that exclamation mark in the night.

"Get his gun, Lesley."

"Aye." And she did. She purloined the protruding pistol from his belt, then gave it to her man. He placed it on the dashboard. Mo recalled how that same tool had near shattered his friend's skull. How was Derek? he wondered. How were the others? He wanted to see them, speak to them, inform them, go home, conk. All in time.

"Get his car keys, Lesley."

She did that, too – raking through the man's pockets till she found them in his jeans. In retrieving them, she inadvertently touched the form of his penis. She held the keys up as if they'd been dipped in dung, with a 'fit noo?' look on her seldom-friendly face.

"The car kin wait," Charlie said, intimating towards the problem of disposing of the giant's chariot. "We'll come back fir it. First thing's first."

He grabbed one of Lex's arms and motioned for Mark to do the same. Mo did as he was bidden. The thug's limb felt like a sopping bag of sand. With ample difficulty, the pair managed to hoist the giant into the back seat of the purple saloon. It was like trying to pack an alligator into a suitcase. Job done, Charlie closed and locked the door. Both men panted from the exercise. They were smeared with the sanguineous solution. The woman's cloth was passed around. The drive would have to be hosed down.

"Right, 'en," said Charlie, after a minute of much nothingness had elapsed. "Dee ye want tae get in the car, Mark? Seems 'is'll be a twa-man job."

"Eh, aye, okay."

"Fine." To his wife, "Maak sure ye pit the rifle awaa. Ah'll taak it back tae the fairmer the morn."

The wife crushed her breasts under intersecting wrists. She shuffled into the house. She didn't lock the door, as she hadn't done for the past seven nights – the aperture to their snare. And now, perhaps, an end to sleeplessness. That dilemma had been eradicated with a bullet, just the one needed. She would secure the door only when her man had returned.

Mo and Mr Mackintosh stood in the cold, standing there staring at each other. Cold, cold night; frost festering by their feet; dying man in car; and they stood there staring at each other. Mo noticed that Charlie wasn't really staring at him, though. The man was staring slightly off to the side of Mo. He adjusted his stance to discover what it was that might've entangled the man's scrutiny. There didn't appear to be anything of note except for the twin garage doors and stacks of darkness. Mo felt: unease; disconsolation; illness; the realisation that everything was now in the realms of death and prison-sentence seriousness.

"Fit noo, mister?" Mo could see his own words: bluish clouds billowing away from a cotton-padded mouth. He'd escorted a man to the barrel of a gun. He'd been ignorant of Lori's parents' plans; but his reaction to their transgression did not broadcast innocence.

Charlie spoke to his vehicle. "We get in the car."

"Then fit? Faar we gaan?"

"Faar else?" A frail confidence; a wistfulness that could engulf. Beneath the lid of Charlie's grin, empty was the biscuit tin. "Tae the hairbour."

*

The reeds seemed to part, and not poke as they usually did whenever Freddy ventured over this way. Normally, those streams of lithe daggers would jig at his legs, like a tight trench lined with syringes. Brave would be the summer fellow in his shorts. The long grass swished with the wind, which was temperate but icy. The moon was the torch on a miner's helmet. If those reeds did grate him to his knees, Freddy did not feel it. And if there were pains to be registered the morn, then that still wouldn't be enough to sully his praise for this most wondrous night. It was. It was. Magnificent.

Those swirling reeds. The moon. Luk at 'at fir a moon. A full moon, waashed an' hung oot tae dry. An' it really wis dry, wisn't it? Like a bone. Nae a drap. Jist brilliant, like. Spectacular.

Caal, though, eh? Bitter kine, no? Nae maitter.

So long, too long, since he'd last walked about up here in the dunes. The eclectic lumps between the sea and the golf course. Dual stars journeyed in tandem along the road to the southward villages. He thought he saw a plastic bag bound over the lower hills. Fit times they'd hid up on the dunes, eh? They used to have a campy around here; somewhere between Tiger Hill and the Philorth River that gushed out by Cairnbulg beach. Their campy: a hut assembled from flotsam. But where exactly? Nae maitter. Gone by now. Cairnbulg, though, eh? Freddy could see from this trail that he strode its short sequence of lanterns, like lures dangling on the end of the captain's line. Freddy interrupted his trek to appreciate the vista. To the north, there was a more intricate procession of lights.

Ach, the Broch's a'right. Folk spick the place doon aa the time. Say Broch's a roch place – a shitey-hole, eh? 'At's pish. Broch's a great toon, eh? Well, it's nae as bad as some places, eh? It cannae be; could it? Ah mean, it is a'richt, though, ken? Ye read aboot dad's gettin battered an' left wi brain damage by young cooncil-estate cunts fir tellin 'em tae keep the noise doon. Ye hear aboot 'at shit happenin aa the time doon Sooth. It's nae jist a Broch thing, ken? Fair enough, 'ere wis 'at cairry on last nicht, bit 'at's nae the norm, like. 'Em cunts will be caught. Believe you me, pal. They'll be caught. 'At winnae stand.

Fit is the Broch, though, onwye, like? It's jist a bunch o light bulbs an' bricks stuck taegither. Fit Broch identity? 'Ere's nae like a 'Broch' attitude. Aa cunt's different. Same onywye ye go, man. Ye'll get the pricks. 'At's the game, though, eh? The decent folk usually aiwyes ootnumber the twats, ken? Bit nae cunt's perfect. Ivery guy's a bit o a dick.

'At right, moon?

Fit ye ignorin me fir? You ken ah'm right. It's aa gweed.

The tide was out. The shoosh of the grey foam chewing on the sand combined with the faraway thrum of Fraserburgh yards, in operation until the old adage was defunct and there really weren't plenty more fish in the proverbial. The noise made for jolly companionship, encouraging him along to complete his task. His task? Find the girl. Derek's niece. Remember? Donnie Wise's wee quine.

'Ere's Donnie doon 'ere, luk. He rolled across the beach at whelk speed, like a punctured full stop. Once in a while, Donnie's drawl blew up over the dunes in Freddy's direction. Raaay-chilll. But Rachel wasn't here. Freddy knew that for a fact. The girl would be home by now. In her bed in her pyjamas, having already forgotten about the fear that she had instilled in her parents. Children were horribleness most brilliant.

Everything was marvellous, simply so. The beach. Jist luk at it. It wis dark, like, bit ye got the gist o it, eh? Flat and smooth, like how Kim's sweet bum once was. Why did they nae fuck onymair? Erectify that tomorrow night. If he could be bothered. He'd make himself bothered. Kim was magnificent. And the sea. Choppy and endearing, like a feisty, wizened alky, as ever forever. Live awaa fae it? Ye're aff yer rocker, pal. The sye's faimily.

'Is is jist great, like. Bin too lang. Get the wife, get the boys – the bairns, nae the *boys* boys – an' come here on Setterda, providin the wither's nae too Broch-like. Shid be okay. Maak a day o it. Why nae?

Woof.

Pardon?

Woof. And once again for your convenience, sir: woof.

A dog up ahead was calling out. Freddy couldn't see the dog, but he could tell that it was up ahead. How long had he heard that dog barking for before he had actually catalogued the sound and distinguished it as being that of a dog barking? Christ shrugged. Freddy kept to the path that led to the dog that barked up ahead.

*

Fuckin fuckin fuck. Scream. Fuckin fuckin fuck. Scream.

Fuckin fuckin fuck fuck fuck fuck. SCREAM.

Performing analingus

On Martina Hingus.

Fuckin fuckin fuck. Scream. Fuckin fuckin fuck. Scream.

Africans an' Asians

Chase 'em wi Alsations.

Fuckin fuckin fuck. Scream. Fuckin fuckin fuck. Scream.

Bang. Bang. Chris. Open up. Open up.

Fuckin fuckin fuck. Scream. Fuckin fuckin fuck. Scream.

Turn the music doon, turn the music doon.

No. Get tae fuckin fuck. Get tae fuckin fuck. No.

Waarnin you, ma lad, waarnin you, ma lad

No.

Waarnin you, ma lad, waarnin you lad, ma lad

No.

Ah will taak this blessed door doon.

Get tae fuckin fuck. Get tae fuckin fuck.

No.

Ah thought ah tellt you tae get tae fuckin fuck. Get tae fuckin fuck.

Oh. Whoa. Chris, ma lad
Ye've deen it noo
Ah'll tell yer dad.
Ach, well, 'at's jist too bad
Bit fuck you, mam
An' fuck you, dad.

Fuckin fuckin fuck. Scream. Fuckin fuckin fuck. Scream.

Fuck fuck fuck fuck fuck fuck. SCREAM.

Jews an' gentiles
The young an' senile.

Chuck 'em in a bag. Chuck 'em in a bag.

Scream.

Chuck 'em in a bag. Chuck 'em in a bag.

Scream.

Taak them doon tae the loch tae droon.

Chris, ye swine
Ye mohican-haired queer,
Listen up
'Cos daddy's here.
Eleven o'clock is too late at night
Too late to roar, to shout,
To fight.
So one mair soon
One sang, one strum
An' ah'll come in 'ere
Tae smack ye dumb.

Ye got ’at, Chris?

Stop taakin the piss.

You,

Jist like me,

Need sleep

Fir work,

Ye see?

Noo awaa, ye pit

Yer guitar an’ amp

Then climb intae bed

An’ switch aff yer lamp.

Fir peace, ah want,

Ah really need,

An’ if don’t, ah get,

Ye’ll be fuckin deid.

Weel, sorry, dad,

It’s sad tae hear

Ye refer tae yer son

As a little queer.

Bit, father, father, ’at’s so absurd

Fir ah’m nae gay

By ony stretch o the word.

Ah baal an’ sweer

An’ cause ’is noise

Fir maim an’ beat,

Did me an’ the boys.

’Is pain, ’is guilt

That drives me doon

Maaks me play an' wail

An' sing like a loon.

Help me noo,

Fir ah confess,

We left 'at aal bastard

In an affa mess.

*

Woof. Woof. Woof woof.

Strecht up aheid, aye? Aye. Ye kin hear it, Fred. Nithin wrang wi yer lugs; it's jist yer brain that's a bit funny. Pretty close by noo, like. Right ye are. Be some aal couple waakin their dowg. In the middle o the night? Ye ken fit like aal folk are. Feel as onythin.

Freddy would ask the walkers – perhaps they would not even be old, just foolish – he would ask the walkers if they'd seen a young girl, which they wouldn't have done because she was in her bed. Probably dreaming about the beach and the sea and treasure islands, and childish things.

Remember how he and the boys – the *boys* boys – had talked about buying a yacht? Years ago. Aye, they would all put some pennies aside for five years or so, then get themselves a sailing boat. A thirty-footer. Had they decided upon a name for it? No. Maybe. Cannae mine. They'd talked earnestly of their plan for at least four months. Where they would go; the places they'd see; everything. It would've been fantastic. Had they started saving at seventeen, when they'd promised to, they would've navigated the globe by now, surely, certainly. Of course, if they had followed through with that project, he likely wouldn't have married Kim, and the Earth's population would be slimmer by two males.

It had been a grand plan, however. Would have to mention it again sometime. No. That's utter stupidity. Fit wid be the point, eh? The plan would be dismissed with the prior swiftness; their interest and excitement in the cerebration would dwindle like the half-life of the flimsiest radioactive material. Fit's the hairm in mentionin it, though?

Freddy, Freddy, Freddy. Ye really think much o yer pals, don't ye? They kin save money, aye? Aye, 'at's wye they still bide wi their mams an' dads. Face it. Yer mates are a bunch o wasters. Fit fuckin use are they? Fuckin ditch 'em. Hoi, 'at's enough. They're drunkards. Sae am ah. No, ye're nae. Ah like a drink. 'At's nae aa ye like. Fuck off. Caain me a lee'er? No, bit 'is the noo – 'is is jist a present tae masel. Present, aye? Aye, 'at's fit ah said. Aye. Keep tellin yersel 'at. Fa the fuck dee ye think you are, like? Some fuckin angel or somethin, eh? Fuckin slaggin me aff, ye cunt? Whoa, simmer, Fred. Calm noo, Frederick. Jist you simmer. Jist think aboot yer yachty, an' hoo ye're gaan tae get it on a welder's wage wi twa bairns an' a wife tae luk aifter. Fuck you. Hey, nae need fir 'at. Ah'm jist sayin, like. Get tae fuck, wid ye? Calm doon, ah said. Ah'm sure ye'll get 'at boat een day. Ah'm sure Fat Ass an' Mo an' Jimmy an' Derek – ah'm tryin nae tae laugh here – ah'm sure they'll aa settle doon, they'll aa get decent jobs, they'll aa be bringin in the money, an' 'en ye's will be able tae save an' get yer yacht. Ye's will be sailin by New Zealand afore ye's ken it. Ah kin see it noo. Sae kin ah. Good. Ah'm only here tae help, Fred. Aye? Aye.

Sailing past the green hills and dark cliffs of kiwi country. Tremendous. It really wasn't too hard to imagine. It wasn't impossible. Derek was lazy, but he was decent. They all were. He just needed guidance. They all did. He'd settle. They all would. They'd all be like Freddy. Freddy had it sussed. Party now and enjoy your youth, but don't wake up when you're sixty and moan because there's no one else in the house.

The dog was barking, closer. He still couldn't see it. Somewhere ahead in the reeds and hills. But possibly downwards, he thought. That inky figure on the beach was drawn by the din, cutting towards the steep verges, along which Freddy ambled pleasantly. Fantastically pleasantly, in fact. Freddy lolloped down the slopes on the golf course side of the dunes.

Freddy thought that he could reach out and steal those urgent woofs, barks, growls and howls from the night sky. Imagine 'at. Imagine bein able tae touch soon, nae jist feel the bass traivellin through the grun at a concert or somethin, bit actually be able to sink yer fingers intae it. 'At'd be crazy, like.

A face appeared. Freddy's heart paused. Then – there we go – started up again. The face was pale and furry, and at shoulder-height. He was going to shriek; his mind sorted through the data that his eyes threw at it and came to the conclusion that he wasn't nose to snout with a werewolf. The dog was merely higher up on the ledge of a dune. The white terrier perused him like a referee deciding whether a fighter was fit to continue. Friend or foe? Friend or foe? The dog did not bark as though threatened. It nattered for acknowledgement.

Freddy, seeing no accompanying walkers, summarised that the dog was alone. Lost wee doggy? The terrier appeared to be tame, not flinching or fleeing or biting when Freddy reached over to scratch its noggin. "Like 'at, doggy? Dee ye like 'at, eh, ye neep?"

Encompassed by a multitude of hidey-holes and peaks, Freddy knew that he might've been entitled to dirty his boxers at this point – an ambush? – yet he knew only warmth and fuzziness and contentment and warmth. The dog trembled under his hand. Wis it really 'at caal? He couldn't tell. Derek's jacket sheltered him like a caravan. "It's a'right, doggy. It's a'right."

He scanned the bushes that receded from the path in clumps and swells. Freddy saw a pallid, oblong shape on the ground. The rectangular configuration lay across the sandy footpath, emerging from a dense cluster of reeds in a manner implying that it was one part of a greater piece yet to be uncovered. At first, he thought it a cricket bat. But no, the shape, though narrow, was too rounded to be a cricket bat. Maybe a baseball bat? He also noticed that the wan flesh of the object seemed to be of a woven texture. Soft and marked like fabric. Like a sock. A sock filled with a wee leg. Freddy near screamed with delight. Hurrah. Hooray. Rachel was out here among the dunes, and he had found her.

*

Charlie said nothing. Mo was silent in reply. The engine was off. All that could be heard inside the car was the chatter of the bay that curved in a shadowed groove around the beach and the dunes to the Broch and its lighthouse: a spark against prodigious space. That and the sporadic, low-pitched drone from the back seat where the giant lay dying.

The two men viewed from their seats, with belts still fastened, the two modest piers of Cairnbulg harbour. The only vessels that massaged the surface of that black soup, of which there were five, were yawls; small crafts with which it would be arduous to chisel out a living. Nobody else, it was needless to say, was about. Broch harbour, meanwhile, was active all hours of the day. A boat would be landing; a boat would be leaving. There was always someone doing something.

A pinched road wound behind them into the village, which was hidden from sight behind sheds and a dip in the earth.

Charlie's plan was simple. The execution would not be.

Mo said, "Ye sure 'is is wise, mister?"

"No," came the answer. "It's nae wise. Bit it's right. An' it his tae be deen."

Both men knew that Charlie was angling for some agreement from his much younger accomplice. Mo offered no consent. Murder, as far as he could see, was simply inexcusable.

"It's nae too late, ye ken?" said Mo. The blood on his collar made him itchy, as when eating whilst being pestered by flies. "We could drap 'im aff somewye an' phone an ambulance tae pick 'im up. He might survive, ye ken?"

"No. 'At's... No. No. Ah think we shid finish 'im aff here. Aye."

The men held their discussion without ever turning to face each other. Mo thought that he heard a dog bark in the distance. Any tone above a shout would carry for miles out here, which was why the rifle had been left in the house and the giant's pistol was stowed out of mind in the glove box.

"We'd be killers."

"Aye, 'at seems aboot right. Aye." There was no intentional mockery in Charlie's response. Everything that he had done or said since this 'Lex MacMurran' cretin had entered his house had been governed by blank acceptance. He had shot the man, would kill the man, would dispose of the man. Charlie stroked his bonnet as if he'd forgotten that he wore a hat over his hair. "Some folk jist seem tae hae it comin."

"Hoo is killin 'is guy gaan tae help onythin?" Mo did attempt to make eye contact with his driver. "Dee ye think he's alone? Dee ye think he's nae got chums or 'at? 'Is winnae be the end o it, even if the coppers dinnae catch ye. Folk'll come lukin fir 'im. Dee ye realise 'at? Please, mister, we've got tae think o anither wye. 'Is solves nithin. Ah aiwyes hid ye figured fir a man o sinse, bit 'is is aboot the least sinsible thing ah've iver kent o. Fuckin hell, min, ye cannae ging through wi 'is. Ye cannae kill ivery scumbag that comes up here lukin fir Lori. 'Is is aa jist like a hole ye're diggin yersel intae. Dee ye ken fit ah mean? Come on, mister. Ye've got tae listen tae me here. See sinse. Please, fuck sake, 'is is jist wrang."

Charlie exhaled, though not to rudely reject the other man's trepidations; it was the act of one whose platform was sinking into the molten lava. He was aware of every problem, every corner of every complication, but he didn't care, and nor did his wife. So why should Mark's remonstrations matter? Step by step. Come what may.

"We'll pay 'em," Mo said. "We'll pay 'im an' the rest o his cronies fitiver they're owed. We'll double it. We'll pay 'em double fit they're owed on the gruns that you, well, shot 'im. Fitiver it costs. We'll aa chip in. Ah could work somethin oot at the bank. We could dee it in instaalments. Think aboot it. Then, aifter 'at, we'll hae aa 'ese shites aff oor backs fir good. Lori could come hame. She could fix 'ersel up. Sort 'ersel oot an' 'at, ken? It'll aa be fine. Dee ye hear me, mister?"

The man resisted from looking at Mo. The serrated silhouette of Fraserburgh had always reminded Charlie, from this vantage point at least, of a cruise ship. He started the engine. The car began to crawl forward. Had Mo's pleas made a dent? The banker couldn't say. The man's face had changed not a crease. The car continued down the left pier, which hooked in towards the longer of the two. Dust and gravel was strewn beneath its wheels. Wakened gulls took to noisy flight. The car rumbled on at slow speed. The pier, being several tiers of enormous blocks, buttered together with cement, was tighter than the road that led from the village. There was no room for a three-point turn on here, and Mo didn't fancy the idea of Charlie reversing all the way back to shore, not in this murk, not in his state. When they were roughly halfway down the pier, just before the path swung inwards to its straighter relation, Charlie shut off the engine.

The grunting giant did not plead. It remained indeterminate as to whether or not Lex could still formulate sentences, or even utter multi-syllabic phrases. He said something; however, it could quite easily have been more burbling. Mo surveyed the viscous mass. That hole in his chest, the hole somewhere between here and there, between his nipples, drained him, like a rent in a Bedouin's water bag. Not a nice man, not a charming man, but deserving of better than this, the assistant manager thought. Anyone, within reason, deserved better than that.

Charlie got out as though a paratrooper on his final jump. He stood on the pier. Mo looked at the wheel. The keys were gone. The pistol was in the cabinet by his knees. Mo could make a stand, save a life, prevent more happenings of this nature. And what would he say? Gie's the kyes, mister, or ah'll shoot ye. Like the man had any reason to believe that he would. Mo found it onerous to recall the precise order of things in this capricious series of events, as if trying to pick out the notes as sundry bands played at once.

He had his mobile. He could, should, phone an ambulance. He could stall the man a while. If need be, he wouldn't have much trouble overpowering Mr Mackintosh. Mo was no scrapper, but he doubted that Charlie had ever thrown a punch at anyone ever. Plus, he had the advantage of youth. Although, the man would, inevitably, end up in jail for, at best, *attempted* murder. There was no obvious happy-ending route for Mo to take. To save the one life meant the destruction of many others. Lose. Lose.

How could he be in such a diabolical predicament? Mo hadn't even liked Lori, and he hardly knew Charlie. The guy was just a mate's ex-girlfriend's dad. Certainly, the man and his wife exchanged Christmas cards with his own parents; the couples occasionally mingled at the same parties. And, incontrovertibly, Charlie did come into the bank about once a week, and they could make effortless small talk as cheques were cleared. Their conversations were usually about golf. After all, Charles William Mackintosh was chairman of Fraserburgh Golf Club. Frequently recently, Mo had dallied with the idea of signing up, renewing his membership for the first time since he was fourteen. Freddy had just got himself a new set of clubs. Mark and Mr Mackintosh had been known to stop for one another on the street, to deliberate like imitation pals the weather and other such instantaneous trifles. But that was it. That was fuckin it, like. Mo certainly didn't know the man well enough to go killing people with him. Now they'd be bonded through eternity for such devilishness.

Charlie chapped upon the driver's window. Mo climbed out and joined the man by the edge of the pier. The boat nearest to them lay low in the water due to the tide. The rope connecting the yawl to the pier forced through recollections of the extension cord for the clunky, old phone that once was mounted to a wall in the O'Connor household.

"Fa's boat is 'is?"

"A chum's," Charlie replied. He pulled his mittens taut. "Dee ye ken the guy that dis the motorbike lessons roon here? The lad Graham? No? Well, it's his boat. Said ah could use it faan need be. Seems ah need it noo, eh, Mark?"

Rusted steps inscribed into the side of the pier reached for the boat like a helicopter rescue. A thousand shattered portraits of the moon belly-danced for the two men, who were each cognisant of just how cold it was tonight. Mo scraped at his cheek. He could do with a coat.

"Charlie."

"Ken fit ah'm thinkin, Mark?" The man indulged a transient musing, as though he might be having a misgiving. "Ah think we might nae need tae finish 'im aff aifter aa."

Mo's relief lingered fleetingly.

"Ye see," Charlie continued, "ah'd bin thinkin along the lines o killin 'im wi a rock. Like 'at folk did tae the aal manny last night. Bit no; noo ah think that aa we need tae dee is drap 'im intae the boat. Ah think the faa shid taak care o 'im. Braak his neck maybe, eh? Fit dee you think?"

Mo stepped away from the brink. “Ah think ah dinnae want ony part o ’is.”

“Bit, Mark, ah might need ye tae help oot wi the rowin.”

“No. Ye’re freakin me oot. Let’s jist dump ’im somewye.”

“Aye,” Charlie concurred, like at excellent news in the obituaries. “We’ll dump ’im oot ’ere. Ah’ve got a life jacket padded wi steens in the boot. We’ll get ’at on ’im. It might be choch, like, bit it shid help ’im sink, no? Bit ’at kin wait. We’ll get ’im oot in the boaty first, eh? Shidnae be too hard. We’ll jist drag ’im o’er the side.”

The man’s resolve disturbed Mo, so single-minded and pitiless was he, like a boy let loose with a pellet gun among myxomatosis-infected rabbits. Charlie yanked open the door and wrapped his gloves around the giant’s ankles. He tugged at the man’s legs as if to wrench a tram off its tracks.

“Come on, Mark,” said the man, as though proffering a game of football, “gie’s a han’ here, eh?” as though a teacher requesting his pupil to aid him in shifting a desk.

“No,” Mo snapped. He blocked Charlie from the door and the dying man. “No. Ye cannae dee ’is. Ah cannae let ye. It’s nae fuckin right, mister. We’re taakin ’im tae the hospital. Ah’m nae bein responsible fir ’is guy’s death.”

“Okay, Mark, a’right. Ah see fit ye mean. Ah’ll drap ’im o’er the side masel. Ah see faar ye’re comin fae, aye. Nae problem. Dinnae worry yersel.” Charlie was dressed as if to shovel the snow from his driveway. He stood as though waiting for his spade. “Bit could ye help me get ’im oot the car. He’s an affa size.”

“No. Ye’re nae fuckin listenin. We’re nae deein ’is. We’re nae killin ’im, an’ we’re nae dumpin ’im in the sye.” Mo had felt better refusing loan applications to newlyweds.

Charlie shook his head, as if he’d been told a funny, though naughty, anecdote back at the clubhouse. “Oh, michty me, Mark. Govvy. Ah’m an aal man. Ah cannae dee ’is aa masel. Behave. Ah’m nae ’at strong. Noo come on; gie’s a han’. Gie’s a lift wi yer young, strong airms.”

Mo wanted to scream. Was the man clued-up to what it was that he suggested they do? It seemed not. It seemed like some integral part of Mr Mackintosh was either switched off or missing. Scream, scream, and forget this night. Between the lifeless giant – how lifeless? – and this nutjob, Mo was tempted to dive into the harbour himself and swim for Sweden. He pressed Charlie away, apologetically, and closed the door, protecting the giant. Charlie returned like an insect to a window. He tried for the handle, to get at the giant, but not in a fierce way. Not in a violent, spitting-mad way, but blandly and weakly, like a baby to a breast. Mo pushed him, roughly this time.

"Ah fuckin tellt ye, ah'm taakin 'im tae the hospital."

Charlie appeared hurt. Had sense prevailed within the man's head? It was the first instance that evening that Mo had seen the man look somewhat sane.

Charlie let his palm fall on the purple bonnet of his car. One stiff arm supported him. He swayed a little. Stared at Mark. Andrew and Sandra's boy. The O'Connors. One of Lori's old mates. One of. One of. The guy seems scared. Why? Ah winnae hurt 'im. It's 'at ither guy. The big guy in the back. Ah want tae. Ah want tae.

"Rip 'im tae shreds wi ma bare hands, Mark. 'At's fit ah want tae dee." The man's glazed countenance hovered above the windshield, like a white dove confused by its reflection. "Ah really want tae. Ah really want tae kill 'im. He shid dee. 'At's fit ah'll. Aye, 'at's fit ah'll. Ah'll kill 'im."

"No, mister. We'll save 'im. Ye shot 'im. 'At's enough."

Charlie's chin fell onto his throat, then raised itself again.

"The things he made Lori dee. He fuckin. 'At scum. He fuckin." The man hung over the bonnet, sobbing. He coughed. His mouth went soft as if his gums had dissolved.

Mo's mobile rang. Charlie did not react to the musical intrusion. Mo retrieved the phone from his cord trousers. He thought it would've been a friend. He was taken aback to see that the caller was SexxyMilf. Mo turned away from the crying man. He did not think that it would be a smart thing to do to speak with her now, but he realised then that he was impotent to refuse her allure. He had to hear her voice. Mo answered the call.

"Yes?" he whispered. He did relocate so as not to see Lex behind the glass. "Hello?" Mo said, when she did not reply.

“Are you Rudie?” Rudie was the pseudonym that Mark had chosen for his Internet connivances. The voice on the other end of the line was not what he had been expecting. It was a male voice for one thing, and a child’s voice for another.

Mo held the phone as though it were suddenly of unfathomable technology. “Who is this?” he asked.

“Leave my mum alone,” said the boy. The child was daunted to near imperceptibility by the challenge of articulating his tribulations. “My dad’s coming back. Let my mum be.”

Mo did not respond after that. He listened to the rustling bay. Eventually, the kid did terminate the call. Mo saw the grown man weep.

Mr Mackintosh whimpered. “Iverythin’s a mess.”

“Aye,” Mo said. He put his phone in his pocket. “It’s a mess.”

Chapter 18

"So, here we are, Derek, Phil, the rest of you people who I am sure are all adequately respectable. Long time no see. Shame really. I'd have liked a more extensive catch-up with my old mateys. Never quite turns out like that, does it? No. Big shame. So disappointing, for I'm sure there are many tales that we could've tickled each other's ribs with till dawn. So much stuff happens in twenty-four hours, and all those things and reminiscences could be multiplied by seven by fifty-two by ten. We'll have altered, no less, but not that much. People don't really change. They tend to modify and adapt if they feel that they might have something to gain from doing so. They unveil themselves in divergent situations. But do people ever go the whole one-eighty in their souls? Nope. That's bollocks. An angry child sprouts into an angry adult. Pure fact. He may be better equipped to control and hide that rage which made him decapitate his sister's dolls as an adolescent, but he's still as likely to detonate now as back then, barring drugs and therapy, which I don't feel are either healthy or helpful. We can't change. We don't change. Same goes: an unhappy infant, for further illustration, is unlikely to grow up to be anything other than downcast. Right?

"And no, I'm not drunk. Does it seem like that? Well, maybe just a wee bit. Spirits. Lethal. The Scottish cure for everything. I'm starting to enjoy myself. You all appear to be hearing me, which is fantastic – thanks a lot. Then again, maybe you're all just eager to watch a man set himself on fire. Me, too, and I am going to do it. But, friends – old and never-before-met, don't make a rash dash at me. Any attempt to retrieve this lighter from my grasp will only hasten the inevitable. But then, like I said, maybe that's what you want. Don't repudiate. No shaking of heads or mumbled insincerities. We're above that. Let's just admit that we want to watch someone die. That's what the Web is for, is it not? The unedited documentation of real-life tragedies. Dismantled bodies and shit-slathered pornography. Beautiful women defecating into each other's mouths, and Brazilian fart porn, lest we forget. That's what your Internet's for, isn't it? Be wary of that over which you wank, though; the Web's a nudist beach beside a motorway. Everything is visible to all. Come on, speak up. If someone were to a pin drop now, I'm certain that I would hear it. Who wouldn't want to see a man reduced to smoke and ash before their very eyes? Liars. Who here has ever witnessed death? Not the noun, but the verb. The very act of death. The losing of life. The slip into the void. Speak out, liars; someone must have. What about the gentry in the corner? The war wasn't that long ago."

The soaking man sat forward on the pool table; his energy transmitted over the room, urging a riposte from his class with raised eyebrows. A verve grabbed hold of the patrons and slapped them awake. Alive and reborn into this curious evening.

English Bob replied from his stool by the table of the two older men. "Sorry, lad, but I wasn't born until after Adolf and his mob decided to run amok. Never seen a man die in my life, I'm afraid. This old man hasn't seen everything."

"Really?" Pagan intoned, with comic disappointment. "What about the rest of you gentlemen?"

"Weel," Albert Thatcher procrastinated, as he did whenever he deigned to speak to strangers, especially young ones. The man who used to be the skipper of a successful trawler tugged upon his large, bumpy beak. "Ah've seen some horrible things in ma time, bit ah dinnae feel like sharin 'em wi you the noo."

Never requiring much of a prod to partake in discussions of such a grim nature, Patrick Hendry said, "Ah've seen it aa, pal. Ah wis in the trenches, an', believe you me, ah've witnessed ivery orra thing that kin happen tae a man. 'Ere's nithin ye kin show me that ah hivnae seen a thoosan times afore. Ye winnae scare me like 'at, no."

"I'm sure you're right." Pagan glowed under the lights, glistening where the petrol slicked his body. "I should make it unequivocal that if anyone wants to leave, then they may do so at any time. I'm not holding myself hostage, and there will be no demands made for you to translate to a waiting police barrage. I aim to kill myself within the hour. Stick around and watch if you like."

None of the other nine patrons moved. A ghoulishness eddied around them all; it contracted quickly within those who comprehended that they were not staying out of some sickening pleasure, as the journalist had insinuated, but rather because of an agreement made to themselves that they would see this Thursday night in The Tart through to its conclusion.

Derek and Phil and English Bob would work to prevent the man from making an indoor bonfire of himself. Samantha would exit when it was over, inconspicuous in the dark, leaving the flirty Brocher and his broken fingers behind. She thought that she would, for a while, long to forget her stay in Fraserburgh. Gazza and Scotty and Alex sat in their booth, like mistreated beasts in a kennel. Scotty had seen death unravel before him. He'd maybe see it again within the hour. Alex began to see dots and flashes and crimson blotches; he also saw ten-fifteen little Progeria kids running around the room. Gazza eyed the fat cunt at the bar and the fuckin, drunken fucker at the back and the aal English bastard on his seat. Gazza waited.

Derek went forth, halting when he was beyond Bob, in the middle of the floor. "Fit's 'is aa aboot, Pagan? Ye dinnae hiv tae dee 'is. We'll get ye cleaned up, an' 'en ye kin get some fuckin sleep. It's rough comin hame, ken? Ye need some time tae adjust, like. Ah kin see 'at. Too much memories an' aa that. It's tuk its toll on ye. Nae buther. We'll get ye sorted oot, Peggy. It's a'right." Half an hour ago, Derek had been the great seducer. Now, he was a counsellor. Could his throbbing brain take anymore?

"Derek, dear friend, I appreciate the gesture. In all seriousness, I do. But did you ever hear the expression that elephants go home to die? I always sort of knew that this was on the cards when I returned to the North. Don't fret. It was unavoidable. It's destiny, Derek. Go with it."

"Peggy, pal," Phil said from his bar stool, with a hand on the shillelagh, "fit's a dee wi ye, min? Tell us. We kin fuckin help, like. So ye came back tae the Broch tae kill yersel; disnae mean ye hiv tae dee it."

Derek nodded. "Fat Ass is right. Mest o the folk that come tae the Broch end up wantin tae kill 'emsels. If aa cunt did it, though, 'ere wid be nae cunt left, wid 'ere? Apart fae maybe a couple o Russian prostitutes an' a Filipino net-mender."

"I believe you." Pagan watched his plastic lighter roam across his knuckles. He laughed. "Suicide is the fastest growing pastime since Sega. Everyone's cottoned on to the fact that Heaven's doors are locked, and all we can expect from our resting immortality is forks up our asses and perpetual sunburn. How does that grab you? We suffer on Earth for a hundred years, then burn with Satan for infinity. Sound fair to you? Fuck it. Why try? It's a con. We've been tricked into believing that if we behave and suckle on the Haloed One's scrotum for long enough we'll end up prancing about on clouds and playing harps in harmony. Mention nothing of the fact that we're all doomed, and all there is is hell. Except, in place of fire and demons, it seems that His preferred method of torture is a ceaseless parade of tedium and antagonism. My fucking God, all I see in this world is aggression and idiocy. And what the fuck is the deal with your eye-patch? Sewing accident?"

Pagan's rant shifted course with such an acute bend that Gazza was left sitting there like he'd missed his stop. Pagan anticipated a retort, neither hostilely nor impatiently, but with genuine zest.

Feeling as though he'd been mocked before the entire bar, Gazza pursed his mouth, which shrank beneath a scabbing nose. The black, leather patch crossed his face like goal posts fallen onto clay. The head decoration that blossomed from Gazza's right eye socket demanded many answers. He offered the drenched reporter one explanation. "Fuck you, ye daft cunt. Ah'll fuckin set ye on fire masel."

Fat Ass gripped the club and got to his feet. "Waatch it, Gazza, or ye'll be needin a patch fir the ither een next."

"Ye want tae get intae it again, aye, fatso?"

"Whoa, whoa, whoa." Peacemaker Derek waved the pair down and back to their seats. Pagan vibrated with a resigned mirth, as though amused by his own incompetence. "A'right, boys, 'at's enough" said Derek. "Nae fuckin fechtin, a'right, ye pair o fannies? Jist calm the fuck doon, eh?"

"A'right, a'right. Tell 'at cunt 'ere. He's the cunt wi the threats."

"Fuck off, ye fat shite."

"'At's it," Derek yelled. "Enough." The gravity in his voice was slightly offset by the manner in which he held out his left hand: cupped, swishing that pretend wineglass still. Gazza decided to compose himself for now, though he didn't take his eye off the bartender. Phil detached neither ophthalmic stud from Gazza. Scotty was coiled, ready to pounce whenever it was that his brother might embark on his incursion. Alex, ill under his floppy do, would like to go outside and vomit in the harbour. A six-year-old Progerian girl bounced on his knee, arms lovingly around his neck like a lobster's pincers. "We got 'at clear noo? The boy's covered heid tae fit in petrol, so less o the japery, aye?"

"Very authoritative, Derek. I'm impressed. People do, it seems, change."

"Nae sae sure aboot 'at, like, Pagan. Ma han's sair; ma fuckin heid's sair. Ah jist want some peace."

"Say it loud and say it proud. And do you reckon that, today, Derek, we live in peaceful times? It was, forget not we must, midway through the antecedent century when last we had a war that we could call a World War. Do our ongoing skirmishes with Muslim maniacs constitute a proper war? Does it? Do we live in an era of peace, Derek, or are these war times? Which is it, Derek?"

"Ah dinnae ken." This was the Pagan that Derek remembered. The version that parents found off-putting. "The world's nae perfect, no," Derek replied. "Bit it is quite peaceful, aye. It's bin worse."

"When?"

"Like ye said, the middle o last century."

"Oh." Pagan was a lecturer who had finally engaged one of his braver students into weighty debate. "So, you reckon that the world was a less peaceful place during the 1940s?"

"Well, if ye taak intae accoont the six million Jews fa were killt, aye."

"Six million? We might have to consult Iran about that. Six million Jews, Derek, whom, at this time, would either be dead or dying anyway?"

"Pagan, 'at's a bit sick, like."

"Of course it's sick." Pagan's mirth stuttered not. "We're dealing with the sick. And so you think that the world was a sicker place back then? Sicker than it is now?"

"Aye." Derek regretted the inflection that conveyed a degree of irritability. He softened his tones, and continued, "World Waar 2 was a shitty time."

"Well put." Pagan tarried along the border between arrogance and encouragement. "And you remember the forties well, do you? You see, I can't, thus you have the advantage."

"Very good."

"I'm only teasing." This was ostensibly true. Pagan appeared as though he were discussing nothing less trivial than his favourite Star Wars character. "Derek, others, would it enlighten you all to know that once upon a time when I was out collecting and collating dibs and dabs for a report on some junkie neighbours, I conducted an interview with a tenant, a seventy-year-old lady, and she said, hand up to God Almighty, she said that she would rather live through the war again than have to endure these times? That's fact, Derek."

"'At's nostalgia, Pagan."

"Well, let's find out. Gents." Pagan addressed the three old men. "Do you think that the world has improved in the interposing years since Herr Hitler shot himself? I feel that you're ideally placed to give a totally unbiased and objective answer to this query."

Albert Thatcher shirked away from the stream of attention that the master of ceremonies had forged specifically for them. Patrick, however, bathed in it, sipping his drink self-consciously, milking the silence. Bob spoke.

"I'm afraid that's too complicated a question to close with a yes or a no," he said. "You can't say that the world's any better or any worse. The world's the world. It is what it is. Some of it's good; some of it's bad. That doesn't change."

"True," Pagan said. He rapped the lighter on his thumb. "Allow me to rephrase. Was it common, when you were a lad, to flick through the paper, tabloid, broadsheet, magazine, whatever, each and every day and always find some story that truly repulsed you? A story like, for example, a child being raped with the shards of a smashed bottle. A blind man beaten to a pulp. Land mines planted in playgrounds. The torture. The murder. The hate. The mindlessness. Or, for instance, an old drunk having his head obliterated like an Easter egg in the middle of the street."

"Is 'is fit 'is is aboot, Pagan?" Derek dropped a note to sympathy. "Yer story?"

Alex pleated inside. Were all the cameras on him? Were they in him? The inside of his skull was like a stadium during the closing ceremony of some major sporting event. The flashing bulbs and lenses. Confetti. Had he and his short friend been found out? Was this all an elaborate set-up? A sting to capture the killers of some pish-stinkin drunk? Confess, confess. Free Scotty, scot-free; Alex had to fight to keep his face from sliding off.

Pagan ignored Derek's question. Instead, he quizzed the Englishman, "Old man, do you really think that our society is not unwell? That it is, in fact, good? Do you honestly believe that we're evolving, and not regressing back to our animalistic state? Animals, though, don't torture, don't derive gratification from cruelty to their own. We're something else. We are separate and mean. Loathsome and spiteful and nasty. This is who we are, and what we are. The riddle to be solved is the why."

"Yes, partner," Bob said. He thought of his wife, alone, in the camper van. "There are people out there who are all the things that you just said. And then there's the rest of us. Folk who strive to be nice and compassionate and empathetic and kind and brave and creative. It's not all bad, son. Believe that."

"Okay, okay," Pagan extended his arms as though to catch a bale of hay, "I know all that. Sweet and sour. Okay. But do you remember being a youth and ever hearing about elderly women being mugged and punched and attacked and molested where you lived? No, you didn't, because it never fucking happened. Seldom, rarely, never. The world's turned on its own. It's ruthless. No one's exempt from its foulness. No one's too young or too fragile to be bludgeoned with the stench of decaying spirituality."

"Ye soon depressed," Derek said.

"Depressed?"

"Aye, Pagan, depressed."

Pagan reacted with the restrained exasperation of a man whose only child has presented him with the equation 2 + 2 = zebra. "You say depressed like you're handing out fliers for some nightclub promotion. Would that explain it to you? I've doused myself in petrol because I'm unhappy. I'm going to set myself on fire, effectively killing me, because I feel a bit stroppy. Does that sum it all up, put the tin lid on proceedings? I'm sure that it's a tidy and sufficient motivation for where I am at this stage. But answer me this, old chum: does my being depressed in any way alter the fact that across all media tomorrow morning there will be a fresh batch of misery to cut and paste to the page? Derek, you're not paranoid if they're really after you. Whether I'm melancholic or homosexual or handicapped or a Zimbabwean cripple with five tumours or any other jumble of a limitless source of social-inadequacies, it doesn't make what I have to say any less accurate. The Earth rolls crookedly onwards through a mist of indifference, regardless of whether or not you care to accept this information. I can't change the pain, Derek; I merely observe and absorb it, and sell it back to you for three silver slices. My interpretation of your misfortune comes at a price. I'm depressed, that's moot. Everyone's depressed. Nobody, apart from the intellectually tranquillised, strolls to their grave in some abiding haze of satisfaction. Simple. We're all crestfallen. We amble along in our puzzled state as if through some endless French film that professes to be about everything but actually doesn't seem to be about anything.

"Are we fans of Gallic cinema here, people?" Pagan turned to the booth nearest to him, and, with the most palpable hint yet of the sedition behind his smile, inquired of the pugilist and his associates, "Do you not watch films that you have to read?"

"Get tae fuck," said Scotty.

Gazza took out a packet of cigarettes and knocked them on the table. "Ah think ah might hae a smoke in nae lang."

Pagan laughed. The edge subsided.

Derek tried to steer the conversation away from despondency and mortality. "So, ye still a big reader, aye, Pagan? Still intae yer buks an' 'at?"

"Yes, I've read a few." Pagan cooled, taking on a reflective posture. His chum's digressional tactics had worked for the time being. "Ever read any French literature? I did. Once. Camus. The Plague. After I finished it, I put it in the sink and set it alight, would you believe? I did not care for it, though I am prepared to accept that the fault may reside with me. I might have pushed the book through my head when I wasn't really of a mood for it. I read a lot of Eastern European novels by authors you've never heard of with surnames I can't pronounce. Read up on Marx because I thought that I should. Read Ulysses because I wanted to say that I had. I read the holy texts, to have ammo against the zealots. I read a fair amount, yes."

"You read Ulysses?" Bob said.

"Cover to cover. Have you?"

"I gave it go, a while back. Two hundred thousand words. None of which I particularly liked."

Pagan looked annoyed, as if his shopping bag had come apart. "It's genius," he countered.

"That may be, but it's also gibberish."

"Then it's worthwhile gibberish."

"Perhaps," Bob pondered. The yellow-haired Englishman went on, "In any case, I never finished it."

"The last chapter is possibly the best bit of the book," Pagan said, pleading the case for the Joyce masterpiece. "Of all books. I guarantee that if you persevere with it, you'll find it to be a richly rewarding and entertaining read. Richly rewarding, very lots. The point is: you'll like it."

"I read enough."

"You should finish it, though. Seriously."

"I'll pass, lad," Bob said. He played to agitate the youngster, and unsettle him from his perch. "I found it clever to the point of being ludicrous and patronising, genius or not. No, young soul, I've better things to do than scour through the drunken ramblings of a dead

Irishman. I could be with my wife. Phone the children. Speak with the grandkids. That's rewarding."

"Did I oversell it? Then I apologise. Complete it in your own time, if ever."

"Apologies are quite unnecessary. Forgive my rudeness," English Bob brushed a lens of his glasses, "but who are you? Whenever I talk literature with half-naked men about to execute themselves by flame, call me traditional, but I just like to know their names."

"I suppose my name is Pagan. That should suffice. So, you read much, whoever you yourself might be?"

"Bob Schell. Sometimes. I go through spells where I read a lot, then don't for some time."

"You derive much joy from reading, Mr Schell?"

The old Englishman spoke as though to an esteemed, longtime acquaintance, as he was in the habit of doing with most people. "Sometimes. Yes. It depends on the author, doesn't it, and whether they could be bothered or not?"

Two clever men talked about books. The others almost felt weirdly intrusive. If they allowed their minds to dim for a second, they could just about forget that one of the pair did plan to casually commit suicide at the end of their chat, and it did all become sleepily normal.

"I appreciate the company of a man who enjoys literature," Pagan said.

The pensioner replied, "I don't enjoy literature. I enjoy books in spite of them being literature."

"Interesting." Pagan paused. "Dubious, but interesting."

"Books are a fine thing," Bob said, "but they are a weak substitute for flesh and blood."

Pagan sat tall on the shaved grass of the table. He accused, excitedly, "You paraphrased. That's a quote. Robert Louis Stephenson, if I can remember correctly. Let's do quotes. My favourite: 'Let him who desires peace be prepared for war'."

"I can't really recall that many, I'm afraid. They come and go, like jokes. Here's one, however, that fits with your theme. 'In peace, children bury their parents. War violates the order of nature and causes parents to bury their children.' How's that?"

"Not bad," Pagan said. "But I do believe that in the actual line Herodutus uses the word inter and not bury. Very well." He then reeled off the next quote like a mechanised dispenser. "'The most persistent sound that reverberates through man's history is the beating of war drums.'"

Bob tapped a leg of his seat. "'Older men declare war, but it is youth who must fight and die.'"

"'Politics is war without bloodshed; war is politics with bloodshed.'"

"'No victory in battle is worth the blood it costs.'"

"'The optimist proclaims that we live in the best of all possible worlds'," Pagan thrust his lighter for emphasis, "'the pessimist fears that this is true.'"

"'Not a shred of evidence exists in favour of the idea that life is serious.'"

"'God made the universe out of nothing, but the nothingness shows through.'"

"'He who has done his best for his own time has lived for all times.'"

"'It is easier to fight for one's principles'," Pagan declared, "'than to live up to them.'"

Bob slowed from the taxation of academic jogging. He struggled to find the right order for the right words. "'It is more shameful to doubt one's friends than to be duped by them.'"

"'It is easier to forgive an enemy than to forgive a friend.'"

"One last," Bob said, brain-drained. "How exactly does it…? 'All the great things are simple, and many can be expressed in a single word: freedom; justice; honour; duty; mercy; hope.'"

"Churchill," said Pagan. "Another from the porky leader: 'Solitary trees, if they grow, grow strong'. 'A nation that forgets its past has no future.' One from Abe Lincoln: 'Nearly all men can stand adversity, but if you want to test a man's character, give him power'. How about Voltaire? He's always good for a sound bite. There's the obvious one: 'I don't agree with what you say, but I'll defend to the death your right to say it'. Or: 'Every man is guilty of the good he did not do'. And: 'It is dangerous to be right when the government is wrong'. Or what about Gandhi? Gandhi kicks ass. 'We must be the change we wish to see in the world.' True, yes?"

An Arctic Monkeys song erupted from a pocket.

Alex was brisk in fishing out the melodious felon. He received the call without ever glancing up at the room. "Hello? Fit? Aye. Aye. Eh? Aye. The Tart. No. A'right. Okay. Right. See ye." He put his mobile away. Scotty pecked his question, like a gull at a cat. The feline rolled his shoulders, as though this act made it perfectly unambiguous that he meant 'Chris'. Alex saw that the bare-chested smarty had deflected the focus onto him.

"And who was that?" Pagan asked, nettled not.

"A mate," Alex muttered.

Pagan said, "You should've told him to come down with some marshmallows."

Derek aimed to keep things light, if he could. "Did ye iver try yer han' at writin?" he inquired.

"Well, Derek, I am a journalist, so the answer would have to be 'no'." Pagan, a mostly magnanimous man, forwent the opportunity to score points off of a friend, as the majority of others might have done. No venom did coat the irony implemented in his retort.

"Ah meant buks."

"So I did gather. Yes, Derek, actually I did begin writing a novel a few years back. Guess what it was about."

"A unicorn?"

"Wis it sci-fi?" Phil speculated. "Or fantasy, like Lord o the Rings?"

"No." Pagan relished the meditative break, like he was an invigilator overseeing studious pupils. "It was a sequel to the Bible," he said, after providing the testers with plenteous time to jot down their suppositions. "The Bible 2: Joseph's Revenge." Pagan cherished this moment every time, when they would all, surely, have to admire the ballsiness and ingenuity of his idea. "The story was based on the premise that Joseph was aggrieved with the Almighty and set out to fuck Him over. Here's a guy, a shepherd or whatever he was, and then one day God decides to shaft his virginal wife, submitting to him a stepson, who is basically the product of rape. Joseph would somehow grow to love this boy. Then he'd lose him in the most gruesome of manners, all for the supposed benefit of humanity. Talk about a slap in the face. And what benefit? If God doesn't like something, He alone has the ability to change it. He shouldn't need floods or sacrifices to make His point. He shouldn't need to kill anyone. But, as Moses sings about the originator in Exodus 15:3, 'The Lord is a man of war: the Lord is His name'. We are also told that 'The Lord is a jealous God'; that's Exodus 34:14, if you want to check. He's quite a vicious character is God; He's Joe Pesci in Goodfellas. He's like the biggest twat in the universe, and the template for every single dictator ever. My book strove to detail Joseph's mission to bring the big man down and make Him accountable for His actions. It was all very anarchic and profound. Witty rather than funny, maybe."

"Ah think yer granny might owe ye a couple o toffee aipples," said Derek. The reference meant nothing to anyone other than the three pals who used to play football together.

"Indeed." Pagan retained a humorous incident. The green felt moistened. "I'd forgotten about that."

"Soons a'right," Fat Ass said. "Fit happened tae yer buk? Get it published or 'at?"

"Nah. The joke wore thin after a few chapters. I gave up on it. Chucked it. I think about it, though. Now and again. Sometimes contemplate going back to it. It definitely had potential. The vision was sound, I thought."

"Ye shid," Derek pressed. The slickness dried on his fingers like he'd been washing the dishes. "Taak a breather an' ging back tae it. Ah'd fuckin read it."

Pagan regarded Derek with an incredulous look. "Have you missed something here, old friend? Derek, I'm Pagan. I'm going to kill myself in about thirty minutes. Before I do, however, I just want to stretch my tongue a little. I hear the dead don't talk much, if at all. A silent breed."

It hurt Derek to hear the man discuss his impending demise with such conviction. He had to replace the gloom with something breezier. Find something to awake the positivity within his mate. "So, fit else ye bin up tae?" Derek asked. "Hoo's yer folks?"

"Never really see them anymore." Pagan moved from a specialist subject on to a topic about which he was unlettered. "I feel that we've outgrown each other. They've both hit the restart button. New lives and new families. That sort of thing. I was invited to both weddings, which was nothing if not considerate. Obviously, I never went to either. The Broch years have been firmly quashed from their memory banks. I never forgot, though.

"Fraserburgh, for fear of sounding like a complete arse," said Pagan, "is who I am. It never left me. London's too massive and isolative to claim to be a part of. Same with any major city. To say you're a Londoner means virtually nothing; it's like saying you're an Earthling. Being a Brocher, I like to think, means something."

"Aye? An' fit dis it mean?" Derek knew that there would be an answer waiting by the gate.

Pagan chewed over his response. "I don't know. It just seems like it should mean something." Pagan appeared lost for a minute, as if he'd misplaced the map of his escape route. "Did I tell you that I used to be in a band? No, I didn't. But I'll tell you now. Derek, Phil, Bob and the room, I used to be in a band. A punky, passionate quartet of the we-can't-play-but-we-can-make-a-loud-noise variety. An experiment during college. Very political. Probably read 1984 one too many times. We were awful. Guess what we were called."

"1984?"

"Close."

"1985?"

"No. Funny, though, Derek. I like it. Give up?" Another recess to strengthen the anticipation. They all knew that the band name, like the book, would be markedly controversial. Pagan said, triumphantly, "We were The Cancerous Cunts." Eyes bulged like scorpion stings. “Yip. You heard correctly. Clearly, we had no aspirations of performing on Top of the Pops or headlining the Queen’s Jubilee. Our goal was humble. To change the world.”

“The Cancerous Cunts?” After having repeated the name for confirmation’s sake, Derek became embarrassed when he thought of Samantha behind him.

“Our lead singer had cancer. We felt justified in using the name.”

“Hoo did ye’s get on?” Derek said. “Crack America, aye?”

“No. We were shit. We played a lot of seedy pubs in rough locales, not unlike your Tartan Rainbow. I do jest. I can see how this place could grow on you, if one were to scrunch down their dreams enough. Back then, I was the muscle: the band’s bassist and bodyguard. Can you believe that?” His exposed physique was solid and his biceps spherical. The patrons just about could. “Got in to many a joust in them days, I can tell you. Won a few of them, too; though, to be fair, I also lost a couple. Well worth it, however. There’s something harrowingly satisfying about landing a clean punch on someone.” Pagan looked from Gazza’s nose to Derek’s hand to Phil’s lips. “Seems like you people have had your own wee battle in here.” Nobody lent any credence to this rumination.

“So, fit happened tae yer band?” Fat Ass was too prudish to utter the name in front of the Irish lass, whom listened at the end of the bar in her quiet trauma.

“Our singer died. We split up. The Cancerous Cunts were no more.”

“Still play guitar?” Derek asked. “Or bass, wis it?” He held an imaginary skull as though to deliver an impromptu Hamlet soliloquy. The pain was apparent even in his back.

“I don’t think you can rightly say that I ever really played bass, but no, I haven’t mistreated an instrument in over five years. Not a great loss to the music industry. Then again, we were always worth watching. The singer was a star. Really, he was insane. A sweet, frail fuckwit who was just about the most intelligent person I ever met. He was also the most crude and obnoxious, but fun with it, mainly. A dangerous companion. If God hadn’t killed him, someone else would have.”

“Dee ye miss ’im?” Derek said. “Dee ye miss the band?”

"I miss everyone," Pagan replied, pleasingly devoid of sentimentality or sarcasm. "It happens, though, dear friends. And tonight, folks, I shall choose the how, the when and the where for myself."

"Dee ye miss her?"

"Who? Who am I missing, Derek?"

"'At quine ye mentioned by the beach." Derek couldn't believe that their esplanade picnic had occurred that same day. "The one ye loved."

"Oh. Her?"

"Aye. Her." Derek tried to pierce that smile; but breaking down Pagan's façade was like eradicating the Sphinx with a toothpick. "Is she the reason ye're here? Aboot tae kill yersel in front o the best pals ye iver hid. Is she the why? The why o the depression an' the petrol."

"It all plays a part, Derek. Do you remember what I told you became of her?"

"Aye. She wis murdered. Ye didnae really elaborate or 'at."

"I told you that she was raped and thrown under a train." They all winced. "As is the way. Our way."

Derek knew that he had to pursue this lead. 'At's fit, like, negotiators and shrinks were mint tae dee, wisn't it? Find the suffering and relieve it. Suck out the poison. "Faan did 'is happen? Hid ye bin seein 'er lang? Tell us, Pagan. I want tae hear it."

"They never caught the guy," Pagan said. "What difference would it make anyway? Whether or not that scum's inside, the conception and motivation behind the act will always be out there. You can't imprison evil."

"Ye kin tell me aboot 'er."

"Evil is out there, you know? It's in here; it's out there. It exists. It's a thing. It's as real and far-reaching as the climate. Derek, best you know, it's everywhere. Paedophiles near playschools. Dealers at your door. Addicts in your house. There is no eluding it. Well, maybe there is. There's maybe one method for evasion." Pagan rattled the yellow lighter; a cheap contraption bought earlier that day, along with a sandwich and a bottle of Lucozade.

Pagan didn't smoke. "No. Possibly, there's two." He gestured towards the rows of luminous and muddied bottles. "Does that do it for you, Derek? Submerge yourself in the watery universe. A cartoon reality where evil dare not tread."

"Ah drink 'cos it's a laugh. It's usually a good time."

"You're twenty-eight years old, Derek. How good of a time is it now?"

"Fairly good, aye." Derek thought about Monday's hangover. "An' ah'm twitty-seven, nae twitty-eight. Ye chicky cunt."

Pagan laughed. The laughter was strained, like a harness packed past its limit. The dark was setting in. "Sorry. I forgot. You're a couple of months younger than me."

"Nae hard feelins. Tell me aboot 'er. Tell me 'er name. Faar wis she fae? Fit did she dee? Wis she aaller than you?"

"She was, as a matter of fact." Pagan had to admire the accuracy of his pal's punt. "But you're not a medium, Derek. And neither am I. That is why I am here. The wrong in this world is too immense for me to take any longer. To endure another rising of the sun is beyond my will. This is hell, people. There is no worse place. No worse race than the one that is human. We know that. Every single one of us does. It drives us here to this kindly pub. But Satan is on the loose, soldiers, and it's coming for us all. I plan to meet him halfway and head-on."

"Evil is not Beelzebub," said Bob, deciding it was time for him to make another foray into the discussion. "Pal, Pagan, you seem to see things a tad one-sided. There is evil out there, as there has always been; it's no passing fad, no new disease for the twenty-first century. And it's certainly not a horned red monster with a tail and a trident. Do you want to know what my interpretation of evil is?"

"Yes, Bob Schell, I do."

"Evil, to me, lies in convenience," the Englishman said. "Let me explain this. Evil – and its potential is in all of us – is choosing the easier, quicker option that best suits us and our pride and our time constraints, largely to the detriment of others. Evil is in the day-to-day things, and exists in infinite degrees. It's ignoring the phone because you think that it might be a cousin or a friend needing your help to load a trailer or paint the kitchen but it's after five and you just want to sprawl there on the sofa for a little while more. Evil is understandable. We've all been there. But it adds up. It makes us lazy and self-centred. After a time, it can turn us into fairly unpleasant beings.

"Germany was not populated by demons," Bob continued, "though it's undemanding of us to dismiss them as such. They were people, like us. It's been reported that, at the time, in and around the towns and out in the Germanic countryside, officers shot Jews purely because they didn't want to look weak and less manly in front of their comrades and pals. Sounds familiar, doesn't it? Reminds you of your first cigarette. Changes things. It's like some people see the storm troopers or the government-backed militias on the march and say 'Oh, so we're being evil now, okay', and then fall in line. It is sad to say, but men have often times found themselves in situations where it is better – more convenient – for them to become beasts than to bear the task of being human, the responsibility of being which entails usually doing that which we would rather not. It is absolutely frightening what a man will do just to save face.

"Little things build and create big problems. Does that make sense to you?"

"Yes," Pagan replied, drawing out the word to impart his scepticism. "Very quaint. A twee notion; one to ponder as I rot in my grave. Bob, no offence, but I don't think that you can ever equate rape, pillage and plundering with not giving Uncle Chucklebutt a hand to redecorate his house."

"It follows the same plan," Bob said, unfazed. "My point was that evil is part of us, and not some bloated mass that hunts in the night and lingers in the air as you so appear to believe."

"I believe that evil *is* a disease," Pagan reaffirmed, "a contagious one, and I believe that it's blooming, growing in scale and savagery, fertilised and nurtured by a disaffected and bored society. We differ on the exact parentage of evil. Excrement doth transpire. I say you hear my thoughts on vaccination. The truth, beyond argument, as to how we should repel this illness, stunt its growth. A cure for what is killing us. You won't like it. Chances are, none of you will. But since I'm pencilled in for a death-by-inferno in about twenty minutes, I might as well tell you anyway. Where's the harm?"

"Go on," Derek said. Inquisitiveness conquered his resolution to talk of more cheerful things. "We're listenin."

"Life is the question, correct?" Pagan halted for a reply that he did not expect to come. "Life is the question. Death is the answer." He could see that no one quite understood. "Allow me to extrapolate. I begin, once again, with war. We'll opt not to argue the point this time: war is good. It's another tragic irony in a history that gives us 9/11, a number which had already gained global prominence as America's emergency number. I say irony, though the sameness of those two sets of digits may well have been deliberate – a joke by the plotters, whether it emerges that those schemers were of Middle-Eastern or Western origin after all, or some labyrinthine conglomeration of both. Yes, it's all ironic, everything's ironical, but you can't build a house with irony, can you? Here are the facts.

"War brings people together; makes them appreciate more what it is that they stand to lose every day. There is a camaraderie and sense of high morale that is evident only when everyone's in the soup together. Faced with the prospect of real death really soon, people tend to start pulling in the same direction. The team works. From the troops out in the front lines to the strugglers back home – raising the kids, protecting the townships, at work in the fields, making the ammunition – everyone has a purpose. A distinct, singular link to everybody else. This is important. Very, very important, folks. Keep up. Amidst this death and dread comes a blinding goodness, as good as man is ever likely to know. Man becomes more than man. The old lady said this. It's what she meant."

"One more final quote," Bob said, proceeding without the young man's permission. "'War is the form nostalgia takes when men are hard-pressed to say something good about their country.'"

Pagan's feathers were ruffled a tad by the old man's interruption. "Possibly. Except that I'm not extolling the virtues of being either Scottish or British. I'm talking about being a people, chained and free. With purpose. A contented race, enlivened for having shared in so much death.

"War is not good in the wholesome, Spielberg sense of the word, but more in the caustic, Kubrickian vein. It's important. Vital. Humanity needs to kill itself to survive, like a tree shading branches to burst through the smothering canopy."

Contentious to the last, Derek thought. Faces around the bar, Derek's included, were baffled. Baffled yet deeply intrigued by the man's ideas. Scotty appeared roused, like it was his go next. Alex seemed queasy, as though he'd just had his turn.

"Man has an incredibly simple plan with which it must adhere to in order to last the distance," Pagan said. "With the mammoth race mankind has to run, it can't afford to ever deviate from said plan."

"Plans? Races?" Derek stepped forward. "Pagan, ye're startin tae soon nutty."

"Nutty? I'm doused in petrol, for flip sake. Of course it's nutty, but don't you dare ever, even for a second, ever think that the insane are wrong purely on the grounds that their mental flightplans alter from what is commonly held to be the sane path. Thin line between genius and madness? Derek, there is no line.

"There is a plan; an order. Man fights, destroys, rebuilds, then fights again. This cycle keeps the evil at bay. Evil is like the sewage foam after a storm of prosperity. First thing's first, you have to get the drainage system working; otherwise, what have you got? Streets teeming with knife-carrying neds, gun-wielding black kids, BNP louts, Asian martyrs – who think it's reasonable and courageous to blow themselves up in trains and buses and planes, and who think that if they do incinerate as many pregnant women and kids as they can then there's a chance that they might get their pick of umpteen flowery virgins, the creepy fucking wankers.

"Hitler was a lunatic, but he was imperative in the conservation of the all-important trend that a fall must follow a rise. He wanted power; he needed a target. He was unhinged. Before World War 2, there were between six and seven million Germans out of work. They'd lost a war; they weren't best pleased. Hitler chose an enemy – the Jews. This despite it being a Jew whom had recommended him for a medal for services during the First World War, and the possibility that he might very well have been part Jewish himself. It's conceivable that, in the end, Hitler even managed to convince himself that he hated the Hebrew nation. He gave his people a war. An objective and an ethos to steady the resentment in the streets. God bless Hitler. Fortunately, we won that war. It was a war that we had to win, really.

"I hear the questions flow with the blood around your brains. What significance does the Second World War bode with us? What does any of it matter to us now? Bear with me, children. Pagan's here to elucidate."

The pool table beneath him became his throne. The nine became legions. The roof and the night drew back to reveal a brilliant day and glorious crowds; the multitudes did blend into colour.

"You fought for us years ago," Pagan said to the most senior duo, "or you were, at the very least, part of a part of the war. Grateful, very much. You came home; you grew old. Our fathers were born. They reconstructed the populous and established a peace among all men. We were born. What the fuck did we have? What could we contribute? All that's left for us to do is to make things smaller, faster and more expensive. And the quicker we get to places, the sooner we realise that we'd rather be at home, in our beds, sleeping till we can't wake up. We never fought; we shopped. A sulking generation of brand-whores waiting for the green light to annihilation. I ask you, I ask you now, who here could really give a poop about reproduction and the assimilation of the family unit? Procreation will not, somehow, save us from our stagnation. Obviously, it will bolster our numbers and retrench the food stocks, but it won't improve us as a species. It won't get us through the writer's block.

"Our design has to be grand, like the canyon, bottomless and wide and visible from space. And the stars will not fill this chasm. The universe is too fucking huge, and we don't live long enough to get anywhere. There's nought but us in this solar system, and the next one's about fifteen trillion light years away. So, it's just us and our fellow Earthlings for the foreseeable hereafter. Stuck together in this pendulous lift. Unless, of course, the aliens want to visit us. Which they've probably done. But if they have and they are, as they say, grey-skinned, bulbous-headed midgets, then they can just keep walking, basically. Come back when you're an eight-legged, multi-skulled flying monstrosity. Give us our target. War is the way."

His eloquence and the velocity at which he unspooled his views had the capacity to astound. Pagan was not yet finished, though. His pause was intentional, leaving his audience time to catch up.

Only Derek spoke. "Dee ye really believe 'at?"

"Most likely."

"Ye cannae think like 'at, Pagan. It's silly."

"Is it? Imagine a real war of the worlds, Derek. Who wouldn't want to be a part of that? Face facts, Derek: we all need the excitement. Life's too flat. The novelty of being upright and having opposable thumbs has worn off. There should be more somehow. But there isn't.

"Ian Brown said 'there ain't no lions in England'. There are no tigers or bears either. No toxic snakes lurking under the tub, ever ready to leap in and take a nibble. We won't fucking starve or freeze in Britain unless we really make a hash of things. Suddenly, the world's too safe, and a century of comfortable mediocrity seems worse than the death that underlines our final paragraph, like puke on the pavement outside some big, cheesy wedding reception. Oh, dear. What do we do?

"We shove needles in our feet, whiskey down our throats, start fights at football matches. Pick on the strong. Take on that which is deadly and not advisable for the preservation of our health. Anything to remind us, however fleetingly so, that we are alive and that we die, and that we are tangible things. It is why we have this attitude, stalking us like a hooded ASBOnite, pushing our age towards frustration and violence and total self-destruction. It's as the pattern of romantic tragedies: affection, rejection, heartbreak, loneliness, madness, mayhem. Derek, don't you see, as Braveheart taught us, as well as historical accuracy being insignificant, we die without ever having truly lived? There is no point to our being here."

"That's just wrong," Bob blurted out. "You're generalising everything. I'm sorry for your sadness – undeniably potent as it is, but you can't say that because you're feeling down everyone else must be as well." The Englishman gesticulated as though his chair bucked. "The world doesn't begin and end with your feelings, son. I'm sorry. I might have a cold, but that isn't to say that you then must also have it. And to suggest that everyone skips merrily along holding each other's hands during times of war is nonsensical. As I understand it, gangsterism and criminalistic opportunism was rife in London throughout the Blitz. We all have our ups and downs, pal. That's what life's about, and it's hardly pointless. Think of all the people you've been close to and have loved. Was all that a waste of time? Doesn't that mean something to you?"

"Yes. Maybe. Of course," Pagan replied. "But an accurate dissection of our times has to be bereft of any and all subjectivity instigated by previous personal happiness that I myself might have derived from individual relationships prior to our chat."

"Fir fuck sake, Pagan," Derek came forth another sly step, "stop spickin like some twat fae Dawson's Creek. Dinnae tell me that ye turned intae the kina cunt that says prophylactic fin he means dury. Ye soon like a fuckin exam question. Spick normal, ye fud."

Pagan chortled. He was the stage. "Sorry there. Sometimes – you're right – I get a bit overconfident with the wordsmithery. I'll tone it down for the masses. But, in all honesty, the only time that I can ever recall using the word 'prophylactic' has been in this very sentence, which I am about to finish.

"To answer your question, Bob, yes, I have been happy. I was happy today, in fact. The happiness, though, never lasts, nor does it carry any kind of substance to it. It sparkles, then dulls, like a festive display in January. As is the way.

"I generalise because, as a reporter of youth and crime and youth crime for a few years, I feel that I have earned the right to paint with the broader brush. There are, in my files, enough column inches and clippings to substantiate the claim that there is a disgruntled attitude of unfulfilment on the rise amongst my peers and those junior to me. This outlook breeds umbrage, dovetailed by a propensity towards brutal action and antisocial behaviour.

This is most common among males between the ages of 16-35, though it is not unheard of amongst females of a similar age group. Do we agree that not only is our society imperfect, but that its imperfections are explicitly expanding? Derek, what do you think?"

Derek dallied until the sentence formulated on the tip of his tongue, then said, "Ah think that if we start lukin at the Holocaust as bein some kina golden age, 'en we really are fucked."

"Beautiful." Pagan rocked back and rolled forward. There was pride in his eyes, as though his son had dressed himself unaided. "I doff my hat to you, sir. See, Derek, I always knew you were sharp. Most people don't get that about you, but I always did. You're not just some passive, placid, seventies-throwback; you're perceptive, and wiser than you'd ever tell. You're a good man, Derek Gibson. Never forget it. Shame you let the alcohol blunt your progress."

"Cheers." Derek echoed the poignancy that rounded off his old friend's compliment.

"Nevermind, though. There's always time." The pub seemed to breathe in. The lull expired. Pagan said, "Think of a war, people. A war that could be all ours."

"If you're so interested in military combat," Bob began, "why didn't you go into the army? That would've given you all the discipline that you'd have ever needed."

"It's not for me, Roberto. Humanity is not about the individual. It's about the group benefit. We all have to be a part of this. Everyone's a shareholder in the company Homo Sapien."

"Like the National Service?" Phil was repulsed. "Fuck 'at shit."

"No. Not the National Service. What could anyone benefit from guarding a chicken shed in Bolivia? I'm talking about a World War, for this generation. Not just firing missiles into caves. Going toe to toe on a battlefield. A serious war. One that would last for a decade. Death count into the tens of millions. Think about it.

"Instead of teenagers idling about outside their local chipshops like gargoyles, terrorising adults, they could be shipped off to battle their foreign counterparts. To defend their lives and the lives of utter strangers. They could learn what it means to be a man by killing another, by killing lots and lots of them. They could perceive the value of life by ending it. Toil not with this. Let the logic prevail. I am not green. I have thought this through.

"Our dissatisfied plurality will have a purpose. Everyone will have a story worth telling. The students and the social workers and the hippies – the pig-headed and the uninformed alike, all will have their chance to shine. They could unite to clog our city streets with their megaphones, placards and dreadlocks. The government will, once again, be worthy of a shouty hatred. Mothers will go on talk shows, sobbing into the microphones of fake psychiatrists. Fathers will raise a glass to the heroic deeds of deceased children. Grandfathers will be able to discard this war as some dolls' tea party compared to the Armageddon that they faced, in the days before the elderly souls ceased to serve a practical function. Everyone will figure. Politicians will become leaders will become legends. Picture it. Great books and songs will be written about our war for the next one hundred years. America's rap artists will have something meatier to drone on about than Cristal and Bentleys. Bling-bling: how odious. Geniuses will deride our war for being meaningless, a senseless tide of barbarity. We will know better. When it's over and our boys and girls return victorious, the world will be fine for the next fifty years. And when the muggings and stabbings and rapings escalate once again, it will be time to resume combat. It is a simple, murderous plan that has to work for mankind to last the distance. This is how you renovate the house of anthropocentrism."

Bob mulled it over. "Poppycock," he exclaimed.

"Fa wid we fight?" Scotty asked. His interjection surprised all.

"Not sure," Pagan said to the bleach-haired enthusiast. "How about China? There's about five billion of them, and nobody likes communism, apart from the fact that that's what everything is and always was. But that'll be our excuse. We hate those slitty-eyed Reds. How do we start our war, though? Same as everyone else does, I suppose. Plant a bomb and blame our enemy. Flawless."

"This is hoo yer mind works, Pagan?" Derek was unable to conceal his dismay.

"Sometimes."

"Sometimes when?"

"Sometimes when I'm going to kill myself. Sometimes when the sun in the sky doesn't shine for me. Sometimes when the grey clouds follow me home, and they're all that I can see when I close my eyes. Sometimes when it seems like life is just not worth the effort. Ever feel like that, my old matey?"

"No," Derek said. "Life's fuckin amazin," he deadpanned.

"Derek, do you want to know what the saddest thing that I ever saw was?" Pagan held the lighter between the finger and thumb of both hands, as though it were some pigeon-delivered dispiritedness. "It was in February. This year. I was leaving the gym and I had to go by the pool. It was eight o'clock at night; the pool was closed except for swimming lessons. So, I'm walking by, looking down over the empty spectator seats, down into the water. A guy was walking around, blowing a whistle and giving instructions with his arms, as swimming instructors do. But it wasn't kids that he was teaching. It was adults. Grown men and women, all between forty-fifty, standing in the shallow end, trussed up in armbands and goggles. For some reason, the sight of those people depressed the absolute living fuck out of me. It really did. I almost started crying right there in the stands. They watched me go, their doleful eyes sagging with their jowls, like I was going to tell their parents on them or something. I just sat in my car and bawled like a baby for near an hour."

"Ah dinnae un'erstan." Derek wasn't alone. Scotty flared his nostrils as if Platoon had been replaced with Pretty Woman.

"Neither did I," said Pagan. "Not at the time. I do now. I felt their shame, Derek. It overwhelmed me. This gigantic sense of the pathetic had flushed me out like a chi enema. I pitied them so much that I could hardly take it, and it wasn't just them. I felt this sorrow for everyone." The room was a sock drawer. Pagan spoke as though he were missing a heel. "The Chinese are sending dissidents to loony bins, telling everyone that they're insane. The Japanese rid the waters of whales in the name of science. Africa's run by corrupt assholes. Christ knows who's in charge of the United States. The Russian Mafia will cut off our power if we don't let them murder their opponents in our restaurants. Democracy has never ever been anything more than a myth, anywhere. You can't vote to improve things, because equality means freeing up the money, and the Smaugs of our mountain will never let that happen. The proles have no chance. We're all to be crushed under a wheel. What is the point, now, of learning how to swim? You're old and you are going to die. They were like fucking kids flying kites as the fucking tornado comes for them. They looked so stupid."

Derek unintentionally motioned a rude gesture at his friend with his damaged claw. "Pagan, we'll get ye help," he said. "Ye're nae right jist noo. We'll get yer heid sorted oot."

"Is that right, Mao Tse-tung?" The final traces of a smirk were vanquished from Pagan's voice. "No. It's too late. I appreciate it, Derek. Very much so, I do. I thank all of you for hearing me out; however, now is the time for the inevitable."

"'Ere's somethin in yer mind," Derek pleaded, "we'll fix it."

"'The mind is not a vessel to be filled, but a fire to be kindled.' Folks, the moment has arrived for me to become that fire." Pagan raised the lighter, with his thumb on its clicker.

A simultaneous gasp, like many beer cans being opened at once. The patrons recoil.

"No," Derek snapped. He seethed. A rage emitted from him like a floodlight. "Fuck you, Pagan." He pointed. He snarled. "Ye're nae jist showin up aifter ten years tae rub 'is shit in ma face. Ye're nae fuckin killin yersel. Fuck you, ye cunt, ye're nae fuckin deein it. Life might be shite, and the world might be run by fuckin pricks, bit it's better than fuckin nithin. It is worth the fuckin effort."

"Oh?" The others watched Pagan lower his plastic ignition switch. "Convince me."

"Convince ye? Hoo dee ah dee 'at, like?"

"We'll go around the room," Pagan said, as though a mist dispersed. "The people will tell us why we bother. Left to right. Starting with you, my swashbuckling friend. What's the point of it all?"

Gazza was inert in his booth. He hunched forward as if in an interview for a job that he didn't need but did want. The one-eyed man announced, "Respect."

"I see," said Pagan. "Respect. Well, thanks for that, Mr Corleone. Next."

"Riches an' bitches." Scotty was manifestly chuffed with his reply, which was also the name of a song that he'd written.

"What's this? Do we have the Sopranos sitting here? What about you? Have you got another wise-guy platitude to contribute?"

Alex didn't respond. He stared, loose-jawed, at all the unwell children dying on the floor. An elbow to the ribs endeavoured to bring him round. Scotty appeared flustered for them both. Alex was unable to consummate Pagan's query with words.

"Moving on. Old sir, can you tell me why life is worth the effort?"

Albert Thatcher grumbled. "Fit tripe. Garbage. Rubbish ye say. Feel question. Fit a neep. Tripe." It was as though a key had been slotted into his face and twisted. Albert glowered at his dried-up glass.

"Okay. You. Any chance of an answer there, captain?"

"Ach, me," Patrick said. His chin was up to facilitate his thinking. "Ah say that ye jist hiv tae get the good o it fin ye can. While ye're young. Govvy, ye shidnae be thinkin aboot 'is stuff at your age. Ye've a hale life tae ging yet. Deary me, ah wish ah could swaap places wi you the noo. Ah tell ye, ah widnae be thinkin aboot deein fit it is that you've got planned fir yersel, ah kin tell ye 'at much. Get yersel waashed an' fin' yersel a fine quine."

"I found one," Pagan replied. "But people just keep on killing them. What's a guy to do? Now, this should be interesting. What say you, Mr Schell? What's it all about?"

Bob put his hands on his knees and let the front of his jumper swell. "For me, young man, life's all about integration. It's about all these billions of people coming together, with all these diverse theories and philosophies and languages. It's about how we communicate and interact with each other, building and maintaining relationships. Developing bonds with loved ones and friends: two-way systems, interdependable partnerships and such. That's not to be sniffed at or taken for granted, which, sure enough, most of us do from time to time. You will know the quote that goes 'no man is an island', yes?"

"Johnny Donne."

"That's right. And it's true as well. We're all in this together, lad. There's no point hiding yourself away, or getting upset whenever someone treads on the back of your shoes. That will happen." Bob pinched the excess saliva from his mouth. "Get to know your species. We all start off as strangers, alone and insecure on this soaring rock. The trick is to create strings of concerned parties that will circle around you. Be like the sun. There's nothing more rewarding than having someone truly depend on you, and you not letting them down.

"Books aren't rewarding, son. Books don't go off to university, get married and present you with grandkids. No one *inters* books. They get pulped. Immerse yourself in life, not paper. Be with the living. Don't be intimidated by crowds. Sit in amongst the throngs now and again. Just be near people. The exposure will do you plenty of good."

"I'm always around people," Pagan retaliated. "I'm a journalist."

"You'll be *next* to people often enough," Bob said. "I'm sure you're *beside* them and *around* them. But I bet you're not that accustomed to being *with* them. Are you? You're probably more likely to be behind the camera than in front of it, aren't you? Get in front of the lens. Get stuck in. Involve yourself in proceedings more often. Don't do things like this."

Pagan bit the lighter as though it were a cigar. "Fine," he said. "Although I rejoice in arguing with you, Bob, in this instance, I shall opt not to. How about you? I would like to hear a female perspective on this debate. Have you anything further to add to our discussion?"

Samantha was inured to male regard; but seldom had a gathering of men been more interested in her opinions than her womanly form. The shame that she had hid behind since the accident with the boy frittered away like the numbers on an overworked television remote.

"I don't know," she said, hearing herself speak for the first time in a while.

"What makes you tick?"

"I travel, and I paint."

"Does that make it all worth the while? Subside the unbearableness of being? Make you happy, girl?"

"Yes."

"Irish?"

"Yes."

"Very well. Phil, how about it? What gets you through the days – besides the obvious?"

Fat Ass smiled at the remark. The truth was that the image of a kebab actually did flicker an inch or two behind Phil's sockets. He was hungry. He was always hungry.

"Ah'm nae sure. Films, probably," said Phil. "Ah like a good film, like. Did ye see 'em Lord o the Rings films? Good as fuck, like."

"Indeed." Pagan turned to Derek. The pub was lit like the interior of an airliner that had ventured beyond dusk. "From Philip the Wide to our very own Master Gibbins. What sayest thou? What can you say to restrain my halting play right now? We've had veneration, gold, sexual magnetism, blank, blank, female attachment, family ties, art and geography, Hobbits. What can you add to that list? Anything? I'm not sure if what we have thus far is enough to stop me from pressing this here button and raising hell. Please, Derek: a suggestion."

"Ah suggest ye gie me the lighter."

"Another suggestion."

How exactly did you talk someone out of killing themselves? What was the answer? Was there one? Derek had not a clue.

"Ah dinnae ken," he said, confidently. "Ah dinnae ken fit tae say tae ye. Ye're a mate. Ah dinnae want ye tae dee it. An' even if ye wisnae, ah widnae want ye tae dee it. Unless ye were a fuckin paedo or somethin, then ah probably widnae care. Ah want ye tae bide wi us a filey langer, Pagan. A good while langer. Jesus, 'ere's nae hurry, ken? Ye've got yer health: ye kin waak aboot an' lift things. 'At's top-notch. An' ye're nae too grotesque. Ah'm sure some quine'll let ye touch 'er boobs. Ah mean, fit the fuck? Fit's the worst that kin happen tae ye if ye dinnae kill yersel, eh? So ye'll be miserable some days, an' nae iverythin will ging yer wye. So fuck. 'At *is* life. Dinnae expect things tae work oot as ye'd like 'em tae. Bit at least ye'll be aroon fir the laughs. It's nae aa bad, ken?

"Like, 'ere seems tae be only one guarantee in life: the last funeral ye ging tae will be yer ain. Ah suppose 'at's nae guaranteed eether. If ye were cremated – properly cremated – then some fuckin twat could cairry yer urn along tae anither funeral. Bit it's unlikely. They might even smoke yer ashes in a doob." Derek pondered what the ramifications of inhaling another person into your lungs might be. "Ah suppose 'ere's jist nae guarantees at aa, is 'ere? Ah might even taak yer ashes, mix 'em up wi some paste, mould it intae some kina dildo-type shape, bake it, 'en let some gay-boy ging wild wi it. Ye jist niver know. Why rush tae fin' oot, eh?" Derek became very aware of the sound of his own voice, like he was the only thing in the world making a noise at that moment. He said, "Ah cannae be arsed wi onymair funerals, Peggy. Gie's a break, eh? Fuckin sick o 'em fuckin shitey hymns. An' fit is the hurry tae be deid, like? Ye think ye're nae gaan tae dee onywye, like, wi aa the rest o us? Jist hud yer fuckin horses, eh? 'Ere's a queue, an' you're at the fuckin back o it. An' ah'm nae convinced aboot the aifterlife, an' reincarnation luks a bit dodgy. 'At's a fuckin gamble. Imagine comin back as a pair o Phil's switey, stinkin pants."

"Fuck you, ye bastard."

"Why taak the risk?" Derek asked. "We'll aa be deid seen enough onywye. Nae cunt here's livin tae see a million – ah widnae've thought. Bit, ah suppose, wi medicine, ye jist cannae be too sure, eh? Christ-o Geppetto, ye're only here the once – that we ken aboot. Maak the mest o it, eh? Dinnae worry yersel aboot 'is nonsense. An' if Putin's butherin ye 'at much, ah'll gie 'im a boot in the baas for ye, the neest time ah'm in the Kremlin, or Stamford fuckin Bridge."

"He's a judo expert," Pagan retorted.

"He cannae be 'at tough," Derek said. "He luks like one o my nuts, faan ah wis twelve."

Pagan was entranced by his lighter; he twirled it around his fingers, but didn't drop it. "You tried, Derek. I think you all did. I think you're learning."

"Learnin fit?" inquired Derek.

"The other reason why our world's a mess. It's probably the real reason." Pagan raised his head towards the square eye above the bar.

"TV?"

"Yes. But no. On the TV."

The volume was down. A rich sort, a silvery man, a lord, was talking, stiff upper lipped; a single tear descended into his peppered beard. The channels were still gorging on the actor's death.

"Do you want to know why he died?" Pagan asked of the room, knowing full well that everyone did. They wanted to hear everything that he had to say, whether or not they concurred with him at all. "He was crammed tight with drugs, right? Pills and whatever he could get his hands on, which was anything. That was his way. Why? Why would a multi-multi-millionaire movie Adonis without a care have any cause to escape his life through pills? Why was he so stressed and saddened that he wound up atop a nightclub, singing some craziness? Why why why? I know. Most people in the media knew." Pagan reclined on his backless throne. "He was gay."

Some offensive flavour landed on Scotty's lips. "He wis a faggot?"

"Imagine being that famous, and being that famous for projecting a certain perception, and that concept made a lot of people content and rich, but that conceit was just a lie. An utter fabrication, and about as far from who you really were as was possible to get. The poor guy must've been breaking to pieces. The papers never said anything, though. Tabloid magnates and studio heads have their understandings. The guy was a billion-dollar industry. He was an oil rig. He was Iraq. He had proper clout. As a straight man, at least. How do you reckon your average cinemagoer would respond to the news that their hero was a cum-guzzler? That when he wasn't saving the day up there on the screen he was having his holes stuffed with massive black cocks in some Belgian S&M dungeon? With joy and praise, or bile and spite? What do you think? It'll all come out now, I'm sure. Kiss-and-tell exposes in all the rags from semen-drenched extras and fellow queers he may or may not have rogered in the backlot toilets? Who knows? What does it matter? Who cares?

"The message is important, however. The message is pure. We don't know how to talk to each other. Everything we feel, that we're embarrassed to feel, is cemented over. Then the concrete cracks and we explode. We're Yellowstone National Park. The worse we feel, the louder we laugh. In this country alone, there's an abundance of puerile, shellsuity, sweary torpedoes, with no way of articulating their sorrows. No offence." The insult flew by a platform-rooted Scotty as debris shed from a passing locomotive. "Were wee ned Billy to say to his pals that he's been feeling blue as of late, chances are that they'll call him a homo and tell him to fuck off, despite the fact that most likely they all feel an analogous ennui. Why? And that's the problem. We are not a nation that knows how to deal with its weaknesses. We are awkward and clumsy and harsh when addressing the sick in the herd. Men aren't supposed to have feelings. We weren't designed for that, were we?

"Everyone's angry. Everyone's stressed," Pagan said. His fist consumed the lighter. "But we're British." The nine patrons of the pub watched Pagan as though he were some stand-up comedian who'd gone off script and decided that to entertain was to demean oneself. "We are far too considerate to inconvenience one another with tales of our demise. How rude to tire an individual by telling them that, quite frankly, you've had enough; it's much more apt and becoming of a man to batter that person.

"I don't know where we go." Pagan was weary, as if wrung by a flu. "But I know that it's definitely not better to remain quiet and be thought a fool than to speak out and remove all doubt. Speak out. At least that way you'll learn and will have rid yourself of foolishness, instead of storing it up like some kind of bank of ignorance. And if people do think that you're a fool, don't despair. Opinions are ephemeral. Last impressions, underrated as they are, are much more important than first. You'll astonish them one day. Anyway, we're far too concerned with what other people think about us than what we think about ourselves. The community of us must learn to open up and be confident to express itself, and resist that impulse for knee-jerk mockery. Or where are we going? Wars wars, more wars. Forever. We seem to have a habit of running headfirst into brick walls. This has to stop, surely.

"We learn to guard our emotions from an early age. Boys are taught that the arts, poetry, literature – anything of any substance or skill – is for poofters. There's a football. Kick it. That's for you. Shakespeare? He's a nonce. Ballet? You're fucking joking, right? At the initial sign of anything that threatens to be inconsistent with the ordinary and challenge us or make us think, we dismiss it and insult it and allege that we're better than it. That's our shield for life. We build ourselves up by knocking others down.

"And then there's the scrapping in the pubs, outside pubs, wherever. A shoal of piranhas scrambling for meat. Can it come as a shock when we reflect that Schwarzenegger was our baby-sitter? Not that I would ever accuse films of making people violent. That comes down to a lack of imagination – which we've never been encouraged to explore, unless we're girls or come from a very specific background. Let's face it, though: we never see disputes settled with anything other than knuckles or nukes. Maybe you had something there with that 'convenience' spiel, Bob. Probably. After all, empathy takes time and effort. Why bewilder yourself and strive to understand why anyone does anything and engage in a lengthy debate about said problem? Punch him in the face. Be done with it. A bloody nose - "

The Tart door gust inwards. The diatribe shrivelled in Pagan's mouth like petals spritzed with acid.

The two darkly clad policemen entered, as though retrieving a ball from the pitch mid-game. Their hats had a tilt like spread bellows, above faces stony and grim. Gazza tensed, as was his ritual when the rozzers were about. Fit did 'ese fuckin piggies want, eh? Derek and Fat Ass had a shared fear. Something had happened to their mates.

What had become of the giant?

The officers surveyed the bar; the topless man, sat wet on the pool table, snagged their attention like a rag nail caught on a sheet. The eyes of the policemen sailed on from him, though, and finished upon the booth with Gazza and company.

"Are you Scott Thomson?" the taller bobby asked the boy with the bleached hair, alert like a cornered rat.

Gazza shot up as if some thing had plunged onto his plate. "Fit the fuck is 'is aboot, eh?" Big brother came out from behind his table.

A youthful voice skimmed through between the policemen. "'At's 'im."

"Fit the fuck?" Scotty screeched; the affrighted rodent had been prodded. Alex was too preoccupied with the phantasms to be distracted by the real.

Derek saw a familiar teen appear by the side of the shorter and younger of the two officers. With his stooped build and sapphire mohican, Chris Fraser identified his friend. "It wis 'im."

The tall copper announced, "Scott Thomson, I hereby arrest you on suspicion of the murder of a Raymond John McLeish last night in Fraserburgh town."

"Eh?" Gazza's thoughts jolted like a truck driving over downed posts. A mistake. A misunderstanding. But the guilt shone bright from his wee bro. Scotty appealed for mercy. His sibling's fierce rejoinder confirmed that he would receive none. "You did fit?" Gazza roared, snatching a fistful of Scotty's T-shirt. He yanked him forward and thrust him back, as though little brother were some sobbing yo-yo. Gazza struck out at him, tearing his cheek. Scotty cried and made jumbled protestations, minus the breath to entreat coherently.

The lawmen intervened to prevent another murder. The stocky, junior officer wedged himself between the brothers. "Gary. Gary, we'll handle 'is. Get back. Ah told ye tae get back."

Gazza screamed at his kin, "Ah'm gaan tae fuckin kill ye." He tried to climb over the policeman so that he could fulfil this promise. "Ye're deid, ye daft wee cunt. Ye cunt, did ye even think about mam? Cunt. Ye're deid. Fuckin deid."

Scotty fell deaf from the toll of his arrest. The yells and threats were muffled like a cassette being masticated by an old stereo. He couldn't see for chlorine. Couldn't feel the distension of his cheek. The tall policeman was calm but incomprehensible, reading out

Scotty's rights like Portuguese played backwards, cuffing his wrists behind his back as though they were prosthetic limbs. Dumb Scotty went dumb.

Alex watched the melting children diffuse into the floor. He got up and he shrieked. The loftier bobby grabbed him. "You're coming as well." When the blood was thick like margarine on his tongue, Alex stopped screaming. He watched the children die; let himself be guided by the tall man; didn't notice himself bump into Chris, who nothing more said; went out the door; into the back of a large, white van.

The short policeman fought to contain Gazza, whose ire had reached a crescendo. He flapped at his brother like a crow with one snared leg. Scotty couldn't lift his head as he waited to be guided out to the van and the station and the cell and court appearances and jail. Gary spat rage at half-brother Scott.

Phil and Derek, wary of his hurting hand, formed a scrum against Gazza, holding back the waves. "Thanks." The twenty-something copper could now escort Scotty outside. And so he did. Chris stood at the door. Raised a weak hand. Then left.

Derek sensed Gazza's resistance lessen behind his sweating shoulder. The one-eyed thug's grunts also diminished in their ferocity. Fat Ass was like a cowboy, with his arms clasped around Gazza's chest, riding out the last few throws of the bull.

Some time after the coppers had come and snatched his brother, the bull fused. Desisted from fighting completely. Sank and thinned in the duo's clutches. They let him go. He shuffled away. Oblivious to the honey stains that would mar his clothes, he leaned against the pool table. The green baize was spoiled beyond repair.

Gazza sloped against the spot where Pagan had sat. Derek's brain did stall. Where was Pagan? Had he vanished? He spun, as Fat Ass likewise did. The room, except for a dazed Gazza, looked to the bar. Pagan was positioned behind it, drying himself off with a rag. He wiped his chest and his face and his stomach and all over. He regarded the room's stupefaction as though they were all of a make unknown to him. What was the matter? he seemed to inquire.

Then said, "You guys alright?"

Derek didn't want to say the wrong thing and jeopardise this dramatic turnaround. It was all about tact. He asked, "So, ye're nae gaan tae kill yersel, 'en?"

"Nah. Not tonight, no," Pagan replied, in chipper style, as though home from a gratifying though exhausting chore.

Phil hoped that his confoundedness wouldn't be misconstrued as disappointment. "Why nae?"

"Well, Philip, I feel better. I've said my piece, and I don't feel quite so awful anymore. I think the talking was enough."

"So 'at's it?" Derek said.

"Yip. Won't be burning myself this evening. Psycho, eh?"

Derek needed an answer. "Bit wis it 'cos o somethin me or somebidy else said?"

"The momentum just sort of took a dip, then died out."

"So, ye're nae gaan tae dee it?"

"Nope."

"Well, 'at's a fuckin relief." Derek was not the only one left grazing their bonce. "Dee ye dee 'is sort o fuckin thing aften, like, Pagan?"

"No. Not often. Only the last time I was drinking."

"My advice," Bob said, "is that maybe you shouldn't drink."

"I'm not so sure about that, Mr Schell. It's good to slacken the valve now and again. I'm feeling pretty okay now. Right as the rain."

Derek felt rejuvenated, like discovering that it was still the weekend, after having woken up believing it to be Monday. Like it wasn't late at night, but early in the morning, and the morning of his eighteenth birthday at that. He'd survived this friggin night. Derek had earned the right to a teeny slice of smugness.

Pagan persisted in the task of clotting the petrol from about his person, under the gaze of the room. He appeared to be towelling himself down after a sauna.

"Ulysses." Fat Ass uttered the name as though it were a query in itself. "Ah taak it ye wisnae spickin aboot 'at freaky French cartoon wi the Bee Gees-lukin guy?"

"No." Pagan's tone tested negative for condescension. "It's a book, written by James Joyce, over the course of, I think, eight years. It's excellent."

"Fit's it aboot, like?"

"Life, I suppose."

"Is it glum, like?" Phil asked. "An' fuckin depressin an' shit?"

"No. Not really. It didn't depress me, and I'm soft. Like a sponge." Pagan flossed the cloth around the back of his neck. "I would have to say that it's rather optimistic, really. Life affirming, indeed. Why, do you want to read it? I've got a signed copy; got it from a car boot sale, believe it or not. Looks authentic to me. I'll let you have it for a pound."

"Nah. Fuck 'at." Fat Ass was back on his stool. He mucked about with the shillelagh. "Ah cannae really be fucked wi buks, like. Ah'll wait fir the film."

Derek's concentration had drifted on from Phil and Pagan. He observed Gazza, whom had removed his patch and was currently dabbing at both eyes. Questions festered like fish bait in a tub.

"Fit's wrang wi yer ee?"

"Ah'm fuckin greetin, a'right?" Gazza's enmity was limp, like the eye-patch that dangled from his pinky.

"Ah mean, why dee ye need the patch?" Derek said. "Fit's wrang wi ye, like? Ah thought ye wis supposed tae be missin an ee or somethin. Is it made o glaiss?"

The juice of Gazza's trademark aggression sapped away. He looked up at Derek, meeting the eyes of Pagan and Fat Ass also. "'Ere's nithin wrang wi ma ee, a'right?"

"Fit? Why the fuck hiv ye got 'at patch, 'en?"

The thug was ashamed. "Ah saw it in some fuckin shop doon in Newcastle. Ah thought it made me luk scary."

This revelation took Derek a second to process. He'd worked alongside the guy for the last four months. "Are ye fuckin mad?"

"Must be."

"I'll do you a deal," Pagan interjected. "I'll swap you this lighter – never been used – for your eye-patch. What do you say? Is it a deal?"

Red around the pupils and bashful, Gazza laughed. A wheeze through his fractured beak. "A'right."

"Perfect."

The two men traded across the bar, tossing first the yellow lighter then the patch. Pagan slipped the leather patch into the back pocket of his grey trousers.

"You should probably give that thing a wipe before you use it." Pagan rubbed the fuel from his ears.

Samantha was heading for the door.

"Stop," Derek said. "Wait."

She halted. She dallied.

"What?" she replied, defiant like the fox confronted by an unarmed farmer. Samantha said to Phil, "Tell Valerie I quit."

"Ah'll waak ye hame," said Derek. She did neither verbally accept nor decline. She only delayed her departure further. He said to his friends at the bar, "Ah'm off. Ah'll hiv tae ging an' get ma han' checked oot, like."

"Oh, aye." Phil's intonation was of one who suspects another of having stolen from him. "An' fit exactly did happen tae yer fingers? Ye niver quite explained 'at bit."

"Disnae maitter. Ah'll see ye's later. Nae mair fuckin surprises, right?" Derek thought about Samantha in her pink top and him in his black T-shirt, and about the night. He inspected a stool at the end of the bar. "Wait a second; faar's ma jacket?"

"Freddy's awaa wi it," Phil said, back to accosting Derek as a pal.

Derek was perturbed for the first time in minutes. "Why? Faar did he ging?"

"Jist awaa oot for a meenty. He shidnae be lang."

"Did Mo ging we 'im?"

"Mo's wi the grite Dundee lad." Phil aimed to reassure himself that external issues might have resolved themselves by now. "Ah think aathin shid be okay."

Derek doubted that it would be. “Ah’ve deen aa ah can fir jist noo. Ah need a tune up.”

“You do remember where I’m staying, don’t you?” said Pagan. The good friends were reunited. “Your bags are in the kitchen. There’s a key under the mat.” He grinned as though they’d somehow nicked a win.

“Right-o, Peggy.” Derek recalled that his chum’s grandmother’s house was a small house in Lumsden Way: a safe, forgettable street that barely registered even as you travelled through it. “Cheery bye, boys. Behave, eh?”

“So long, Derek.”

“Cheerio.”

“See ye later, Gazza.”

“Right.”

“Gentlemen.”

“Goodbye.”

“Samantha. Ye ready?”

“Yes,” she said. She hid a smile. “Yes. Why not?”

Chapter 19

They intersected the Broadgate from the harbour road by traversing up the hill between the Woolworths and a church. The shopping district was deserted. They crossed the road and passed the off-licence, which was closed at this hour. They travelled away from the town centre. There was no greenery there; it was like they'd fallen into a vat of cement: the mess splashed up and settled around them as stalagmites. They strolled up soundless streets; front gardens began to appear like opened tills. He spoke sparsely. She said little. This was not as a result of any discomfort triggered by their earlier liaison. The mortification had since waned. They didn't need to talk. A radio-wave succour flowed between them that speech could only harm. There was a mutual need for the silence that the evening supplied, excluding the intermittent growl of a modified engine.

He wanted to take her hand. He asked her where she was staying. She told him an address. He knew the street; it was nothing special or unique, as it wasn't likely to be in a town like the Broch. It was her relative's house, she said. Good stuff, he replied. He didn't really care. He wanted to take her hand.

They took the route through the academy grounds. It was an unnecessary deviation, but he was in no hurry to depart from this fair maiden. She'd go to the hospital with him, she had said, though she wouldn't have known how near or how far the hospital was from her digs. It wasn't awfully far. The hospital was close to the academy; only a couple of rows of toffee shards to the west of it. Atop a grassy mound, the academy was like a lair assembled from cereal cartons. During the day, the building was stirred by teachers and spiced with prospective do-gooders and dole-bums. It was empty at present, as it should be.

She asked him if he had gone to school here. Yes. He had. He remembered those with whom he had shared classes. Where were they now? Mairriet or deid, mestly. He had known them all before they'd met that special someone, or had strayed off into the chemical wastelands. He'd known them as they had become junkies. Nice enough folk, some of them.

They'd simply lacked the ability to say no. In the years to come, he'd wager that some of them had even forgotten how to spell no. Fine folk. Derek didn't, as much as it could be helped, talk to any of them anymore.

I'm sorry, she said. Dinnae be, he replied. It's nae ma fuckin problem.

They continued on by the building. They walked past a block, which, if the infrastructure of the school hadn't been changed drastically, he knew to be the gym hall. 'At's faar ah did PE, he announced. He'd got his first blow job in there, in the changing rooms – from a girl. He kept this to himself. This had been whilst the others were out playing hockey. Whatever had become of that girl? he wondered. Moved away, I think. She was a slut, he thought. An unattractive slut, and she'd been in love with him. He'd had no qualms back then about treating her like a recycled condom. Her name was Heather Noble, he recalled. They'd dubbed her Heather Gobble. She, as he'd never find out, lived above an arcade in Bristol with her abusive partner and her autistic son; the lover was not the father of the boy. 'Em were the days, Derek said.

It was cold. She held her elbows; her nipples were as hood ornaments. He'd have given her his coat, if Freddy hadn't inexplicably went off with it. She'd explained that she didn't have a jacket with her because her cousin was scheduled to be picking her up after her shift, which, because of events unforeseen, Samantha had not concluded. Caal, eh? he said, as though the acknowledgement would precipitate warmth. She shivered; she nodded. He tried not to stare at her chest.

He wanted to pause and give her a hug by the enormous shed, inside of which he'd received his first lesson in oral sex. With all the hubbub in The Tart, he'd almost lost sight of how glorious she was. His Irish cutey: she was as adorable as a hen party. He'd cuddle her till the moon dropped and the sun bounced and Fraserburgh's teens, as well as those of the surrounding area, returned to their educational spa. He wanted to tell her so. He wished to express to her as eloquently as he could that he thought of her as being more than just the girl who broke his fingers with her vagina. He'd like to hold her hand and hug her and kiss her and take that band out of her blondish brownish hair and sit on a wall somewhere and talk to her as if they had Physics in the morning. Listen to the stories that she had accumulated on her travels. He was in a listening mood.

They walked. They dawdled. They exited the grounds of the academy. They could take the cold that chilled. There was no hurry. She never looked far from smiling. This has been the oddest night of my life, she said. I don't think there's anything left of me. He would assure her that there was plenty of her left. But that might sound either sleazy or like an insult. There's more to you, he'd say, than any girl I've ever met. You're rich and sweet and fascinating. Marry me. He could marry her. He knew that. She would offer him something new every day. She didn't seem the predictable type. There was a spikiness about her. A shifting in the eyes. She'd always be the same: ever changing. He wanted to keep her for himself, before someone else thought to do so. It was inevitable that somebody would think to hatch the selfsame plan. She wouldn't grow old alone. She wouldn't be allowed to. She was a prize. Every man that she would ever meet would come to realise this about her; although, her modesty would buttress her blindness. She was special. Unique. A one-off. One to keep. She was a keeper, definitely.

Phil would've loved her. But Phil was fat. A fat man didn't deserve such a delicately prepared dessert. Such feasts were reserved only for men whom had the decency not to scoff their grub. Gluttonous fat people. Fuck the fatties. Shovel your asses off the ground and move to Florida.

She wasn't fat. Not skinny either, however. Samantha wasn't envelopes-in-a-bag thin. When Derek was with a woman, though, he wanted to feel that he was with a woman, and not as if he'd caught his dick in the slats of a deck chair.

The streetlights embraced her like she was a visiting granddaughter. They sauntered along the pavement, as if both untroubled that they tail-feathered at the rear of some race. He thought about his digits. He wanted to nourish his smell receptors with her scent. He wanted to taste her. She would be thinking. What would she be thinking about? The episode in the pub? In all probability. A man threatening to set himself alight was an incident not easily dislodged from the cerebral hemisphere. Pagan. She'd be thinking about him. About how

Derek had intervened. He'd talked Pagan out of doing it, kind of. He had acquitted himself well, possibly. Done himself proud, he thought. She'd maybe think better of him now. He thought that she must do. She might be thinking about his pal's six-pack. Derek could obtain those ridges for his stomach. He could do the requisite exercises, if that was her thing.

She could be dreaming about her adventures across Europe. Men she'd left lonely. Canadians. What the fuck was Canada? It was like America, but not. The arse-end that the French had managed to get their garlicky mitts on. This isn't America; this is Canada. There's a difference. We don't use our guns on each other. We don't even use them against our enemies. We don't have enemies. We don't do war. We're not going to go to war. We're against wars.

Benders.

Would you go off to war, Derek?

Aye. Ah'll be shinin bright.

Remember, young knight Sir Derek, with which place Fraserburgh is twinned in the world. Bressuire. A town in France, if I'm not very much mistaken, my lad.

'At's right. Ah forgot aboot 'at, like. Long live the French. The Frogs are a'right.

It was Spain with its Civil War and its Franco. It's Italy with its mopeds and Mussolini. Germany? Das ist nicht sehr gut. The Middle East with its Bin Laden and bombs and rage against the West. He was part of that West. What did that mean? Nothing to him. It was North America with its Christians and capitalists; South America with its she-males and cartels. Asia and its Ding Dong Pings and Hoo Flung Dungs. Australia with its spiders and shades-wearing kangaroo souvenirs. Corks on hats. It was the North Pole. The South Pole. Great, big Polar bears and furious penguins. Eskimos in houses made of snow. It was last week. This week. Funerals. His own death. How would he die, and when? And what would he leave behind? In this world, or in the next. It didn't matter. For he had the life and he intended to live the fuck out of it. What time of day/day of the week was it when he had been conceived? Had his mother cum? Did she pretend? Had he disappointed his parents both? Had he let down every person that he'd ever met? It wasn't good versus evil. It was grey against grey. It was the fire in the sky above this play that cast them all as charcoal. You won't scorch me, you giant, yellow swine. I won't die young. I'll die aged and hideous, shrivelled like a bollock. A heart attack aged ninety-one. My children crying; their kids apathetic. I will be missed. And all the pain I will miss when I am gone.

Och, it wis aa a'right.

What are you laughing at? she asked. She was better than alright. She had wandered ahead. He lagged behind. She was better than best. She waited for him to catch up. She looked like she, too, wanted to laugh. He could tickle her and grant her permission. Are you feeling alright? she inquired, as they resumed their journey to the hospital. He'd like to tell her that he'd never before felt better. He would stress to her how truthful this statement was. He never had felt better. He wasn't stottering about after her, drunk, on his toes, erect. He was lustrous like the sunshine of an unclouded winter. Practically sober.

He would've quoted a poem, had he known any. Sonnet, come to me now. A stanza. A line. One elegant line to rival the grace of her skin. What could he say about her hair that he wanted to stroke? That it had the sweep of desolate glens? Her eyes to marvel? Were they like the rock pools of a Mediterranean alcove? Her mouth to kiss? Did it bear the elixir of an oxygen mask to a faint man? If he could but split the cosmos and take her to the valley of undying light and time that could never fade. Hold her, he said inside his head. Adorable Samantha so adorable. Her proximity cushioned him like bubble wrap, but it also made his heart thump like a collapsing city. Are you feeling alright? she asked. Tell her the line that would make her ours. Mine until death. I could love you, he thought. I really could. Be mine. Propose to her. Are you…? Aye, he replied. Ah'm a'richt.

They walked onwards. Down this street. Turned right into the next. Then left down another. Then right again, up the drive to the hospital, which was fortified by a square of swarthy semis. The hospital was like a flattened version of the academy, and might possibly have been designed and built by the squad that did construct the aforementioned comprehensive, most probably in the same period, about a decade before Derek's conception. The building was both peculiar and blank; it was a dirty white in the night, like a slumbering

Goth. It seemed no less vacant than did the academy. He'd been born here. They followed the path up to the doors. Most of the lights in the wards were out. A few cars were in the car park, like void tins by the fridge. An abandoned ambulance was on stand-by.

They stood by the doorway. They could see that, as they'd rightly anticipated, there was no queue. There didn't appear to be any staff on either. He turned to her. Would she slap me now if I kissed her? Was the conflagration that had resulted in his being injured now extinguished? Did she beam for him? Was she waiting for him to do something? Was it the lights? Was it the stars? Was it

Ach. Fuck it.

He kissed her. Tenderly, not pornographic like before. She kissed him back. They kissed. They unfastened. He was smitten. He could only pray that she felt something approaching the same cosiness as he did.

"Samantha," Derek said, "ah think maybe ah kina, like, love ye, ken?"

She did not reply. She wrapped her arms around him; she sank her head into his chest. He smooched her on the crown. They cuddled.

A skirling motor skidded round the corner and tore up the drive. It had been fortunate not to capsize. It demolished the speed limit on its jaunt towards the entwined couple. There appeared to be a tussle going on behind the wheel. The car swerved, jumped the kerb, and smashed into a squat wall that shepherded a lawn down to the street. The boot popped open. A life jacket and a set of golf clubs bounded out onto the road. Steam had automatically begun to spout from the purple car's crumpled front like an ill-tempered kettle.

Derek knew the car. It was the car that had come to take some items away from Jimmy's flat, not long after Lori had jilted him.

Samantha pulled away from Derek. He shook his head in reply to her facial gymnastics. He shook his head. He watched the car. He waited for anyone to emerge from that crash and penetrate the stillness of the random picture rammed at them.

The front passenger door sprang wide. A man got out and started to run. He made off across the grass; a cautious glance over his shoulder to assess the scene prompted him to stop, however. The man stretched his neck as though he were at the back of a crowd, to make sense of what he saw. "Derek?" said the man. "Is 'at you, Derek?"

"Aye. Mo. Fit the fuck are you deein here? Fit's gaan on?"

Mo crept towards the car, but halted again when the driver's door swung out. Two brown shoes fell upon the pavement. Mr Mackintosh sat sideways in his car. He got out and reset his hat. He tucked the tails of his scarf under his coat. Charlie went over to sit upon the kerb by the hospital doors, as if a deluge had postponed his sport. He ignored Derek; it was as though they were on independent channels.

Samantha moved away from Derek. "What's going on?" she asked him.

"Ah dinnae ken." Derek utilised a pitch that he thought would persuade her that none of this was in any way his fault.

His and her understanding of occurrences prior to the crash were shaken to lucidity when a third door was punched ajar and out oozed a bleeding giant. The zombie pushed himself up and sat back against the car. He grasped his black pistol as though it were a lively thing that might wriggle loose. Lex MacMurran did not, it seemed to be, have a full comprehension of that which transpired about him.

Derek seized one of the golf clubs, a nine iron, from the road. He held the club in a manner as to indicate to the giant that he should relinquish the gun immediately. Lex leaked like a breached hull. This may have been his premier taste of canvass. He was in as bad a shape as Derek had ever seen a man.

"Fit the fuck happened? Fa the fuck shot 'im?"

Mo mimed towards Lori's dad like it was he whom had put the Frisbee into the greenhouse. Mr Mackintosh counted the atoms in the air.

"Ah cannae fuckin believe 'is shit." Derek's sweat churned the frost. "'Is is aa too fucked up."

Neither a nurse nor a receptionist had yet come out to investigate the thud and smash that must've been heard from inside. Surely someone had witnessed the rumpus through the cameras, if there were any.

Lex studied the weapon in his hand as though it were becoming gradually apparent to him for what purpose the metallic device served.

The golf club strained the one arm that Derek could afford to brandish it with. Out of the corner of his eye, he noticed a figure heading down the drive away from the hospital, absconding at a fast trot.

"Stop. Samantha, wait."

She didn't stop. She didn't wait. She called back, "I'm sorry. I can't take any more of this." Samantha reached the street; she was briskly obscured by garden foliage.

Fir the love o

"You, listen tae me." Derek was poised like a fly-fisher, solid to the currents. "Drap 'at fuckin gun. We'll get ye in 'ere. We'll get 'at hole o yours cleaned up afore it's too fuckin late, ye cunt. Ye listenin?"

The Dundonian was no longer recognisable as being the gargantuan might that had entered The Tart that very evening. This same one. What a day. Lex's grip grew firmer around the handle; his finger found the trigger. From somewhere, he discovered the power to raise the pistol; it wobbled upwards to an angle that could severely hurt Derek and his plaything.

Mo rounded the smoky vehicle to see what was going on. He kept his distance. "Will ah get a doctor?"

"Shut the fuck up," Lex spluttered out, like his teeth were made of card. His face was as corrugated iron. "If ah'm deein, sae are you." He said this to Derek. "Ye're fuckin brave, aren't ye? Ye fuckin brave?"

"No, bit 'at winnae stop me fae buryin 'is club intae yer skull. Drap the gun."

"Fuck you." The rubble of Lex wished to clamber up and reconstitute itself, but it could not. "You're comin wi me."

"Luk," said Derek, "nae cunt his tae dee."

"Some cunt shot me. Somebidy's gaan tae fuckin dee. Might as weel be you, tough guy."

Mo came forward, mindful that the gun barrel should shift towards him. "No. Lex, we kin save ye, like. 'Ere's nae pint gettin saved an' 'at, 'en comin oot tae ging tae jile, like. We'll fix ye, 'en we kin forget aboot iverythin that's happened." Mo spoke as if he were trying to convince someone to exchange their lemonade for urine.

"Forget? Nah, nah. Lexy boy's bin shot." The giant's words crawled out as if through a narrowing hatch. "'At cannae be forgot."

"We'll pay ye fit ye're owed," Mo pleaded.

Derek intervened. He said, "Ah'll pye ye. Me personally." The gun wavered. Derek rested the head of the golf club on his trainer. "Ah've got five grand." This was, indeed, the downpour about which his father had forewarned him. "'At dee ye?"

The receptionist, a chubby, middle-aged woman with a puffed-up do and an alarmed face, came through the doors to behold the drama.

"Wid ye taak five gran'?" Derek asked him. "Wid 'at settle it?"

"Fit's gaan on oot here?" She saw the car, the club, the pistol. "Ah'm phonin the police." She scurried back towards the entrance.

"Fuckin stop," Derek roared. The impassioned directive compelled the lady to freeze. "Nae police. Nae yet. We kin handle 'is. Bit we'll need a doctor. Ging in 'ere an' get een o 'em fuckin rolly things. Please." She did as she'd been instructed, disappearing into the hospital like a puff of rotund smoke.

"Ah've got fuckin five gran'," Derek repeated, angered more than frightened by the giant and the gun. "Ye'll taak 'at fuckin money, an' 'at'll be the fuckin end o it. A'right? Ye got 'at? Ye fuckin listenin?" Derek struck the club on the tarmac as though to convoke sparks. "Nae fuckin aboot. Ah'll gie ye five grand; en' we'll niver fuckin see ye again. If ony cunt asks, ye fell on a bullet."

"Five grand?"

Derek couldn't decide whether the giant had thought the sum a lot or very little. "Five grand. An' 'at'll be it. Feenished. Ye kin fuck off back tae yer Dundee slum aifter 'at."

Lex was weighing this up, balancing out the money with his desire to shoot Derek, when another car blitzed the drive. It hurtled towards the Mackintosh mobile; its brakes cried out; the car steered sharply to impede collision. Otherwise, the purple car would've smacked into the giant and folded him in half. Derek did fathom that this new car, a blue vehicle, belonged to Freddy. He watched it scream to a halt. The receptionist returned with a nurse and a gurney. Derek could not contemplate the whys or the whats of the matter. Freddy leaped out of his vehicle, yanked open the back door, dragged something out – no, some*one* – that Derek could not yet identify – someone small? – Freddy rushed up to the hospital, carrying this person – a girl – nearly clattering Derek over in his frenzy. The cogs reeled and clicked. Freddy wore Derek's thick, navy jacket. Derek saw Donnie in the front seat of the blue car. Donnie did not move. Derek turned to see Freddy barge past the two approaching women. "Faar's the fuckin doctor?" Freddy was yelling inside the hospital, at no one. "Faar the fuck – faar the fuck – get me the fuckin doctor." The receptionist and the nurse were as bunnies caught between multiple sets of oncoming headlights. Derek saw the tubby receptionist make the decision to go indoors and see to the blaring man with the unmoving girl in his arms. The nurse pushed the gurney onwards. She was slim and almost pretty, he observed; she passed him by, taking that trolley to the dying giant. Without vocalisations being bartered, Mo agreed to assist the nurse in the hoisting of Lex, whom had let the pistol slip from his talons. Derek watched the pair aspire to shift the pale colossus. Derek advanced towards the wide parting of the hospital entry. Mr Mackintosh sat to the side, dreamily reading the nothingness ahead. Derek went through those hospital doors. On the corridor floor, which Derek thought looked both cream and lime, his niece lay flat, moon-coloured – unbruised, uncut, undamaged, seemingly. And wordless. Freddy paced around her. Muttering aloud. Blaming himself. Blaming everyone. Shrieking, suddenly. "Fuck. No. Fuck." The receptionist ran back into sight from around a corner. Two doctors pursued her. The two men were uniform, attired both in their trousers and shoes and ties and white coats. They were of the same build, had the same shape of face, and their hair also was alike. The only discernible divergence that split the pair was that one was a Caucasoid whilst the other was Asian. The white doctor waved Derek on. Then Derek realised that the white doctor wasn't motioning to him, but at the nurse who pushed the stretcher. The white doctor guided her and the bleeding giant around the corner; the trio evaporated. Mo materialised by Derek's side. Mo kept on moving; he finally stopped beside the receptionist's desk, from where he viewed the efforts of the medical team. The Asian doctor was knelt over Derek's niece. He massaged her chest; he breathed into her mouth. Did those things that doctors did when they attempted to bring a patient back from the dead. He rubbed; he exhaled. Freddy paced. Frantic. Ranting. Mo stood. Voiceless. The receptionist bit her fist. The Asian doctor did what he could. Derek did pivot. He saw Donnie by the doorway. Startled and hirsute; a knee-length, black, leather coat. Derek was the first to perceive that Lex's pistol was in Donnie's hand. The Asian doctor desisted with the inconsequentialities. He looked at his watch. Derek saw Donnie put the gun under his chin. Derek heard a bang; the man-made thunderclap scared his eyes temporarily shut. Derek watched the brain and the gore drizzle down from the ceiling onto Donnie's slumped corpse.

Chapter 20

"Amen."

Derek sat back down onto the bench.

Roof high. Frescoes. Church. Bandaged hand. Sweating. Two coffins instead of one. One bigger than the other. Not big, though. Normal size. It's the other one that is small.

Derek cannot look away from those two boxes. It was as if he were the nail from which they hung. He knows that the room is full around him. Young, middle and old, the Broch is out in force. Benches packed. People stripe the back wall as though around a fence at a farmer's market. The balcony is stocked like the detachable heads of a screwdriver set. His family sits along from him. Dad by his side. Yet to speak. Further on, nextwards to his father on the left, was Derek's sister. Catatonic. Heartbeat sluggish; like a tap almost off. Watching her life end from within, possibly. Taken something to prevent feelings. She will improve, Derek thinks. He'll make sure of it. Mum sobbed beside wee Trace. They'd taken her in. We'll get ye help. There, there. Come back tae the castle. No one's invited Derek back home as yet, though the nod that his dad had given him when they'd taken their seats did appear to indicate a relenting of animosity. Should his father ask him to return, however, Derek would abstain. The Wise clan occupies the parallel bench. They seem like they'd be of a nature more inclined to read the sorts of books that Pagan read. Derek didn't know those people too well.

The minister began to tell the story of how it was that many great tragedies had often acted as springboards for reconciliations long overdue. Derek could feel his liquids circulate, but not as though they were set to burst out of him. They were secure, in steel pipes, between crust and core.

Pagan was not present, and neither was Fat Ass. Both were at work. Mo was here, somewhere, with his parents. The weekend was fast in passing; their nights went unused.

Another Monday afternoon. Not been in The Tart since Thursday. Looks unlikely that Pagan's grandmother will ever leave the hospital with a pulse.

All ears tracked like hounds the tale of that Thursday night. Too many ins and outs and strange bits for the public to assimilate. A minimum of ten clashing stories abound. One legend goes that there wasn't a giant but a gang, and that Donnie was murdered and not the victim of a grief-induced suicide. At least three versions imply that Rachel was abducted and abused most horrifically. Few suggest the truth. Death by misadventure. Disorientated by the cold and in the dark, she tumbled. The seven-year-old fell down the dunes and broke her neck.

Derek discovered that he could tolerate those hymns when he wasn't hungover. He didn't sing along with them; he could, though, stand for them without complaint, for however long they took, when there wasn't that sickness inside of him, plotting like Palestinians against the Israel of his stomach. A song played through the sound system. Derek didn't recognise the song initially. He must have heard it at enough post-pub parties. It was Fleetwood Mac. Derek thought that they were an okay band. It was one of their songs. Donnie had liked them. Tracy loved them, or had done, when Derek had kind of known her. Evidently, she was still a fan. This, apparently, had been Rachel's favourite song. Sara. She'd mimic Stevie Nicks whenever it was played, even when junkies had commandeered the living room. The song stimulated a breeze of lamentation. The coffins were wheeled down the aisle. The Gibsons and the Wise folk followed them into the street.

Outside, Derek stood upon the pavement and watched the people – there were a few hundred of them. The way in which they spilled out from the church and onto the Broadgate reminded him of how he had emptied his guts the week before. The mourners homed in on the bird feeders of their chosen transport, craving not to be delayed by others. The day blazed but was not especially sweltering; clouds sneaked about on the periphery like rats by the canal, as though to blatantly convey a sense of approaching doom. Into a future uncertain. Then again, Derek thought, it was just the weather.

"You comin wi us?"

Derek averted his gaze downwards. His Aunt Rosie was across the street in the car park, next to a graffiti-stained monument. A door of her and her partner's carriage was agape in expectancy.

The twin black beacons led them along the harbour road. They pursued those two hearses in the midst of the procession. "Fit ye going to dee wi yourself noo?" inquired Sylvia's reflection in the rear-view mirror. The car was spacious and luxurious, like the cabin of a yacht, but the engine lacked oomph. They passed the yards. Broch rock segued into country crispness.

There wasn't enough spite in Sylvia's question to warrant a burst of roaring indignation. Derek replied, "Dinnae ken." He wore the same suit as he did last time, though the women did not; even their hair was styled in a slightly dissimilar manner. "Why?" he asked. "Fit hiv ma two favourite dykes got planned?"

Rosie refined her throat. Derek saw the pair exchange a look. They wouldn't rise to the bait. His aunt said, "We're going tae adopt."

"Adopt, aye?"

"That's right, Derek." His father's sister seemed different to him then. Her ferment revealed a vulnerable – dare he think it? – likeable side. "The forms are bein processed. We're going tae have a wee Afghanistanian boy tae look after. What dee ye think about 'at, Derek?"

He decided that he would respond positively, whether he meant it or not. "Good stuff," he said.

The graveyard crowds scattered. His parents were arms by Tracy's side. They escorted her through the far-off gates like a thing that walks on its fists. Derek tarried by the open pit. The seeds had been planted. He'd helped to lower them into the muck. Her little box did rest upon his. That was it. That was them. That was their go at being alive. It had been a terrible thing that had happened. If he were ever going to cry, he would cry about this. Maybe later. Freddy and his wife came over. She was starting, at last, to shed the pregnancy padding.

"Fred Zeppelin. Kim."

"Derek, hoo ye deein?"

Derek could not be definite about his status. By way of being polite, he replied, "Fine, ah think."

Kim, like the preponderance of ladies at the funeral, had been tearful. She didn't talk for the lump in her throat that pained her to her eardrums. She was brittle like a bread-stick chairlift. In contrast, Freddy was a sombre obelisk: a tribute to reticence. Frederick was smarter than usual in his burial suit, and for having smoothed off his stubble.

"Fit aboot you, Freddy?" Derek was pleased that he also had thought to shave that morning. "You're the een that fun' 'er. Hoo you copin?"

"Nae great."

The husband and his wife left after a minute of ungarnished repose.

Derek's Great Uncle Willie was the next to come over and commiserate. Drunk, and in clothes too small for him. His shrunken sleeves unveiled his wrist bones. The bump at the acute pinnacle of Derek's left forearm was concealed by his stookie. Willie said hoo affa it aa wis. Derek did not disagree. Then his uncle talked about the fitbaa. Willie expressed his wish that the Dons wid hae a gweed season 'is year. Div ee 'ink they will? Derek thought that they would not, and told him as much. Willie considered this point, as though it were of the mightiest significance, and drearily supplied his concord. The uncle then ambled away across the grass, over the graves of all those whom he had miraculously outlived.

"Derek, dee ye need a lift?" It was Mo whom called to him from down the path. The assistant manager scratched at his head, though he likely had no itch.

"Nah. Cheers. Ah think ah'll bide here a file."

Mo was gone. They were all gone. The buses and cars headed back along the road into town. Derek stood in the graveyard alone. Alone except for the two men whose job it was to put the piles of mud back in their place. The pair were of the fading, gradually but perceptibly, age of his dad. Both men were visibly dyspeptic, veering towards resentful, having Derek there to observe every shovel's worth that they dropped onto the boxes. They did not converse with one another as they would normally have done, for fear of displaying insensitivity. The boiler-suited men would have anticipated that the family of the deceased would have pissed off by now. Derek knew that as soon as he turned to leave, the duo would be cracking jokes and perhaps regaling each other with bawdy limericks. They'd probably even fetch a radio from their van. Derek couldn't blame them for eyeing him with mild hostility.

As yet, no stone marked the hole that would prove to be the eternal bedsit for his brother-in-law and his niece. Those two men did tuck them in forever.

Derek decided to give the workers a reprieve from his fixed inspection. He had himself a stroll around the cemetery. Initially, the older, craggier stones – those with dates that began 18somethingorother, they were the ones to captivate him. These tombstones inspired thoughts of pirates and were engraved with fairly suspect grammar. Entire families were represented by a solitary erection. He passed, though, sleeker stones, for dead people that he might've known. Many that he had done. Emblems for plantings that he'd attended. Many began 'For our son' or 'In loving memory of our daughter'. If Derek couldn't put faces to some of these names, then he would know someone who could. As was the way in small towns. Everyone was connected in this Petri dish.

Derek found it quite disconcerting that a lot of these polished rocks towered above coffins crammed with the bones of his generation.

There was Debbie Walker: the blonde minx with the lisp and the highly exalted melons. Derek had, or so he'd been told – he could recall no such rendezvous – been there, done that and wiped his jizz off her chest with a T-shirt. She OD'd a couple of winters ago. Chrissy Reid. The Welshman. He was a laugh. Not a bad player, to boot. Chris had a vein in his neck cleaved by some girl with an alcopop bottle. When was that? Some New Year's night. Ah, yes. Bringing in the millennium. Next to him: Edgar Jennings. Crazy Edgar and his ginger afro. A drink-driving accident. The same crash had proved fatal for the subsequent three stones: Paul Mackie, Alisdair Stuart and Alan Lobaczewski. And, of course, there was Lloyd Cardno – another OD. At the time of his demise, it is said of the former skin-headed Nazi-admirer that he had taken to jacking-up into his rectum. His wee brother Brian followed suit a year later. Last summer, that was. Whether or not Brian, too, had resorted to spiking his ring-piece, it remains unclear. Then there was David Smith. Pagan's brother. And Daniel Miller. He killed himself; he was found naked and dangling from a beam in the garage after his wife had jettisoned him for the joiner hired to sort their conservatory. The joiner – a Malcolm Downey – was the next to be discovered on the end of a tight rope. Brochers took exception to his involvement in the Miller divorce and resolved to swerve his business. Big Downey went bust. Malcolm tied a noose. The wife, Michelle – maiden name Brown – by all accounts, she lost the plot after that. Derek first became aware of Michelle when they both showed up at the academy after the summer break with the same school bag. He was not altogether fond of her from then on. She landed in here as a result of, well – the rumours had it that she took a knife to herself. It was all none too pleasant. Many people were in here because they'd jumped to avoid a predicted push: Andy Bananatime, Rory Chalmers, Gavin Tait, Japanese Ian, Martin 'Marty Poohs' Cowe. These were just a few of the suicide Suzies whom were so desperate to move in here. Derek thought about this sunken crowd. His fellow humans: a rather bizarre collection of crayon strokes, they were.

Movement down by the gates. The minister stepped aside to allow access for a returning hearse. This new coffin was led to another hole, away from where Derek reminisced. Derek pursued the gravel path around the decomposing residents to where the minister beckoned for the box. He noticed that there didn't appear to be any mourners or nosy people gathered about in this instance, not including himself.

The two shovellers halted their immediate task to aid the driver of the hearse and a passenger. Derek watched from a couple of rows distant the submergence of the box by the four men. These men weren't pals or relatives of the dead. They dropped the ropes and trudged off to contend with more relevant matters. The driver and his accomplice reversed away in the hearse. The boiler suits did unload more soil atop Donnie and his daughter. The minister read from his Book; he was just out of Derek's hearing range. Derek approached. On his way, he tapped a stone, which read, 'To a beloved father, grandfather and great grandfather, Stanley Gibson'. The minister closed his Book. He whistled at the men across the yard. One raised his spade to indicate that he was listening. The minister spotlighted the grave in front of him. The shovel nodded its understanding, then resumed the chore of covering young Rachel with six feet of earth. The minister made to leave; he was stopped by Derek's inquisition.

"Fa wis 'is?"

"Raymond McLeish," the minister replied. This was as close as Derek had been to the sixty-and-a-bit-year-old with the raven summit. It was surely a dye job. Derek thought that he would do likewise once he went grey. "A pensioner. You must've heard about him."

"Aye." Derek didn't want to keep the man standing about all day. The minister looked like he had somewhere else to be; his gelatinous frame could also have been giving his knees some jib. But Derek was driven to interrogate. "Naebidy showed up?"

"No. It seems that Mr McLeish was a recluse."

"'At's nae right, 'at." Derek peered over into the gash. "Ye wid've thought that somebidy wid've showed up."

The minister made a sound that was neither a yes nor a no. "We reap what we sow. You were here for the Wise burials?"

"Aye. Faimily."

"Weren't you here last week as well?" the minister asked. "I remember you. It was your grandfather, wasn't it?"

"Aye," Derek said. "Almost."

"Yes. Stanley Gibson. The big man." The minister smiled as though some amusing clip played just for him. However, his body language briskly became everything but rolling up his sleeve and rapping at his watch.

The question came to Derek. He felt as if he'd been cajoled by the collective will of these here ghosts. He asked, "Dee ye believe in God?"

The minister tapped the Book against his thigh. It was not an action of unease. It was one of knowing. "I believe that there is a goodness in us all that will prevail always, though we want it to or not."

"Aye. Ah ken." The cold sunshine filled the cemetery like a bath sat too long. Derek said, "Bit, like, dee ye really think 'ere's a God an' 'at? Ah ken it's a bit o a stupid thing tae ask – considerin, like."

"Not at all," the minister said, in a suit not disparate from Derek's. His collar thirstily absorbed the light. "We should never forget to ask questions, whether the answers may seem obvious or straightforward. The learning's in the asking."

"So, God: dis he exist?"

"In what sense? I'm not predisposed to see God as the man with the white beard in his throne." He clasped the Bible in both hands. The palings of his spectacles shone. "It is as my late father once said to me: 'It's better to believe in a God that doesn't exist than in a Devil that does'. I hope that casts some helpful illumination for you."

Derek wiped his nose with a handkerchief that he had found in his coat pocket. "Ah sort o see faar ye're comin fae."

"Do you believe in God?"

"Me? Nah. Nae affence, like." Derek did award the inquiry some contemplation. "Ah think maybe it's jist wishful thinkin. Ah could be wrang, like. Ye jist niver know."

The minister took an interest in the lad of the shaggy barnet. "But do you believe in that which exceeds our grasp of concrete logic and science?"

"Hoo dee ye mean?"

"I mean," said the minister, "do you believe that all you see is all there is?"

Derek digested a beat before replying. "No."

"Weel, ah suppose 'at's somethin, eh?"

The minister walked off down the path and through the gates. Derek looked into the pit. The box opted to ignore him.

Derek ventured upon the grassy pathway alongside the road to get back into town. The high dunes to his right currently blocked his view of the North Sea. He couldn't see the golf course for the receding graveyard. The sheds across the road from him on the left were, he believed, where some engineering work was done. In the foreground of those sheds, on the path opposite his, a group of foreign types returned with their shopping. Their bags divulged that they'd forsook the larger supermarket for its cheaper neighbour. He did not wave to them, for they did not wave at him, though he was not adverse to the idea. He might have greeted them warmly, had they intimated a desire for him to do so. He could appreciate that they may be anxious around the indigents of this outpost. The fishyards were ahead, after the esplanade with its changing rooms and café. The pitches and parks where he'd played as a laddie roamed towards him, up there beyond the engineering huts, as well as the rooftops and spires, and the academy on its brae. These inanimates crunched together to form the Broch.

An American evangelist once proclaimed that 'Scotland is a dark land'. A famous disc jokey, originating from yonder Southways, labelled it a barbaric nation populated by barbarians. Some of this, Derek would rightly concede, was true. The DJ had since spent time in jail for acts of buggery on young boys. Such is life.

Derek strolled along the grass. The good thing about the town, he noted, was that its leaders weren't shy about sending the barbers out when nature's hair got a bit scruffy. A layer of cool gratified Derek's skin. There was profuse chill for him not to have to worry about his clothes sticking to him. A tangerine car pulled up to his side. A grin poked out of the passenger window.

"Hiya, Derek."

"Lee. Fit like?" Derek saw that Lee Johnstone, along with his chauffeur Catherine and some unknown chick in the back seat, were all dressed up – subtly, however. They'd also been in attendance at the Wise burials.

"Oh, ye ken me, Derek," said Lee. "Cannae complain." The three bods in the car were all sprightly; Derek knew that they'd be doing their best to quash their genetical good cheer so as not to upset him. Their struggle was akin to a cat befriending poultry. "Hoo aboot you?" Even with Lee in toned-down mode, he still had a glitz about him like an Eurovision rehearsal. "Oh me, fit happened tae yer han'?"

"Ah fell."

"Oh?"

"Aye."

Lee implied by biting a nail that he, too, could feel the pain that had been inflicted by Derek's plummet. "Ouch," he said.

"Yip."

"Oh," Lee said, as if he'd espied his keys, "did ye hear aboot Lori's dad?"

"No."

"He's in Cornhill. He's bein rested."

"Ah didnae ken 'at." Derek, like everyone else in the northeast, knew about Cornhill.

"Oh, aye. 'Ere's folk sayin he's went a bit doolally."

"Aye?" Derek gazed off towards the playing fields, oblivious to how sexy he appeared to those in the car. "Cannae be easy pittin up wi fit he's hid tae ging through. Hopefully the break'll dee 'im good."

Lee skipped the song on their stereo. "Sorry, Derek, fit wis 'at? Oh, onywye, so fit's new wi ye? Are ye a'right aifter…?" Lee allowed the query to die amid a series of solicitous, oh-so-concerned gestures.

"Ah'm fine," Derek said. "Luk, ah hiv tae ging noo. Ah'll see ye's aboot."

"Okay, Derek. Taak care. Oh, wait. Ah forgot tae say."

"Say fit?"

Lee Johnstone sucked on his bottom lip. "On Thursda night, 'ere wis some brute askin fir yer pal Jimmy. 'At wis at aboot seven o'clock, back o seven kina time. Ah tellt 'im tae try The Tart. Ah niver tellt 'im faar he bides, though. Ah niver caased ony trouble, did ah?"

"No. Nae trouble at aa. See ye's."

The cute one in the back smiled. "See ye, Derek."

The car lunged onwards as though the driver were being timed. Some Britney Aguilera Pink noise rattled in its wake.

Derek continued his trek. He might've guessed that it had been Lee whom had steered the giant in his direction. Well, nae pint girnin aboot it noo.

Jimbo.

He'd tried to kill himself: that was the story that Derek had been hearing. Broke both of his legs in the attempt, apparently. Another whimsical episode in the charmed life of James Stevenson. He was still in the hospital; through in the invalid ward in Aberdeen, Derek had been told. Derek would have to go see him, sooner or later. He'd possibly take his guitar through with him, for Jimmy to practise on; maybe he'd get some use from the instrument. The lad would have nothing better to do with his time.

As Derek passed the promenade from up on the road, he noticed the silver machine in the car park; it arrowed out towards the sand and the sea and the polluted blue like a fish on a chopping board. The clouds were water-filled pails, sliding, by increment, down a seesaw. Pagan propped himself against the railings as though at the bow of a craft. Derek sauntered down a verge to join him.

"How do, Peggy?" Derek was surprised to hear the zip in his own voice.

Pagan held a tray of chips. "Ah, Derek. So, how did it go?" A white terrier sat by Pagan's side, patiently waiting for its feed.

"Ach, it wis a fuckin funeral, ken? Could've gone worse. Could've fell in o'er the hole. Ah'm fuckin kina amazed ah didnae, wi ma luck."

Pagan propositioned a chip. Derek declined. Pagan dropped it for the dog; it didn't let the morsel touch the ground. The small dog was ravenous.

"Fa's yer pal?"

"A hungry wee sod," Pagan replied. He had himself a new pair of brown trousers; he'd ruined the last ones. "'Gordon' says his collar. I've tried his contact number, but no joy. I'm thinking about making him my first ever pet."

"Aye? Faar did ye fin' it?"

"Here. I was standing here and it just came over. The moocher singled me out; didn't you, you bugger?" Pagan fed the dog another chip.

The two men looked out across the bay. Derek's eyes were drawn to the yellow-jacketed loner poised by the edge of the waters.

"He's been standing down there like that since before I came along." Pagan picked at his portion. "You know him?"

"I've seen him around. I think he might even be crazier than you," Derek said. He appropriated a chip from his pal's tray. "So, fit are ye workin on the day? Dee ah need tae ask?"

"I'm sorry, Derek. This is a story. This is how it goes."

"Ma sister's a shambles. She disnae need tae be blamed fir fit happened."

"Relax, Derek. I don't plan to. It was a tragedy. The blame should be shared equally between everyone and no one. I'm not the sort to do a hatchet job. The cut will be fine."

"Cheers." Derek sprawled over a post. Pagan slopped what remained of his dinner down for the dog to devour. He put the container into a bin. The twosome in their dressy ensemble were soothed by the spectacle of the crawling sea. The scarce souls on the beach did ensure to alter their trajectories so as to sidestep the curiosity in yellow. Derek said, "Fit neest, eh, Pagan?"

"I say we go somewhere. Myself, you, Phil, and Mo if he wants to come with us; Freddy, if he's up to it. I think we should travel. Go somewhere where they don't speak any English."

"Ye're a'ready 'ere, pal."

"Somewhere further afield, I was thinking. We could have an adventure. If I'm going to be alive, then it should fucking well feel like it. And not just some long weekend in Amsterdam, smoking hash and giggling like idiots. Nothing cosmopolitan or overtly domesticated. Peru or something like that. Jungles. Glaciers. The Antarctic. Cannibals chasing us down the Amazon with poisoned darts, or lightning bolts hitting the masts. That kind of thing. Anywhere where we're unlikely to see any holiday reps."

Derek pushed himself back off the post. "Ah'll hiv tae get a job first, like."

"Don't worry about that, Derek. I'll see about getting you something in the presses. You could maybe deliver the papers out to the newsagents."

"Sounds fantastic." Derek put his foot on the lowest of the rungs. He confessed, "Ah dinnae hae a licence."

"Well, then, it's about time that you did, isn't it?" Pagan brushed his hand back towards his silver car. "I'll give you lessons; free of charge, as long as you start washing a plate now and again."

"Ah kin dee 'at. Cheers." Derek couldn't see Bob Schell's camper van among the transients on the coaster of grass by the nearest fishyard. The Englishman and his partner must've moved on. Derek perused the green and orange cliffs, over which young Rachel Wise had been found. He was hit by a sensation like a refrigerator door being opened in his face. The clouds had finally caught the sun. "Ken somethin?" Derek said. "Ah sort o regret the fact that in the mair than ten years that you've bin aa o'er the place, ah've practically niver left 'is toon. Is 'at nae jist sad as fuck or fit, Peggy?"

"Yes, Derek. It is." They both laughed, though Pagan wasn't the sort to audibly express his enjoyment of a self-said quip. "But we all need some regret. It's the regret that fuels us and keeps us striving forth. Who would be content?"

"Aye, Pagan, ye're a'right."

"Yes. I am."

Derek tickled the dog's ear with the tip of his shoe. "Ah tell ye, Thursda nicht, Peggy – ah wis fuckin sure that ye wis gaan tae dee it, like."

"I was."

"Bit ye're nae insane onymair, are ye?"

"No. I'm not insane, as such. I'm just simply not quite right."

"Indubitably."

"Derek, I should be okay. But who's to say? Nothing's easy, is it?" Pagan studied his newly acquired pet. Then he said, "While we're on the subject, I think it felicitous that we give the last word to Hemingway." Pagan thickened his vocal cords accordingly. "'Man is not made for defeat. A man can be destroyed, but never defeated.' You should keep that in mind. Of course, Hemingway wound up shooting himself. But he'll always be the dude. Derek, you shouldn't have to hide the matches from me."

"'At's fit ah like tae hear." Derek left Pagan and his dog by the railings.

From the tentacles of the graveyard and the esplanade, Derek went next to Fraserburgh's belly. He travelled by some of the fishyards where he had, at some stage, pretended to work. No sign was there of his uncle in the office out front. Tommy would be changing out of his funeral attire and into his Toories' garb. Derek walked along the harbour. A boat went out. A boat came in. A sailing ship was up on the stocks. Scurries were flummoxed by sudden dusk. Derek crossed the street. To the side of the street where the pubs marched.

One week. A to B by way of Z. And what had he learned from all of these weird incidents? What hast thou been taught, Sir Derek?

Mucho nada.

A pea-tinged sports car lounged outside The Tart. Derek knocked on a pane. The giant jolted awake in the passenger seat. Derek could see a triangle of cloth beneath the neck of the giant's shirt. The bandages spanned the circumference of the Dundonian's chest. Lex was stiff and drowsy. He was also, however, fairly gladdened to see Derek, and not in a sly or fiendish way either. They'd been through the wars together; Lex had class enough to revere thine foes. He bipped down the window.

"How goes it?" Derek said.

"Nae too bad. Niver bin shot afore."

"First time fir iverythin, eh?"

A few boat-painters trudged along across the way, arguing. One flicked a lit cigarette at another. They took a breather from their bickering to salute Derek. He waved in kind.

"Hoo's yer heid?" Lex asked. "Ah niver did 'at tae yer han' as well, did ah?"

"No. Ma heid's a'right. Same as it wis onywye."

An emission from the giant's throat signified that he found this to be satisfactory. "'Ere wis mair gaan on 'at night than jist me an' you, wisn't 'ere?" inquired Lex, wedged into the trainer of his vehicle.

"Aye."

"'Ere wis a girl? A guy shot 'imsel wi ma gun, didn't he?"

"Aye."

"Did ye ken 'em, aye?"

"Yip."

"Nae fine, is it?"

"No."

"Ah kina feel bad that things turned oot the wye they did." Lex was not rendered timid through wounding; he spoke as one bewildered by mess.

"Aye."

A van passed them. A horn sounded. Derek gave a nod.

Lex said, "Aboot the last thing ah remember is you wi a golf club. Faar the fuck did 'at come fae?"

"The dad's boot. He's the manager o the Broch clubhoose or somethin like 'at."

"Play golf yersel, like?"

"Nah," Derek replied. "Ye'll niver fin' me oot on a golf course, ah kin assure ye o 'at. Yer boss in 'ere, aye?"

"Associate. Aye. He's bin waitin a while. Try nae tae piss 'im aff, eh?"

Derek patted the car roof. "Right-o." A handshake would've been much too much. He entered The Tart.

The giant's superior or fellow henchman or whatever it was that his role description declared him to be sat at the bar, accompanying Fat Ass as a spectator of the actor's cortege that unfolded live on the television. The blinds, as always, were tilted downwards. Neon fought the gloom like glow sticks chucked into a barn. Both of the booths were empty. The pool table was minus competitors. Monday afternoons in The Tart were usually deathly.

"Fuckin shame, 'at," the gangster told the barman. "Han'some guy like 'at; he could've hid aa the flange in the world." The crook had yet to respond to Derek's presence, so intently did he watch that hearse drag itself down roads lined with a million Brits. The movie star was to be buried in London, as per his wife's request.

The criminal was both fashionless and unpretentious in his demeanour. His clothes were of stretchy materials to compensate for his build. The man was broad like a toad; he was a blatant steroid fan.

Phil dried a glass; he saw Derek surveying his only customer. The man reacted to the barman's resulting shift in attention by swivelling around on his stool.

"You Derek, 'en?"

"Aye." Derek brought a chequebook out from inside his black coat and went forth to the bar. He perched next to the man, whom could've been in his forties. The man looked like he'd used his face to push over a truck. Derek split the book. "Pen?"

"'Ere's een here, luk." Fat Ass provided Derek with the required tool. The toad-man stood over Derek as he scribbled upon the paper.

"Fa am ah writin 'is oot tae? Lex or…?"

"Jist pit doon Frank Jones," came the reply.

The information recorded, Derek tore out the slip and handed it to the crim.

"'Ere better nae be onythin suspect aboot 'is cheque. If it disnae cash, boy, ye'll be fuckin in fir it." The man was rustier of complexion and more volatile of temperament than his associate was. "If 'is disnae work, the next thing that bounces will be my fuckin nuts aff yer mum's chin."

"'Ere's nithin wrang wi it." Derek put his elbow on the bar. "The money's 'ere."

Phil twisted the towel into a mug.

"Well, 'at's a-fuckin-right, 'en." The cheque vanished into the gangster's tracksuit bottoms. His T-shirt fit him like a windbreaker. He was by the doorway and near to fresh light. The man hesitated. "Ah heard shite things aboot 'is toon, like. Ivery cunt says the Broch's a dump. Ah dinnae ken, like. To me, it's a bonny kina place."

"Aye." Derek regarded the mobster from his seat. "Noo, get the fuck oot o ma sight."

The man was predictably tousled by this closing assertion. "Easy 'ere, chief. Ye dinnae want yer right han' tae luk like yer left."

"No?" Derek said. "Ah could aiwyes ankle-wank."

The gangster punched the wall; he dallied for some seconds. Then he stormed out. An engine howled and whined into nonentity.

Phil put an up-turned pint glass back onto its rack. "Nae bad, Derek. Fit kin ah get ye?"

"Let me see." Derek paused. "Fit dis a vodka an' cola taste like withoot the vodka?"

"Only one wye tae fin' oot." Phil poured the drink, slapped in a few chinks of ice, and set it down under his chum's nose. Derek took a sip. Phil asked him, "Hoo much did ye gie the guy?"

Derek sipped again. "Five thousand pounds, Philip."

"Fuckin hell. Five gran'? Dee ye ken hoo much Lori owed 'em, like?"

"No." Derek did not. But his cheque covered it, and that was that.

"A thoosan quid," Fat Ass said, providing the solution to his own riddle. "She only owed 'em a grand."

Derek took a longer sip. No mercy would he expect to find in that dollop of weak fizz. "A grand, eh?"

"Aye. 'At wis aa."

Derek saw that the felt from the pool table had been removed. "Well, the guy wis shot. Ah think 'at's worth a couple o pennies extra."

Phil flattened his palms on the bar as though pressing down on the bonnet of a terminal machine. "So," he said, "ye gaan tae try an' get some o 'at money back fae Lori's dad? Surely he shid pye some o it? He's the een that got tae blast the cunt."

"Nah. 'At's me back tae zero. Ah'm skint, Fat Ass. Let it lie."

Phil pursed his lips as if in discernment. Then his focus slipped upwards to the image of a bairn crying for an actor whose films she'd likely never seen.

Derek bore holes in his friend. "Phil, hoo are ye?"

"Eh, nae bad." The barman lifted his cap to wipe his brow. "Fit like yersel?" He'd become suspicious of the patron.

"No. Seriously. How do you feel, Philip?"

Fat Phil's incredulity depressed to the vicinity of most genuine meditation. Philip Davidson Ironside said, "Ah'm kina miserable, like."

"Me an' aa," Derek replied, almost propelled from his chair with enthusiasm. "It's great, in't it?"

They observed the parade without any need to elaborate on this dual confession.

Fat Ass rubbed his neck; he scanned the ceiling for a brief period. "Hoo ye gettin on bidin wi Pagan?" Phil said, once the pong of honesty had disseminated.

"Fine." Derek traced the rim of his cup. "Ah saw 'im jist noo."

"Aye?"

Derek sank the rest of the cola. "Aye." He got to his feet.

"Fit's the plan, Derek?"

"Fitiver happens, happens."

"Aye, Derek. 'Ere's aiwyes somethin happenin."

Derek strode away from the bar. "You said it, ye fat fuck."

"Ah sure did, ye ugly cunt."

Derek lingered at the doorway. The toad-man had left indentations in the frame.

"Fit aboot Samantha?" Phil asked, as though to the present occupier of his childhood home.

Derek hadn't seen or heard from the Irish lass since that Thursday night. "Is she still in the Broch?"

"Nae sure, like. She hisnae bin in here."

Derek fingered the navel-like bumps. "Maybe she'll swing in by on 'er wye back fae John o' Groats." The tip of his digit caressed the grooves in the wood.

"We aa like ye, Derek."

Derek chose not to look up at the barman. "Right," he said. He parted the door. It had begun to spit down outside.

"Faar ye gaan?" Phil asked.

The elements spattered Derek's cheek. "Ah've got folk tae see; things tae say."

"It's gaan tae start pishin doon in a minute."

"Fuck it." Derek went out into the vertical tide. "Ah like the rain."

Phil rinsed the glass as used by his chum. He polished it with a cloth. He waited for Adrian Campbell to phone; he was supposed to definitely call today. The procession droned on. The ebony limb slithered forward as if it had hooks for tyres. Fat Ass changed the channel. In other news. TV watchdogs had reprimanded the comedian Roy Complain for crass remarks made on his show relating to the movie star's death.

Phil laughed. That cunt was one funny fucker.

*

He lay, fractured of peg, in this hospital bed. He was snugger now that his casts had been changed. The room was light and clean; he had no cause to whinge about the temperature. It was not stuffy; his flesh was not clammy beneath his loose apparel. The two poorly men on either side of him slept. He could sleep, too, Jimmy thought; although, sleep was all that he'd done for the past week. He'd slept himself tired. His brain needed to be zapped. The curtains were wrapped around the bed in front of his. A doctor was in to see that patient, along with some nurses. That patient was older, considerably. Jimmy thought that it must probably be serious business. With all the commotion, he sensed that something might be shutting down. He could concentrate on the television up in the corner. The funeral. Were all of the channels devoted to that ceremony? Wasn't there anything else on?

Most likely not. He could read. His mum had dropped off a bundle of books. Horror and sci-fi stuff, because that's what he used to read when he had the energy to read. She'd bestowed him with the seven chunky tomes that comprised Stephen King's Dark Tower cycle. He'd heard that they were pretty good. But Jimmy wasn't in a reading mood either.

A restlessness hollowed out his joints. He felt like part of the floor. He was, for the time being, paraplegic. He was a stone in a field. It could be long enough before he'd walk again. The next phase of his recovery process would see him in a wheelchair. Then perhaps after that he'd manage to manoeuvre himself about on crutches. Then he'd be out of here. Back to the Broch. Back to his flat. To unemployment and loneliness. They'd refer him to his GP, though. She'd forward him on to a counsellor. He'd already spoken to a psychiatrist since being admitted here. That was standard procedure, for cases such as his.

He could've been dead right now. Imagine. The final question answered. What's out there, and what does it look like? He would've now known everything. He doubted that there was anything to know.

He didn't think that God existed. He did not think that he'd incurred His wrath. It was just how things were. The road had been replaced with dirt, at least for a while. He couldn't see where he was going. The path had disappeared. Maybe now it was starting to resurface.

He pulled himself up against the pillows, careful not to cause further aggravation to his legs. The window was a blue poster on the wall. Pasty wisps of tumbleweeds drifted across it.

Just going to have to get used to being alive, Jimbo. Imagine. You're alive, James. Think of it. Really think about it – Einstein, Mozart, Picasso, Newton et alii: each fellow a brilliant specimen; but every man a dead cunt. They were as dead as shite. They were gone for good, irrespective of how sensational they were. They were dead. You are not. Tenants of boneyards universal would give what nothing they had to be in your bandages.

Aye, wi twa broken legs.

They'll heal.

Ah'm a laughin stock. Cannae even fuckin kill masel right.

So? Nobody that really matters to you is laughing. None of your family or friends want to see you this way. Cheer up, Jimbo. Be grateful that your plans did go askew. Suicide's the one action where failure is the best outcome for the person involved.

He would read. He would try to read. He would regain control of his mind. He grabbed the first book of King's opus from off of the cabinet. He nearly toppled his juice. Pain coursed through his lower half as if he had a mole-infestation. He steadied himself. He rested the book on his chest. He opened it. He took out his bookmarker, which his eyes embraced once more, as though he hadn't yet scrutinised it sufficiently. That postcard continued to delight him. His parents had delivered it to him on the Sunday afternoon. The card was addressed to him and his abode. On its front, an excitable font yelled 'Perth'; the encircling pictures disclosed that it wasn't the Scottish rendering being heralded. The hand-written paragraph merrily imparted trivialities. Its final line had made him want to shout with joy, and still did. But he would not. People thought him mad enough already. Those last two words were the equal of any bridge: Love Lori.

Eventually, he put the postcard back on top of his bedside cabinet. He began to read his book.

*

I control the sea. I control the water. I control the sand. I control the dark clouds. I summon them to me. I control the weather. I made it rain.

The rain poured down onto him. The sea swirled around his ankles. He took off his right glove. He let it fall. The water collected it. He slipped his hand up through his beard and under his black, woollen hat. He felt his deformity. He was a mutilation. His ear was like a photograph withered by flame. It was a rosebud. He tossed his tammy out into the froth. It was night. The esplanade was abandoned. The beach was bereft. He thrust his bare hand outwards.

I control the sea. I will make you flow as I wish. I will make you part. The sea will part for me. You will part.

His nose started to bleed. The sea climbed to his knees. His jogging trousers were sodden. The waters did not conform to his instructions. He took off his left glove. That, too, was discarded into the swishing murk. He obtained the garden scissors from his yellow jacket. He'd merely intended to punish the canine, for being as it was, for being a nipping, gnawing corruption. He jammed the thumb of his left hand between the blades. He squeezed the grips. He collapsed. He held onto his scissors. His thumb bobbed away from him. The sea did not part.

He stumbled up the sands. He scaled the steps onto the promenade. He crossed the car park. He walked out onto the road.

I control the moon. I control the stars. I control the lights. I control the cars. Car, stop.

The red car ploughed through him; it flung him into the air. He crashed onto the tarmac. The car screeched to rest. The red-haired driver got out. He screamed at the man, whom gathered himself like a mop being raised from a muddy pool. He hobbled towards the driver. He put the pinky of his own left hand into the scissors, then cut. The driver shrieked, and went silent, then backed away. The damaged man pursued him, offering him the detached finger. The driver was not enamoured with the gesture; he continued to elude the shuffling man. The man buckled before the car, sinking in front of its headlights. He'd wanted to tame the mutt with sharpened metal. The girl had intervened; he'd only pushed her. Not that hard. He relieved himself of his yellow coat, and his zipped top, and his vest. He was thin like a dust jacket. The human race was a smudge. He was a separate blotch. They were all the same thing. There was no rape; it was aggravated masturbation. There was no violence; it was sadomasochism. There was no murder; it was only suicide. It was just suicide. They were all too close to see that they were the same thing. He could see that they were one, for he was not of them. He was not among them. He was somehow wrong, the wrong form, the wrong shape. Something. Somehow.

He severed the bicep of his left arm. He plunged the scissors deeper into the gushing rip. The blades clamped the bone like a dog biting into its leash.